Praise for *Aether Ones*

"Science fiction gourmands have a succulent new dish to devour in *Aether Ones*, Wendi Coffman-Porter's debut novel. . . . A delicious . . . adventure novel that not only keeps you turning those pages but makes you think. . . . [Coffman-Porter] combines theoretical physics with superb storytelling to create something new and unique for the modern age. Coffman-Porter and *Aether Ones* are the big bang of science fiction."

—John Kindervag, Cybersecurity Leader

"Engaging throughout . . . [*Aether Ones*] kept me guessing . . . leaving me in happy anticipation of a sequel. . . . Intriguing characters, unique cultures, and plots within plots."

—Ben Zittere, Commander, US Navy (Ret.)

"Fantastic and imaginative story that draws you in until the very end."

—Travis Fachin, Operations Specialist Petty Officer First Class, Surface Warfare and Aviation Warfare, US Navy (Ret.)

AETHER ONES

WENDI
COFFMAN-PORTER

BROWN BOOKS
PUBLISHING GROUP

Aether Ones

Brown Books Publishing Group
Dallas/New York
www.BrownBooks.com
(972) 381-0009

A New Era in Publishing®

Publisher's Cataloging-In-Publication Data

Names: Coffman-Porter, Wendi, author.
Title: Aether ones / Wendi Coffman-Porter.
Description: Dallas ; New York : Brown Books Publishing Group, [2020]
Identifiers: ISBN 9781612544557
Subjects: LCSH: Women detectives--Outer space--Fiction. | Murder--
    Investigation--Outer space--Fiction. | Outer space--Fiction. | LCGFT:
    Detective and mystery fiction. | Science fiction.
Classification: LCC PS3603.O323 A38 2020 | DDC 813/.6--dc2

ISBN 978-1-61254-455-7
LCCN 2020905347

Printed in the United States
10 9 8 7 6 5 4 3 2 1

For more information or to contact the author,
please go to www.WendiCoffmanPorter.com.

This book is dedicated to my best friend and partner, Richard.
You never once doubted me or my ability to tell a story.
Thanks for always wanting to know more. I love you.

1

CONSCRIPTED VOLUNTEER

"Next!"

The line shuffled forward about three feet, and Leilani Falconi looked down at her wrist. The device there was annoyingly blank, just like it had been for the last twenty hours. Nothing. Not even one response. She was beyond annoyed or angry; now, she was well into acceptance. Luckily, adapting was something she did well—a side effect of her line of work.

"Next."

The line shuffled forward again as the person in front of her walked up to the table.

"Education?" The young male seated behind the table had been repeating this question for the last five hours. He was clearly bored and frustrated.

That made two of them. Lei looked again at her wrist, but it was pointless. The conversation in front of her was drowned out by her own thoughts. She barely noticed when a man in a local military uniform who'd been standing off to the side stepped up, cuffed the man in front of her, and led him off. That had been happening all day.

"Next." Waving to her, the seated man watched her step up to the table. "Name?"

"Amanda Thompson," she lied casually. She'd been playing the part of Amanda for a week now—though, at this rate, she might have to play the part for longer than she had intended.

"Sherin 254 regulations require that we supply the Kassian Empire with five hundred volunteer personnel every three years." The man's tone was dull and bored. He never even looked up at her. "Do you volunteer?"

Lei raised an eyebrow. She was starting to understand what was going on now.

"What's the alternative?"

"Ten years in mining service." Which was a nice way of saying "prison-work detail." Not even a nice prison, either. Sherin 254 was infamous for its mining programs—programs in which the average survival rate through term of service was a spectacular 65 percent.

Lei chuckled. The sound caught the man off guard, and he glanced up at her.

"I guess I volunteer, then."

The man looked down at his pad and tapped something.

"Education?"

"PhD in abnormal physics."

"Right." He shook his head, obviously assuming she was being sarcastic. "Go through that door." He cocked a thumb over his shoulder to indicate the plain door behind him.

Lei sighed. Someone's head was going to roll for this. The door popped open just as a buzz on her wrist alerted her to an incoming call.

"Move it, recruit!" a youthful voice yelled at her. "I want you through check-in in three minutes and locked into the shuttle in five!"

Ten minutes and a ludicrous string of belittling slurs later, she was strapped into a gravity-compensating chair aboard an Imperial Kass troop shuttle. This particular shuttle was designed to carry about one hundred troops through a high-speed scenario. Older models of vehicles like this had poor gravity compensators and were nicknamed "vomit comets" because of the typical physical response of the troops who used them.

Strapped into the hard seats were easily thirty nervous and fidgety new recruits wearing dark-blue jumpsuits with green trim—the traditional colors of the Kassian Imperial Navy and Marines. The face of the man sitting next to her was already a disturbing mixture of ash gray and green, and that was before she even sat down.

The traditional age group targeted by these snatch-and-grab recruiting techniques was between twenty and thirty. Leilani appeared to be just under thirty. Of course, the reality was much different; thanks to the special tools of her trade, she was easily five times that. The other new recruits were closer to the twenty-year mark.

Two of the younger recruits threw up into the vomit bags attached to their seats. She raised an eyebrow; the shuttle was still on the ground. This was going to be an interesting flight.

The recruiting check-in had involved her stripping in front of a scanner and two naval ratings. She had been handed a storage bag for her personal effects and given fresh underwear, the traditional jumpsuit of dark blue and green, and a pair of black boots. Her belongings had been taken and stored in a box sealed with a biometric lock genetically assigned to her. She was then issued a large duffel bag containing three uniforms, underwear, personal basics, a pad, and a wrist comm.

The entire process was designed to humiliate and embarrass the new soldiers. After all, the original scan had cleared her and the other recruits of parasites and diseases. So rather than give the recruiters the satisfaction of a response, she had remained calm and collected throughout.

With her head resting back against the chair, Lei closed her eyes and tried to nap. She knew from experience that the first few days of boot camp would include sleep deprivation in order to make it easier to break the new soldiers, so any short naps she could manage to fit in, she needed. She wasn't sure how long it would take command to find her without her belongings, so she would just get comfortable for now.

It took them three hours to finish filling the last nine seats in the shuttle, meaning Lei got plenty of sleep despite the crying and vomiting going on around her.

"We good, Gunny?"

Lei's eyes were still closed, but the presence of a calm, quiet voice drew her attention toward the rear of the vehicle. She took a deep breath and pulled herself fully awake. As she opened her eyes, she saw an older human male standing near the rear of the main compartment. He was handsome, with strong, masculine features and hard eyes. He wore a marine uniform bearing gunnery sergeant stripes on the arm. He had only one ribbon on his chest, but Lei knew that was because he was never allowed to remove that particular ribbon while in uniform. The embroidered name tag said Smith.

"Yes, sir," he answered.

"It looks like a crappy haul this time." The younger voice belonged to the annoying young ensign who had screamed at them all through check-in.

She was surprised he wasn't hoarse.

"If you say so, sir."

"I'm going up front. They're all yours."

"Thank you, sir."

The young male stormed past on his way to the cockpit and slammed the heavy bulkhead hatch. A few seconds later, the shuttle roared to life.

Lei ignored it. In this model of shuttle, the startup of the engines couldn't be heard, which meant some asshat was simply feeding the sound into the main compartment from the tiny engineering compartment in the rear of the shuttle. The volume was far too high to be believable. Hell, it probably wasn't even that loud right next to the engine.

Several people screamed in fear, and Lei furrowed her brow in annoyance. She hoped the young lieutenant wouldn't be around for the actual basic training.

The ride up, while loud, was uneventful. The g-forces were a little high, which meant the lieutenant either had shut off the compensators or was far exceeding port speeds. More than likely, it was the former. After about forty-five minutes, the roaring sound suddenly stopped.

"Listen up." The gunny was now standing near the intercom next to the cockpit hatch. His calm voice was a welcome respite from the crying and engine noise.

The new Kassian recruits all turned to look up at him—all except the recruit next to her, who had passed out. Lei quickly checked the man's pulse. Her eyes had been closed, and in all the noise, she hadn't realized that his breathing had become so erratic. His pulse was very weak.

"The navy is full of assholes," the gunny continued.

Lei looked to the rear and caught the attention of one of the marines who wore a medical insignia. She pointed to the recruit next to her and waved her hand back and forth with the palm down, indicating that his life signs were iffy.

"Our enemies are full of even more of them. People willing to make your life a living hell. Or just outright kill you." His voice slowed as he allowed the words to sink in.

The medic—his name tag said Morrison—got up and came over to her. He crouched in front of her to prevent drawing too much attention from the gunny's speech. Lei tapped her neck and gestured to the unconscious man. The medic nodded and checked his pulse.

"The lieutenant up there wants you so terrified of him that you wet yourself every time you see him." He jerked a thumb toward the hatch next to him. "It's my job to make sure that never happens. I'm going to make you so tough that if you met the emperor, you wouldn't balk. You will know exactly what to say and do in all situations. This includes what to do when you come across an enemy who pulls a gun on you. By the time I'm done with you, nothing will rattle you. You'll be rock solid in all aspects of life and war."

Morrison put his hand to his ear and mumbled something into his subvocal comms.

Lei, meanwhile, was resisting the urge to chuckle at the gunny. He was expecting a lot from basic recruits. She knew admirals who couldn't stay calm when meeting the emperor, let alone with a gun to their head.

"My name is Gunnery Sergeant Smith. You will all call me Gunny. Is that understood?"

"Yes, Gunny!" Lei answered loudly, trying to inspire the others to do the same. She got about half of them to follow suit. The others were too scared.

Morrison tapped her on the knee as the gunny yelled a little louder. "I didn't hear you!"

"Yes, Gunny!" most of the ship yelled in response.

Lei undid her harness and leaned forward so she could hear the medic. The g-forces were a little much out of the chair, but she ignored them.

"I've turned grav compensation up in his chair and given him a shot, but I can't do anything else till we land," he said in her ear.

"ETA?"

"Eight minutes. Can you monitor him?"

She nodded.

"We're going to try that again until every single one of you is answering me as one voice. My name is Gunnery Sergeant Smith. You will all call me Gunny. Is that understood?"

"Yes, Gunny!" the ship answered in unison, including Morrison and Lei.

The medic nodded to her and moved back to his seat, keeping low as he went.

"Much better. Now, here's the next step. The lieutenant is going to come out here and yell some more. I want a 'Yes, sir!' so loud that he wets himself from fear. Do you think you can manage that?"

Lei grinned as the entire compartment yelled, "Yes, Gunny!" so loud it seemed to rattle the ship. That much was purely her imagination, of course, but it was a good sound nonetheless. She scanned the room and found that the recruits' fear was quickly being replaced with anger. Stage two of grief.

Allowing her gaze to travel around the large troop shuttle, she assessed the actual marines she could easily see. Most of them were keeping an eye on the recruits, but a few of them had trained in on her specifically, including Morrison. Inspecting the name tag of the man next to her, she saw that his last name was Walker.

Without moving, she brought up her heads-up display. Microcomputers—or, in her case, an oracle—were systems designed to interact with communicators, pads, and networks and built into the skull. In Kassian space, heads-up displays were so commonplace that it was considered strange not to have one. They were usually implanted once the skull was fully developed, unless there was a need to place them in earlier. Leilani had been one of those who'd had hers put in when she was very young. Of course, hers had been updated and adjusted several times since then.

She mentally performed a quick search to see whether there was an open link with a roster. Luckily, the Kass navy standards held. Kevin was Recruit Walker's first name.

"Hey, Kevin. It's going to be okay, but I need you to breathe. Try to breathe evenly. In—one, two, three. Out—one, two, three."

He was unconscious, but quite often, unconscious people could still hear what was going on around them.

She took the young hand in hers and squeezed gently as she kept repeating, "In—one, two, three. Out—one, two, three."

His breathing started slowing. Then she heard the *dong* of metal connecting with metal as the shuttle started the docking procedure with the larger ship orbiting around the planet. The sound caused the man next to her to skip a breath.

"Come on, Kevin. You'll be okay. Breathe with me." She squeezed and continued counting until his breathing calmed again.

The gunny started walking down the aisle toward her. He stopped right in front of her, his back to her, facing the rest of the new recruits.

"All right. I want everyone to reach up and punch that large round circle on your chest that's holding your harness in place. Punch it hard—some of them stick."

The compartment clanged with loud sounds as everyone did as they were told. Some of them had to hit theirs several times before the harness came loose. Lei didn't move. She knew what the gunny was doing.

"And stand up. Hurry up! Get your neighbor out if they seem stuck. Kassian marines leave no one behind."

The hatch to the front still hadn't opened, which meant the lieutenant was waiting for his cue. Finally, as the last person stood, the hatch whooshed open.

"Who turned off my damn speaker?" The lieutenant stormed right up to the gunnery sergeant, which put him annoyingly close to her. "How dare you disobey direct orders!" The man went red in the face again. "Are these wastes of space ready to get off my damn ship?"

"Yes, sir!" The scream from the ship was enough to cause the man sitting next to her to jump slightly.

Leilani knew better than to speak, but she began pumping her hand in the breathing pattern again. It wasn't enough. She could feel his breathing getting weaker. Looking toward Morrison, she shook her head slowly.

"Then get the hell off!" the lieutenant screamed and stomped back to the cockpit. He didn't go inside, however. He waited, his eyes glued on Lei and Walker.

"File out, starting with seat one. Grab your duffel, and follow Corporal Henderson out." The gunny pointed toward a woman near the hatch.

"Move it!" Henderson yelled loudly. "Faster!"

But there were a hundred souls on the shuttle. They could move only so fast. As her row cleared, Lei kept one hand on Walker's wrist, monitoring his pulse. Only half the recruits had made it off before his pulse stopped. They'd run out of time. Disruptive or not, if she didn't do something, he would be dead.

She swung her hand hard and hit the man in the dead center of his chest, triggering his harness to release. She then pushed her way past the gunny and pulled the man to the deck.

"Get back in your seat, Thompson," the gunny growled in a low voice.

Ignoring him, she laid Walker flat and began compressions. Morrison suddenly realized what was going on and rushed to her.

He yanked an object from his bag and shooed her off. "I got it, Thompson."

She leaned back as he set a device in the center of the man's torso. Six strands leapt out from it to surround the chest cavity, and his body convulsed as the device began compressions. Morrison then strapped another device over Walker's mouth and nose. This one forced oxygen into his lungs.

A hand grabbed hold of Lei's arm, and she twitched as her reflexes yearned to defend her. There were still a few people trailing out of the ship. Glancing toward the owner of the hand, she found one of the heavily armored marines. A private, it looked like, but his armor was designed to mask rank.

"I told you to sit back down, Thompson." The gunny's voice was cool, and his eyes were calculating. He was deciding how to escalate from here.

The private almost threw her into the chair behind her, and again she fought the urge to defend herself.

In the aisle, Walker had begun breathing on his own again. He would survive, though she wasn't sure he would be all that pleased about it.

The ship finally emptied of all but the four marine guards, the lieutenant, and the gunny. A stretcher and a naval medical team had come in to haul Walker away.

"All right, Thompson. Here's how this goes," the gunny said. "Either you will fall out and follow orders to the letter, or I'll throw your ass in the brig."

Ironically, the lieutenant in the hatchway said nothing.

"Refusing a direct order has a rather severe penalty in the Kassian Navy, and as a recruit, you have no rights at all. You belong to me, and I will do with you whatever I see fit. Is that understood?"

Lei's eyes hardened as the two of them locked gazes.

"Yes, gunnery sergeant." Her words were slow and deep.

She saw the gun butt heading toward her abdomen and resisted the urge to parry it. When it struck her, she barely moved, bending only slightly and standing back up immediately. The gunny had already moved off, preventing her from locking eyes with him again.

Outside the shuttle, the recruits had been lined up in two platoons inside of a large bay. The bulkheads were exactly the same stark dark gray as the metal deck. On the bulkhead was stamped the name of the ship—IKSRC *Phenom*—in large black letters.

The sound of distant voices echoing off the hull was hollow. A little farther down, the cargo container carrying the individual storage boxes of each recruit's personal belongings was being unloaded.

As her large duffel swung toward her from behind, she glimpsed it in her peripheral vision and caught it just in time to prevent it from slamming into her. Shouldering the bag with practiced ease, she took off at a jog to fall in with her unit across the large bay.

2

TARGETS ARE US

It took forty minutes before they finally got to their barracks. They were given twenty to read their manuals and learn how to properly stow their gear and make their beds.

Not bothering to read, Lei instead began stowing her belongings. The woman whose bunk was below hers watched her carefully.

"Aren't you going to read how to do it right?"

"Nope." Lei finished stowing her gear, then closed the locker. Turning back to her bunk, she unfolded the sheets and blanket and began making the bed.

The whole process took about three minutes. She then moved to the end of the bunk and stood with her hands clasped behind her back and her feet slightly apart. Her stomach hurt where she had been struck, but she ignored it. Leilani's oracle, her advanced internal computer system, had been mostly shut down due to the level of undercover work she'd been involved in as Amanda. But her heads-up display, or HUD, was showing only minimal damage. The pain would go away in a day or two.

"Wow. You did it exactly like the docs." The girl was peering into Leilani's drawer.

"Careful," Lei said without looking back over her shoulder. "There's a pretty serious punishment for going through another recruit's belongings."

"I hear they're going to just come through and tear it apart anyway if you do it right." A nervous male recruit looked up from across the way, where he was busily trying to make his bed.

Lei said nothing.

"Hey, Thompson?" another male called to her from farther down the long aisle, where he, too, stood at the foot of his bed, also at parade rest. "I wanted to say thanks." He was slightly older, like herself. She recognized him as one of the four recruits on the ship who hadn't been freaking out.

"For?"

"Walker."

She nodded. "No man left behind."

"Oorah," a female even farther down called out.

The female behind her stepped into the aisle. "What does that mean?"

Lei shook her head. "No talking unless you're done packing and making your bed!" she yelled loud enough for the entire barracks to hear her. The sound came out with such practiced authority that the woman next to her jumped slightly.

"Damn, you sound like them."

"Don't insult me like that." Lei grimaced. "I just know you can't learn something new and talk at the same time."

The room grew fairly quiet, with only the occasional questions.

When the hatch opened at the end and the gunny stepped in, every single recruit was standing at parade rest at the foot of their bed.

There was a long pause.

"Company! Attention!"

The Kassian Navy had several recruit-training vessels, designated IKSRC, or Imperial Kassian Ship Recruit Carrier. Each had a regular crew that ran the ship itself, but the bulk of the vessel was set up for the basic training of the hundreds of thousands of recruits needed to maintain the 1,143 solar systems in the Kassian Empire. The ships were so massive they were often called small planetoids, though that description was not accurate, as they were not able to affect system-wide gravity wells.

Leilani had seen these vessels in passing, but the military had never really been a part of her jurisdiction. This little sidetrack, while tedious, was at least informative. She was learning about the minor crew skills that had just never come up in her regular training. After all, in the navy, all members were smart hands. They had to be.

"In space, you're on your own," the petty officer first class at the front of the classroom stated flatly. "You'd better be able to count on the guy next to you to know enough to follow your orders. No matter what their job on the ship is." He tapped his pad, and a word appeared on the screen. *Hydro-inserter.*

Almost in unison, each person in the small platoon reached down into the toolbox in front of them and pulled up the same tool.

"Good. We're done for today." He looked down at his pad and furrowed his brow in confusion. "Apparently, you now have PT. Head to the field. You'll be on mat nine for hand-to-hand training."

One of Lei's fellow recruits, a man named Simmons, turned and frowned over his shoulder at Leilani.

"Move it!" the petty officer yelled.

He got the reaction he was looking for; several people jumped and jogged toward the hatch.

Over the last week, the petty officers in charge of their unit had gotten very frustrated with Leilani. She knew all of their tricks, and she ensured that the rest of her unit learned them quickly with minimal friction. She knew good and well that she wouldn't be staying here for long, but the recruits in her unit would be here for their full term. She did everything in her power to protect her unit by drawing the ire of the trainers toward herself rather than the others.

"Today, we're going to learn basic hand to hand." The tall marine in front of the group had dirty-blond hair and multiple scars on his face and arms. Based on the look and pattern of them, they were more than likely from fighting rather than from gun combat.

"Does anyone out there think they can beat me in hand to hand?" His shirt had the name Keller printed on it and two stripes, denoting the rank of corporal. They really hadn't seen much of this corporal, but based on his size and movement, Lei had a sneaking suspicion he was one of the guards from her first day.

She had briefed the unit about this particular tactic. There were seven martial artists in the group, but she'd told them all to just do as they were ordered. This was more for the people who couldn't fight than for the people who could.

"Thompson, front and center."

She heard sighs from the people around her.

Behind her, Anderson mumbled, "This is getting old."

She agreed. This *was* getting old.

"Remember what I told you," she said loud enough for most of them to hear.

"What did you say, Thompson?"

"None of your concern, Corporal Keller." She kept her voice low.

His posture tightened in anger. "I think it *is* my concern, Thompson."

"Very well, Corporal. I told them to ignore your blustering." Leilani kept her face neutral. If she could get him to attack her first, then any response on her part would be self-defense. Hopefully, that would draw the attention of someone higher up the chain of command.

The young corporal was easier to instigate than she had expected. He swung at her with a clearly practiced sucker punch, but she simply stepped aside.

"You enjoy punching people when you think they can't defend, don't you, Corporal? Not a very honorable trait in a marine," she added, making sure to speak quietly enough that the audio sensors wouldn't pick it up clearly.

The man roared and charged, which surprised her. With one deft counter, she sent him flying a good ten feet into the air. She hoped he knew how to land.

Indeed he did. He tucked and rolled heavily, obviously injured by the distance. The display, however, drew the attention of the officers who were overseeing the training.

He approached her more carefully this time. After a deft feint, his foot came up in a blow intended to kill. That was all she needed. It was now self-defense, and the cameras would prove it. She stepped into the kick and punched the side of his knee with just the right pressure to snap it audibly.

He screamed, and several instructors who had been standing by in case something like this happened rushed to the mat to attack her.

Leilani decided that if they weren't going to teach the class, she would.

"Occasionally, when engaging in hand to hand, you will have more than one opponent." She changed her stance to defend against multiple opponents. "The trick of multiperson combat is to keep track of where all your opponents are at all times."

The purpose of her lecture was twofold. It was designed to drag out the fighting as well as to educate. Forty-five seconds later, all five instructors were lying on the mat with debilitating injuries. But it didn't look like she was going to have any shortage of opponents anytime soon. Five more marines approached slowly, this time with stun batons. Remaining calm as they approached, she continued to teach.

"Remember, if your opponent has a weapon, then so do you. There's never a shortage of weapons in a fight." She smiled and looked to the guards. "Which one of you would like to give me your weapon first?"

Two minutes later, they, plus four marines in armor, were also lying on the mat. The addition of the stun batons had made it even easier to take out her opponents without serious injuries. Not that medical wouldn't be able to put them all back together, regardless of the damage she dealt—so long as she kept them alive.

"Hold." A stern female voice spoke up.

Lei turned toward the voice and saw a one-star admiral step onto the mat. She snapped to attention, dropping the stun batons. When the admiral's gaze shifted to Lei's right, she instinctively ducked and stepped back in time to dodge another stun baton swinging at her head with enough force to easily crush her skull. With a skilled spin kick, she dropped the attacker to the mat. It was Gunny Smith.

Figures.

"What part of *hold* is difficult for you two?" The admiral towered over the prone gunny. "Gunnery Sergeant, I'm putting you on report for refusing a direct order," the woman growled. "And you." She turned her attention back to Lei. "Recruit Thompson. What is going on here?"

"Self-defense education, ma'am."

The admiral looked around at the unconscious and broken bodies on the mat. She walked over to one of the armored marines and picked up the baton lying near him. When she glanced at the setting, her eyebrows drew together, and her jaw clenched. She pointed to one of the batons that Lei had been using and held out her hand for it.

Lei grabbed the baton lying at her feet and placed it in the admiral's outstretched hand.

The woman looked at Lei's setting and sighed.

The marines had theirs set to lethal. That had become painfully obvious the first time one of them connected, but she was far tougher than she looked. Leilani, however, had turned hers down. She had no desire to kill a bunch of morons. Hurt them, yes, but there was enough death in her life. There was no need to kill anyone today.

The admiral gestured to one of the men who had followed her onto the mat. "Chief?"

The master chief stepped forward.

"You will take over this class. Take them to training mat eleven."

The chief stepped forward and bowed to Lei.

"With your permission, Recruit Thompson, may I have the class?" His face remained neutral, but his bow had been respectful and genuine.

Lei smiled and returned the bow. "Of course, Master Chief. The class is yours." She went back to attention.

"Come with me, Thompson." The admiral turned and approached a colonel standing near the edge of the mat. She handed him one of the batons. "Take care of this."

"Which one was hers?"

"This one." She handed him the second baton. He looked at both of them and shook his head.

"Yes, ma'am."

Brigitta Gremm, rear admiral lower half, and Amanda Thompson, recruit, walked with four guards up the catwalk to an office that had a rather spectacular view of the training field.

The admiral sat at her desk and started flipping through data on her pad. Two marines had come in with them, while the other two remained outside. Lei stood at attention in front of the desk and waited to be addressed.

"So. I have reports here that you have repeatedly refused to follow orders and that you are a detriment to the training in your company." She leaned back in her chair. "At ease."

Lei shifted her weight and relaxed with her hands behind her back.

"Yet your company has the highest marks of any to come through here in the last five years. You are already two weeks ahead of schedule. And according to one of my lieutenants, you have been nothing but the model recruit, caring more about your team than your own well-being." She waved the pad in the air gently. "He recommended you for a promotion, which my trainers immediately denied."

The woman steepled her fingers in front of her. "What do you have to say to that?"

"I have no comment at this time, ma'am."

She raised an eyebrow. "I highly doubt that. But I recognize your right to say so."

The admiral looked off to the side, no doubt getting a message in her heads-up display. "Not even one serious injury. That is statistically unlikely."

The hatch behind Lei opened, and the admiral stood to attention.

"Admiral Gremm." Lei didn't move as the male voice spoke up behind her. "I need you to step out, please."

"No disrespect, Admiral Dorthy, but this is *my* recruit."

"I understand that. I just need a few moments with her."

"I will be filing a protest." The woman stood and strode past him into the passageway, or p-way.

"Understood." The three-star admiral, who had white hair and a charming smile, stepped up next to Lei as the woman left.

As the hatch was closing, he set a small device on the desk. It started spinning and growing taller. Then a translucent bubble expanded from it until it surrounded both of them, at which point it seemed to vanish. The device hummed softly.

"Report?" Admiral Jason Dorthy asked.

"What the fuck took you so long?"

He raised an eyebrow at her.

"Sir," she added somewhat indignantly.

"It took me longer to get off world than I expected. Luckily, there was this massive naval vessel in orbit for me to catch a lift on."

Lei chuckled.

"I'd like to point out . . . you missed your debrief." He leaned back on the desk and crossed his arms.

"Ya think?"

He shrugged. "Do it now."

"I can't. They locked up all my gear."

"You can give me a verbal, at least."

"Target was corrupt and eliminated as ordered."

"Any complications?"

Lei shook her head. "Just this shit." She spread her arms out to encompass their surroundings.

"Yeah." The look on Dorthy's face did not make Lei happy. "About that . . ."

"Don't you dare," she growled.

"Command says you stay."

"No."

The admiral's white eyebrows formed a tight line across his forehead. "That is not a request."

"At least make me an officer."

He unfolded his arms. "How did you end up enlisted, anyway?"

"I have no idea. The idiot rating either didn't understand my degree or didn't believe me." She shrugged.

"I'll see what I can do. But this far from command, I can't promise anything fast."

"What about this Admiral Gremm?" Lei went back to parade rest. Things like lip reading were impossible with the shield around them, but reading her basic body language wasn't.

"It's her you're investigating."

"And I'm supposed to do that as a recruit?"

"Your orders are to stay navy. How you do that is up to you. You know how this works. The more involved command gets, the more likely you are to be found out."

"Which means we're doing a veeshali on this, then?"

The admiral nodded.

Veeshali—the elari word for forgetting. The Imperial Investigative Service possessed a number of fun toys that were not available to regular Kassian civilians or even the military. In this case, Dorthy had a device on his person that, when triggered, would send out a wave of energy designed to affect all biological entities within range.

Such devices were often preprogrammed to delete specific memories or eliminate a certain time frame from a person's mind.

"Right, then, you'd better get out of here. I'll be in touch when I get my gear back. I'm guessing she's the bottom tier of the investigation?"

Admiral Dorthy shrugged. "Probably. All command knows is that the death rate on these recruit vessels is too high, and we think the issue might fall under our jurisdiction. She might be part of this, and she might not. That's for you to figure out."

"You people don't make my job easy."

The admiral tapped the device on the desk, and the bubble popped. He then walked over to the hatch and pushed it open. On the other side, Admiral Gremm was talking to a lieutenant.

"Thank you very much for allowing me to use your office, Admiral. I apologize for taking up your time."

There was a pulse behind Lei as the veeshali triggered. It started at Dorthy and would most likely travel through the whole ship . . . or until it had made all the needed adjustments. Behind her, the conversation paused briefly before he began the memory insertion.

"You were right, Admiral. I don't believe she *is* the criminal I'm looking for, but I thank you kindly for allowing me to interrogate her in your office."

"I'd like to help in catching your criminal. Do I have a full profile?" Gremm's words came out slowly, no doubt because her mind was trying to fill in the gaps that had just been made.

"My date stamp says you received it yesterday. Wasn't that why you brought her up here? To interrogate her?"

"Yes, that's right. She was causing trouble, so I thought she might be your suspect." She was talking faster now, her tone more confident.

"Thank you for your assistance, Admiral Gremm. But this woman is simply a handful. Her record appears to be clean." His tone grew quieter as the last of the energy waves passed over the room and he planted a last subtle thought. "Though I highly doubt she is enlisted material. You might want to ask if she has any education."

"Thank you for the assist, Admiral Dorthy." As Dorthy left, the woman walked back into the room and sat in her chair again. "Have a seat, Thompson." She picked up her pad once more and tapped a few things, then swiped through a file.

Lei sat down.

"According to this, you have no schooling?"

Lei shook her head, rolling her eyes.

"Not true?"

"I informed the rating that I had a PhD in abnormal physics. I'm not sure he even understood what I said."

"I'm not sure *I* understood what you just said. What is abnormal physics?"

"It encompasses M-theory and abnormal phenomena that can't be explained with typical physics, such as dark matter." When the admiral continued to look confused, Lei resisted the urge to roll her eyes again. "Think of me as a private investigator who researches things no one else understands."

"Do you work for a university?"

"I did, until I was kidnapped and coerced into military service." Lei shrugged. Her words seemed to imply she was referring to this time, but in reality, that had happened many, many years ago.

"Hmm. Well, this ship isn't really set up for OCS training at this time, so for now, I'll have you assigned to me, and we'll do your training personally. When we get to Oltherian Prime, I'll transfer you to the OCS there." The woman made some adjustments to the data on the pad and tossed the file into digital oblivion.

Lei smiled and nodded. "That will work just fine."

3

INFORMATION GATHERING

Lei sat in the galley, reading through the data on her pad as she sipped a cup of hot coffee. The last week had been spent dealing mostly with administrative crap. Inputting reports and data management. Today was the first day she had been given something more interesting. It seemed the incident that had led the admiral to her hadn't been an isolated one.

In the last three years, the ship had suffered more than a hundred deaths per class cycle, which meant anywhere from three to eight hundred deaths per year. For a ship that cycled through more than a hundred thousand recruits a year, that number was fairly low. Admiral Gremm had done a little digging into historical records, however, and found that the death rate had jumped exponentially around ten years ago. Gremm herself, though, had been assigned to the training vessel only three years ago, which eliminated her as a suspect.

"Anything interesting?" A female voice next to her caused her to set the pad down, which automatically forced the screen to go blank—a basic security feature found in all military pads.

Lei glanced to the woman sitting next to her. Senior Lieutenant Carson oversaw one of the many firearms training fields. She had been trying to cozy up to Lei ever since Lei was pulled from recruit training and assigned to the admiral's personal staff.

"More stupid paperwork." Lei shrugged and glanced into her cup. It was too full to justify getting up and walking away for a refill. She took a bigger drink, hoping to remedy the situation.

"Funny word—paperwork. I mean, paper is that ancient stuff made from trees, right?"

"Yes."

"So then why do we call it paperwork?" The woman pushed her food around on her plate. "I mean, there's no paper involved. Pretty sure paper was *never* involved. That's just for those antique books."

"You think mankind has always had digital pads?"

"Haven't they?"

Lei stared at her for several seconds. Her mind was having a difficult time assimilating that answer. "Wow. And on that note, I need more coffee."

The woman looked confused, pointing with her fork to Lei's cup.

"But you still *have* coffee."

Lei drank the rest in one gulp, then shrugged. "And now it's empty. Have a good meal, ma'am."

"See ya, Thompson." The woman waved, but Lei ignored her.

After refilling her cup and putting a lid on it, she wandered from the galley.

She glanced at her pad and frowned. The data wasn't looking good. She was fairly sure, at this point, that it wasn't the admiral, but there was definitely a problem. In a situation like this, there was usually one clear line of troublemakers that got transferred in, beat people up, and left. But this time, that wasn't the case.

A voice in her ear caught her attention. "Amanda?"

"Yes, ma'am?"

"Come to my quarters."

Lei changed directions and wove her way through the passageways in officer country until she came to the admiral's personal quarters. The marine at the hatch nodded.

"She's waiting on you. Go ahead."

There were four marines on the admiral's personal staff. They'd come with her on every post. Their presence clearly marked her as noble, but that wasn't entirely unusual for higher-ranking officers. Nepotism was alive and well in Kassian military echelons.

She stepped into a large living area featuring two couches, a conference table, and a comms station. There was no one inside but the admiral, which was unusual. She didn't generally meet with Lei alone.

"Come in, Ensign. Will you look at this, please?"

The woman was sitting on the couch with several flimsies and pads laid out on the small coffee table in front of her.

Lei stepped up and looked down at the mess of data. She recognized several ship names and what looked to be medical reports.

The admiral waved her hand above a pile of data pads. "Take a minute. I need a refill. You?" She picked up her own cup and pointed to Lei's.

"No, thank you. I'm good." Lei shifted some of the pads around. "These are all of the recruiting ships in the various fleets."

"Yes," the woman called through an open hatch.

"According to this data, there are three ships with this kind of death rate, but it hasn't been going on as long on the others." Lei picked up a pad that had sensor readings on it. The readings were wrong. They had to be. "What is this sensor readout?"

"Yesterday, after our slip, I had the captain scan the ship. Then I had him scan the fleet as a whole. Most of the data was normal, except for that. That's when I thought of you and your degree." She smiled. "Besides, without you, I wouldn't even be looking into this."

"Where did these scan results come from?"

"This ship." Admiral Gremm sat back on the couch with her feet tucked up under herself.

"I need access to my gear," Lei blurted out.

The admiral raised both eyebrows in surprise.

"That might be difficult. The storage containers of recruits' gear aren't really set up for easy access while stowed aboard the recruit carrier. Though I suppose yours should be pulled anyway, since you've been removed from your company. I'll have it done immediately." She lifted a pad and tapped a few things. "I assume you know what that is?"

She gestured to the flimsy in Lei's hand.

"I've seen it before, yes. But without my gear, I can't prove it."

"We have regulations about the use of civilian gear aboard military vessels."

"You also have regulations about murder aboard military vessels."

"Touché." The admiral took a deep breath, then sipped her coffee as she looked the scattered data over. "Do you think this is an accident?"

"No, ma'am." Lei was still standing, and she held out the flimsy with the sensor readings. "This proves that it isn't."

Somehow, Admiral Brigitta Gremm's brows furrowed without showing a single wrinkle on her perfectly smooth face. She sipped her coffee cautiously.

"This won't look good on my record." She patted the seat cushion next to her. "Sit. I don't like people hovering over me."

Lei sat on the edge of the couch. There was no way she was going to relax in this woman's presence. Something about her just made Lei feel edgy.

"Wow, you really *are* uptight." The admiral tried to smile, but it was halfhearted. "I don't blame you. I've been uptight since I took this post. There's just something wrong with this ship. Too bad it took one of my recruits almost killing my entire hand-to-hand team before I looked into it."

Lei didn't know what to say. The woman was right.

"So, Doctor, what's the next step?"

Lei tossed the flimsy onto the table. "I need my gear. Then we find the source of the energy readings."

"Is it an item?"

"Sometimes." Lei shrugged. Any method she had of finding the information without her gear was strictly forbidden. Well, it was when there were possible witnesses, at least. "It's hard to explain."

The woman grimaced at her. "What are the odds that something like this would exist on my ship, and then suddenly an expert falls in my lap?"

"Strangely, the law of large numbers would say it's higher than you might think."

"I doubt that." The admiral took another sip of her coffee. "After all, secret investigators like you exist all across the imperium, and if this has been going on for ten years, one of you was bound to show up eventually."

They stared at each other for several long heartbeats.

"Relax, Amanda. Despite what you might think, I'm happy you're here. This one is out of my wheelhouse. Why do you think I put you in charge of the investigation? You're new on the ship. And as for knowing what you are? A three-star admiral shows up off the same planet I found you on and feels the need to immediately talk to you individually? Don't get me wrong, I believed his story . . . for a while."

Lei slowly scanned the room, shifting a filter in her internal heads-up display as she did so. She was not all that surprised to find several minor telltales of aether technology in the room. But as she got to the hatch, she realized what was going on. There were two very bright spots outside the room on either side of the hatch. If all four of the admiral's guards were aethers, that would explain why the memory insertion hadn't held.

"They're genies. Assigned by my family. I go with them everywhere—or they go with me. I suppose it depends on how you look at it." Admiral Gremm answered Lei's unasked question.

Lei narrowed her eyes at the admiral. The admiral was not an aether, which was odd—why, then, would she have aether guards? She quickly searched the ship's secure files until she found the admiral's.

Since she hadn't been on the ship when the death rate started spiking, Lei hadn't looked too deep into the woman until now.

Firstborn of House Shovalli. Brigitta's father, Duke Ferdis Steven Shovalli, owned three solar systems and ran a multi-trillion-dollar mining company that supplied materials for ships to the imperial naval shipyards. Gremm appeared to be using her mother's maiden name rather than her father's. Running the Shovalli name through her own internal database, Lei found a surprising match.

"You're royal." Lei's statement was flat. Annoyed.

She had been ordered to investigate the loyalties of the woman and, if needed, eliminate her. How the fuck did they think eliminating a royal would go? With aether guards, it certainly wasn't going to be easy. Did Dorthy even know she was royal? And how had she hidden that fact all this time? Someone had to have helped her cover this up.

"That is not common knowledge, and I prefer to keep it that way." The admiral was watching her carefully. One didn't make it to admiral without experience, and this woman was carefully calculating Leilani's every move.

"Understood, ma'am, but it does change the parameters of my job."

"I disagree." The woman smiled. "You're navy now. And your job is to find out what's causing the deaths and, if possible, to stop it and arrest those responsible." She took a deep breath before adding, "That includes me, if need be. Do we understand each other?"

Lei was suddenly very uncomfortable having her back to the aether genies. Even though they were on the other side of the hatch.

"Yes, ma'am."

"Good. Now take this order, and go get your gear."

Lei stood and turned toward the exit. "Yes, ma'am."

The hatch slid open, and one of the armored marines stepped in with his helmet removed. It was the first time she had ever seen one of their faces. His eyes were a deep red, almost black, and his skin far pinker than a typical human's. The tiny horns on his forehead either had been filed down or were oddly small. He nodded curtly and stepped aside before snapping to attention in front of the admiral.

As Lei passed him, she saw the traditional barcode tattoo on the inside of his pointed ear, indicating that he was not fully human; rather, he had been genetically engineered. Genies were common all across the galaxy and generally engineered for a specific purpose. These ones were a mix she had seen before. They had been specialized for aether combat and general guard work, making them much faster, stronger, and tougher than any pure human being. Anyone who knew anything about royals would certainly know for what—and for *whom*—these guards had been designed. Likely, that was the reason they were always in uniform.

"Fuck me," she mumbled under her breath as she walked out of the admiral's quarters.

4

RAMPANT MORBID ANGER

"And I don't fucking care who you think you are!"

The angry male voice drifted to Leilani's ears as she entered the cargo hold.

The massive warehouse was filled with stacks of large cargo containers. Each corresponded to a particular recruit unit and held several smaller containers, which belonged to the individual recruits. When recruits' personal belongings were taken from them at processing, they were securely sealed with each person's own biometrics to ensure that only the owner could open them.

"Back off, Lieutenant, before you find yourself going on an unscheduled space walk."

Lei blinked several times and resisted the urge to shake her head. Such hostility aboard a ship like this was highly unusual.

"Fuck off, Chief." There was a loud slam from somewhere inside the maze of cargo containers. "I'm telling you that you will follow the order or I will throw your ass in the brig!"

Lei wound her way through the racks, trying to find the source of the argument.

"Then who's gonna do all this work, Lieutenant?"

Lei walked around the corner in time to see the lieutenant pick up an enormous wrench and charge toward the chief's back.

She cleared her throat. "Lieutenant?"

Turning his head toward her, the smaller man ungracefully ran into the larger one. This resulted in a loud thump and clang as the wrench struck the smaller lieutenant on his own shoulder, at which point he and his weapon both fell to the deck in a heap.

The chief turned to face her. He was clearly a genie. His arms were longer than was typical for a human and his legs slightly shorter, giving him a build like an ape, which was likely what his genetics were mixed with. At about seven feet tall and nearly five feet wide, he looked like he could bench press an antigravity car.

On his lapel was the insignia of a chief, which meant he probably had a decade or more in service over the lieutenant currently lying on the deck. The chief glanced down at the younger man before stepping over him and walking up to her.

"How can I help you today, Ensign?" His smile was bright and calm. His green eyes sparkled with humor.

"I need container 247-JCX." She handed him the pad she was carrying.

The chief pointed upward without looking at the pad. Above them, attached to the crane, was a large cargo container.

"I'm moving it for off-loading. What do you need it for?"

"I was reassigned and am no longer with the company. So I need to recover my belongings."

"Sounds reasonable, Ensign, but I can't pull anything from the container without approval from fleet."

Lei pointed to the pad, and the chief began skimming it.

"Hmm. Well, damn." He glanced up at the cargo container currently hovering over them in the lifter's arms.

"Looks like you were right," the chief called to the lieutenant, who was sobbing and holding his shoulder. "All right, Ensign. I was moving this anyway to get ready for transfer. Give me a few minutes to get it in place, and I'll pull the box you need. That okay?"

"Thank you, Chief. And the lieutenant?" She glanced down at the injured officer.

"He's a big boy now, as he keeps reminding me. He'll be fine. Besides, I didn't touch him." The chief shrugged as he lumbered off.

A few minutes later, the lifter began gliding through the narrow aisles toward a massive cargo hatch in the outer hull of the ship.

Lei knelt down next to the injured man.

"Lieutenant, are you okay?"

"No, I'm not okay, you idiot!" he snapped at her.

It was rapidly growing clear why this lieutenant was not well liked.

"Help me up, plebe!"

She stared at him for several seconds before finally reaching out and lifting him, carefully avoiding his injured shoulder—even though she really wanted to do the opposite.

The man shrieked and took a swing at her with his good arm. This, of course, caused him to drop the bad shoulder, which in turn caused more shrieking and another wild swing. It was so off the mark that he slammed his fist into one of the massive steel beams used to hold the containers in place. The screaming began again, and he quickly fell into a ball on the deck.

Lei took a step back from the insane lieutenant and wrinkled her nose in pity. She tapped the comms unit on her wrist and got a soft chime in her ear.

"Medical," she requested through the small computer.

"Medical one, how may we assist?" a female voice from the other end called back.

"I have an injured lieutenant in cargo three."

"Again?" The woman sounded exasperated. "Fine. I'll send a tech with a sedative. Just try to keep him from hurting himself any further."

Not for the first time that day, Lei really wished she had her gear.

The man curled into the fetal position on the deck, sobbing and rocking himself back and forth.

Lei took another step back and scratched her head. Something was very wrong here. The hairs on the back of her neck stood up, and she dropped her weight, spreading her legs slightly as she prepared to fight. She shifted her internal systems to display aether and saw a small flash zip past her.

"Shit."

Another flash; then two tiny ones moving in opposite directions. There were more than one of them, and she had just inadvertently told them she could see them. She was in trouble. Something leapt at her extremely fast, and she felt a tiny claw rip across her cheek. It stung, but it was nothing compared to the poison she knew she would feel soon enough. Without her gear, she was vulnerable. And now that they knew she could see them, the shera weren't likely to let up.

She closed her eyes and focused on her internal systems. As they started booting up and coming online, she felt two more slashes: one across her shoulder and a second on her opposite thigh.

Suddenly, the world slowed down as one of her combat systems came online. She opened her eyes. She could now clearly see it streaking past: a tiny, naked creature with a large head and spindly arms. Shera were no more than a foot long, but they didn't need to be large to cause chaos. They literally fed off the fear and anger of other creatures. Their presence explained a lot about the state of the ship. They were likely everywhere, yet most Kassian sensors would never notice them.

Her hand snapped out, grabbed the tiny thing by the head, and squeezed. It splattered easily, shooting bluish-black blood everywhere. There was a quiet squeak of surprise—a total deviation from their nature. Lei spun toward the sound and swung at the other creature. Her fist knocked it into a nearby cargo container, and it dropped. She felt a slash on her back, which luckily missed her spine, and pivoted toward it with her hand already out. The creature crashed into her palm. She squeezed. Another down.

The creature that she had punched recovered itself and began whispering. She could barely make out the words.

"Come. Help! Have aether warrior. Come all!" His tiny voice was high pitched. To anyone who couldn't see the creatures—which was everyone aboard the *Phenom* except her—it would sound like the squeak of an ungreased wheel.

Lei scooped up the wrench on the ground and chucked it at the creature. Her aim was true, and blue-black goo splattered everywhere. But it was already too late. Tiny screeches could be heard over the soft hum of the ship's engines, and the sound was growing into a deafening roar. Lei turned and started running. She wound her way through the containers as fast as her enhanced legs could carry her.

As she slid around a corner, she saw the chief pulling a small personal box from the cargo container. Her luck was changing. She leapt into the air and roughly planted both feet against his chest. He was so surprised that he was kicked clear of the area and slid back into the deck wall. The action might knock him unconscious, but regardless, it would force him clear of the fight.

Slamming her hand down on the box, she waited half a heartbeat while it scanned and processed her identity. When it slid open, the gear inside was already shifting itself in anticipation.

"*Rosh!*" she yelled as the first wave of tiny creatures washed over, through, and around the cargo containers where she was standing.

The items in the container leapt into the air and started hurling themselves at her and locking into place. The device that wrapped around her wrist immediately triggered, creating a translucent blueness that slid across her body and enveloped her in a protective barrier just before the first of the creatures began to tear into her, shrieking vehemently.

She stumbled as she pulled her feet under herself and braced for more impacts. She began swinging at the tiny creatures, but there were so many of them that her swings were useless. In her HUD, the various pieces of gear checked in as ready. Then, finally, she got the green light for her weapons.

She pulled two pistols from the straps that had fastened themselves to her legs and began firing into the fray.

"Switch to spray!" she called to the internal computer, and the HUD readout that displayed her current ammunition changed. The next shot was more like buckshot, spraying out tiny little fireballs in a mass array. She kept firing as the creatures continued to come. She knew good and well that the blood and dead bodies were clearly visible to the chief behind her, but containment wasn't really a concern at the moment. Survival was.

"Holy shit!" the chief exclaimed.

"Get the lieutenant, and get out of here. They'll ignore you!" she yelled over the screaming creatures as he scrambled away from the fray. To herself, she added, "I hope."

She needed to create a distraction. Holstering one weapon, she reached into a bag on her belt and pulled out seven small balls. She tossed them in a wide arc along the cargo hatch. In her HUD, she triggered the balls, and seven similarly dressed people appeared and began firing into the cloud of shera. They were only holograms, but the creatures were too stupid to know that.

This is Agent Leilani Falconi. I have a class-five infestation and need a cleanup team ASAP!" Lei's thoughts projected through her embedded IIS comm unit, or silcomm. It allowed transference of information via thought rather than vocalization, but it was otherwise fairly similar to a normal communication device.

She knew the sounds of gunfire would travel across the comm. She then switched the frequency to the *Phenom* and tried to recall the name tag on the chief. Fredrickson. She searched for that name in the roster, but the distraction was enough that she missed a rather organized attack and found herself lifted off the ground and slammed into the bulkhead.

"Chief. You clear?" she called after letting out a soft *oof.*

"Yes, ma'am, and I got the brat too," he answered.

"Do you hear any more screeching in the hall?"

"No, ma'am."

"Then seal the hatch."

A painfully loud alarm sounded in her HUD. Her armor was at 20 percent. It was now or never. The shera swarmed over her, biting and clawing as they tried to tear through her protections. She turned her head, getting the lay of her surroundings.

Her luck was holding. The creatures had pressed her into the bulkhead directly next to the control panel. She slapped her hand into the emergency button.

"Armor integrity at 12 percent," a female voice said calmly inside her head.

"Emergency override. Commander Leilani Falconi, ID number 34A5F697 Jasper!" she yelled into the control panel on the hatch.

"Voiceprint verification accepted. Emergency evacuation sequence commencing," the ship computer chimed.

Red lights flashed, and a massive warning alarm sounded. The creatures on her chest screamed in fright. They turned and ran, flying toward the inner hatches and vents, but those sealed as the emergency evacuation protocols enacted. The massive cargo hatch next to her snapped open, and she, along with thousands of shera, were sucked out into space.

In her HUD, the warning lights kept flashing. Six percent. Six percent. Six percent.

"Ma'am?" Her internal oracle spoke up. *"At this rate, you will not be able to handle even space dust. I recommend getting to safety as soon as possible."*

"Gee, that thought never occurred to me. Thanks, Sarah." The sarcasm would be lost on the computer, but it somehow made Lei feel better.

"You are quite welcome, ma'am. Did I miss anything interesting while I was off-line?"

"Not really, no."

Nearby, there was a bright flash in space as a much smaller vessel appeared just off the port of the massive recruit carrier. It was sleek, with a striking black-and-red paint job—nothing like the hulking blue-and-green military vessel. The brightness dissipated as the ship fully entered real space again.

"You are being hailed, ma'am," Sarah chirped.

"Well, hello there, Agent. Want a lift?"

Leilani chuckled. *"Hello again, Admiral. And yes, I could use one right about now."*

5

CLEANUP

"How long do you think it will take to get the ship operational again?"

Captain Jessica Veridith was the lowest-ranking command person in the conference room, but the IKSRC *Phenom* was hers. As such, its mission parameters were time sensitive. She had to make drop-offs and pickups on time, or they would fall behind.

"Well, the agent needs to finish her investigation, and we have quite a bit of cleanup to do before we can clear the ship for service," Dorthy answered.

"What about the other training ships?" the general in charge of ground training asked.

"We will take care of them individually."

"What's left to finish with the investigation? I was told some sort of device was creating an abnormal energy field that was causing unnatural levels of aggression." Gremm seemed mildly annoyed. "Then what's left?"

"While it *is* true that we found the cause of the aggression, we still don't know how it got here or why."

"And what does that have to do with us?" General McDowell snapped.

He was another genie, slightly taller than a typical human, with somewhat elongated features and sharper teeth. Likely one of the combat models, with some sort of carnivore in his DNA. The fact that this particular genie had made it to the level of officer, let alone general, was amazing.

It had taken Leilani and the other agents five days to find the portal generator—or PG, as they called such devices—that had allowed the shera to sneak aboard the vessel. It had been hidden deep within the ship's bowels. The delay was causing problems within the fleet as well as within the recruit carrier itself. General McDowell and Admiral Gremm were growing frustrated.

"How is it taking you more than a week to take care of this simple situation? You find the device, remove it, and move on." Gremm's lack of tolerance for the delays was evident even as Dorthy tried to explain.

"It isn't as easy as you suggest, Admiral. For starters, this is a 1.2-million-ton vessel, and the device was smaller than three centimeters by four centimeters. It was hidden inside a heavily armored casing. This was not easy to find and was likely even harder to place."

"Regardless, you have your object and all of the ship's data files for the past ten years. Now get off my ship and out of my hair!" Gremm slammed her fist on the desk and rose from her chair, glaring at the higher-ranking admiral.

"My team still has people to question and loose ends to investigate, not to mention ensuring the ship is clear of any residual energy readings," Dorthy replied calmly.

"You've had five days to interview people. Not that it matters. You said yourself that, based on your scan data and the maintenance logs, the object was placed ten years ago. No one on this ship was here ten years ago." Gremm crossed her arms, her patience officially gone. "If you do not release my fleet in the next twenty-four hours, I will be forced to call my uncle and demand your resignation."

Admiral Dorthy smiled. "You're welcome to call whomever you wish, Brigitta, but it isn't going to change how I or my people do their jobs."

The use of her first name was completely within naval parameters for a junior officer, but in noble circles, a royal outranked an admiral. Dorthy was pushing the admiral's buttons on purpose.

"How dare you take a familiar tone with me! You will address me as 'ma'am,' 'Admiral,' or 'Your Grace.'"

Lei had been rolling a small marble between her fingers for several minutes now, but she'd finally had enough of the woman. She tossed the object into the center of the table, where it shattered into a wave of yellow smoke. As it rolled across the room, everyone froze except one guard at the hatch and two people in black trench coats with red trim.

The guard by the hatch took a step forward, and Lei drew one of her pistols. The energy chamber that fed into the barrel glowed a bluish green as she pointed it at him.

He froze.

"Get back to your post," she growled.

The man took a step back and went back to attention.

Jason sighed and leaned back in his chair, crossing his arms. "She has a point, sadly. We aren't going to be able to delay the fleet any further."

"I know. I was just tired of listening to her." Lei sat on the edge of the table next to her admiral. "Orders?"

"There has to be a link we're missing. Someone hides a microportal generator capable of opening a tiny hole between aether and kuldain space on a recruit carrier, allowing thousands of shera to sneak aboard. The little creatures then create enough hatred between the crew and recruits to gorge themselves and to potentially breed at an alarming rate in kuldain space. This wasn't a casual thing. This was premeditated and requires a clear understanding of both realms.

"Take the PG with you. Have Gellar make a copy for evidence lockup. And then go ask the prof. He might know more about it or be able to give us a maker's mark."

"All righty. But we still have twenty-four, right?"

"I'd rather not go that far, but yeah. What do you have in mind?"

"There've been a couple of things bugging me since I came aboard. I'm going to look into them."

The smoke was beginning to dissipate.

"Make it fast."

"Roger that." Lei holstered her pistol and walked up to the guard at the hatch. She couldn't see inside his visor, but she doubted he was smiling. She put her face up close to his and grinned.

"Good dog," she whispered as the others in the room coughed and the last of the yellow smoke vanished.

Leilani was done with this ship and everyone on it. When she was playing the part of Amanda Thompson, she had been polite and respectful because that was the role. But Leilani Falconi was sarcastic and short tempered. A much more entertaining character, in her opinion.

She stepped out into the p-way and found the other three guards waiting for her. One of them reached out with lightning-fast reflexes and grabbed hold of her hand; the other grabbed her other wrist.

She grinned. "Aw, c'mon, boys—you can't take a joke?"

She responded with reflexes they hadn't expected. Before they realized what was happening, the one's arm was cuffed to the other's with a sealband. In a split second, the aether technology crawled up both arms and encased their elbows and hands in one solid metal band.

She swung under their arms and wrapped her legs around the neck of the third guard, who was in front of her. With a snap, she yanked him to the ground and slapped a small patch on the back of his helmet. Inside, an electrical charge triggered, destroying the electronics and giving the genie a strong enough shock to knock him unconscious. He fell limp.

The first two reached for her with their free hands, only to find themselves restrained once again.

"You know what I love about royal guards?" She smiled down at them as she stood. "Your training regimen hasn't changed in more than a thousand years. You're predictable, boys."

She pulled the guns from their holsters and tossed them down the hall, well out of easy reach. Just as with her own weapons, their technology would prevent anyone else from using them.

"Especially you flunkies who wash out of the main program." She turned away and strode off to find a few people with whom she needed to have *words*.

6

AETHER VS.
KULDAIN REALITY

"Did you find anything interesting?"

"Yes, actually. It appears there's more going on here than I originally suspected." Lei tossed a memory stick on the desk and flopped none too gracefully into the overstuffed leather chair. Propping her feet up on the desk, she shrugged. "Who knew? Toss a few hundred thousand souls together in a confined space for years at a time, and corruption crops up someplace."

"Knock off with the sarcasm." Admiral Dorthy stood and walked around his large wooden desk to push her feet off. He then leaned against the desk to prevent her from putting them back on—a ritual that had become all too common between them.

She gestured to the memory stick.

"There's the full confession, but suffice to say, the admiral isn't as innocent as she portrays herself."

"That doesn't really surprise me. They usually aren't."

"She's been doing a few naughty things, but nothing in there is enough to arrest a royal."

Jason picked up a pad and inserted the stick. As he flipped through the pages of data, he shook his head.

"I don't know. Putting dead bodies for sale on the black market is damn close, but you're right. We wouldn't be able to make that stick. Man . . ." He let his words fade as he continued reading.

Finally, he tossed the pad to his desk and crossed his arms in frustration. "Gambling, extortion, bribery, and black-market dealings. But still not enough to tie directly to her—only to subordinates. That won't bring down a royal, even an extended one."

"Yeah. The enlisted are too afraid to talk, and the officers are getting paid too damn much to break their loyalty. The kickbacks alone on that ship are astounding. She did a damn good job of keeping her hands spotlessly clean." Leilani shrugged again.

Delving through the dark and dirty rooms of back-alley dealings was her specialty. Nothing really surprised her anymore.

"Well, either way, she wasn't the one who placed the portal generator, so she isn't really our problem right now. I'll pass this info to naval intel and let them take over."

"And if she has them in her pocket?"

Jason shook his head. "Doesn't matter. This isn't our investigation. Let the peons deal with it. It's a kuldain matter, not an aether one."

"She had aether guards!" Lei sat upright in the chair. She may not have been surprised by the woman's dirty dealings, but she also knew that if IIS dropped it, Gremm would walk away scot-free and likely continue down her dangerous path, killing more and more souls along the way.

"Doesn't matter. She isn't aether. Therefore, she does not fall under our jurisdiction, and you know it. Neither does any of this." He picked up the pad and shook it at her.

"What if she's somehow tied to the PG?"

The admiral's lips quirked, as though Lei had just walked into a trap. "Then prove it."

Yep—walked right into it. She blinked at him several times, then slouched back into the chair. "I guess I deserved that."

"Indeed. Now get out of my office, and go do something productive."

"Bite me." She stood up and walked toward the hatch.

"Excuse me?"

"Bite me, *sir!*" she snapped back and stormed out of his office.

Just as the hatch swooshed closed, she could hear him say, "That's better."

~~~

Leilani made her way through the ship to the transport hub. As she strolled along the p-ways, she thought back to her first lectures on eldrilin theory at Eldrich Line University many decades ago.

"In the beginning"—Professor Eagleton had been pacing in front of the class, slowly rolling the digital pointer between his fingers— "as many of my counterparts in kuldain space like to say—there was a big bang. We, however, simply call it the Great Sundering. Either way, there was a massive explosion. During that explosion, the entire universe was torn into two distinct realms. One we call kuldain, and the other we call aether. The weave of eldrich that tied all life together was ripped from kuldain space, and each planet was duplicated or ghosted. Each now existing in both planes."

He'd tapped a crystal on the desk, and a massive illusory hologram replaying the Great Sundering had erupted over the lecture hall. Hundreds of first-year students oohed and aahed.

"The universe was copied in every detail, save two." The image had shifted to show massive lines of pure power crackling and sparkling as they connected several planets in an eerie weave. "The first: only aether reality still has eldrich lines—or eldrilins, as we call them—tying each living planet together."

The image shifted again to show an immense ruined city of buildings that looked like they had once reached the lower atmosphere. It was now mostly overgrown rubble. "The second: only the planets that remained in the aether still have the ruins of the ancient civilizations associated with the cataclysm."

Later on in her college career, when Leilani had begun her graduate work, she'd been required to take a more advanced class from Professor Eagleton that explored how the two realms interacted with each other. That was where she'd learned about the IIS and its function—and, inevitably, how she'd been recruited into the IIS.

"Due to unique differences in the physics of each realm, kuldain space and aether space developed differently," the professor had explained in one of Leilani's most life-changing lectures. "One developed electronic and psionic technologies, while the other developed aether technology and magic." When he brought up a display of a Kassian battle cruiser, Leilani had been amazed. She'd known she had to see one of those ships someday.

"Kuldains moved into space and traveled between worlds on ships, colonizing as they went, while aethers built trams and moved between worlds using the massive rivers of eldrich energy that flow between and throughout the planets."

Leilani had only partially listened after that; instead, she had brought up different types of ships on her aether pad and begun reading about them.

"Eventually, gates—also called doors—were formed and made permanent between the two realms. The doors were added to the tram stations, allowing both aether and kuldain to move back and forth freely." Eagleton had gone on to explain that in kuldain space, like in aether space, there were many different governments and races. But the one that had expanded the fastest was the human government of Kass.

The first time Professor Eagleton had used that name, Leilani's head snapped up from reading about the ships. She found the professor looking directly at her. *Kass*; she knew she'd heard that name used before. At the time, however, she couldn't remember why or where.

"The Kassian government was too rigid for the average aether citizen. Their strict laws seemed overly oppressive to the free-thinking and free-acting aether. So, an antikuldain movement formed and grew, fed by fictional stories and a ratings-hungry media. Eventually, tensions rose, and war broke out between the Kassian Empire and the aether people."

Eagleton switched the image to that of a lone human man wearing a black trench coat with red trim. He was tall and well built, with white hair and sparkling blue eyes. It was then that Leilani remembered where she'd heard the name Kass. She knew this man. He'd brought her to her stepfather when she was just a child.

"After the death of some of our greatest heroes at the Battle of Grelashi, a treaty was signed to end the conflict. It was then that a group of kuldain and aether soldiers formed the Imperial Investigative Service. It would be their sworn duty to police the gateways between the two realms and ensure that the chaos of the aether never again affected the law and order of the Kassian people."

Then the professor opened the door to the lecture hall, and in strode the white-haired Dorthy.

"May I introduce Commodore Jason Dorthy. He will be explaining the IIS and answering any of your questions for the rest of today's class."

Leilani smirked as she recalled the heated debate she and Dorthy had gotten into that day over the strict regulatory controls the Kassian Empire had imposed on the aether people. They still got into the same debate regularly, even after she joined the IIS.

Several minutes later, Leilani stepped through the door into the small transport room. An annoyingly cheerful face smiled up at her from the transport console, and Lei groaned a little louder than she probably should have.

"Where to, Commander?" The tall, thin female beamed brightly at her. She had extremely angular features, and her tiny ears were clearly tattooed; Lei already knew she was a genie. A seriously annoying one, to boot.

In the IIS, certain flagships had transport rooms. They were small, with usually four to seven manual doors mounted along one bulkhead. Without power, the doors went nowhere, but when eldrich power was fed to them, they acted much like the tiny PGs that Leilani was investigating. Dorthy, as a three-star, had seven of these doors in his transport hub, one of which connected directly to the Imperial Palace.

Each door had a limited number of connections, and due to power constraints aboard the ship, those locations had to be at least somewhat nearby.

"Hey, Sheelie. What station are we closest to?" Lei walked across the room and stepped up onto a teleportation pad.

"Grenthali. According to the latest feeds, though, they're having some issues right now."

"What kind of issues?"

"I don't know. Some sort of protest has gotten out of hand."

"Joy—more antikuldain protesting. When are they just going to get over it? Both realities exist. No amount of protesting and rioting is going to change e-theory."

"Well, they could close the doors between the two." The annoyingly thin genie shrugged when Lei glared at her.

"You're in the wrong line of work." Lei opened the door that had a faint glow around it.

"Maybe, but to paraphrase your own words, no amount of protesting is going to change the fact that I'm here." She smiled sweetly. "Transport engaged. Have a nice trip, and try not to throw up. The compensators are still a little wonky."

"You—" There was a bright flash as Lei's body was yanked through realities from the dark ship to a brightly lit platform. Several automated weapons spun on her and began their charge sequence with a loud hum.

"—bitch," Lei finished as the wave of nausea washed over her.

"Entrance visa accepted," an automated voice chimed, and the weapons powered down. "Welcome, Agent."

Lei walked over to a small booth where a tall, thin woman with pointed ears was moving her hands through an illusory panel. The display was a lot like Lei's own HUD, but this one was visible to everyone, as most interactive displays were. It was also much higher resolution—the benefits of size and power.

"Still fighting with Sheelie?" The elar pointed to the abnormal reading hovering in the air in front of her and shook her head. "When will you learn to just let it go."

"When I get to shove her avian ass out an air lock."

Aleka pursed her lips together, trying to be sympathetic. "It was more than two decades ago."

"It was treason." Lei shook her head, refusing to do as her friend wanted. She couldn't let it go, even if command had decided to let the genie off with a warning.

"Well, command didn't see it that way."

Lei clenched her jaw. "You are way too forgiving."

"No, I'm not, and you know it. I just follow orders." The elar chuckled.

The Imperial Investigative Service was a small branch of the government, so it wasn't unusual for members to know each other, even in an empire this size. But Aleka Levit'dei—or Leka, as she was often called—wasn't just a passerby. She and Lei had been partners once.

Two years ago, they had been split up by the palace after a particularly nasty investigation went horribly wrong. Several innocent people had died publicly and horrifically, including a highly placed senator.

Lei still maintained that the senator had not been as innocent as he'd had everyone believing, but the proof had disappeared with him. Afterward, Aleka had been put on probation—and apparently demoted to door guard.

A warning symbol flashed on the display, alerting of an incoming transport.

Both agents placed their hands on their guns and turned toward the platform as the automated weapon systems began to cycle up with a loud whine. A bright flash appeared on the platform, and sirens shrieked through the area, alerting everyone in the vicinity to the imminent threat.

"Warning: unauthorized teleport," the computer chimed, but it was too late.

Both women had already pulled their weapons and fired large balls of blue plasma at the coalescing body of an unusually large, fur-covered creature with wings—a crashilor. It didn't have the chance to fully form before it disintegrated, but that was the point of firing so quick.

If the creature had had the chance to fully materialize, it would have rapidly turned the crowded tram station into a bloodbath. The technology and weaponry possessed by even one crashilor scout would be highly devastating, even with the two IIS agents on-site.

"They have IIS transportation coordinates now?" Lei twisted her face in a pained expression.

The elar nodded in response. "That's been going on for about six months now. It's why we've been posted here instead of civilians."

"Well, at least you aren't behind a desk."

Aleka glared at her. "Your tram will be here in about ten minutes. Where you off to?"

"ELU. Need to talk to the prof."

ELU—Eldrich Line University, a massive aether university dedicated to the research and study of the eldrich in all forms. It had originally been founded, however, to study eldrich lines: massive rivers of eldrich energy that traveled from planet to planet. Some historical documents called them ley lines, but as technology advanced, so had understanding of the eldrich rivers, and the term used to describe them eventually evolved as well.

Eldrich lines connected all life in aether space. At some point in history, aether researchers had figured out a method of using the rivers as transportation. It was dangerous but effective—almost a hundred times faster than the Kassian method of using slipstreams in kuldain space.

The ELU campus itself was not in any particular city-state; rather, it stood in a created reality built on top of the largest nexus point in this half of the galaxy, generally referred to as a meganexus. Who had created it? That was a historical mystery still researched to that day.

Aleka nodded as another teleport triggered on her display. "Let's do dinner."

Lei shrugged. "Maybe when I come back through?"

"Sounds good."

Lei turned and walked away from the small booth. As she headed toward the stairs that went down into the vast tram station, a loud pop sounded behind her, followed by the computer saying, "Entry visa accepted."

Several large trams were already waiting down below, but they were across the multiple tracks, over in the main part of the station. On the far platform—the local side—were more than a thousand people carrying signs and marching in erratic circles. The signs were made of holograms, paper, plastic—even one or two of wood. They depicted large, catlike creatures that stood on two legs and had two arms, two large wings, and huge manes that flowed down their backs. All of the signs had red marks through the creatures—clearly denoting that they wished them to go away.

Despite the signs showing crashilors as basically naked except for loincloths and flint spears, they were actually a highly advanced kuldain species, which was evident by their standard electronic equipment and lack of any eldritech. Yet they were continually appearing in aether space rather than kuldain.

As Lei continued across a catwalk, lost in her own thoughts, she almost missed a man in an expensive Kassian-style suit stepping out of a door to her left.

He nodded to her and turned to make his way toward the stairs. She glanced along the wall of doors and, in the back of her mind, tried to contemplate just how many places the various doors went. Each door was capable of holding up to a thousand addresses due to their direct connection with the eldrich line running beneath the station.

Witch hunts had started up again in kuldain space, and the number of aethers living or working there was dwindling. Of course, the witch hunts just provided fuel for the aether media outlets and the antikuldain movement.

Lei made it down to the tram platform, and a nearby city-state officer waddled in her direction.

"Identification?" The short, large-eared creature in the local black-and-gold uniform waved his scanner at her. His eyes, like his ears, were disproportionately large, giving him a slightly bug-eyed appearance. His skin was a goldish green.

Lei held out her hand and her badge. Her ID projected up from it, and the creature used his bulky pad to scan the image.

"Welcome to Grenthali, Agent. I assume I don't need to tell you the laws here? No shooting anyone, and all the rest of that garbage?" The creature's voice was slightly higher pitched than she had expected. It was likely female, not that anyone could tell by looking at it. But that was how the gobishili liked it.

"Yes, thank you, officer. I think I'll be okay. Just passing through." She bowed her head respectfully.

In aether space, each city-state—also called a city-planet—had its own government. Most of them had treaties with the Kassian Empire but didn't recognize its authority. And the ones that didn't have treaties . . . They generally didn't have laws either.

"Well, I gotta say it anyway. The freaks are out in force today." The small officer gestured to the crowd on the far platform.

For a brief moment, as the trains passed, Lei could see that the crowd was getting aggressive. The protest was about to become a riot.

"Oh, goodie! We might get to test the new suppression system!" It cackled and rubbed its hands together. Suddenly, Lei was forgotten completely as the short creature waddled off excitedly.

Lei shook her head and looked over the trams. Far to the left was a small black one with red trim. That would be her ride. She needed to get out of here before the station was locked down. Judging by the sudden surge of people around her, it seemed like many of the eldrilin travelers had the same idea.

No one attempted to get into her small tramcar. More than likely, that was due to the turrets set on the outside of the vehicle, which locked up anyone who got closer than ten feet. As she stepped inside, a person in a black jumpsuit with red pinstripes turned toward her.

"Where to?" The voice was slightly mechanical sounding—likely, the person was an automaton.

"ELU Station. And move it. They're about to lock this station down."

"Understood."

The tram jolted forward even before Lei could sit down. She dove for the closest seat and began to fasten the harness as the vehicle sped toward the slowly closing iris hatch.

"Hold on, Agent. We need to pick up speed." The person at the controls ignored the warning light on the tram's comm station and triggered the emergency engines.

Behind them, Lei could hear screaming as whatever new weapon the Grenthali security forces had invented fired into the crowd. Their weapons were generally nonlethal, but with the addition of the crashilor attacks, who knew what they would be crazy enough to do now. That was one of the problems with aether space: life was not terribly precious, and as such, it could get a little chaotic at times.

Lei stared out the back window toward the station. On the side that had eldrilin travelers, there was a shimmering orange dome of protection, but on the other side, bodies were flying onto the tracks and bouncing off trams as something she couldn't see knocked them away. She watched the chaos until the security hatch snapped closed behind them, blocking her view.

"We are clear."

Lei shook her head. Aether reality was tearing itself apart. The protests and rioting were escalating exponentially, and the media was having a field day with it. Each report was wilder and more dramatic, increasing the frenzied attitudes. If they would just treat the crashilor like any other criminal, the frenzy would likely die out, but that wouldn't make ratings. Ratings equaled sponsors and money, and it didn't matter where you lived: money equaled power.

"Please fasten your safety belts. We will be entering the line momentarily."

In these smaller cars, even as armored as they were, the initial cross into the ley line was always violent.

The car grew bright on the inside, then, as the light shielding initiated, dimmed back to a normal level. It slipped into the line with a powerful jerk. It felt as if it were a toy car in the hands of an angry child.

No amount of gravity compensation had ever managed to handle the effects of entering the eldrich line, so while the car was equipped with compensators, they never made enough of a difference to let riders avoid a full five-point harness. Once the car settled into the stream, the seatbelt light dimmed.

"ETA?" she asked the pilot.

"Twenty minutes."

7

FIELD RESEARCH

Lei stepped into the library of the highly acclaimed Eldrich Line University and took a deep breath. All around her were towering shelves lined with leather-bound books—antiques in any space. Between the various rows floated slow-moving railed platforms just large enough to hold one greduna or two humans.

Far above, near the vaulted ceilings, flew dozens of fluffy-looking creatures. Some were carrying books back to their shelves, while others circled lazily, waiting to be called on to do something. Each of them had hands and feet with carefully manicured claws and long, fluffy tails. Their cute little faces hid rows and rows of tiny, razor-sharp teeth that could rend the flesh from anything that didn't belong in the university library. They hadn't been used as security in decades, but they didn't care.

"Well, I'll be a thazorian's uncle!" a nearby voice called. It sounded male and slightly muffled.

Lei looked down the aisle to her left. There stood a three-and-a-half-foot-tall creature with dark-blue skin and leathery wings. He had craned his head in what looked to be a rather uncomfortable position in order to barely peek around the towering mound of books he was carrying.

"I highly doubt that, Krelor." Lei smiled and stepped foward to lift some of the stack so he could see more easily.

He blinked up at her with bright-green eyes oddly magnified by the glasses he wore on the bridge of his elongated nose. He smiled, showing rows of once-sharp teeth.

"Perhaps not, but the metaphor remains true enough." He chuckled and began his slinky shuffle down the main aisle toward the massive desk at the far end. His dark-blue wings were sitting lower on his back than she remembered, but then, it had been a good number of years since she had been a research student here. His long tail slid back and forth on the ground as he waddled across the massive library.

Lei did her best to avoid stepping on it. She had learned long ago that his response often required a visit to medical.

"What is the occasion that causes you to grace us with your presence once again, little Leilei?"

The tone and the use of that annoying pet name grated on her, but she chose to ignore it.

"I'm looking for Professor Eagleton. His office said they hadn't seen him in a couple of days. His ID was last used here."

"Hmmm." The creature tossed the books onto the large desk with grace that hinted at the true strength hidden in his tiny body. His wings flapped slightly as he climbed up after them and sat on the edge with a loud grunt.

Krelor tugged at his well-worn beard. "I suppose I have seen him. But first you must tell me why you seek such a distinguished person at this point in your dark and dirty career."

Lei frowned. There was no way the small imp should have known her current profession, grand librarian or not. She set her books on the stack.

"That's not how this works." She held up her hand, and a holo of her identification appeared and began to rotate.

The little blue imp smiled, showing his dulled teeth. Utterly ignoring her ID, he straightened the long silk jacket he wore over his soft green sweater.

"I know whom you serve, child, and I know who you are. This information changes nothing in the greater fabric. And the person you seek is firmly folded in that fabric. I shall not reveal him unless you do as I request." He looked up and met her gaze firmly. "And possibly not even then, depending on your answer."

Lei stared into the creature's eyes. Something wasn't right. A sensation that often warned her of danger was crawling through her bones. She was missing something. "I could just arrest you," she stated flatly.

"Could you?" The small creature crossed his legs, his smile gone. "You might want to check on that."

In her HUD, she pulled up the file on the librarian. His name appeared, alongside a picture of a younger him, but the rest of the profile was utterly empty. Under the heading for race was the word "UNKNOWN."

At the very bottom of the file was a note: *Under no circumstances will any agent of the empire touch or hamper this creature. He has an imperial pardon for all things past and future.*

Lei glanced at the little imp. He had opened a small notebook and was checking in the books next to him on the desk while he waited. A strong breeze blew past her as one of the small, flying creatures dove past her to snatch up a book and fly off with it.

She chewed on the inside of her lip as she considered her next move. When she was a student, Krelor had helped her through many sleepless nights of study. In fact, now that she thought of it, she had never seen him leave the library. He had never once stopped working. The hairs on the back of her neck tingled. Whatever she was missing, it was big.

The imp set his notebook down and looked up at her, hands in his lap. "Well?"

"The empire needs his help."

"Does it, now?" He chuckled, some unknown humor sparkling in his large black eyes.

She decided to test her theory. "But you knew that already."

The librarian grinned proudly.

Lei took a deep breath, resisting the urge to toss the small creature into a nearby bookshelf. "But if you knew that already, then you likely know why I'm here."

"I do indeed."

"Then why ask me why I want the professor?"

"Now, that is the question of the day, isn't it, young Leilei?"

The little blue creature had always enjoyed his verbose puzzles, but Lei hadn't been in a good mood since she was drafted by the Kassian Navy. Well—in truth, it had been a lot longer than that. She took a deep breath and centered her mind and emotions.

Krelor nodded his approval. "Better."

Lei gave in to his games. "Have I ever told you how annoying you are?"

"Yes, young one. Two hundred and forty-seven times." His laugh echoed throughout the library.

Above them, the flying creatures screeched in panic at the noise and flapped their wings erratically.

He quieted his laugh to a soft chuckle.

"I'm not sure why you feel the need to protect the professor, but I mean him no harm. I just need his particular expertise."

Krelor stroked his small beard again as he considered her request. "Perhaps. But the others?"

"What others?"

"Those who sent you here." He tapped the desk he was sitting on.

Lei scowled. It suddenly dawned on her what he meant. The professor's office had been pretty upset when she showed up. Several people she hadn't recognized—obviously not university staff—had been talking to his research aides in the back of the office. She'd talked only to his personal assistant, asking where he was. She hadn't even shown any ID to the woman, who had freely told her that the last place the professor had been seen was the library. Lei had left after that.

In reality, she had ignored the entire scene since it hadn't seemed relevant to her mission, but now she began to replay the details. The students had been scared. The aide, whom Lei had met several times—which was why she hadn't bothered to show her any ID—had also been scared. And now Lei was pretty certain she had been trying to get her out of the office as quickly as possible.

She reached up and tapped a button in her HUD.

"*Switchboard*," a male voice chimed in her head.

"*Charlie Nine*." She carefully masked her thoughts as she communicated with the switchboard.

"*Location?*"

"*Professor Eagleton's office, ELU.*"

"*Units en route.*"

"*Roger. Out.*"

The line fell dead, and Lei felt another stiff breeze as one of the creatures dove past her for another book.

"Someone else is hunting him." Lei was stating the obvious, but she got a nod of acknowledgment for her effort. "Then I definitely need to find him first. Do you know what they want?"

The small creature looked up at her and smiled. "The fabric knows all."

"And you have no intention of telling me." It wasn't a question.

Krelor said nothing.

"Okay. Well, I sent agents to the office to deal with whoever is causing trouble there. Hopefully, we'll get some intel out of them."

Again, the small librarian said nothing.

"I really do need to find the professor."

"Aye, you do." He grinned in agreement. "If you wish to move your questions through the fabric."

Lei took a deep breath and closed her eyes. Right now, she wanted to skin the damn imp.

"Where is he?"

The small creature leapt to his feet and clasped his hands together in excitement. "The young student finally asks the real question!"

Lei's shoulders slumped as she resisted the urge to punch him.

"I will not tell you the answer you seek, for the walls have ears." The librarian walked across the desk and hopped down into the tall chair made especially for him.

He reached into a drawer, pulled out a small glass marble, and tossed it to her.

"Go, child. There is a wrinkle in the fabric here. Go before you find yourself lost in it."

The magic in the tiny sphere transferred to her, and the marble itself became inert. The sensation was so weak and fleeting that she almost missed it, but this wasn't the first time the grand librarian had given her a marble like this. She knew exactly what it was. It was a bookmark.

The hairs on the back of her neck began to itch almost painfully as she walked away from the desk. Turning into one of the aisles, she began to sprint through the library. As she did, a commotion broke out near the main doors.

A loud male voice echoed through the bookshelves. "The library is closed!"

The only people able to cast spells in the library were the librarian and the president of the university. That voice, however, didn't belong to Krelor or to the president, who was female.

"Everyone out!"

Lei sped up her mad dash through the maze of bookshelves till, finally, she arrived at the location indicated by the bookmark. She glanced up and saw the book she was looking for highlighted three-quarters of the way up the massive shelf. She jumped onto the closest lift, then over onto the next one. It slowly began floating toward the highlighted book.

Down below, footsteps rushed out of the library as the students fled. The grand ELU library had not been closed in more than eight hundred years. The lift was taking too long, but there was nothing else near the book that she could jump to.

"C'mon!" she urged the lift quietly.

"Librarian!" the demanding voice called out to Krelor.

"Yes, Mr. President?"

Interesting—the president had changed. She must have missed that news somehow. The odd thing was that Lei wasn't anywhere near the main desk. Why was she able to hear what was being said at all?

"Where is Professor Eagleton?"

"You have no need for such information, Mr. President."

"You will tell these men where he is, or the university will find that it has no need of you."

"Will it, now?" Krelor sounded amused.

The lift finally got within reach of the book. As it did, she heard the loud crack of a weapon discharging. Above her, the cute, furry little fliers screeched angrily. Their casual, chaotic flight sped up and began to coalesce into a rapidly spinning circle. Lei turned toward the noise just in time to see the creatures break the circle and begin diving toward the intruders.

She had read about the last time the library had been closed. During the war, a group of opposition forces had fought their way into the grand library. Nothing had been found of those 139 soldiers except their weapons and armor. Not even a single soul remained. Every part of their existence had been eliminated.

Lei looked at the spine of the book. It read *The Beauty of the Nine Pillars*. If she pulled the book from the shelf, it would automatically end up in the read pile, and anyone who came after her would know the time and date of the last read. She left the book where it sat.

Leaping over the railing, she pushed off the edge of the lift and dove toward another one. With several deft jumps, she made it to the floor and jogged off toward the back corner of the library.

One of the benefits of spending so much time here as a student: she knew all of the ways out.

8

MATHIOUS MOON

Several hours and aether doors later, Lei landed in a forward base station that had been stood up—obviously recently—on Mathious Moon. The files she'd read en route didn't say why they had suddenly needed to deploy a ground unit to the moon, but she hoped it had nothing to do with her professor.

The Nine Pillars were an ancient historical site found deep in the wilds of the moon's surface. It was a huge Kassian tourist site, purported to be the oldest man-made architecture in existence—though several scholars argued that it hadn't actually been made by man.

Lei had been informed that no technological devices worked within twenty-five miles of the Nine Pillars, so she'd made arrangements to land her vehicle at the base and go in on foot. As she climbed out of the car, she was saluted by a marine corporal. "Welcome, Agent Falconi. The general would like to speak to you."

Gesturing for the marine to precede her, she sighed.

She was led into a drop-cube command hub, which had all of the necessary equipment for a ground team to manage thousands of troops and could be picked up and dropped anywhere within hours. In the middle of the room was a holo table. Behind it stood three naval personnel in digital form as well as two physical marines. They all looked up when she walked in.

"Welcome, Agent." The marine with the markings of a one-star general nodded his head in her direction, then glanced at the others. "Please continue. I'll be back after briefing the agent."

The others waited quietly until she and the general left the building.

"I'm sorry for the circumstances of our meeting." Once they were outside, the handsome general smiled at her and held out his hand. "But I have to admit, I've wanted to meet you for some time now. My name is General Anthony Marshall."

Lei shook his hand. He waved for her to follow him through the camp toward a smaller building.

"Why?"

He chuckled. "Because I was a captain on Dalori Eight during the Kamorian incident."

Lei skipped a step as she walked, and the general turned to look at her. He smiled again, but this time it was more a look of gratitude. "You saved my life and the lives of more than three thousand of my fellow marines."

Lei didn't know how to respond. She and Aleka had taken such a severe beating for that incident, despite the lives they had saved. They'd both known the senator was corrupt, but because of the way he'd died, there had been no way to prove it. Because of his aether meddling, hundreds of innocent civilians had been slaughtered. He had gone out of his way to set Aleka and Lei up, making it look like they had been the ones to release the creature.

In the chaos that followed the incident, Aleka was removed from active-duty status, and Lei was shipped off to the rim for training she never wanted—or needed, for that matter. Their records were severely black marked.

Lei, however, had recovered. Aleka, being an elar, had been categorized as a kuldain risk and demoted to aether duty only, which was how she had become a telepad guard despite her five hundred years of excellent imperial service. The ultimate form of racism. The memories were painful, and she had worked hard to forget them.

"Personally"—the general touched her arm—"I think the reaction by the crown was asinine. You saved more than just those of us on Dalori Eight."

Lei frowned. There was no way he should have remembered that. There had been a planetwide veeshali put in place as soon as main command entered the system. She adjusted her vision and looked the marine over. He had a faint aura around him. He wasn't aether capable, but he was protected against it. She skimmed the camp. All of the marines there had the soft hue.

She waved her hand to indicate the nearby marines. "Is everyone here from Dalori Eight?"

"Yes. Like you, we were sent to places where we couldn't easily interact with civilians." He shrugged. "But most of us also received security clearances, pay raises, promotions, and, in this case, honor duty. So it's not all bad, I suppose."

The aura of protection wouldn't have been missed by command, but she had never heard about it—not that her being left out of the loop was a big surprise.

"Leilani?" His voice was quiet. "Everything okay?"

She blinked several times, then met his gaze, her confusion hardening as she refocused her thoughts on the mission at hand.

He raised an eyebrow apologetically. "Sorry."

"For what?" she asked.

"Using your first name."

For the first time in a long while, she smiled. In another place, at another time, her response would have been different.

"What's the situation here?"

He stood straighter. "We know something unusual is happening. We requested IIS assistance two days ago." He shrugged. "They told us that they didn't have an available agent in the area but that when they had one, they would route them in our direction. We are a pretty low priority. Honestly, I was surprised to hear that you were here."

"You requested IIS?"

He raised an eyebrow and motioned for them to head to a smaller drop-cube building. "You aren't here because we requested you." It wasn't a question.

She indicated the building. "Secured?"

He confirmed.

The two quickened their pace.

Once inside, he inclined his head in the direction of a gunnery sergeant across the room. "That's Gunny Lairn. I had him pack you a hiking kit. It's a long hike in; however, if you can ride a horse, we happen to have them available to speed up the trip."

Lei smirked. "I can." She chose not to mention just how long it had been since she'd ridden.

"I'm not sure why you're here, but I will say this. The natives are freaking out. The ones who aren't evacuating are rapidly growing violent, claiming it's the end of the universe as we know it."

Lei raised an eyebrow. "And you?"

"I've been here just under two years. My men and I were the first ground troops to ever be stationed on the surface long term. In the past, troops have developed severe psychological trauma when they remained on the surface for more than a few weeks. The reactions have been as severe as suicide or murder and everything in between. So it's imperial regulation that troops stay off the surface except during emergencies. My men and I . . ." He shrugged. "The moon never bothered us. So when things went weird, we set up a forward base to try to find out what was happening."

That told her a lot about what to expect.

"About five days ago, the weather suddenly cleared. The raging storms just stopped. That feeling that we were always in danger left." Anthony shrugged. "I know that sounds strange."

Lei shook her head. "No, it sounds about right."

The general let out a short grunt. "Tell that to the admiral. He recommended me for a psych eval when I told *him* that."

"Do you think this is the calm before the storm?"

The general suddenly looked uncomfortable.

"No." A gravelly male voice spoke up; the gunnery sergeant hefted a large set of saddlebags onto the table next to her. "The stupid moon is just happy for once. Stranger shit has happened."

"Gunny, that's enough."

"You have to be kidding me, sir. This woman fought a creature that we all know good and well was not of this plane, and she did it using crap that shouldn't exist. She knows far more about this shit than we do. Stop pussyfooting around and tell her the truth. We all hear the stupid thing ranting and raving."

Lei looked from the gunny to the general and found him watching her carefully for her reaction.

"Are you sure it's the moon?"

He shook his head. "No. We don't know what it is, but it doesn't mess with us like it did the others. Even though we hear it, we're able to just ignore it."

Another set of bags was set on the table.

Lei glanced down at them, then up at the gunny. "You think you're coming?"

"I know I am," the general next to her said.

She turned to look at him and frowned. "No way I'm going to be responsible for a general."

"You're not. I am," the gunny spoke up. "The horses are outside. We're ready to go, sir."

Lei glanced out the window and saw a rather large herd of horses. Riders were mounted up and waiting.

"This is not how this is going to work, General."

He picked up his own pack and tossed it over his shoulder with a chuckle.

"You know the best part about this particular post?" He opened the door and looked back over his shoulder. "I get my orders directly from the emperor himself, which means only one man outranks me. And last I checked, you weren't him."

The gunny bowed slightly and held his hand out, palm up, toward the horses outside. She grabbed the saddlebags that had been set out for her, tossed them over her shoulder, and followed him out of the building.

Fifteen horses waited outside, as did a group of marines, each of them sporting an old-fashioned bolt-action rifle and basic flak armor. The horses, all of which were all black, had unusually large bones and thick-looking hides. Even the mares were very muscular. They were a little shorter and wider than the horses she was used to, but that really only meant that she'd have a shorter fall.

One of the soldiers on the ground handed her a set of reins. After tossing her bags over the horse, she swung herself easily into the saddle and patted the horse on the neck. One of the horses moved up next to her, and she glanced over to find the general smiling at her.

"Besides, we know the countryside. You don't." At a gesture of his hand, the unit wheeled and began to ride away from base camp, splitting up into small groups as they entered the grassy countryside.

"You have to stay spread out here." He waved his arm in a large arc to encompass the horses and riders as they spread out around him and Lei. "If the weather suddenly decides to go south, you have to be ready to move quickly. He'll take out an entire group with one hit if he gets the chance."

"'He'? What do you mean, 'he'?"

"We're pretty sure whatever it is that talks to us—whatever it is that's controlling the weather—is male."

A nearby lieutenant added to the conversation. "And he is one angry . . ." She allowed the statement to go unfinished, but Lei got the idea.

"Well, most of the time, anyway." The general looked up at the beautiful blue sky overhead.

"Yeah, this is pretty creepy," someone else behind them said.

The group grew quiet as they rode toward the distant tree line. Everyone in the unit kept within visual range so they could use hand signals—a logical choice, since they would lose digital comms the closer they got to the pillars.

Leilani felt a strange sense of calm settle over her as she rode. It seemed almost as if it were coming from the direction they were heading. Yet all around her, the riders and horses were tense, as if they were expecting a sudden but imminent doom. Experience told her that a sense of calm could mean two things: something very big was very happy . . . or something very bad was being masked.

9

PILLAR GUARDIAN

Darkness crept in around them and found Lei and the general looking down into the valley as they sat astride their mounts. She could barely make out the massive pillars far below. The landscape seemed quiet and empty.

"We will make it by midday tomorrow." He veered his horse away, back toward the spot where the team had chosen to make camp.

Once he had moved far enough away, Lei pulled a pair of binoculars from her personal bag and flicked the switch on top that allowed her to see into the aether plane. Aether was a different sort of energy source than the traditional electromagnetic energy used in kuldain space and, unlike electromagnetism, was highly visible. However, seeing it required either a special tool or an individual capable of casting spells.

When she looked through the lenses, the colors brightened so immensely that she had to jerk the binoculars away from her face. She rotated a dial on the left side to dim them to a tolerable level.

Down below, its body woven between the pillars, was what appeared to be a massive winged serpent. Though extremely rare, some places and creatures had a high concentration of aether energy, even in kuldain space. This creature, however, didn't just have a concentration of aether energy; it was made purely of it. That meant it wasn't fully in kuldain *or* aether space; somehow, it was between the two worlds.

Zooming in farther, she found what she was looking for. Sitting in the middle of the circle was a white-haired greduna. He appeared to be playing three-dimensional chess with the creature. The massive serpent lifted its head and looked in her general direction. It said something to the professor, who followed its gaze.

Through her binoculars, Lei did as well. There seemed to be some sort of winged bird flying high overhead. She was pretty sure she had seen it several times during the day, but it had carefully avoided being noticed by the marines. It turned and flew slowly toward her.

"Shit." She spun the horse toward the camp. Anything a serpent of pure aether sent her way wasn't going to get along with a horse.

She trotted into camp and hopped off. After tying the horse to the grazing line, she removed its tack and put her things in a cleared area.

"Hey, Agent. You want some chow?" one of the marines called to her.

"In a few. I need a bio really quick." She headed back out of camp toward a nearby tree line, grabbing a roll of toilet paper as she went.

The moment she could use the trees as cover, she set the paper on a branch and ran back toward the ridge. There, she could look out over the valley below without her location being easily visible from camp. She hoped the creature, whatever it was, wasn't too big.

As she approached the ridge, she glanced up at the huge winged animal; it was now drifting in a small loop as it slowly circled down to land. Its front half was a massive eagle with beautiful blue eyes. The back half was a heavily muscled lion.

"A griffon?" she grumbled.

As it leaned back and beat its wings to land lightly, she noticed that the creature was wearing a saddle and a rather unique blue-and-silver chest plate.

"Daison? Are you kidding me?" Lei snapped at the creature as it settled to the ground and shook out its feathers.

The creature squawked, bobbing its head.

"I don't care what your excuse is. You know for a fact that this breaks at least five treaties!" Lei strode toward the creature, balling her fists at her side.

It squawked several more times and cocked its head to the side.

"Really?"

The eagle head bobbed up and down.

"How did you get here?" Lei was losing steam. If the creature was right, she couldn't blame it or the professor.

The griffon cocked its head several times but said nothing.

"Fine. Take me down there, and I'll ask him."

The bird shifted its position to a more aggressive stance.

Lei suddenly realized it wasn't looking at her anymore. Darting a glance over her shoulder, she saw Anthony standing perfectly still at the edge of the clearing.

She took a deep breath. "Fuck. Today is not my day."

He surprised her by holding up a hand. "It's quite all right, Agent. Go. We'll wait here. Just be careful."

Lei cocked her head in surprise. In her peripheral vision, she could see the large beast behind her do the same, which caused the general to chuckle before heading back toward camp.

She hopped up into the enormous gredunian saddle and held on tight. It would have been easier to ride the creature bareback than in the oversized saddle.

Greduna were, on average, ten to twelve feet tall, hence why they were often called giants by those unfamiliar with genetics. In fact, the two species were not related at all, despite their similar size. Much like their descendants, the dwarves, greduna were generally known for their bad tempers and sheer enjoyment of fighting. Unlike their descendants, however, they had a nasty habit of destroying things—even their own things. They had very few scholars and mystics, as well as a very small population base overall. Historians theorized that perhaps their low population was because too many of them died young, but really, it was simply a side effect of a long lifespan and a preference for war over scholarly pursuits or breeding. Occasionally, there were exceptions, however—such as the professor, who chose not to live among his own people.

The griffon flew lazily through the darkening sky. It was almost like she was flying among the stars. Several times, she had to remind Daison where they were going. He seemed so happy that she almost felt guilty. She knew she had to return the professor and his mount to the university. There, the sky was merely a magical representation, and there were no stars.

Finally, they landed in the circle. Lei had already shifted her vision to see aether reality on top of kuldain reality. It would be stressful to hold both for too long, but she needed to see and hear what she was dealing with. The serpent ignored her as she dismounted. The professor, however, charged toward her with his arms out wide. This was going to hurt.

He snatched her up into an embrace that gave a whole new meaning to the idea of a bear hug. She heard a rib crack and her shoulder pop free of the socket.

"Leilei!" Professor Eagleton had pale, blue-tinged white skin and pure white hair drawn back into the traditional braid of his people. His beard was braided with glass and gem beads. Each of them was like a medal, representing some kind of special event in his life. Several of those beads were now embedded in her skin.

Fighting to remain conscious as the unusually excited professor hugged her, she managed to get out a small amount of sound. "Prof . . ."

"I think you're crussshing itsss tiny body." A hissing noise crawled across her skin. It wasn't a comfortable feeling.

"Oh." The professor suddenly lightened his grip. "I'm sorry, little Leilei."

She nodded. "It's . . . okay."

He set her down gently, and she bent over to regain her breath.

In her HUD, a soft chime was followed by a female voice. *"Physical integrity 96 percent. I am detecting two broken ribs, a dislocated shoulder, and a minor perforation of the left lung. Starting restoration sequence. Requesting permission to activate nanites."*

"Negative. Activate h-nodes."

"I will need override to activate within kuldain space."

"Override Juliett-November-Alpha-Quebec."

"Roger. H-nodes active." The entire conversation took place over only a split second after the special aether system spoke directly into her mind.

The pain subsided enough for her to stand up straight. She took a couple steps over to the griffon and grabbed hold of one of the straps on its harness. Clenching her teeth, she jerked backward, popping her shoulder back into the socket with a grunt.

She blinked several times, then looked up at the professor and smiled. "It's nice to see you in such a good mood, Professor."

"Quite!" With a squeal, he gestured to the area around him. "Do you have any idea how amazingly peaceful it is here?"

A large humanoid pawn in full plate strode forward across the enormous chessboard and swung its massive maul at a griffon. The blow crushed the griffon in one swing, and the pawn took its place in the square as the body vanished.

"Your turn, Professsor." The creature looked up from the board as it spoke and bobbed its head politely at her.

The same sensation crawled across her skin, but she nodded back.

"Greetingsss, little one. Would you like to play a game?" It seemed genuinely curious.

"Yes. Sitharus here hasn't had a good game since the kuldains came and killed his chess partner." Professor Eagleton walked back to his resting spot by the chessboard and plopped down with a loud thump.

Lei followed him.

"Dreadful creaturesss, thossse." The creature gestured with his head toward the small camp on the ridge. "Although thessse have been rather interesssting."

Lei smirked and shrugged in agreement. "I wouldn't make a good opponent. I've never been able to master this game. I'm afraid I would be no challenge at all."

The winged serpent snorted.

"Professor, may I ask how you got here?"

"I brought him here." The serpent carefully watched the professor's move.

"What?"

They both looked at her with almost disappointed glares.

"What part of that wasss too complicated to undersssstand?" the creature hissed.

Lei took a deep breath. If this creature was disrupting the weather of a whole moon merely because it was annoyed over a board game, she needed to be more careful with her temper.

"I apologize. I simply meant that I would appreciate more information on how and why?"

"Then why didn't you say so?" the professor admonished her. He had been her graduate adviser for eight years, and in that time, they had grown rather close.

She sighed.

"I went to Krelor when I realized people from the government were hunting me. He talked to a friend of his"—the professor gestured to the serpent—"who agreed to keep me company while Krelor dealt with the problem."

Lei frowned. "They shot Krelor."

The professor laughed so hard that he fell to the ground, holding his sides. The creature the professor had called Sitharus laughed, too, until what looked to be a meteor shower started streaking across the sky. The moment he noticed it, he stopped laughing, though his face took on a very comical expression from trying to hold it in.

"I am sssorry about that. Please tell your people that I will refrain from laughing." The serpent gestured to the sky with his nose, then moved his enormous body in what seemed to be a shrug.

Lei glanced up at the meteors, her eyes widening as she realized that several of them seemed to be trying to correct their orbit. She pulled up her binoculars and looked closer. They weren't meteors; they were vessels from the fleet. His laughing had pulled them into the atmosphere! She lowered the device and stared at the still-chuckling creature in shock. What the hell *was* it?

A wing slid forward, and even though the creature was purely aether, it poked the laughing greduna.

"It'sss ssstill your turn."

Professor Eagleton pushed himself upright, tears streaming down his face. "What I would have given to see the look on his face!"

"Indeed." The serpent grinned, baring a frightening pair of fangs.

"I'm guessing he wasn't harmed?" Lei asked, though their reactions had already answered the question.

"Of course not." The professor shook his head. "Nothing any of them possess could hurt Krelor."

"That librarian issss tougher than me, and that issss no easssy feat." The serpent smiled. "Relax, young one. Thissss game is jusssst that. Nothing but a way to kill time."

The greduna finally stopped laughing and frowned. "Maybe to you two. But I don't appreciate being a piece on the board."

The serpent shrugged its wings. "You are both piecesss on the board."

Lei actually chuckled. "I'm always a piece on the board. You'll get used to it, Prof." She patted him on the back. "Oh—that reminds me. I need you to take a look at something for me."

"Ah, you brought me a bauble?" He seemed pleased by the thought.

"Something like that, yes." She withdrew a small glass vial from her bag and held it up to him. "Do you know the maker of this?"

The professor gestured to the board. A piece began moving, but he didn't watch; his hand closed around the vial. Pulling a large magnifying glass from his own bag, he began to examine the vial and its contents.

"Hmmm . . ." Both chess players mused in unison as they examined their own puzzles.

"There are only two who could have made this. But they are both dead."

Under her breath, Lei grumbled, "Of course they are." She looked up at him. "When?"

"One died before you were born; the other more recently, I think." The large humanoid used a pair of tweezers to tug the top off the vial and pour the small device into his palm. He looked it over again with the magnifying glass. "This one is elari in make, which means it was made by Elaris Shoomer of Markes and Shoomer. The shop can be found on Masaquin Eleven."

He carefully dropped the device back into the vial and replaced the cork. A light tap resealed the spell, keeping the portal generator in stasis.

"You've made my day, Professor." Lei carefully slid it back into her bag.

The serpent flicked his tongue in the direction of the camp. "The insssectsss are ssswarming."

Lei could see lights moving around on the ledge.

He shrugged. "I believe my laughter hasss created a ssstir. I forget how fragile you are." He snorted, shaking his head in irritation.

"Prof, you know you can't stay here, right?"

"Yesss," both chess players said together as a piece floated across the board.

"Now that the immediate threat is gone, I will return when I am done with this game." Eagleton watched the piece carefully.

"Checkmate." The serpent hissed, a huge grin sliding across his massive face.

The professor laughed. "That's what I get for being distracted." He stood and walked over to his griffon. After swinging up into the saddle, he waved to her and the serpent. "It was an honor to meet you, Sitharus. Perhaps we will be able to play again someday."

"Perhapsss, young one." The creature stretched his wings and bowed his head to the professor.

"Come talk to me when you are done with your investigation, little Leilei. I have more for you."

"Understood, Professor."

The two shimmered briefly into the same ghostly state of being as the serpent, then vanished completely.

"Pardon me, little mortal. May I call you Leilei?"

Leilani looked up at the giant winged snake. She resisted the urge to grimace. "I prefer Leilani or just Lei."

"Very well, Agent Leilani. I have a requessst of you, if you are ssso inclined."

"How may the imperium assist you, Sitharus?"

"May I have this mortal?" A translucent illusion of General Anthony Marshall appeared to stand in front of her.

Lei frowned. "The imperium does not condone slavery. As such, he is not ours to give." She glanced over at the lights moving on the ridge. They appeared to be traveling down into the valley.

The creature blinked several times, almost as if he were trying to understand.

"May I ask why?" she asked.

"Yesss. The good professsor reminded me how good it is to play chesss. I feel better. Happier. I require a new chesss partner." He shook his head, as if that wasn't right. "No, I *requessst*. It was the insssectsss who killed my lassst partner. They ssshould give me a sssubsssstitute."

"I would be happy to ask him for you."

The smile that spread across his face was incredibly comical. "Then we go." He dove at her suddenly and swept her up faster than she could dodge.

They flew across the valley floor at impossible speed. The massive serpent's head bulldozed through the trees so fast that they were thrown aside and appeared to explode. Lei, however, was not affected by the speed in the slightest. Atop the serpent's head, the gravity and the breeze were exactly as they would have been if she had been standing still.

The creature came to a sudden stop, and Lei found herself the target of fourteen soldiers all aiming at her chest and head. It took her a second to realize they couldn't see the creature, meaning she appeared to be standing in midair.

She turned and looked back over the destruction left in Sitharus's wake. She could clearly see his elongated body stretching in a straight line back to the standing stones. There, the end of his tail remained tightly wrapped around one. He probably never left them. So either he was bound to them or he was their guardian—or both. That explained why he was allowed to remain in kuldain space. There was no way something this massive and this powerful had been missed by IIS.

"Agent?" The general's voice was slightly strained.

"Pardon me, Sitharus." She jogged forward and slid down his scaly nose to hop to the ground.

The weapons remained trained on her.

The giant serpent remained silent.

"General. Just the person I need to talk to." She chuckled as several of the marines backed away from her. "If it makes you feel better, I didn't do that." She pointed over her shoulder with her thumb.

A couple soldiers turned hesitantly to look at the massive hole in the forest.

"What's going on?" The general pointed to the ships in the sky. They were still fighting gravity as they attempted to get back into space.

Lei hadn't realized some of them were stuck—likely because they were either damaged or lacked the power to fight the gravity because they hadn't been designed for the atmosphere.

"Sitharus, can you do something about that?"

The serpent turned his huge eyes to the ships, then back to her. "What issss wrong with them?"

The sudden sound was too much for the marines. Several shots were fired in the serpent's direction, and all of the marines, with the exception of the general, began a hasty retreat, reloading and preparing to fire again as they did.

"Hold your fire!" Anthony yelled loudly.

The frightened marines obeyed the order and slowed to a stop when they realized their general wasn't following them.

The general answered Sitharus even though he couldn't see the source of the voice. "They aren't built to come into a planet's or moon's atmosphere. They're falling, and if they crash, thousands will die."

"And thisss isss sssomething you do not wisssh, General Anthony Marssshall?"

One of the younger corporals startled and opened fire again. However, his actions were quickly remedied by the gunnery sergeant next to him, who yanked the rifle from his hand and slapped him on the helmet.

"I said hold your fire," Anthony growled, then turned his attention back toward the hissing speech. "I would prefer that my people did not die. If you can arrange that, I would be in your debt."

Lei grimaced and shook her head. "Poor choice of words, sir."

His brow furrowed.

Far overhead, the ships that were fighting for their lives suddenly began moving back out into space—likely faster than their hulls could handle. But then, Sitharus *had* said they were far more fragile than he realized.

"I put them back where they came from. Now you will come with me."

Several marines stepped between the hissing and Anthony. Frightened or not, there was no way they were letting anything they couldn't see take their general.

"Hold, everyone!" Lei lifted a hand to stop them. If she didn't intervene, there were going to be several dead marines.

"Let me explain what's going on." She turned toward Sitharus and shook her head. "We discussed this. You cannot own him. You must ask, and he can choose to decline."

"But he agreed to be in my debt," the serpent pouted. That was almost more disturbing than if he'd been angry.

She glared at him.

"Whoopee, you breathed out and a few ants moved. That does not entitle you to ownership of him. It might equal one game. Maybe."

The serpent's wings sagged.

She turned back to the general. "Now, Anthony, you need to understand what you're dealing with before you can make any decisions." She reached into her bag and pulled out an antique-looking pair of glasses. "Put these on."

He did as he was bid and jumped slightly when he saw the pouting serpent. He started to pull the glasses off, then opted to leave them in place.

"This is Sitharus. He's the cause of your weather, the whispering, and the accidental pulling of the fleet into atmo."

"Accidental?" The general didn't seem to believe that.

Lei shrugged. "Evidently, when he laughs, weird things happen?" She wasn't sure how the creature was able to affect his surroundings with only his emotions.

"I do apologizzze for that. I forget that you are ssso incredibly fragile." The serpent shrugged. "But get on with it, Agent Leilani."

She nodded. "Sitharus likes to play chess. He would like you to be his new partner. It seems his last one was killed by the insects."

"Something tells me that he considers us 'the insects'?" the general murmured.

"I believe so, but I'm not sure if he means the military or the civilians. Though I doubt he knows the difference."

"Okay, where do we play this chess?" Anthony seemed concerned, but he obviously had a grasp of what was going on.

"At the loom," Sitharus answered.

Lei cocked her head in confusion. "You call the Nine Pillars 'the loom'?"

He nodded. "I am the guardian of the loom."

Her mind flashed back to Krelor talking about "the fabric."

"Does the loom create the fabric?"

The serpent nodded, though he seemed surprised she understood.

"Doesn't a loom need a weaver to make fabric?" Anthony asked next to her.

The serpent smiled. "I have chosssen well." He lifted his head up high. "I will allow the noissse again. You will come play chesss with me at leassst once a rotation around the sssleeping giant. Though if you can play more, know that I will be happy. After one thousssand rotationsss, I will consssider usss even. Perhapsss you will one day meet the weaver."

The creature spun and returned to its stones even faster than it had come from them. A few more trees exploded.

"Um, General?" The gunny tapped his ear. "We have comms again."

10

TRANSITIONS

"Will someone please explain what the hell is going on?" Admiral Haltorn's holographic image leaned over the battle table.

"Sorry, Admiral," Lei answered. "You're not cleared for the details at this time. All I can say is that the issue is under control for now."

"Although, based on new information the agent was able to retrieve, I do recommend moving the fleets farther out in orbit," General Marshall added.

"Agreed; we're already trying to limp in that direction. But we received a lot of damage, and some of our ships are dead in the water right now."

"Understood, Admiral. Ground Team out." Anthony killed the link and turned to Lei. "So, how about you tell *me* what's going on?"

"Well, let's start with: welcome to the Imperial Investigative Service." Leilani waved her arms flamboyantly and grinned.

He chuckled. "I saw that coming."

"I still have to put my report together, but based on the brief I was able to give my command, you're to be instated. You'll keep your current rank and position for now, though, while they research what's happening here." She shook her head. "None of us know everything. I have no idea how much command knows about Sitharus. I do know that we have no idea who was killed here, when they were killed, or by whom. I'm betting that will end up being your assignment."

"What did it mean by being happy?"

"It meant that you and your gunny were right. The weather was nice because he was happy." She shrugged. "When I arrived, he was playing chess with the person I was looking for."

"Really?"

"Hey, it wasn't what I expected either." She clapped him on the shoulder. "But that's something you get used to in this line of work." She didn't have the heart to tell him he wasn't a kuldain citizen anymore.

Leilani hadn't realized it until they got back to the base, but when Anthony and Sitharus had agreed to a thousand years of games, the massive serpent had magically adjusted the human marine to ensure he would be able to fulfill the deal. The kuldain marine now had a strong aether pattern woven throughout his body. It seemed amazingly intricate, but aether research wasn't really her job. IIS would likely send someone to learn more about what had happened. Dorthy could explain it to the general when he got here. He had the staff aboard to deal with any fallout or necessary education.

"Now what?"

"Now you wait." Leilani gestured in the direction of the fleet far overhead. "A ship will come in system. You will be taken aboard, debriefed, trained, then likely given a mission."

Onboarding in the IIS was highly random and specific to the instance.

"Do you know how long it will take?"

"IKS *Eldrich Sun* hailing Ground Team Alpha," a female voice called into the command center.

Lei smirked and gestured at the comms panel. "About thirty seconds?"

He frowned at her. "How is that possible?"

"Well, I commed them a while ago. It's not like it took them thirty seconds to get here." Since they were having a secure conversation and space was limited, it was just the two of them in the room. She walked over to the panel and answered.

"This is Falconi. Go ahead."

"Ah, Leilani. He says to get your ass up here, and bring the general."

"Roger that. Movement here is limited by environmental factors. We may be a little slower than he likes."

"I'll let him know."

"Falconi out."

"I'm not going to like this."

"Probably not. Actual military have the hardest transition." She walked over to the main terminal and sat down to requisition a shuttle. "I can give you some advice that may help."

He stepped up behind her, pointing to a particular ship in the list of available vessels. "What?"

"You have now seen two fairly large creatures with some pretty spectacular destructive powers."

"And?"

"Remember: that is what we deal with on a daily basis." She left him to consider that in silence. She finished requesting her shuttle, then turned to look up at him. "When you've spent the day arguing with a creature that can rip your ship in half just because it got annoyed, you find that an angry politician threatening to have you fired for some dumbass scandal just doesn't seem all that impressive anymore."

She crossed her arms. "I've told the emperor that he was wrong and that his behavior was childish and petty. Of course, he *was* a child at the time, but nonetheless."

The general cocked his head in disbelief.

"Don't get me wrong, I spent a week in the brig for it. But in the end, he did as I suggested, and we avoided a war that we would have lost. Hard." She gestured in the general direction of the Nine Pillars. "You're going to spend a lot of time with a creature that is likely older than some planets. You'll learn, whether you want to or not, that there are things much larger than you or me . . . or even this empire."

She stood and gestured to the door. "We need to get going."

The two walked silently out of the command building. As they got to the waiting shuttle, she grinned mischievously at him. "Want to hear the worst part?"

He grimaced. "Not really, no."

"It makes going to the mall an utter letdown."

He chuckled, and she smiled. This transition was rough on kuldains. Their reality was always so organized. No matter how chaotic it felt to them, it was nothing compared to the chaos of the aether. Fact was fact, even in the philosophical sense; there was still at least *some* order. But in the aether, anything was possible. No matter how impossible it seemed.

11

THE SHOP

Lei rounded the corner of a rather nasty-smelling deli and stopped cold.

"Your destination is twenty feet ahead," her internal oracle system chimed.

The neighborhood she'd been walking through was dilapidated. Many of the buildings hadn't seen paint or even minor repairs in decades. Masaquin Eleven was a particularly poor moon that housed miners for one of the largest water companies in this arm of the galaxy. There were three ice planets in this solar system, orbiting a dying sun along with more than thirty moons. Much as was the case in kuldain space, the city-state that ran the lone populated planet had only limited control over the corporations that owned just about everything else, including the workers on Masaquin Eleven.

This, however, was different. Across a severely damaged cobblestone street stretched a blackened crater. Not a burned or broken-down building—a pure, glassy black hole in the ground.

Several young children were watching her from a safe distance to her right. When she met their gaze, all but one of them bolted down an alley and out of sight. The one remaining child looked to be a rotund little orishon.

The child's larger lower jaw caused its bottom teeth to jut out over their top lip. It had a deep brow and wide brown eyes. The tuft of hair coming out of the top of its head was matted and greasy, and it wore an adult-sized shirt as if it were a dress, using a piece of twine wrapped around its belly several times as a belt.

He or she was maybe ten years old, which meant that it could probably talk and understand her but would not understand complex ideas. Orishon adults were not the most intelligent lot, and the infants were, well, infants. They matured far more slowly than human children. But this one might be able to answer a few questions. She started walking toward it.

The child didn't move. It simply watched her approach and continued munching on whatever it held in its chubby little hand.

When Lei got close enough, she crouched so that she could be closer to the child's eye level.

"Hey, there." She smiled brightly.

The child just blinked, watching her. Now that she was closer, Lei could tell it was a little girl.

"Can you understand me?"

It was rare that such a child not be able to speak the common tongue, but not unheard of. In aether space, local dialects often ruled over the more widely used common tongue.

The child nodded.

"Do you live around here?"

She nodded again.

"Do you know when this happened?" Lei pointed over her shoulder to the black hole in the ground.

The child shook her head slowly, and Lei sighed.

"If money's involved, *I* might know a thing or two," a high-pitched voice chimed in from above her.

Leilani looked up from where she was crouched. Far out of reach, sitting on a burnt-out streetlight, was a purple-skinned imp. His wings looked a little more muscular than normal, which meant that this one might know how to fly short distances, at the very least. Like the orishon, he was clearly not an adult, though it was much harder to tell age with imps.

"I'm sure I can arrange that." Lei reached into her bag and pulled out a nutrition bar.

The little orishon's face lost its bored expression as her eyes locked on to the bar in Lei's hand. Leilani couldn't be sure in the dim light, but she almost thought she could see the child beginning to drool.

She handed it to the kid and stood, patting her on the head. "Thank you, little one."

"*I'm* not that cheap." The imp folded his arms in defiance.

"What's your name?"

"Max."

"Mine is Leilani. Do you know when this happened?"

"Payment?" The kid was good, she had to admit.

Pulling a couple of local silver coins from her pocket, she splayed them between her fingers so he could see that she had more than one.

He shifted his weight back and forth on his perch as his gaze locked on to the coins. Leilani smirked. It was a reminder that even as smart as he seemed to be, he was still an inexperienced kid. He had probably never seen silver in his entire life.

"Three years ago. Two guys showed up." He shrugged, then made a gesture of something exploding. "Then, boom."

"Did you see it happen?"

The imp shook his head. The right side of his skull was heavily scarred, as if he'd been in an explosion or a fire. "Nope."

"You're a bad liar."

He snarled at her, baring a row of sharp, tiny teeth. "No, I'm not!" he spat.

She flicked a silver coin up at him.

Leaping off the lamppost, he dove with amazing control and snatched the coin out of the air. He needed both his tiny hands to catch it since the coin was larger than one. He flapped his wings and glided to another post.

Lei felt something touch her hand and looked down to find the little orishon taking hold of one of her fingers. The child started leading her toward the hole in the ground.

"Masha, you're a little tattletale!" the imp taunted.

But the girl ignored his blustering. They walked all the way to the edge.

"Bo Bo scare," she whispered quietly. "Bad men hurt."

Leilani knelt next to her. "The men hurt him?"

She nodded.

Lei sighed. If the other child was scared, getting information out of him might be harder.

"I need to find them so they can't hurt anyone else."

The girl nodded and pointed into the hole.

Lei looked down into the perfectly glassed crater. Whoever had done this had known exactly what they were doing. The black walls of the crater were a razor-sharp mix of melted glass, stone, and metal, all of which had reached the right temperature to melt perfectly. There was nothing left. The precision was almost military. *Almost.*

"Sweetie, there's nothing there."

The girl shook her head and pointed again.

"Ha!" The little imp had followed them, though he was still easily out of reach. "She's an outsider, Masha. She's too stupid to see anything."

Lei could almost feel his hatred.

The imp growled. "They're all stupid."

She furrowed her brow and shifted her vision so she could see the aether. When she looked back into the hole, she could now see the ghostly outline of a tall, thin male elar standing in the center of the crater and watching her carefully. When their eyes met, he smiled and gestured for her to come to him. Lei reached out and patted the little girl on the head again.

"Well done, Masha. Wait here. I'll be right back."

The little orishon smiled and happily chewed on her nutrition bar.

Lei pulled on gloves to prevent being sliced by the edges of the crater and slid down inside. As she approached the ghost, she realized he looked familiar for some reason.

He reached into the pocket of his jacket and pulled out an ID. It marked him as a retired agent. He then pointed at her jacket.

She wasn't sure that the residual energy of the entity could read a hologram, so she reached into her pocket and pulled out a physical copy of her ID.

He nodded his understanding, then pointed at his feet.

Now that she was close, she could see that he was weak. The ghost had likely been waiting three years for someone to come find him.

"Are you Elaris Shoomer?"

The elari ghost nodded.

"Did you make this?" She pulled the vial from her bag.

Without doing more than glancing at it, the entity nodded again.

"What happened here?"

Again, the ghost pointed at his feet, this time with more energy. It caused him to flicker somewhat. He was losing cohesion.

"Yes, I know, you died here."

"Oh, good grief, you idiot. He means that you need to go underground." The imp started to fly off. "You're on your own, Masha. I'm done with stupid today!"

Lei looked down at the ground. Even with aether sight, she couldn't see past the floor of the crater, which meant that either the glassing had formed an aether barrier or there had already been some kind of barrier in place below the crater.

"You mean there's a vault of some kind below this?" she asked the ghost.

He seemed to relax and nodded.

"Will my overrides work?"

He nodded again.

"Were you on assignment?"

He nodded again and began to flicker softly.

"You've been waiting to give your debrief," she said, more to herself than to the entity.

He smiled and nodded as he slowly dimmed.

She sighed. This would likely be her someday—dead and waiting for someone to notice so she could give her final debrief. As he flickered one last time and then vanished, she grimaced. How had he been missed? Someone had to have known that an agent hadn't checked in. Three years was a long time, even for a deep cover . . . unless he'd been missed on purpose.

She glanced around herself. Now that she was in it, she could see that the crater was even more perfect than she'd originally assumed. The buildings all around it were undamaged aside from a little blackening, and the razor-sharp glassed walls of the crater meant that even any enchantments were gone.

The explosion had taken out the building, the basement, and likely a little bit of the ground, just to be sure, which meant the agent had hidden the reports off-site. Lei looked up at the little girl, who was still standing at the edge, watching her.

"Is there another way to get underneath this?" She pointed to the floor of the crater.

The little girl nodded.

"Can you show me?"

She nodded again.

Lei looked around the crater. There was no easy way out of it, but she wasn't a big fan of spells if she could avoid them.

"Sarah?"

"Yes, Agent?"

"Warm up the boosters."

"Yes, Agent."

Her boots shook slightly and gave a loud hiss.

"Twenty percent for three seconds. Then cut."

"Yes, Agent. Ready when you are."

Lei grimaced. This was going to hurt. Unlike some of her colleagues, she didn't use these things enough to have perfected flight. She preferred to walk or drive.

She positioned herself so that she wouldn't land anywhere near the child. *"Go!"*

The boots activated with a loud whoosh as gravimetrics kicked in and triggered a small engine in the bottom of each boot. It was enough to launch her up into the air rather ungracefully. As she flew out of the hole, the orishon child just watched, craning her head as Leilani flew past high above her, all the while still chewing on her bar.

Lei tucked herself into a ball as the boots cut. She hit the ground hard, but her training kicked in, and she rolled off the majority of the impact. By the time she stood, she was on the far side of the street. She'd have a couple bruises, but she was otherwise none the worse for wear. Dusting herself off, she walked back toward the kid.

"All right, you ready?"

The child smiled up and her and nodded. She reached out to take Lei's hand, then led her off again.

Several minutes later, the girl pointed to a grate in the street, likely one used for runoff. Whatever usually ran off into it did not smell nice.

"In there?"

The child nodded but refused to get closer to the grate.

"I take it I'm on my own from here?"

"She's not allowed in there. And if *you* go in there, you're insane as well as stupid." Max's voice wasn't much of a surprise. Though he had left earlier, he hadn't stayed away long.

"I am assuming that either you're worried about Masha or you're afraid you'll get in trouble if something happens to her." Lei turned and looked up at the imp.

"She's my little sister."

Lei resisted the urge to laugh. Despite the obvious age difference, the little ogre was already easily three times the size of the imp.

"Come down here. Unless you're too scared."

His eyes narrowed, but the taunt worked, regardless. The imp flew down and stood between her and his sister.

"There was no need for that," he grumbled.

Leilani knelt in front of both of them. "Not all outsiders are assholes." She presented three silver coins and held them out to the little guy.

"Yeah, right." He strode forward on his tiny legs and snatched them up. "Some of you are stupid suckers."

She chuckled. "Or we're just generous because we were here once, and we remember what it feels like to grow up on the streets." She smiled warmly. "Though I didn't have such a great big brother."

She stood and dusted her hands on her pants. "Save some of that. Don't blow all of it at once." She turned and headed for the grate.

"Hey, lady?"

"Yeah?"

"How did you get out?"

"I met a sucker like me who took an interest." The lie came just as easily as the smile that followed. "Don't worry. You'll see me again."

She reached down and pulled back the grate. The smell made her eyes water. From her bag she pulled a fitted rebreather and placed it over her face. "Stay smart, Max, and take care of that adorable little sister of yours."

She hopped down into the sludge below and grimaced. She wasn't sure a sterile shower was going to be enough after this. Four hours and fifteen dead creatures later, she found herself in front of a door. It was sealed, but thankfully, it still had power.

"Sarah, query the door."

"Unable to comply," the female voice replied. *"It does not appear to have any wireless connections."*

"How antiquated," Lei grumbled.

"Or just secure," her oracle replied.

"Oh, hush."

"Yes, Agent."

The door didn't even have a physical panel, though it did bear writing that she didn't understand.

"Do you recognize this language?"

"No, ma'am. It is not in my data banks. Without searching the command databases, I have very limited information."

"Then never mind. Like I said, none of this goes to command."

"Understood."

There was a long pause as Lei ran her hands over the frame, looking for something that could be used to trigger the door.

"Agent?"

"Yes?"

"May I ask why?"

"Why what?"

"Why aren't we communicating with command?"

"Because I think there might be an insider."

Another long pause.

"Is that why you didn't file a report about the investigation while we were aboard the Eldrich Sun*?"*

Lei wasn't entirely sure why she hadn't filed a report. She had told herself it was because she was pissed at Dorthy for selling out the prof, but that wasn't really the case. Dorthy was going to do what was right. Now she was beginning to suspect something else had prevented her from filing her report—some nagging suspicion in the back of her mind.

Something was very wrong with this investigation. The trail was leading in strange directions that didn't feel right to her. There was something much larger in play here than a ship full of angry soldiers.

Taking a step back, Lei examined the door carefully. She tried to consider what she knew of the owner. Markes and Shoomer had been a pair of aether inventors. Shoomer had been elari, and Markes was a dwarf, or so the public listing had indicated.

"Ye can stare at it all ya like. Ye no be gettin' in," a deep male voice rumbled from nearby, startling her.

She stepped backward, whipping her gun from its holster and aiming it toward the sound. The resulting maneuver caused her to lose her balance on the slick surface and fall backward into the muck. She regained her balance, now chest deep in sludge but with her weapon still aimed at the short, wide humanoid.

He was clearly a dwarf and had probably been a redhead in his younger years, based on the peppering of red in his otherwise white beard. He wore a heavy rubber suit, a rebreather, and a large metal helm with a spectacular array of gadgets and lights. Over one shoulder, he carried a heavy bag, and over the other, a large rifle.

He tilted his head to the side slightly, obviously impressed. "Nice weapon control. Who ya be, and why are ya here?" He gestured toward the door with an elbow.

Lei glanced at her weapon and grimaced. Today was not turning out the way she had hoped, but then again, nothing had gone smoothly since she was assigned to this stupid mission.

"Gordon Markes, I assume?"

"Ah-ah." He shook his head. "I asked first."

"Agent Leilani Falconi." Lei climbed back up the nearby ladder to the slightly less disgusting walkway.

He dropped his bag as the rifle that had been resting casually on his shoulder snapped into his hands.

The laser sight above the large-caliber barrel flashed faintly. Based on his aim, there was likely a red dot in the center of her forehead. She blinked several times, trying to ignore it. She could swear that it hurt, but that had to be her imagination warning her of the danger.

She lifted both hands. A large drop of slime fell from her arm with a splat, and not for the first time since coming down here, she resisted the urge to vomit.

"Easy, Markes. I came to see what happened."

"You people know what happened," he almost growled. "Ye killed mah partner and trashed mah place tryin' ta kill me." He glared at her. "Ya missed. But I ain' gonna miss you."

The rifle spun up, and the barrel glowed red and yellow.

"Are you saying that IIS attacked you and your partner?" She furrowed her brow.

He cocked his head. He wasn't as sure as he had been a few seconds ago. "Yer not gonna fool me inta thinkin'."

Lei resisted the urge to laugh, but she couldn't fully hide her smile.

He considered what he had just said and grimaced. "Damn it. Now see what ya done? Now yer laughin' at me."

She finally chuckled. "I'm sorry, Markes. I couldn't help it."

The high-pitched whine of the weapon quieted, and the barrel darkened as it started to cool.

"Shoomer sent me down here."

The dwarf shook his head. "That damn elar is loyal to a fault."

She shrugged.

"Why'd ya come?"

"I found a PG hidden on an imperial kuldain ship. I was told Shoomer made it." Her hands were still up, but she really wanted to pull the vial out, so she started to lower them. "I have it here."

The dwarf waved at her, shaking his head. "No need ta show it to me. We made 'em. That's why they tried ta kill us." He grumbled under his breath in dwarven.

Dwarven used to be the technological language, used in all oracles and aether tech, but now it was nothing more than a smattering of words written down in obscure books. For the most part, the language was dead. Even most dwarves didn't know it anymore. If this one did, that was a fairly spectacular feat, and she knew at least five professors at the university who would love to pick his brain.

"I guess ya better come inside. Canna keep standin' out here. We're gonna attract the wildlife." He walked up to where she stood in front of the door, then pushed past her.

Several feet down the wall, he stopped and said something in dwarven again. A section of wall just vanished. He turned and grinned at her.

"See? Ya can play with tha' door all ya wan. It don' lead nowhere. Save ta twenty feet of magsteel." He laughed, looking her up and down. "Why in tha world would ya come down here dressed like tha'?"

Lei shook her head and resisted the urge to shrug. She already felt disgusting. He didn't need to make it worse.

"Yer gonna make a mess. Make sure ya clean up before ya come all tha way in." He stepped inside, and she heard the sound of an iris door cycling open and then closing.

Stepping up to where the wall had vanished, she found another door set deeper in. It looked like a lock door to a ship. On the other side, she could hear what sounded like a sterilization sequence happening, which, considering their surroundings, made perfect sense.

She waited until the light turned green, then stepped into the chamber.

12

SECRETS WITHIN SECRETS

It took her just over an hour to pull off her gear and clothes and sterilize everything. Once she was done and redressed, the light finally turned green and allowed her to pass further into the facility. Inside, she was met by the smell of some sort of stew and fresh bread. If she wasn't mistaken, she could also smell beer.

"Took ya long enough," Markes spoke up from a neatly organized kitchen area.

Despite the extremely advanced sterilization area she had just come through, she found she was standing not in a research facility but in a decent-sized apartment with a kitchen, a living room, and a well-furnished office area. In the office were bookshelves, two large wooden desks, and a workbench covered in tools and machines that she couldn't identify the purpose of at all. Past the living room was a hallway that led farther back, likely to bedrooms.

"Everythin' ya need is on the workbench over thar." He gestured past her with his nose. "I'm makin' us dinner."

Lei started to argue, but her stomach growled at her, so she opted to smile and nod a thank-you instead. On the workbench, she found a digital pad and several leather-bound notebooks. She picked up one of the notebooks and began to skim the elegant, handwritten elari script within.

As she flipped through the pages, she learned far more about the two partners than she really needed to know. But she also learned about Agent Elaris Shoomer's suspicions.

According to his notes, the buyer who had contacted him about making PGs was an IIS agent. Originally, he'd requested fifteen microportal generators. Shoomer commented that in each of their dealings, the agent seemed scattered. He always had the right paperwork, but his body language and behavior left Shoomer wondering what was really going on. Their dealings had always been in person, and nothing digital had ever been logged. Not entirely unusual, but it still seemed to make the elar nervous. One entry from after the tenth PG was collected caught Lei's attention.

I think Gordon might be right. I hate to admit it, but there might be something wrong. Agent Caris was far more nervous this time. Constantly looking over his shoulder. He's obviously scared of something. He kept mumbling that she was getting angry at how long the PGs are taking to make. I've checked with command. His superior is Commander Dorthy, who is definitely not a woman. So who does he mean by "she"? I will report this to the commander and see what he wants me to do about it.

Several pages later, he'd continued:

I talked to Dorthy. He agrees that this is unusual. He also reinstated me, which caused Gordon to lose his mind. He smashed all of my work, saying that he refuses to go back to constantly looking over his shoulder. I can't say I really blame him, but I also can't refuse a direct order. Dorthy wants me to keep a detailed record of my next meeting with Caris. If we're lucky, this next meeting will be the last. I should be done with the final PGs he ordered.

Leilani set the book down and looked through the rest of the pile for a holo recording.

"Food," the gruff dwarf barked at her from the table. "Come eat."

She walked over to the table and sat down. She wasn't really sure what to say to him.

"It ain' tha best food. But it'll fill yer tummy. I been in this bolt-hole for a while."

"If I'm able to find out who's behind all of this, you'll be able to come back out." She tried her best to be positive, but it wasn't really her style.

"Prolly." He shrugged. "But ta wha?" He gestured upward. "A hole in tha ground?"

"Well, you could rebuild. Or move?"

"I ain' movin' nowhere. I was born in this neighborhood. I'll die in this neighborhood," he snarled. "But that ain' yer problem."

They were both quiet while they ate. For not being "tha best food," as he had put it, it was still damn good. When he'd finished eating, he stood abruptly.

"Now, get yer data, an' leave. Take nothin' tha's handwritten. Only tha digital stuff belongs ta yer precious IIS." He growled and stormed from the room with a beer in hand.

Lei returned to her bag, which was resting on the table next to the pile of notebooks. She spent another two hours poring over the digital data, looking for the dates and names she needed. Then she sat back in the chair and stared at the screen in her hand.

"*Sarah, pause playback.*" She stared at the face of the man depicted holding the elar by the throat. She recognized him. It was one of the royal aether guards assigned to Admiral Gremm.

"*I know I am not the agent, but that looks pretty incriminating,*" the oracle said.

"Yeah, but it's not enough to do anything but arrest the two of them for murder."

"Based on my learning parameters and our time together, am I to understand that you do not intend to do so?"

"No. I need more than that. I need to know just how involved Gremm really is and why. I have to know what her overall plan is. This doesn't make any sense yet."

"Well, the why is easy to extrapolate. They were attempting to prevent this very thing from happening," the oracle stated blandly.

"Your ability to state the obvious continues to astound, my dear."

"Thank you, Agent."

"That wasn't a compliment."

"Oh. Well, what's next?"

"We find them and make them pay."

13

BACK DOORS

At the small door set into the side of a massive megastructure, Lei swiped one of her fake IDs. There was a soft chime, and the door slid open silently.

"Welcome to the Mountainside Chalet," a voice cooed from invisible speakers. "You are expected, Ms. Smith. Please follow the arrows on the floor to the penthouse elevator."

Lei ignored the lights. She already knew where she was going. As she approached, the elevator doors slid open, allowing her entry. Stepping inside, she reached over to the panel and popped it open. Inside were several wires leading to the main panel and a second ten-key pad. She typed in a thirty-number code and hit the pound key. The lights in the elevator went red.

"Step back so I can see you," a high-pitched male voice commanded flatly through the digital circuit.

She took a step backward and looked up at the camera.

"The scans say you're armed." The voice was clearly unhappy.

"Your point?"

"I said come unarmed!" the voice shrieked.

"And I told you to stuff it." She crossed her arms and smirked. "I've never once come here unarmed, and I'm not starting today. We both know how this plays out. You bluster, I threaten, and in the end, you just shut up and let me in." She reached up, closed the panel, and gestured to the back of the elevator. "Can we please just skip to the end? I have something I need you to help me with."

The elevator began moving down.

"The great and powerful Leilani Falconi needs help?"

The lift stopped, and the rear of the elevator slid aside. It wasn't a door per se, but the lift had been modified to open when, where, and how this particular hacker told it to. She walked into a dark room filled with machinery, some of it working and some of it just piled up in seemingly random locations, waiting to be used.

She wound her way between several of the piles and through a door set into the far wall. There, sitting in a reclining chair that cradled his whole body, sat a small male who was so thin she could see the bones in his shoulders and elbows. His face didn't look much better. His eyes were sunken into his head, and his cheekbones stuck out from under his cheeks. He stood on shaky legs and turned toward her.

"Aw, BB, you look like hell." Lei stepped forward to give him a hug. "You really need to stop the stims and eat something."

He waved his hand dismissively. "I'm fine."

Lei sighed.

"What do you want?" He turned and sat back down at the massive full-immersion rig, too weak to even stand for long.

Leilani looked around at the empty vials of various illegal drugs that littered the rig. Gesturing to them, she shook her head.

"I called ahead so you could clean this shit up before I got here."

"You're not going to arrest me, and you and I both know it."

She shook her head. "Maybe not, but that doesn't mean I want to look at it."

"Get over yourself." He glared at her, already beginning to shake from being out of the rig for too long. He was much worse than the last time she had been here. But then, it had been a few years.

"You're going to kill yourself at this rate."

"I know. I'm working on a plan for that. But that isn't why you're here. Can we please move this along?"

She nodded and gestured to his rig.

He hit a button on the arm of the chair, and it began to enclose him. She knew from experience that it was also piercing him with needles that injected sustenance, drugs, and anything else he needed or wanted.

Around her, the room flickered to life, and a hologram of a much younger and healthier BB appeared next to her, smiling brightly. The walls seemed to vanish, and it now appeared as if they were standing in a well-kept and decorated office. The walls were lined by bookshelves and corkboards pinned with various projects. In the middle of the room was a large wooden desk, against which her childhood friend leaned.

For Lei, the holograms were laid over the junk-filled reality, but for him, it was all real. BB was a perfect example of the dangers of full-immersion virtual reality.

"Whatcha got?"

Lei sighed. This was suicide each time. If she were caught, her life would be forfeit.

"This is about a case. So the usual preamble applies." She walked over and inserted a data stick into a panel on the side of his unit.

The files it contained gave him a somewhat sterilized version of the data. He was kuldain, just like she had been in the beginning. He had seen enough shit while hacking that she doubted he would be all that surprised even if she did tell him the whole truth. But she had limits, and that would be too far over the line even for her.

"I'm having trouble connecting the dots." She brought up the IKSRC *Phenom*, a picture of Admiral Gremm, the PG, and the glassed area where the PG inventor had been killed. Each image came with far more data behind it. In his virtual state, BB could access the information almost instantly.

He stood up from behind his desk and walked over to examine the images. "I'm assuming you need me to query the IIS databases securely?"

She nodded. "I think there's an insider."

"Who's not in this list?" He gestured to the floating images.

She shook her head.

"Still don't trust your best friend, huh?"

"Do you trust *me?*"

"Nope. Not even a little." He reached up, plucked one of the images from the array, and studied it more closely for several seconds. He then turned and strode to a large board with several pictures and strings pinned to it. "Hmm . . . Well, this is interesting."

She followed him, carefully stepping over a pile of partially bagged garbage.

On the board were images of several people, most of whom had "deceased" written across their faces. All were connected by string to one central image. The man in the center wore an Imperial Investigators uniform—not of her department, but IIS nonetheless. He, too, was marked as deceased.

BB pinned the image of her PG next to another that looked almost identical. Apparently, it had been found at the scene. According to the report next to it all, however, Agent David McConnell had been killed by a bullet to the head.

"You have this marked as a PG. What does that stand for?" He met her gaze, and the two stared at each other for a long time while she considered how to answer.

"It generates a micro wormhole. We call them portal generators."

He blinked at her for a split second before reaching toward the board and beginning to quickly shuffle things around. Some pictures came off, and several others were put up in their place. It took him a good twenty minutes to arrange everything until he was satisfied. Stepping back, he looked over the board while rubbing his chin.

"Great. You fixed the number-one thing I was having trouble with—the how—but now I don't have a suspect." He turned and walked back over to her display, where he tapped the picture of Admiral Gremm. "I know this woman. She's a serious bitch."

"How do you know her?"

He waved his hand, and a news article from three days ago appeared. "Admiral Brigitta Gremm to Receive Her Second Star." The article cited her exemplary service in the face of an unknown hazard to the crew and recruits aboard the IKSRC *Phenom*, stating that she was a credit to the empire and to her family.

The reporter then went on to explain how she'd called in a microbiologist to help her track down the cause and find a cure for everyone aboard her ship. All of this had been done without any concern for her own safety.

Lei couldn't help but chuckle. She was used to not getting any kind of credit, but the article didn't just leave her out; it made up entirely fictional accounts and people that never occurred or existed.

"To make herself look good, Gremm arrested her own people, who were running her drug and gambling rings," BB snarled at the picture of the woman. "Then had them all killed when they got to prison."

Lei frowned. "Can you prove that?"

"Well, yes, but not in a way that your bosses will accept." He folded his arms as he considered her files. "And you're saying that she's somehow related to these PGs?"

"Her personal guards murdered the inventor after picking up the last of the order."

"When?"

"A little more than three years ago."

BB gestured, and the whole board flew over to where they were both standing in the middle of the room. It grew in size, and her new images were added to it. He shuffled things around so Gremm's image was in the center.

"My IIS agent was shot from long range, inside a room with no windows and no holes." He shrugged and gestured to the picture of Agent McConnell. "It was what attracted me to the case. The impossibility of it. But then you brought me the how. What you will find interesting, though, is when. Forty months ago."

Lei stepped closer and began looking the whole board over. The unusual murders seemed to fit into two different categories. One covered a fifteen-year period more than three hundred years ago, while the other started about eight years ago. She circled the older murders, moved them into a folder, and set them aside. "Different maker. And likely different ringleader."

BB nodded in agreement.

The IIS agent had been on an internal investigation, according to the file attached to his picture.

"Do we know what the investigation was about?" She stared at the image of the agent. She'd never met him, but that wasn't all that unusual.

"The data was missing when I went looking for it."

"Figures." She tapped the picture of Admiral Gremm. "The PGs have a minimal activation range. Let's see if we can find where our admiral was at the time."

BB's holographic image froze as he searched through the net for information. Several moments passed before he came back.

"Imagine that. She was on-world. But at the time of the murder, she was in a public interview with one of the Kassian Navy's public relations officers. Something about a new command."

"Yeah, she took command of the IKSRC *Phenom* around that time," Lei agreed. "But she really isn't the type to get her hands dirty. Can you see how many guards she has with her?"

"According to this footage, two. But here, when she's leaving, there are two more with the car. That was about an hour after he was killed."

Lei frowned. "I went through the *Phenom*'s records, though. She wasn't aboard when the PG was planted ten years ago."

"Maybe an accomplice?"

"What about the rest of these?" She pointed to the various other unusual murders pinned to the board.

"Mostly contractors, miners, and one senator, Silo Gittleman."

"Miners?"

"Yeah. I originally assumed it was some sort of plot involving a couple of mines owned by Gedrin Mining Conglomeration."

Lei shook her head. "I don't know them."

"They supply the Kassian naval shipyards. The senator was investigating rumors that the shipyards were taking in low-grade materials in order to cut costs and skim off the extra money. That was eight years ago." He tapped the image of the senator, then shrugged. "The others were two contractors who were arranging and delivering the inferior goods. One was a mining foreman, a Mr. Duan Forren, and then there was his son Marcus, who was also a miner. That was about seven and five years ago."

BB grinned at her.

She didn't like that grin.

"In fact, all I need is for some legs to go check out that office for me."

"Why?"

"Because they keep their data off-line, and each of the shootings—except the son—happened in that office. The PG has to still be there someplace."

"You want me to sneak into a corporate archive and find a live PG that has been used multiple times to kill people?"

"Isn't that your job?"

She stared at him blankly. He was right. It *was* her job. Somehow, though, wording it that way made her job sound suicidal.

He chuckled. "Besides, it'll take me time to research Gremm. I've run into her people several times online. Hell, some of her people have hired me for work. I'll have to be careful so we don't alert her. Can't catch our prey if they run to ground."

"Fine, I'll go take a look. Can you look up the name Caris in the IIS employee files? I've never heard of him, but that isn't all that uncommon."

"Your insider?"

"Possibly."

Discreetly, Lei reached into her bag and pulled out a small, cylindrical device with a button on the end. When she pressed it, the digital world around her flickered even as the illusory version of her continued to look over his files. That version, however, was now being controlled by Sarah.

She set the device carefully in her coat pocket and reached into her bag again. This time, she pulled out several IV bags. In addition to the usual fluids, these bags also contained nanites. She hung the first bag on the pole attached to the rig and began switching out the lines.

"I felt that," he said.

She said nothing.

Instead, Sarah, who was running her illusion, asked, "Felt what?"

"Stop messing with my IV."

"BB, I'm standing right here." The illusion frowned, feigning concern. "Do you need me to check something?"

BB furrowed his brow in confusion. "No, it seems to be working. Maybe I'm just being paranoid."

"Imagine that," Sarah's version of Lei mumbled under her breath.

"I heard that."

"You were supposed to." The oracle had been with Lei as long as she could remember. She had no trouble mimicking the agent at all.

While the two of them argued, Lei finished what she was doing. She threw out every single drug vial she could find and replaced them with nutritional supplements that would feel similar but were less likely to kill him. They would last him about a month or so.

She really needed to remember to come back more often. For a while, she had been paying his dealer to give BB only what she supplied, but then the dealer got busted for selling his regular stuff to someone else. She'd pulled in a favor to get the man a reduced sentence, but it hadn't been enough to help her friend. She just hadn't had the time lately to find his new dealer. Telling herself that she'd be back more often was a lie, and she knew it. In her line of work, time for family and friends wasn't really an option.

Triggering the device again, she stepped back into the illusion and took her substitute's place as it faded. "All right, BB, I'm tired of arguing with you. I'll go check out your mining office. I assume you uploaded the loc?"

"Yeah, it's on there." He walked across the room and looked up at her. "And Leilei?"

She chuckled. He was the one person who could call her that without annoying her. He'd been using the nickname since he found her in a garbage chute at ten months old. "Yeah?"

"Be careful." He shook his head. "Because no one will tell me if you die."

She nodded and patted the large container that cradled his body. "You too."

14

LOST IN THOUGHT

"And on this side of the mine, we have production and refinement. This is where we refine the materials and prep them for shipment to the naval yards." The man speaking had deep brown hair that was graying slightly at the temples.

The mine's head foreman, Johnathon Mason, was clearly proud of his profession; the young female lieutenant next to him could hear it in his voice as he described the mining facility. "As I'm sure you'll see, we run the mine with precision and attention to detail and safety at all times."

He gestured out the projected window, or prosee window, as those like it were often called. There were no actual windows inside ships, but human beings liked having the ability to look out, so the outer hulls were made with a special photosynthetic material. When power was applied, it relayed the view from outside to the inside.

"I'm sure everything will be in order, sir." Leilani smiled up at the foreman of the Gedrin mining facility in Grelashi System. As with her last alias, Amanda, she'd taken on the persona of a petite, blonde-haired, blue-eyed naval attaché of Admiral Forsythe.

"The admiral just sent me for the yearly oversight." She shrugged. "He isn't expecting me to find anything."

"I have to admit"—the older gentleman smiled down at her—"you're certainly easier on the eyes than the last few lieutenants."

She chuckled. "Thank you, I think."

He laughed and turned toward a table with coffee and snacks laid out on it. "Would you like some coffee or tea, Lieutenant?"

"I understand the tour takes about ten hours?" She almost grimaced at the prospect of spending that much time in a vac suit.

"About that, yes."

"Then yes. I think some coffee might be a good idea."

The man laughed again and poured her a cup.

"Don't worry. I'm sure we can cut a few corners." He took a sip of coffee. "It'll cut off a little time, at least."

Lei took the cup and moved toward the table to doctor it up with cream and sugar. "I can't allow that. The admiral expects me to document everything. And I'm new to his staff. I'm not willing to lose the job just yet." She stood up straight and smiled brightly. "After all, 'admiralty staff' looks really good on my personnel jacket." She smirked, winking at the man. "Being removed from admiralty staff does not."

He bobbed his head in agreement, then shrugged his shoulders. "Very well, then. The whole tour." He watched her over the rim of his coffee cup as she walked back to the prosee window to monitor the shuttle making its way toward the dock in the distance.

The mine was situated on a moon-sized asteroid floating in a solar system with a small gas giant and three other useless worlds far out of the life belt. The asteroid ring encircled the full orbit of the single sun and was smack in the center of the life belt. Based on the unusual elements occasionally found in the belt, many scientists postulated that the asteroids had once been a life-bearing world that had been hit by a random planetary killer.

Lei, however, knew better. In certain circles, it was well known what had happened to this particular planet. Just over eight hundred years ago, there had been a war between the planetary citizens and the aether citizens on the other side. Neither had survived the aether bomb that was inevitably set off. Even the aether line on the other side had been severely damaged—almost cut completely, in fact, which would have damaged the galaxy as a whole. This asteroid belt was the reason for the current treaty between aether space and kuldain space . . . and the whole reason her job even existed.

As she looked out the window, she could almost hear Professor Eagleton giving his lecture on the asteroid belt and how it shouldn't be in kuldain hands. The war that had raged between the two spaces had caused all kinds of damage to the fabric of the universe, and the asteroid belt hid so many dangers for kuldain and aether alike. He'd kept saying that at some point, someone would stumble across the heart, and no amount of treaties would be able to stop the catastrophe that would follow.

"We're here."

The sound of the foreman's voice startled her, and she flinched as she was brought out of her thoughts. Her mind raced. What if *that* was why they'd tried to kill the professor? What if it had nothing to do with the PG at all?

Lieutenant Jessica Jones grinned happily, expertly hiding her rising concern. What if they had found something? She took a deep breath. "Well, I guess we'd better get this over with."

"Don't worry, Lieutenant. It will be over before you know it."

As she followed him through the lock, a warning flashed in her HUD. *Warning: toxicity levels increasing.*

Her daydream had prevented her from getting the warning in time. She could already feel her body growing weaker, and her vision was beginning to blur. She'd been poisoned.

Shit! She triggered her internal stealth and a cleanse protocol in her HUD, trying not to fall even as her vision darkened at the edges.

Two men on either side of the hatch reached out and caught her as she inevitably collapsed. She saw a medical insignia on the lapel of the man closest to her head just before consciousness left her completely.

15

MINING DANGERS

"How long will she be out?"

Leilani recognized the voice of the foreman.

"Well, she's younger and healthier than the last couple, so I would say about eight hours."

"Fine. Do the rewrites, then send her to the office."

"Sir?"

"If it's anything other than, 'Yes, sir,' I don't want to hear it."

She heard the hatch swish as it opened and closed behind him. Once he was gone, several people nearby sighed.

"Yes, sir," the second voice said quietly.

"She may not be capable of rewriting," a third voice spoke up.

"I know."

"What do we do now?"

"If we don't at least try, none of us will be going home tonight." There was a pause. "Or ever again."

"Cameras?" Lei silently asked her stealthed internal oracle.

"One, easily subverted. It is waiting for my orders."

"Aether sensors?"

"None here. However, I am sensing at least one somewhere nearby. It is too far away to detect anything you do in here."

"Understood. On my mark." Lei reached into her sleeve with the hand farthest from the medical staff and pulled out a small device similar to a marble. With a deft flick, she tossed it over her body toward the voices. *"Now."*

A yellow cloud exploded, freezing everyone in place, and Lei leapt up and darted across the room to where her bag had been left resting on a desk. The outside of the bag bore an array of decorative markings; she tapped several of them in a specific and intricate pattern. A copy of herself materialized next to her, and on the desk appeared a copy of the bag. She pointed to the table she had been lying on, and the other version of Lieutenant Jessica Jones nodded and moved to take her place.

By sixty seconds later, when the smoke had begun to dissipate, Lei was invisible and standing in the hall outside of medical. The sterilized copy of herself was still lying on the bed. Unlike her, it had no special cyber- or mageware and was otherwise utterly human and average. While the copy was able to pretend to be a naval lieutenant, however, it wouldn't stand up to any detailed interrogation. She tapped the bag once more, and her doppelganger fell unconscious. It would stay that way until Leilani made it back. She was clear—for now.

"Sensor?"

"Approximately one mile, almost directly ahead."

"Do we have a map of the mine?"

"Oddly, no."

"There is nothing in the computer?"

"No, Agent. It's strange. The computers are utterly empty of anything having to do with the mine itself. When you consider the sheer amount of data that must be required to run a facility this size, that is highly unlikely."

"BB said the system was air gapped."

"Perhaps, but this level of air-gapped segmentation, even on-site, is improbable."

"Yeah, I agree."

A security team of four meandered past Lei as she stood at the prosee windows, looking down at the main floor of the mine. They didn't seem to notice anything amiss.

"This is insane." Lei shook her head.

"I do have the layout of the main command center, which means the offices. Including the foreman's office."

A video played in her HUD. It showed Mr. Mason standing over a drafting table covered in flimsy printouts. He seemed to be alone.

"Agent?"

"Hmm?"

"Have a look at this."

The image of Mason slid to one side, and next to it appeared an overlay of the structures situated around the main mine shaft. The facility she was currently standing in was massive, like a small space station, designed to house and hold more than fifty thousand people along with support facilities. However, on the far side of the shaft was another facility, similar to the first but much smaller. According to the date stamps, it had been marked off limits six and a half years ago, only a few months after the murders.

"Maybe we can find something there. If nothing else, it gets us out of here, which I'm all for."

Lei began working her way toward the nearest mine lock. As she rounded the corner nearest it, she almost ran into several individuals in vac suits also heading for the lock. Sarah patched herself into their local network so Lei could listen in on their conversation as she approached.

"Hey, Mac."

"Hey, Sam. Back to the grind."

"Yeah." The reply didn't seem terribly happy. "How's Janet?"

One of the vac suits shook his head slowly. "Not good, but if she misses another shift, medical's going to come looking for her."

Lei slipped a device across her mouth, and a shielded skin suit slid over her to seal her from the effects of space. She'd had the suit repaired since the attack on the IKSRC *Phenom*, so unless she ran into more trouble, it should be perfectly fine. She slid into the lock with the other four people.

"Aw, man, that really sucks. Have you talked to her about what happened?"

"She still won't talk about it. In her nightmares, she keeps crying about the kids, then wakes up and runs to their room. I have a hell of a time getting her to come back to bed. She just holds them and cries."

"Maybe you should take her to medical?" a female voice spoke up.

"Yeah. I hate that, but I'm not sure she's going to get over this."

"Maybe she needs a mind wipe to help forget it?" The fourth voice was male.

Lei frowned deeply. Kuldains shouldn't have had mind-wipe technology.

"So, Gracie, where do they have you working this week?"

"Section 1290."

"Whoa. Aren't there a few living there?"

"Yeah, I've found two specimens so far. The rest are recyclables."

"Wow! That must be a nice bonus!"

The female nodded as the outer hatch cycled open.

"Yeah, padded my paycheck nicely."

She got several congratulatory pats on the back as the group moved out of the lock. They joined several other individuals in vac suits and waited for the lift that would take them down to the mine floor.

Lei snuck off. She carefully avoided everyone but kept an eye on the group as she climbed her way to the far side of the shaft using the support struts that maintained the shaft's integrity. The group grew to about a hundred people before the large mining lift finally reached them. Once it was there, they all got into a line and started boarding while a second line of miners disembarked.

When Lei had finally cleared the newer station safely, she used her boosters and kicked herself free, allowing herself to take huge leaps along the support beams like some sort of comic book hero.

The asteroid was too large to let her really break free of its gravity completely, and though she had never mastered flying with thrusters in regular gravity, moving around in lighter-g areas was a different story.

It didn't take long to make her way around the shaft to the mostly dead station. It seemed to still have a trickle of power from the main station but was otherwise laid up. The minimal power would be just for maintenance crews, which meant everything was going to be manual.

"Agent?"

"Yeah, Sarah?" Lei found a hatch out of sight of the other station and began to manually crank the outer lock.

"I have been attempting to parse the conversation we overheard. I have come to the conclusion that, based on Section 4159-J of the Treaty of Grelashi, we are required to investigate this."

Lei grimaced. She had come to the same conclusion, but she was technically already on mission. Knowing her luck, though, the two were related. *"Yeah, I know."*

"And your plan?"

"My plan for what?" She grunted as she cranked the hatch the rest of the way open, then tried to squeeze through the hole. Thankfully, she fit. She pulled the crank free, reattached it inside, and began to do the same thing to close the outer lock.

"For investigating the possibility of living specimens on a kuldain/aether contact location?"

"Relax, Sarah. I'm sure they just meant living tissues, not actual living citizens. We'll get to it."

"What if you're wrong?"

Lei furrowed her brow in thought as the outer hatch closed all the way. She tried to ignore Sarah as she turned to the inner hatch. If there was a vacuum on the other side, it would be easy to open.

"Agent?"

"If I'm wrong, a few more hours won't make a difference. They've been at this for who knows how long. I am one person. Besides, odds are both investigations are related."

"That was a flimsy excuse."

"Shut up, and let me work." She wasn't really angry at the oracle. She was angry at the possibility of what might be happening here. But the aether computer made for a good target.

There was pressure on the hatch, and because of the potential for aether sensors, she wasn't willing to risk doing anything overt. It took her almost an hour to crank her way through several hatches into the station and find the office she was looking for. She opened its hatch only about an inch before triggering her own aether sensor. Sure enough, it lit up positive in her HUD. The PG was there, and it was still active, which seemed odd.

Reaching into her bag, she pulled out a large, round ceramic jar. The outside was decorated with several beautiful and intricate aether designs, all of which meant something different and had a separate effect on the jar itself.

Unscrewing the lid, she set the jar down on the deck. After only a few seconds, a small head popped up out of it. It was brightly colored and had what looked to be two massive eyes but were, in fact, thousands of microscopic eyes, like a spider's, arranged in two clusters. The eyes blinked at her, and the creature's head cocked to the side curiously.

"Hey, li'l guy. I need your help."

The creature crawled farther out of the jar. Like an arachnid, it had eight legs on its lower thorax. But the legs and the eyes were where the likeness ended. The ulthari had a humanlike upper thorax with four arms and tiny little fingers capable of rather advanced and intricate work. The creatures were occasionally used in aether space to make amazingly detailed artwork, silk weaving, and, very rarely, clockwork. But that only worked if the person using the ulthari was open minded and willing to accept that the creature was intelligent. Such people were fairly rare.

Leilani pulled out the vial containing the inert PG and showed it to him. "There's one of these in there. I need you to find it, push this button to turn it off, then bring it back here."

"Agent?"

"Yes, Sarah?"

The small creature cocked its head and put its hands on the vial, studying the device inside.

"What if the other end is monitoring it?"

If that were true, shutting it off would alert them.

"How about, instead, you take the camera?" Lei asked the little creature.

It nodded curtly, then scrambled into the jar. Several moments later, it came back up with a tiny camera attached to its lower thorax.

"Good job." She held her finger out to the creature, and it punched her fingertip with its fist, mimicking the human gesture.

The creature was no more than three inches long and four inches high, which made it an amazingly good sneak thief. In fact, ultharis tendency to "borrow" things was the reason there weren't more of them throughout aether space. They were often considered pests and hunted, much like rats on a ship.

The creature squeezed carefully through the opening in the hatch and disappeared inside.

Lei pulled a data pad from her bag and kicked it on. As the camera software came online, she could see the small ulthari weaving its way around the leg of what appeared to be a chair. Using webs, he expertly climbed, jumped, and flew as he searched the room for the device. Finally, the camera stopped. A small face appeared on the screen, and a tiny finger tapped the lens.

"Yes, I see you."

The creature nodded, then turned and pointed to something on the bulkhead. It looked like the deck, but she was fairly sure she could make out what appeared to be some kind of painting. She peered through the crack in the hatch. There was a painting on the bulkhead facing the hatch. The camera scurried around some more until it stopped again. Then it swung around erratically as the little ulthari removed it from his back and pulled it under the frame of the painting. It zoomed in close on some wires.

Well, that explained why they'd left it in an otherwise empty room. "Can you disarm it?"

His face appeared, blown very large as he looked directly into the lens.

Ulthari communication was always complicated, since most of it consisted of sound and body language. They couldn't really make facial expressions like humans did, but this particular li'l guy had been trying to mimic them for years. His eyes were slitted, which was unnerving at this proximity. He uttered a long series of clicks and screeches that came through the pad far too loudly.

"Woah, easy. I'm sorry. I meant nothing by asking. It was just a question." She held up one hand in a gesture of surrender.

Making him mad was often very bad. The creatures could be extremely lethal if they chose to be. Luckily, they rarely chose to be. This one, however, had been taught when and how to kill, which was why she had bought him in the first place.

"Go ahead, and be careful."

She got a noise that sounded a lot like profanity.

"*Sarah?*"

"*Yes, Agent?*"

"*Do we have any hard lines or wireless leaving this area?*"

"*Not that I have been able to detect. This facility seems to have had its hard line cut.*"

"*Man, they really wanted this place forgotten.*"

"*So it would seem.*"

"*Any aether activity?*"

"*Actually, yes.*"

"*Besides the PG?*"

"*Yes, Agent.*"

Lei sighed and scanned the p-way. "*Where?*"

"*It's hard to pinpoint. It's heavily stealthed, but it appears to be approximately five decks below us and farther away from the mine shaft. If I had to guess, I would say it's in one of the old galley areas. But that really is just a guess, taking into account basic space station design and the population density this station most likely housed."*

That was an odd location for aether activity. Lei looked back at the pad. "You going to be a while, li'l guy?"

Another series of profane remarks was all she got in response.

"I'll take that as a yes."

"Sarah, is it a mine sensor?"

"No, ma'am. I am unable to get a good scan of it."

"Then let's go take a look." Lei studied the information on her pad. "Be careful, li'l guy. I'll be back in a few."

16

REFUGEES

Lei had dropped the lieutenant disguise and changed into her normal clothes. In the event that she found herself in a fight, she'd need her tools nearby. She wasn't really interested in repeating the fight on the *Phenom*; space was unforgiving, regardless of your status as aether or kuldain. As she approached the cafeteria, she kept her shield up and began adding cover and her stealth system. What she found as she rounded the corner, however, stopped her cold.

A troll of no older than maybe six was kneeling on the deck of the large passage, his butt up in the air as he focused intently on the marbles spread out in front of him. Next to him, an elari child of probably eleven laughed quietly. The troll was larger than the elar by easily more than a foot, but he ignored the boy. He flicked his own marble, and several others cracked away from its impact and rolled past the chalk line drawn on the deck.

Looking behind the kids, Lei didn't see anyone else down the p-way.

"Hand away from the gun," a soft voice demanded firmly.

She lifted her hands slowly as she turned to find a male, six and a half feet tall, standing well out of reach. He had a makeshift gun pointed directly at her head. It looked like it had been made from metal piping and wires.

The phrase "muscles on muscles" popped into her head, and she resisted the urge to chuckle. His soft brown skin and shoulder-length black hair contrasted nicely with his dark-green eyes. His neck was almost as wide as his rather large jaw. She could see a faint hint of enlarged lower canines barely protruding over his upper lip.

Despite the stealth system she had in place, his cold gaze locked with her own. Clearly this male crodoc was accustomed to killing and was equipped with better internal gear than her own.

Crodocs were uncommon in aether space—mostly because during the Kuldain-Aether War, they had been the main shock troops. Millions of them had been lost to the fighting. This particular crodoc wore a uniform she didn't entirely recognize. It was tattered and worn, but something about it tickled the back of her mind.

"Easy, now," she replied in the same language he had spoken, which obviously surprised him.

Her words were loud enough for the kids to hear, but only because she needed them to run so they didn't get hurt. It worked. The kids leapt up.

"Shit!" the older boy exclaimed. "It's Rothar!"

"But my marbles!" the small troll whined.

"Leave them! C'mon!"

The two combatants didn't take their eyes off each other as the children scurried away. The crodoc's gaze flickered briefly to the insignia on her lapel, and his jaw clenched. It was then that she suddenly realized where she had seen that uniform before.

"Ah, fuck. Of all the damn luck."

"Agent, I think I know who this crodoc is," Sarah chimed in.

"Now, Rothar," she began, repeating the name the boys had used, "take it easy. I am not your enemy." If this was indeed one of the aether soldiers belonging to the Fifth Brigade, she was in serious trouble.

His eyes narrowed dangerously.

"Agent. I believe I have an ID match. This is General Rothar Horrison."

"The Rothar Mathias Horrison?" she exclaimed out loud. That would make him more than a thousand years old. "That's impossible!" Her eyes widened, and her hands lowered slightly, only to rise back up when the crodoc growled at her.

"Yes, Agent. His internal oracle is registering the identification. Its protocols are very old but operational."

Lei lowered her hands, ignoring his gesture to put them back up. "General, if you want to shoot me, feel free. To be honest, I would consider it an honor. However, I am also your way out of here, and I'm betting you have questions I would be happy to answer."

The look on her face must've matched the mix of awe and confidence she was feeling. Every young aether loved to dress up as the great General Rothar Horrison.

"Ma'am, this has to be reported!"

Leilani nodded her agreement. That the crodoc hadn't responded, however, was concerning. He did seem to be considering the situation, though.

"I would give just about anything to shake your hand, sir." She stood perfectly still. She was still in danger, and she knew it.

"Who *are* you?" His voice sounded angry, but she could hear the ire fading somewhat.

"My name is Special Aether Agent Leilani Falconi. I am a member of an organization that was stood up in response to the Treaty of Grelashi." She gestured to the mine shaft in the distance, even though it couldn't be seen from this deep into the station.

The crodoc's grip on his weapon tightened, and his eyes narrowed dangerously.

"The mine I'm assuming you escaped from is what's left of the planet Grelashi, the place where you and your people spent so many years warring." She shook her head slightly. "I know it's a lot to understand."

"I understand it just fine. I'm not a moron."

Lei shrugged in apology. "I meant nothing by it. It was just a long time ago, and a lot has happened since then."

"I'm aware." He gestured to the p-way down which the children had run. "Get going."

This was not going as smoothly as she'd hoped. She stepped in the direction he indicated.

When he had pushed her several yards down the hall, she saw two crodocs and a large, angry-looking troll heading their direction, all of them armed with similar makeshift weapons. The troll carried a large magsteel beam with spikes driven through it. That would hurt, regardless of her armor.

As they drew close, the two crodocs made no unusual moves, but the troll began to swing the massive maul in anticipation.

"It's Kassian." The troll spat on her face.

She wiped the spit off with the back of her hand. The crodocs lifted their weapons slightly but simply tracked her movements.

"Let's just kill it and eat it," the troll growled.

"I wouldn't recommend that," Lei said.

"Are you threatening me, human?" The troll took a step forward, but one of the crodocs put its hand up to stop her.

"No, ma'am, I'm not. I just happen to know that I give your kind rather severe indigestion."

The troll snorted, then looked confused.

"How did you know I'm female?"

Lei smiled warmly. "Because you're too pretty to be male."

The crodoc that had stopped the troll actually smirked while the troll laughed.

"Take her to the professor. I'm going to look around and see if there are any more of them." Rothar had moved into her peripheral vision somewhat, enough for her to see him gesture to the crodoc who had restrained the troll. "Sergeant, you're with me."

The remaining crodoc and troll glared at her as the other two headed back toward where Rothar had found her. The remaining crodoc wore a uniform much like the general's, but the troll wore simply a gray jumpsuit.

"You be a good human. Don't make us kill you before we get intel out of you," the troll grumbled.

Lei chuckled. "Leilani. My name isn't 'Human,' it's Leilani."

"Who asked?" The troll swung the beam lightly at her, more in an effort to make her move than to connect. It worked.

"May I ask how long you've been here?"

"No," the troll snapped.

"Marta," the crodoc said quietly.

"Bah." Again, the troll spat.

They walked down the hall toward the cafeteria hatch. As they approached, the two guards stationed at the hatch eyed them suspiciously. They said nothing, though, as the two escorted her inside. There, in the massive galley hall, she found rows and rows of tents. Outside the galley, it had been utterly quiet, but inside, hundreds— if not thousands—of voices were talking over each other. Tents had been erected even up on the sides of the galley using ramshackle platforms. Imps and fae'ana stood at the edges of their small hovels there, watching her.

They galley grew quiet as her escorts marched her through. Again and again, she could hear the same whispered word: *Kassian*. This was an impossible amount of refugees. There was no way this had gone unnoticed by the IIS. She was led through the group to an area in the back where a more permanent structure had been erected out of scrap metals and scavenged plastics. There, a human woman in a dingy white lab coat was treating the arm of a young gobishili girl.

"Professor. Look what we found," the troll cooed.

The only other human Lei had seen so far looked up at her, and her face paled.

Her lab coat bore a logo Lei was extremely unhappy to see here. She resisted the urge to pull her weapon. There were far too many innocents in the vicinity to start shooting, and she wasn't willing to risk another incident. Lei stayed quiet as she and the two behind her waited for the professor to recover.

Finally, the woman ushered the child off. "You'll be fine, Mena. Go back and tell your mom."

"I'm assuming that you, unlike the rest of these people, know who I work for?" said Lei.

The woman swallowed and stood up straight, trying to project an air of confidence she obviously didn't feel.

"You are from the IIS. I assume you're here to arrest me?"

"Over my dead body," the troll growled.

The researcher raised a hand. "Marta. It's okay. I knew this day would come."

Lei kept her face neutral as she studied the woman.

"All I ask is that you listen to me and that after you arrest me, you take my son to his father at Kass Core."

There was some movement behind Lei; she shifted so she could see her two escorts out of the corner of her eye. The crodoc's grip on his gun had tightened, and he had lifted it slightly.

"You're Kassian military?" His voice was dangerously low.

Before this could get any worse, Leilani took a step toward the human woman.

"Do you mind if we talk inside, Professor?" She used the same honorific the troll had used.

The woman seemed nervous, but Lei didn't give her a chance to argue. Instead, she took advantage of the confusion to grab the woman's arm and lead her inside. The professor seemed to be operating some kind of medical facility. Some of the items were aether tech, and some were electronic. Near the door, a symbol had been scratched into the crude wall. Leilani reached up and tapped it twice. A shimmer rippled across the room as it sealed.

The woman looked utterly shocked. "How did you know to do that?"

"All right, Doctor, I assume?"

The woman nodded.

"Explain. And quickly. I'm not sure how long they'll stay out of this."

"How did you . . . ?"

"Doctor!" Leilani interrupted her. "Now!"

The woman shook her head, obviously flustered. "I work for"—she gestured to her jacket—"well, I guess I used to work for Qualidine Biomed. My team and I were sent here to research what we were told was unusual genetic material found in the rocks." She seemed to grow lost in the memory.

"When we arrived, we were given samples to work with. I grew suspicious when I realized the samples were not only alive but recently harvested. After a lot of research—and help from Marcus, one of the foremen—I found out the samples were coming from subjects that were being kept in some sort of stasis bubble. We still don't understand how the stasis works."

She shrugged as if something were weighing her shoulders down. "I suppose how the stasis works isn't as relevant as the fact that Gedrin Mining is digging up people along with the metals and other materials from the planet. They part out and recycle the humans they find, even though most of them are alive and healthy. And they capture and imprison the other races."

Tears gathered in the woman's eyes.

"They have thousands of them down there. The compliant ones are being used to mine deeper into the more unstable areas. The others, they either dissect for research or kill." She wiped her eyes and met Leilani's gaze. "They have children and parents in chains. I had to do something." She waved her arm in a wide arc to indicate the galley filled with refugees.

Leilani sighed. *Perfect*. This was worse than the last incident, and she had been fairly positive that was impossible. Clearly, she was wrong.

"Squeak!" A loud sound emanated from her bag.

Lei fished the pad out. Popping it open, she found her little scout tapping the camera lens and yelling into it.

"Yeah, yeah, I hear you!"

"Squeak, click click huurrrr," it chittered at her.

"Really? Both ends?"

It nodded.

"Why?"

A lot more chittering.

The researcher had come closer to try to see what she was looking at.

"Hmm. Can you shut it off?"

It nodded.

"Then shut it off, and pack it up. Put everything else back exactly as you found it."

Excited chittering.

"What do you mean?"

The camera moved to show what appeared to be a leather portfolio under the device. When it moved a little farther back, she could see a metallic seal embossed into the leather. It had the royal markers.

"Fuck." Lei resisted the urge to toss the pad. At some point, this had to stop getting worse, right? "Stay there. I'll be there as soon as I can."

"Squeak."

"How do you understand that?" The doctor pointed at the screen.

"Practice." Leilani looked up at the woman and killed the vid. "How much do they know?" Lei gestured to the refugees outside.

She shook her head. "I've told them the date and that they were in some sort of stasis. The rest I've kept kind of vague, because I know they were at war with humans."

Leilani shook her head. "No, they were at war with Kassians, not humans."

"What do you mean?"

"It's a long, sordid story. And to be frank, whatever I tell you isn't likely to stick anyway." She stepped over to the emblem etched into the wall and tapped it twice. Clearly, someone in the refugee camp was an enchanter—a mostly lost art, since that sort of thing was done with aether technology now. "The less I tell you, the better off you are."

She opened the door to find the general standing there. Quickly, Lei stepped back so she was out of reach, then took a deep breath and nodded to him.

"General Horrison," she said in Kassian.

He narrowed his eyes.

"'General'?" The woman behind her was once again shocked. "What do you mean, 'General'? The others said he was a political official."

Leilani chuckled and cocked her head in agreement. "Yeah, that's what I'd tell you too."

She lifted a yellow marble in her hand and showed it to him. Leilani knew very little about the aether military, and what little she'd gleaned from her research into General Horrison himself had been hearsay and conjecture. What she did know was that he'd been able to see through her stealth, so odds were he wouldn't be affected by a simple time-stop grenade.

He glanced at it, then past her to the professor, before nodding.

Lei tossed it behind herself, and the world around the two of them slowed to a stop. Even the crodocs behind him seemed to stop moving.

"This is bad. Very bad," Leilani said.

"Agreed."

"I'll explain more later, but I'm an investigator who works on both sides to keep the peace."

"You are Kassian." He crossed his arms.

"True, but again, later. I have to keep working on my investigation, but I need your help if we're going to stop this, rescue you and your people, and put you back where you belong."

"I am willing to listen."

The cloud was beginning to dissipate. The crodocs would recover faster than the human woman. She was out of time.

"She can't know any more than she already does. She's not cleared for this. My people will take care of her when they arrive to help, but until then . . ." Leilani allowed the thought to go unsaid.

"I will take care of it." The general nodded, then stepped back and gestured to Leilani, who sighed. "Arrest her." As he walked off, he added in crodoc, "*Sha na fa'a moritha.*"

Hopefully, the professor didn't understand the language. Doing as he'd suggested, Lei tried to "make it look good."

"You can't do this! I'm an imperial agent!" Leilani yelled so that everyone in range could hear. She swung clumsily at one of the crodocs and was quickly overwhelmed by extra soldiers who seemed to step out of nowhere.

If any of her people had seen this, they would've teased her for decades about it. But she needed to be believable without actually pissing off members of the Fifth Brigade. She wasn't sure she'd survive that.

It wasn't long before one of them hit her in the back of the head. The pain that arced through her entire body was something she could have gone a lifetime without feeling. As the world fell dark for the second time that day, she wondered whether Sarah had been damaged too.

17

NOTES FROM THE PAST

The pain that rolled across Leilani's mind was strong enough to wake her. At about the same time, an awful smell passed under her nose, and she jerked away from it—a movement that was rewarded with a regrettable wave of pain.

She groaned.

"She is waking up, sir." A voice with an elari lilt drew her to the present.

She opened her eyes to the sight of a bizarrely augmented woman with pointed ears and accented cheekbones. Her hair was shaved to her scalp on one side of her head but long on the other. On the shaved side, various aether tech devices stuck out from her skull. Each was connected by cables or antennae to various other parts of her body.

"Her vitals are stable, and her oracle is reporting minimal damage, though her head probably hurts a lot. So I would keep your voice down."

"You talked to her?" Leilani grumbled silently to Sarah.

"I wasn't given a choice, Agent. She is like nothing I have ever seen before. She is like BB, but for oracles."

An aether hacker? That was impossible. Well, no—*improbable* was a better assessment.

The general stepped into Lei's field of vision and gestured to clear the room. Before the elar could leave, he touched her on the arm.

They looked at each other for several seconds; then the woman uttered a terse, "Yes, sir," nodded, and left.

"All right, Agent. I'm ready to listen." The general sat down in a chair next to where she was lying propped up.

Lei tried to sit up further and grimaced as more pain washed over her. What the hell had they hit her with?

The general answered her thought. "The tech that they use here. They use it to control us. It inflicts maximum pain with minimal damage." He gestured to her head. "Pain meds don't work, but it should wear off soon."

Leilani lay back. It would be easier to just hold still for a bit. "All right, General. I would like to start by saying that I'm sorry it took the IIS this long to find out what was going on here. But I will make sure this gets solved."

He frowned. "Solving a problem can mean many things."

She sighed. It could, and she wasn't sure that the IIS would solve this one correctly. It was more likely that they would kill everything and sweep it under the rug. The rights of aether citizens in kuldain space were limited, to say the least.

"That's what I thought."

She nodded, gritting her teeth at the pain. "You're right. So we need to find a different path. Do you, by any chance, have a gate master with you?"

He shook his head. "Don't you think if I had one of those, there would be nothing to find here?"

"How long was I out?"

"Thirty minutes."

"Shit—I need to get up to the foreman's office."

"Okay, I can arrange that, but I'm coming with you."

"It'd be my honor." She grimaced as she stood up but otherwise ignored the pain. "May I ask a question?"

He nodded curtly, grabbing a pack and a rifle that were resting near the hatch.

"Why didn't you take my weapons?" She patted one of the guns on her hip.

He gestured for her to precede him out of the room. They weren't near the cafeteria, and she knew why.

"Experience." He fell in next to her as they walked through the station. "Those are aether weapons. They will defend themselves, and I seriously doubt I have the overrides anymore. Not that I ever would have, with a special operator."

He shrugged and gestured for her to head in a direction different from the one Sarah was indicating she needed to go. "This way is safer." He was silent for a long moment, then circled back to her original question. "It wasn't worth risking my people."

Lei chuckled. It hurt, but the pain was finally receding. "I'm not sure who would win, anyway."

He stopped at the end of a p-way and lifted his finger to his lips.

It was enough to suddenly put her in a business mindset again. She pulled a weapon and switched her HUD to combat mode. The general was initially indicated as yellow; Lei flipped his color to green.

"Sarah, I need you to start considering how to bring up a link between us and BB."

"We have the emergency bands."

"No, the miners might hear that. And so will any military or IIS ship in range."

"Well, there's always the back door."

Leilani frowned as she considered that. It would blow everything, and afterward, she would have to either read BB in or kill him. Neither was a pleasant thought. Slightly ahead of her, General Horrison made a military hand gesture that indicated she should cross the hall and approach the intersection.

"Agent, you are receiving a comm from the general."

"Let it through, but feed it through the firewall."

"Apparently my firewall is garbage," the oracle grumbled.

"Agent, I apologize for intruding on your comms, but the miners often send patrols through here, looking for us. It's an ugly game we've been playing for a few years. I believe there's a patrol ahead of us now."

The fascinating thing about aether silcomms was that they were silent, because they allowed individuals to speak via a telepathic link. An oracle could bridge multiple links together into a single channel, but that required a lot of power, so it was generally used as a burst only and usually with only two minds.

An experienced user knew how to hide everything but the intended communication. An inexperienced user would often accidentally leak some form of emotion or stray thought as they spoke. Oracles were programed to filter this, but they never managed to filter 100 percent. Silcomms, on the other hand, were so precise that what could feel like a long thought or an entire conversation could generally be communicated over only a split second, moving as fast as the brain was capable without the limitations of speech or hearing.

Between the general and the agent, the speech was extremely clean. There were no leaks. No feelings or emotions behind the thoughts at all.

"Roger that. Checking right." Glancing past him into the p-way, she saw a brief movement. *"Contact right."*

He signaled for her to go high. They both leaned out as if they had been working together for years, found their mark, took aim, and fired. Both weapons were utterly silent as the spells on the barrels triggered.

There was a soft whistle as the bullets cut through the air, then two thumps as one bullet struck the guard right through the faceplate and the other sliced through his chest plate and embedded itself just to the right of his sternum. His body collapsed to the deck.

Almost in unison, the two shooters tapped the control devices on their wrists and vanished from visual sensors of any kind. They continued down the p-way, moving in a staggered pattern to the next section.

Again, that was the benefit of a combat system built on telepathic communication: each of them not only knew where the other was but was marked by a faint halo to ensure that they didn't shoot each other in combat. That was likely how he'd seen her in the first place.

Leilani had forgotten how nice it was to have a partner she could trust. *Why* she trusted this crodoc, she wasn't entirely sure; possibly, she was starstruck, but she had a sneaking suspicion it was more than that. They were working toward the same goal. And real trust went two ways. She trusted him to cover her back, and he trusted her to free his people. What she wasn't sure of was whether or not she would still be the enemy when all was said and done.

They ran across a security patrol three more times as they made their way toward the foreman's office. These patrols were in groups of two but were still no challenge. They had no way to see the agent and the general.

"Does it always go this way?" she finally asked as they neared their destination.

"No. This is unusually easy." There was something hidden behind that statement.

Oddly, him keeping secrets from her made her feel better. It made sense that he didn't fully trust her. As they approached the office hatch, Leilani pulled her hand crank from her bag and began to hook it up.

Horrison watched her curiously. *"Are you wanting this open?"*

"I am opening it, yes. I need to get inside."

He shook his head at her crank, his chuckle buzzing across her comms. Then he reached past her with a small device. When he set it on the panel and tapped it, the hatch whooshed open quietly.

She stared at him for a second before stepping inside. He followed and reached around to pull the device free. As he did, the hatch closed all the way.

"Li'l guy?" she whispered into the room.

Movement near the open painting caught her attention. The spiderlike little creature roused from where he had been sleeping inside and waved at her.

Horrison stepped up behind her and nodded his approval, then moved back to the hatch to listen.

Having pulled the jar from her bag, she set it down inside the safe, and the ulthari crawled up to the edge and saluted her before climbing inside.

"Thank you, li'l one. You'll get your usual pay when I get someplace where I can buy some," she said.

She got no answer. He was likely already asleep. As she put the jar away, she looked over the items in the safe. Why in the world would they have left the safe untouched when they emptied the place?

She scanned the PG carefully. It was definitely the same design as the first one she'd found. It had the same markings, and the end point was a single disk no larger than an aether copper coin. The other end, however, was slightly larger and had several tiny buttons around the outer edge. From the operational end, the user could set the diameter of the portal to be generated and the distance of the portal from the generator, which seemed to be limited to ten feet.

She pulled out another stasis vial and slid both pieces inside. Once the cork was in place, the enchantments on the vial would put the PG in a suspended state. She dropped the vial into her bag, then removed the papers and the leather portfolio from the safe.

She spread them out on the table and began to read. Oddly, they didn't say much about the mining activity; they were mostly contracts and payment statements to unmarked bank accounts, all regarding a Project Phoenix. She examined the portfolios carefully before opening them, but they held no residual magic at all. The topmost paper was a letter, handwritten on actual paper, to a foreman named Duan Forren—the man who had been killed seven years ago.

Forren,

We need to ensure that the project stays on schedule. I have too many pieces on the game board to let Senator Gittleman's investigation slow us down. Eliminate him. The pieces are already in motion. Everyone needs to be in place when we finally reach checkmate. SS will fall.

FSS

Leilani shuffled through the next few pieces of paper. Like the others, they were personal letters signed by FSS, and they all referred to a chessboard and eliminating SS. Then she skimmed a letter that said that it was time to "take the bishop off the table so that he can return later to eliminate the king." FSS was telling the foreman to use a "special asset" to fake his own death.

Her mind put the abbreviations and pieces into place. "Holy shit!"

SS was the emperor, Steven Sargeras. They were planning to kill the emperor!

Horrison popped open the hatch and waved for her to hurry. *"We need to get moving. My people say there is a large group heading this way."*

She snatched up everything and stuffed it all in her bag. At the general's signal, they jogged to the intersection opposite from where they'd come. Once around the corner, they waited.

Several moments later, five individuals in vac suits stopped in front of the foreman's office. They cycled the hatch open, and one stepped inside. Several seconds later, he stepped back out.

"Is there a problem, sir?"

"Yes."

The man lifted his pistol and shot all four of the people with him.

"Yes, there is, and I can't have you telling anyone about it." Looking around himself in both directions, he seemed to be pondering his next action. He then stepped over the dead security officers and strode off quickly, heading deeper into the station.

Lei never got a clear look at the face inside the suit.

"Well, that was new." The general sounded slightly amused. *"My people will follow him and see what he does. Should we kill him?"*

"No. If we eliminate him, they'll put backups in play, and we might not find them in time. I do need to know where he goes and what he does. And, if possible, who he is."

Rothar nodded. *"I'll take care of it."*

"I need someplace secure."

"This way."

18

THE SCIF

Several minutes later, the two of them walked into what appeared to be an IIS SCIF—a secure compartment information facility. The hatch was hidden behind a fake bulkhead in one of the mining staff quarters. It shouldn't have existed on a civilian station.

"This room has shielding. My people found it on a scavenge a few years ago. We use it for storage." Sure enough, one corner contained a pile of weapons, ammo, and a loader.

Leilani walked up to the panel and tapped a sequence on the keys. The room lit up, but then the lights went red. The general look surprised.

"Unauthorized entry," the computer chimed.

"Emergency override. Commander Leilani Falconi, ID number 34A5F697 Magenta."

"Identity accepted. Agent, you are accompanied by an unauthorized user. Are you in distress?"

"Negative. Distress code is magenta."

"Understood. Please be aware that it has been nine years, eight months, and twenty-one days since I was last accessed."

"Status?"

"Power at 83 percent. Hard link down, but aether links are active and available. Last and final report of Agent 21957 has not been sent. Do you wish to view?"

"Yes."

"Displaying on screen three."

"This is one of your people's SCIFs?" Horrison asked quietly.

Leilani nodded. "Yes. I wasn't aware there was an agent here, but we have segmentation for a reason."

He nodded his understanding.

"This is Agent Christopher Caris. I'm not sure this report will ever get anywhere. If you're reading it, then I'm dead, and I'm sorry. I should have reported what was going on a long time ago. It's too late now, and I know that."

There was audio overlying the actual typed report, with gigs of more data attached. "About six months ago, I finally made it into the inner circle and was brought into the deep mining chambers. It was all I could do to remain calm. They had aether citizens mining the rubble of what appeared to be some kind of government building."

Leilani glanced up at the enormous crodoc next to her and saw him glowering at the image of Caris on the screen.

"It was then that I learned that they had found pockets of aether stasis. They were pulling people from stasis, killing them or forcing them to mine. When I returned home that day, my wife and two children were gone. I've never seen them again. I'm not sure if they're alive or dead, but they show me video of them occasionally to make sure I remain compliant."

There was a slight pause as the IIS agent on the screen glanced toward the hatch. "Evidently, they do this to every miner who goes into the stasis mines or the deep mines. They watch me closely, but they need my expertise, so they keep taking me farther and farther in. Today, I learned they're looking for an artifact. They call it the heart. After some digging, though, I believe that it's not a heart but rather a crown of some kind."

Next to her, the general flinched. He knew what it was.

"If it's the crown that I think it is, it's the one thing that links all of the aether city-states under one banner. This could have serious consequences to aether space. I can't let that happen. I know that if these people don't kill me for what I'm about to do, my own will. But I'm willing to sacrifice myself and anyone who gets in my way to stop them from finding that crown."

There was a long pause. "Everything I've gathered to date will be in this file. If you find my wife and children, tell them that no matter what I've done, I love them dearly."

The room grew quiet, Lei and Horrison both lost in their own thoughts.

"My worst fears realized." The general nearly choked on his whispered words.

"This does not bode well for anyone."

"My tech told me about your treaty."

Lei turned toward him. The tech had likely gotten that data from Sarah, who had every last line of the treaty in her memory because she and Lei needed it to do their jobs.

"It is a worthy goal. Peace."

Lei bobbed her head in agreement. They both knew where he was going.

"I was willing to sacrifice myself and my people once to protect the heart of the aether. I will do so again."

Lei offered him a shaky smile. She reached for the panel and began typing in commands.

"Emergency override acknowledged. Objection lodged for later review."

It took several minutes, but suddenly she heard a familiar voice.

"I was wondering when you were going to use this thing. Wow, those readings are awesome!" BB sounded pleased and smug all at once. "Whatcha need?"

"Did you do the digging?"

"Yep. I found your files and a whole bunch of other very interesting info."

"Such as?"

"Did you know that your Admiral Gremm actually *was* aboard the *Phenom* ten years ago?"

"How? I checked the ship's logs thoroughly."

"Yep. That tidbit of info isn't anywhere in the archives, naval or otherwise. However, while digging around, I found out that there's a division within IIS that specifically handles royal security. They track the whereabouts of royal members at all times. They alone had information showing that the IKSRC *Phenom* picked up a cadet named Brigitta Gremm and escorted her and her four guards to the naval academy on Oltherian Prime."

"Holy shit."

"Yeah, that is some serious long-term planning. I also read your own report and know what the PG was being used for there, which got me looking into other reports. It's being used like that in two other places. One is a brand-new ship, straight from the naval yards— the yards owned by Gedrin Mining Conglomeration. And here's another fun fact. Guess who chairs the board for that particular conglomeration . . . ?"

"Duke Ferdis Steven Shovalli. FSS," Leilani mumbled.

"Dude, snatch that wind right out of my sails, why don't you?" He laughed. "Yep. Precious Brigitta's daddy."

"Okay, BB, I need you to do something for me."

"Yep?"

"Did you find anything on Dorthy?"

"Nope, he's as clean as you agents get. As for you, my dear . . . Wow, I didn't need to know that about you. And you aren't allowed to bitch about my illegal activities anymore."

Leilani sighed.

Next to her, the crodoc raised an eyebrow and pointed to the panel in a questioning gesture.

She sent him a telepathic response that was more a collection of nonspecific memories and feelings than any particular words.

He nodded his understanding.

"I need his private comm."

"I think I can connect you to his aether comm," BB answered.

"How?"

"Do I ask you how you murder someone?"

Her eyes narrowed. His bait had worked. She took a second to calm down before answering, "Go ahead."

"It won't translate perfectly, of course, since I have to translate the telepathic to the electronic, but the words should come through. One sec. Explaining to his oracle. Got it. You're a go."

"What the hell?" Admiral Dorthy's words came through the speakers perfectly clear, and though she couldn't feel his anger, she didn't really need to. She knew from sheer experience how pissed he was.

"I'm really sorry, Admiral. I'm breaking protocol because we have a class-one situation."

Silence. Then she heard him speaking, but not to her.

"Yes, Senator. I understand, but I need to step out for a few minutes. No, sir, I don't need your permission."

Next to her, the general chuckled and smirked. "I've literally said those same words to a senator."

"Who was that?" Dorthy asked.

"You wouldn't believe me if I told you, sir."

"Try me."

"Okay. I'm standing next to General Rothar Mathias Horrison."

A long pause. It took almost two minutes before Dorthy replied.

"I'm secure. Report."

"I'm at Grelashi, the mining facility here. I have proof in my possession of a plan to assassinate the emperor. But I don't think the attackers plan to stop there. They also know about aether space and are using captured aether citizens to mine for the heart of the aether.

Which we"—she looked at the general as she spoke—"think might have been on Grelashi when it was destroyed."

The general frowned but nodded slowly. "That's a close enough description, yes."

"Are you telling me that's actually General Horrison?" Dorthy's voice held complete disbelief.

"Yes, Admiral." She nodded her head even though he couldn't see it. No video ever left black rooms.

"So, what's with the utterly unorthodox communication?"

"There is, at minimum, one insider in the IIS. Possibly more. I don't think he's acting alone."

"Contact me again in twenty minutes."

"Roger. Out." The comm cut without her doing anything, and then another voice popped up.

"Wow—when you go all out, you go all out." BB laughed. "But while I didn't really get all of that, I get the gist. And no one kills my emperor without my permission. How else can I help?"

"I'll need you to contact him again in twenty. Meanwhile, go through this data and see if we can fill in some of your map. We still don't know what part Gremm plays in all of this." She sent him Agent Caris's data files.

"Got it." The room fell silent.

"You love your emperor," the crodoc said quietly.

"Sometimes it's important to have an ideal or a person you can get behind. It gives life meaning."

"True, but they do not always deserve your loyalty." The general seemed somewhat jaded on the idea.

"Yeah, there is no perfect ideal or person. Whether it's a god, an emperor, a philosophical idea, a parent and their progeny—it doesn't matter. They're all flawed. But sometimes it's the flaws that make them worth following . . . and easier to identify with."

Before now, Leilani hadn't ever really taken the time to articulate why she respected and served the emperor. "In my particular case, I follow my emperor because he cares about his people. He's human. He does make mistakes, but every soul matters to him, no matter the vessel. It's why he fights so hard to protect the peace between aether and kuldain. And to me, that's worth dying for."

19

REACH OUT AND TOUCH SOMEONE

The general had stepped outside to contact his people while Lei brought BB up.

"Heya," BB chimed happily fifteen minutes later. "So, I have a question for you."

"Hmm?"

"Will you take me to aether space some day?"

She sighed. "BB . . ." The fact that he even knew about aether put him in her jurisdiction. The IIS wouldn't be happy about a kuldain hacker knowing about aether.

"I really want to see a real troll up close. I've been watching some of their illusory plays, and damn! They look awesome!"

Leilani folded her arms. She wasn't sure what to do with him. Odds were this wasn't new. He'd known about her override and hadn't done anything with it. In truth, she'd been using him for several decades. There was no way that hadn't gone both directions.

"How long have you known?" she asked.

"Do you remember when you were five?"

"Not particularly."

"Well, I was fourteen, and I remember it clearly. We were in that foster home with the huge lady who kept dropping the baby. She got mad once because you spilled your juice on the carpet. She came after you with a stun baton. You got super scared and curled up in a ball, and suddenly the lady started floating. Then everything in the room was floating, except me and you."

Leilani stared at the console in surprise. This was not something she had any memory of. She didn't even remember ever being in foster care.

"I picked you up, and we ran. I kept you hidden for several years, but I couldn't keep your abilities in check." His voice grew sad. "I knew you needed help that I couldn't give. So I found some people that seemed to know what was happening. I leaked them some footage of you doing various things. Eventually, they started putting things together and figured out who and where you were."

"You're the reason I was kidnapped and taken away?" Lei knew she should be mad at him, but in her heart, she wasn't. He'd known she needed help, so he'd found it for her.

"Yeah. I kept an eye on you for a while, but when you joined IIS, it got harder. Their systems were too integrated with aether and kuldain tech. I can do one or the other, but both is hard for my systems because I don't have a real oracle. So I started focusing on other stuff, only checking in on you occasionally."

"So you've *always* known."

"Yep."

"And yet we play this annoying fucking game. Every time I show up."

"It's what you expected."

In her mind's eye, she could picture his shrug.

"It's time."

The hatch popped open, and Horrison walked in. As the comm line went live, he bent over and whispered his team's situation report in her ear. "He has another PG. He got it from a second safe in the engineering section."

She nodded. Something told her that a man willing to kill his own people could cause some pretty serious harm with a PG. She probably needed to figure out who the man in the vac suit was.

"You there?" Dorthy asked.

"Yes, Admiral."

"Is the general with you?"

"Yes, sir."

"I would like to start out by saying that the emperor would like to thank you, General Rothar Mathias Horrison, for your service to the galaxy. When all of this is over, he would like to meet you in person."

The general seemed surprised but nodded. "Thank you, Admiral."

"Now that the political crap is over, we have a very serious problem. First and foremost, we have to protect the emperor. So whatever information you can give me about the assassination is paramount."

"I believe we know the who and the how but not the when." She jolted as an idea struck her like a physical blow. "However, I think I might be able to help his security reduce his risk."

"Go ahead."

"They're using PGs to carry out the assassinations."

"Wait, multiple?"

"Yes, sir. We know they have carried out, um . . ." She counted them off in her head.

"Nine to date," BB chimed in on the line.

"Who was that?"

Leilani shrugged. "Let's just say that he's my comms officer."

Next to her, Rothar chuckled quietly.

"Ah, your little hacker. Can we trust him?"

"Do you have a choice?" BB laughed on the line.

"In this case, yes," Lei answered firmly, addressing both questions. Her friend took the hint and fell silent.

The admiral cleared his throat. "Would someone . . . Never mind. I'll get that info in person. How are the PGs being used?"

"Actually, they're using them to gate bullets into their targets. PGs can be placed on anything or anyone, but they're trackable using gate sensors."

"Roger that. I'll pass that info on and leave you to find the when and the where. What about the who?"

"That one is a little trickier. We've narrowed it down to Duke Ferdis Shovalli. But the proof is a tiny bit circumstantial. Now, don't get me wrong—we have proof that a lot of illegal stuff is happening, but when we're talking about the actual assassination attempt, that's when the evidence gets a little weaker. It's not enough to stand up to his lawyers."

"I might be able to help there," BB piped up, shifting to a more serious tone. "I know I'm the outsider here, but that might actually help you in this situation. You see, I do a lot of illegal work for various well-funded entities . . . including Duke Shovalli."

He let that information hang in the silence for a moment. "The duke is very, very good at keeping nothing incriminating in digital form. However, his lawyers do not have that annoying little quirk. They have a lot of data in a highly secured database that I am currently in charge of keeping secure."

"Careful, BB." Lei could see where his plan was headed. She also knew her caution would be ignored.

"And if you're willing to deal, I'm willing to give you enough to arrest him and his daughter."

"I'm listening."

The admiral's acceptance surprised her. He wasn't usually the type to deal. He was far too black and white for that—or so she'd thought.

"I want a full pardon for my past, a job within the IIS, and the ability to visit aether space."

"I can't grant the last one due to the treaty. And before I answer to the other two . . . Leilani, what is your level of certainty that the duke is the key to both issues?"

"At least 90 percent, sir. Likely higher."

Suddenly, one of the monitors in front of Leilani flared to life, and several images appeared. One of them was a scanned copy of a letter from Duke Shovalli to his daughter, signed with "Your loving father" and his full name. In the letter, he laid out his plan and her place in it. She was to take over as secretary of the navy and eventually as director of the IIS.

"Well, on that note, I guess . . ." Dorthy's voice trailed off. His attention seemed to have been diverted elsewhere.

Apparently, Dorthy had received the same images. It bothered Leilani only a little bit that BB could force his way into a SCIF. She should probably be *hugely* bothered by it.

"Sir," she interrupted, "I advance that certainty to 99 percent." At her gesture, Horrison leaned forward to skim the screen.

It was silent for a long moment as they all read.

"I need this stated clearly and for the record. You are saying that you are 99 percent sure that Duke Shovalli intends to assassinate the emperor, assume control of the Kassian throne, and attempt to assert control over aether space?"

Dorthy's tone was oddly formal considering the communication method. Lei suddenly realized why. Because of the method the oracles had to use to link multiple silcomms together, BB likely hadn't been able to see when the direct comm had become a channel.

"Yes, Admiral. I believe Duke Shovalli is attempting a coup." She gave him the one word he needed in order to take the next step.

"General Horrison. It is my understanding that you are assisting Agent Falconi in this investigation?"

"Yes, Admiral."

Leilani tried to tell Horrison what was going on, but he was already standing at attention and ignoring her.

"Do you intend to continue assisting her until this case is concluded?"

"Yes, Admiral."

"Jacob Mercede Reede, a.k.a. Backstreet Boy, a.k.a. BB. It is my understanding that you are agreeing to turn state's evidence and assist the IIS in this investigation until it is concluded, on the understanding that you will receive a full pardon for your actions up to this date and employment within the IIS?"

"Um, wow. I don't know where you got that name, but yeah, I suppose I am."

"Very well. I hereby assign Mr. Reede and General Horrison to the IIS on an interim basis and give them security access equal to Captain Leilani Falconi, ID number 34A5F697. I am assigning them under her direct control."

A new male voice came over the line. Leilani automatically stood up when she heard it.

"We second the order. We give our signature to the promotion of Agent Leilani Falconi and grant her the rights and pay commensurate to her new rank of captain. We also hereby sign the pardon—up to this date only—of one Jacob Mercede Reede and thank him for his service to us. We hope to hear better things from him in the future."

"Thank you, Your Imperial Majesty," the admiral replied before anything else could come over the line. "IIS Unit Forty-Two will deal with your problem and alert you when they have a viable solution."

"You all have our thanks and our best wishes." The voice left the call, and Lei relaxed slightly.

"Wait, did I just get promoted?" Thankfully, she hadn't stuttered.

"Yes. You are now in charge of Unit Forty-Two, which, for the moment, consists of the three of you. Unit Forty-Two will have ten seats. You may bring seven more recruits up to speed if you feel you need them. How the team operates together will determine whether the unit stays together after the current mission. You will report your progress to me, and when you have an overall solution, you will report it to His Imperial Majesty. Oh, and BB?"

"Was that really the emperor?" BB was practically squealing into the comm. "I mean, the voice pattern matched, but . . . that was wicked cool!"

"Yes, but I need you to focus for a second." Dorthy was used to dealing with agents with all kinds of weird idiosyncrasies.

"Huh?"

"You have exactly three minutes to pack up anything you want to bring with you."

"What? Wait, what? I'm not going anywhere!"

"Two minutes and forty-nine seconds," the admiral calmly continued.

The call suddenly cut, probably because her childhood friend was freaking out, which would stop him from hosting the comm.

"What now?" The general raised an eyebrow, crossed his arms, and grinned smugly at her. "Captain."

"'Agent' will suffice. Now we find your heart, before they do."

He nodded his understanding and knelt to look through the pile of spare weapons and ammo. "May I ask a question?"

"Only if I get to as well."

"Agreed." When he stood, he was holding a civilian version of a semiautomatic weapon. "Why does your emperor want to meet me, and why are all of you trusting me so completely? I am your enemy."

Lei chuckled. "No, you're not. The current emperor is an aether."

General Horrison stared at her in disbelief.

"You see, after the"—she waved her arm toward the mine—"*incident* at Grelashi, there was an opportunity to make a peace accord. You had lost your new president, Mai Lenali, and the city-states were arguing amongst themselves pretty hard core. They were threatening even more war while they argued over who would take over. Some wanted to backtrack the election to the past president, but most did not. They wanted their own figurehead. You don't have a royal line, but you did have a pretty amazing set of heroes who had just sacrificed everything to end the war. So the Kassian emperor capitalized on that. He proposed a marriage between ex-president Jeria's daughter and his eldest son, the heir to the throne."

She popped the hatch open and stepped out, nodding politely at the four crodocs waiting for their general there.

They nodded back and looked past her to the general, who now followed her out attentively.

"Once things had calmed and the cleanup had started, the emperor stepped down and let his son take over." She smiled brightly at all of them. "All direct-line heirs from there on out have attended kuldain primary schools but then received their secondary education at Eldrich Line University. IIS formed a new division. Secondarily, our job is to deal with treaty issues and to police the aether that live in kuldain space. But our primary duty is to protect the royal aether line and to keep their secret."

"Are you saying the current Kassian government is run by an aether?" The elar with the mageware sounded skeptical.

"Yes."

"Is this common knowledge in aether space?" The asker was obviously the ranking NCO, and he didn't seem curious so much as he seemed to be weighing the potential security risk.

"No."

He smacked the elar in the back of the head. "Pull that recording."

"But . . ."

"That's an order." Horrison nodded his agreement.

"Yes, sir," she grumbled.

"What was your question, Agent?"

"Why are you agreeing to help me?" Aside from freeing his people from the corporation, she didn't see his angle.

"Because, tactically speaking, we are on the same mission. We're just on opposite ends. You have information and resources I need. If we work together, we both get what we want. I get to send my people home, and you protect your emperor and arrest your criminal." He gestured to the unit in front of him. "My people are at your disposal."

Lei looked them over. In their current state, they weren't of much use. Their tech was antiquated, if effective. Their weapons were makeshift, which made them less likely to be reliable, and their armor was nonexistent.

She glanced back into the SCIF and grinned. "I have an idea."

20

SECRETS DO NOT SAVE LIVES

As Lei crouched near the railing, looking down into the massive cavern below her, a small part of her felt sick to her stomach. She had seen a lot in her fifty years of service in the IIS, including massive rings of enslaved women and children, but this was beyond disturbing.

The Gedrin miners were literally mining bodies from the walls. They would occasionally find what appeared to be stasis bubbles of some kind, which contained people, most of whom were alive. If they were human, they were killed while still in stasis, pulled out, and then tossed into carts. When the carts were full, they were driven along mine tracks to the next stage, where the bodies' organs were harvested and parted out. Then what was left was recycled for food.

She wasn't sure even a veeshali would be enough for these people. Especially the children. They might need full-blown reprogramming, which would require a massive medical staff and surgery units. There were thousands of people here. She knew what Dorthy was going to say: it would be easier to put them out of their misery. And she almost agreed with him.

When she turned to look over the group of twenty soldiers with her, however, she smiled. The general's personal squad had mostly been recovered. They were now all equipped with IIS gear, weapons, armor, and toys. At the moment, the unit was stealthed. Their oracle net had been updated, and not only did they look better but their morale had improved as well. A couple of them had argued about wearing Kassian uniforms, but in the end, they'd followed orders.

"What now, Captain?" Horrison asked over the silcomm.

"To be honest, this is your area. I'm an intrusion specialist and an assassin. I deal with one or two people at a time and let the regular IIS deal with big stuff. You're the actual tactician."

"Huh. I didn't expect that." The elari technician's shock bled into the line.

Then the general surprised everyone on the channel by saying, *"Perhaps, Captain, but your approach may be the best option here."*

"How so?" the elar snapped.

Several members of the team were really having issues taking orders from a human, aether or otherwise. That struck Lei as odd, considering that humans were all over aether space, and at the time these troops had served, their president had been human. Lei just chalked it up to her being Kassian.

"We don't have the numbers to deal with this." Rothar pointed to the guards below them. *"Even if we did kill all the guards, which we could, we would have chaos among the miners. Right now, there's order."*

He turned toward Lei. *"Our primary objectives are the heart and the potential assassin."*

She nodded. *"All right. You have scouts that keep an eye out here. Where do the miners have an unusual amount of security and not allow the slaves to go?"*

At the far end of the train, a female waved her hand to catch Lei's attention. She was crodoc, too, but much slighter than the others.

"The rest of you take up defensive positions. Thorny, maintain the net."

"Yes, sir," replied a male standing along the wall near one of the aether detectors. The small device he was carrying was masking their presence without activating the sensor.

Leilani smiled at him and nodded reassuringly. She had been very relieved to find out that instead of any modern mage tech, the mining company was using a sensor that was more than eight hundred years old. It was effective but easily subverted.

Four of them moved off—Horrison, Lei, Slips, and the young scout they were following. Why the elar was named Slips, Lei had no idea, and she had opted not to ask.

They wove silently through and around guards posted in the catwalks until they reached an area much farther in. The small female crodoc—Corporal Gressa, according to the label in Lei's HUD—pointed to a door in the cave wall about twenty feet up. There was scaffolding leading up to it, and it was heavily guarded by armored security carrying weapons that were borderline illegal. But things such as whether or not a corporation had a license for military-grade hardware weren't really in Leilani's jurisdiction, even if they were creating an obstacle.

She pulled her binoculars from her bag, then glanced around for scanners before turning them on. The odd thing was that the only real sensors were at the entrance to the lower levels of the mine, which meant they could bypass most of them simply by using the air vents rather than taking the lift down. It was the same way they regularly came and went to free individual slaves.

She scanned the door carefully. It was some kind of hatch, like you would find in a ship. It sat at an odd angle, but then, nothing here was on any sort of even keel. The explosive nature of the accident had left everything with its own rotation relative to gravity. The door slipped open, and she triggered the recording.

A male crodoc paused in the argument he was having with someone inside. He stepped over the lower right corner of the door and out onto the scaffolding. Once the door had closed behind him, he slammed his hand into it angrily.

"Sir?" Slips's voice was cool and collected.

"I see him."

Slips raised her rifle. *"Orders?"*

"Leave him be."

"But sir!" she growled across the silcomms.

"I said leave him be. If you can't follow orders, I will relieve you. Permanently." Lei raised an eyebrow at the faint hint of anger that bled across the general's comms.

Being an outsider was often rough. There was always some data missing.

The rifle lowered. *"Yes, sir."*

"One of yours, I assume?" Lei gestured to the crodoc now walking down the last set of stairs.

"He was, yes."

"Did you lose him before or afterward?"

"He was removed from the unit and arrested during the fighting. When we started waking up and found out he was still alive, I issued a standing order to have him shot on sight."

"Is the why relevant?" Lei watched the crodoc through her binocs.

"Yes. He shot President Mai Lenali."

A long pause. There was a lot of conjecture in the history books about the president and the general, and Lei wasn't sure how much of it was romantics juicing up the story versus how much was true. She didn't want to ask, but the nature of their relationship might affect his decisions. For him, it hadn't been that long ago.

"How long have you been out of stasis?"

"Two years." Like usual, there was no emotion in his answer, and his body language revealed nothing. *"My team and the professor recovered me about a year ago."*

"You were kept by them for a year?"

He nodded.

"Doing what?"

"Being interrogated by them daily. They were looking for the heart." He was still utterly unreadable.

She admired his control. If he stuck around after this, he would make a great partner.

"How did they find out about the heart?" Lei asked.

Below, the male walked from the stairs to a small group of similarly dressed crodocs and began talking to them while keeping his back to the security guards.

Horrison nodded toward the crodoc. *"We're fairly sure Thoris told them."*

Lei clicked a button on her binoculars, and sound fed into her ears. "This isn't good, sir."

"I know."

"What do we do now?"

"I'm not sure. We can't let them continue torturing her. But if we die trying to get her out, then we still fail."

"It's been a week. I'm not sure she can hold out much longer."

The original crodoc lowered his face to the slightly shorter one and growled, "You think I don't know that?"

"They're too close, sir! We really need the general right now."

The larger one backfisted the smaller one, knocking him into the neighboring crodoc. He remained standing though and didn't reach up to touch his jaw where he was bleeding.

"He ran away like the coward he is. You mention him again, and I'll shoot you myself." The man turned toward the door he had come from and whispered something.

The group moved off into a separate area of the massive set of interlinking caverns.

Lei leaned back slightly and replayed the footage, blowing up his face to read his lips.

"I'm coming, Mai," he'd said.

Lei raised an eyebrow and looked toward the general.

She created a new private link with him. *"Okay, let's try this again. What happened while you were held by them?"*

He turned to look at her.

"Why?"

"Because I need to know the truth about what's going on before we can proceed."

His eyes narrowed—his first sign of emotion since they entered the belly of the mine. *"They interrogated me, looking for the heart."*

"I need more than that. How did you know Thoris was alive?"

He sighed. *"He came to see me several times. Fed me a bunch of crap, trying to get me to tell him where it was."*

"What crap did he feed you?"

Horrison frowned deeply. *"Why?"*

"Why are you fighting me on this? You were a special operator and a master tactician. You know good and well what's at stake here." Her eyes narrowed as she replayed the discussion below. *"Unless you're hiding something?"*

His glare faltered. She had hit the nail on the head.

"He told me I'd arrested the wrong person . . . and that she was here someplace, and he would find her."

"President Lenali." She wasn't asking.

He nodded.

"And you didn't believe him. Why?"

He looked away from her, allowing his gaze to fall over the people below.

"Please tell me this isn't something basic, like you were both in love with her."

He didn't reply, and Leilani resisted the urge to punch him.

"Oh, good grief. Are you fucking kidding me?" She lifted her hand to smack him but then thought better of it. He likely wouldn't react, but the other two might.

"Look down there!" She allowed her anger to wash through the comm. *"See that child dragging the dead body of another child someone*

just killed in front of her?" She took a deep breath and tried to get her anger back under control. *"How does that stand up to an argument over a fucking woman? I don't care who the woman is!"*

"Was." His voice sounded almost broken. Likely this wasn't the first time he had considered this particular argument.

"Is."

His gaze snapped around to her, his eyes guarded.

"Apparently they found her and are torturing her right now."

He bolted to his feet, but Lei grabbed his arm and yanked him back into a crouch. If his face was any indication, her strength had surprised him. This time, she did slap him on the back of his head. *"Head first, heart later, you idiot."*

He turned and glared at her. Behind him, two soldiers were pointing weapons at her.

"You knew he was innocent when you had him arrested, didn't you?" she growled.

His gaze didn't falter, but he didn't answer, either.

Lei knew better than to poke a crodoc, especially a male. They had nasty tempers. But so did she.

"Look, this is bigger than you or your petty problems. To him, you're a coward. To you, he's traitor. To me, both of you are assets. You don't like that, you're free to walk away from this agreement, but may I remind you that you agreed in front of our emperor to follow my orders."

"Your emperor," he retorted.

"Fine. You're dismissed."

"If I go, my people go with me."

"Works for me."

General Horrison stood and walked past her back the way they had come. The elar stood and followed, glaring at Lei as she passed. The small female scout, however, hesitated.

"General?" The unit comms triggered as the young scout spoke.

"Agent Falconi has decided to go this alone. RTB," he ordered, telling them to return to base.

The scout slid up next to her and tilted her head down toward the mine floor below. *"Is this because of Major Thoris?"*

Lei nodded, and the crodoc scout rolled her eyes. She pointed to the cavern into which Thoris's group had disappeared. *"That heads toward what the corps call the barracks. I know a way there that's fairly safe."*

The group silcomm interrupted them. *"Gressa, RTB."*

"If you want to retreat and pretend like this isn't going on, sir, more power to you. But the reality is that our army is gone. All that's left of our entire government is just a ragtag group of tired soldiers and the secretary to a senator who has been dead for more than eight hundred years. The people down there need us, and the local government has asked for our assistance. I for one am not going to walk away. Not this time."

The woman next to Leilani may have looked young, but clearly she was not. That was the number-one problem with aethers—there was never an easy way to tell one's age. Even in kuldain space, the period that humans considered middle age lasted around a hundred years, so apparent age could be variable among humans as well—but with some aether species, that period could last multiple hundreds of years.

Silence crackled over the silcomm.

"What do you need from us, Agent?"

Three more crodocs were heading Lei's direction.

In the distance, the general slid into one of the air vents. The counter that marked how many individual oracles were attached to the link began to count down in her HUD. When it eventually stopped, five people remained on the circuit.

21

THE TRAVELERS

It took them almost two hours to reach what they called the barracks. Like the refugee camp, the massive cavern was filled with tents, ramshackle huts, and hanging dwellings. Some areas had been highly decorated using paint, bits of metal, stones, and other shiny bits of garbage.

It took another hour to wind their way to the cavern's far back wall. As they approached the area, several greduna stepped in their way. Each was easily twelve feet tall, and they all towered over the group menacingly.

"Who's the new one?" one of the younger males asked.

"Someone who needs to see the Hodair."

"We decide who sees the old woman," a rather melodic male voice spoke up from a nearby table. "You don't."

Such a voice was a sound rarely heard in aether space anymore, and it drew Leilani's attention. Sitting at the table were three individuals playing cards. They each wore cloaks of different colors with their hoods drawn up over their features. But the hoods didn't hide their unusually sparkling eyes. One had blue, one gold, and the other a beautiful shade of lavender. Each had fine features and a very angular bone structure. The result was a natural beauty that every runway model in the Kassian Empire would have killed for.

"Your kind don't usually survive collection." The one with lavender eyes was staring intently at Leilani, like he was looking right through her. Her disguise would never work against an igranu.

"She needs to talk to her," Gressa demanded again, holding her ground.

"I think she might after all." The one with gold eyes had a slightly more feminine lilt to her voice, though Lei wondered if it was an actual female. With igranu, sex was impossible to verify from appearances alone due to their ethereal beauty. She'd never seen a female, but then, no one had in more than eight hundred years.

"You sure?" The large greduna next to them sounded disappointed.

"Let them in," the blue-eyed one ordered as he played a card.

"Damn it." The lavender-eyed one threw his cards to the table and glared at the other. "You're cheating."

"We're all cheating. What's your point?" The golden-eyed one laughed. It was a musical sound, like wind chimes on a soft breeze.

Ignoring them, Gressa squeezed past the two giants into a small courtyard that actually had plants growing in it. How, Lei had no idea. Magic, most likely.

They stepped through a hatch that appeared to be embedded in the hull of a ship. This hatch, however, had been built for people who were at least ten feet tall. There were no guards outside of it. Inside, however, was a different story.

Two ten-foot-tall entities stood inside, barring their path. These entities were completely sealed within armor, making them appear more robotic than alive. Even the large wings folded perfectly behind them were encased in the same strange metal. Armored suits like this could fly, Lei knew, even in space. Their weapons were of a make Leilani had never seen, but they appeared highly lethal. These people were here because they chose to be. The local corporate guards had nothing that could stop this hardware.

"*Leth.*" Lei wasn't familiar with the language the guard spoke in, but the intonation was clear enough.

The group stopped.

"*Hann fa alath ierilam.*"

"Yes." Gressa nodded. "Please switch to crodoc. She understands that."

"Understood." The guard to the left spoke flawless crodoc. "You are armed. Why are you seeking entry?"

Leilani pointed to the crodoc next to her. Gressa answered for her. "She needs to see my father and the Hodair."

"We don't allow locals to see the Hodair."

At Leilani's twitch, the other guard raised its weapon in warning.

"I understand, but she isn't what you think. She represents the government."

The one who had been speaking looked to the other one.

"Threat level minimal," the other answered in a softer voice. "She may proceed. But know this, outsider. We do not give warnings."

Leilani raised an eyebrow and decided not to mention that she had just gotten one.

Gressa walked between the two guards and beckoned for her to follow. The rest of the team waited outside.

Gressa and Leilani wove their way through the ship. The p-ways contained a few scattered guards but no one else. The bulkheads and deck were made of a smooth metal that didn't show seams or markings of any kind. Nor did it seem to have any battle damage. Once again, Leilani wondered why the ship was here—besides the fact that it was trapped deep inside the asteroid. Gressa said nothing as they made their way through the passages.

After one particular turn, Leilani recognized a bulkhead manned by a familiar guard. They had passed the same guard before. Gressa was walking her in circles, making the ship seem larger than it was . . .

or just trying to confuse her. Either way, it had worked. Lei had no idea how to get out.

"You have anything, Sarah?" Leilani asked as they stopped in front of an unmarked hatch. No answer. *"Sarah?"*

The hatch opened, but a crodoc barred their entry. "Meela?"

"Hey, Jost. We need to see them."

"Your dad won't be happy about this."

"I'm aware."

The crodoc stepped aside. On his cheek was a bloody mark showing where he had recently been backfisted.

Lei stepped into an unusually spacious room containing several padded, backless chairs. Across the room stood a well-built crodoc and a tall, thin creature with white wings, long, golden hair, and golden eyes set into the most beautiful face Leilani had ever seen. The dress and slightly pronounced chest suggested that the being was female.

The crodoc hadn't noticed them yet, but the igranu had, and she was watching them carefully. Nearby, two of the armored guards turned toward her. They, too, were igranu. Military? Did the igranu even have a military?

The crodoc major noticed the igranu's inattentiveness and turned. He frowned. "Meela, what are you doing here? And who is this?"

The female igranu answered. "This, Major, is Special Agent Leilani Falconi, a captain of the IIS special aether division. And she is the one I've been waiting for." She sighed deeply. Leilani felt it pull at her. "And she came alone? This is disappointing."

"Wait. Did you say IIS?" The major reached for the weapon at his side. The three other crodocs in the room followed suit, and Leilani found herself at gunpoint once again.

"Coming online, ma'am," Sarah chimed in her ear.

"What happened?"

"Enemy detection online." In her HUD, the four crodocs lit up orange. The three igranu, however, were green.

"Now, Major Thoris, Agent Falconi is here as my guest. Please do not shoot my guest."

The crodoc looked to the igranu with surprise.

"But the IIS is working with *them*. I saw the agent and the foreman together myself."

"Would that be Agent Caris?" Leilani remained unconcerned despite the weapons still pointed at her.

"Possibly. He and I didn't talk."

"Agent Caris is currently wanted for treason against the empire. When I come across him, he will be arrested and tried for his crimes."

The crodoc shook his head. "No, he won't. They killed him and recycled his body three weeks ago."

Sighing, Lei shook her head. "Okay. Well, one problem down. Only thirty-nine thousand to go."

Her sarcasm was not really intended to be funny, but nonetheless, the tall igranu laughed—a beautiful sound, but one that made Leilani's skin crawl. There was danger in that sound. She resisted the urge to reach for her weapons.

"How oddly appropriate." The creature nodded to her, then made a shooing gesture at everybody else. "You are all dismissed. I wish to talk to the agent alone."

The crodocs started to argue, but then one of the armored guards turned its head toward them. The movement was enough to convince them not to protest.

"You'll be okay," Gressa whispered to Lei. "I think."

"Don't take a job on a suicide hotline," Leilani advised. "Don't worry. I'll be fine. You'd be surprised what I deal with on a daily basis."

22

MEETINGS IN TIME

The igranu smiled and beckoned for Leilani to approach. "I have seen your face since the day you were born."

"You're an oracle, then."

"Something like that. You don't have a true word for what I am." She shrugged. "By most, I am referred to as the Hodair."

"Igranu are rare nowadays." Lei traced the outline of the woman's wings with her gaze.

"I suppose from your perspective, that is true."

"What do you mean?"

"My people are travelers. When the war began, we left. We are not keen to destroy others simply on the basis of intolerance."

"Then why were you here?"

"I was the arbitrator trying to negotiate peace between the two factions."

"You failed." Leilani couldn't hide her disdain.

"Did I?" The woman smiled that calculating smile again, and a shiver went down Leilani's spine. She waved her arm in a small arc.

"Both the aether and the kuldain, as you call them, are at peace. The fabric is wrinkled but whole."

There had been many theories about the bomb that had torn the fabric of the universe and almost severed the eldrilin running through the solar system. Most attributed it to the now-extinct aether military, assuming that the bomb was a powerful but utterly lost technology of destruction. But there were a few historians who postulated an outside source. For the first time in her career, Lei couldn't help but put her weight toward the second option.

"But you trapped yourself here."

The woman shook her head and looked toward a hatch on the side of the room. Another igranu with lighter wings was bringing in a tray of food and drinks. They set it on a nearby table and left the room.

"I am no more trapped here than you are." She pointed to the food on the tall table.

Leilani frowned. How could they not be trapped? Their ship was buried in the middle of the asteroid. "I don't understand."

The creature smiled. This time, it didn't trigger her sense of danger.

"That is a good place to be. Confused and seeking information." She nodded. "My ship remains here, as do I, because I am the one keeping the people alive." She gestured to the bulkhead, and it lit up.

Lei saw a large room filled with people all huddled together. None of them were moving. Close to wherever they were viewing the room from, one human-looking girl had spilled her drink, but the pouring liquid was frozen in midair.

Leilani's face paled. "You're holding them in stasis."

The woman nodded. "Yes. It is disappointing what the kuldain corporation is doing to them, but so long as there is one left in stasis, I will remain. This is but a small collection of the two worlds. I believe the proper term is 'city'?"

Leilani looked from the screen to the igranu.

"You mean both worlds are here?" As she considered the size of the asteroid belt, it suddenly made sense to her. The belt contained far too much mass to have come from just one planet, no matter how big the planet had been.

"Yes."

"And you're holding all of it in stasis?"

The woman seemed pleased that Leilani was finally grasping what she was saying.

Lei realized the reason some of the igranu's facial expressions were so overwhelming was because she was feeling the woman's emotions. She wondered whether that was an igranu thing or a creepy Hodair thing. She wasn't sure she really wanted to know the answer.

"All right." Taking a deep breath, she closed her mind to protect herself from the projected emotions. "Then I apologize for my remarks, ma'am."

"Aethianu," the woman replied.

"Excuse me?"

"My name is Aethianu. My friends call me Ae. You may do so as well."

"Thank you, Ms. Aethianu. You already know my name. Can we move on to why I'm here?"

"Of course." Ae lifted something that looked like a piece of fruit and began chewing on it. "Please eat. It is all mae'lacan safe."

Leilani furrowed her brow. "What is a mae'lacan?"

The woman paused midchew. Leilani had finally taken her by surprise. "How do you . . . ? What?" The woman blinked at her several times.

"Yo, yo, li'l sis. How ya doin'?" BB's voice popped into her head.

"BB?"

"Who else?" He sounded smug. *"So, I'm patched into the mine. And you've got a problem."*

"How?"

"A story for another day. Hey, did you know that you people have some pretty spectacular toys? And I mean, like, wow! Did you know that there's a—"

171

"BB!"

"Oh, yeah. There's some sort of alarm going off. And security is racing deeper into the mine in some serious numbers . . . with some pretty heavy artillery. I'm trying to get into the lower network, but it'll take a bit to get my drone down there."

"Roger." She took a step back from the table.

"No—BB."

"What?"

"My name is BB. Did you get hit on the head?"

She rolled her eyes. "I apologize, ma'am, but I need to get moving. Was there anything specific you wanted to tell me?"

The igranu blinked several times, as though clearing her head. "Not really, no." She suddenly looked up into the empty air and frowned. "They found the heart."

Leilani frowned as well. That was not news she wanted to hear. "Excuse me?"

The creature smiled sadly and nodded. "They found it. It's time for you to go and do what you came here to do."

"You're the first oracle I've ever met who didn't spout some nonsense about destiny."

"I am not an oracle. Destiny is only for the superstitious. The future is always fluid. It does not become fact until it is the present." The woman walked her to the hatch. "Agent, I would like to talk more, but for now, I leave you to your job. I wish you luck in your future."

The hatch slid open. The small crodoc was waiting outside.

"Hodair?" She nodded respectfully to the igranu, awaiting her orders.

"Meela, the heart has been found in cavern nine. Would you please take the agent there?"

Meela's eyes widened in shock.

"I'd rather the falair didn't self-destruct again. That might be difficult to stop a second time."

"Yes, ma'am."

"Is falair a name?" Leilani couldn't help but wonder if the heart was a who rather than a what.

"It means *heart* in igranu." Meela took off through the ship at a run.

Leilani raced to catch up.

Outside, they found more than fifty crodocs standing behind Major Thoris. The soldiers snapped to attention and saluted Leilani when she emerged from the ship. At least these ones weren't in makeshift gear like the refugees.

They almost looked as if they'd been equipped by the mining company, but who would be dumb enough to give their slaves weapons and armor?

"Agent, we are ready to move."

She smiled and shook her head in amazement. These people sure were resourceful.

"They found the falair," Meela spat out.

The major nodded. "Yes, but thankfully, they don't know what's happening except that they've found something hostile." He bobbed his head to Leilani. "We have the element of surprise, but not for long. The moment we start shooting, they'll know we've switched sides. For now, they'll let us move through the area without trouble. Stand in the middle of the unit so they don't notice you."

Leilani nodded, understanding that Thoris had stayed and agreed to work with the miners in order to keep an eye on them.

The unit jogged through the station as quickly as possible. Lei, however, had no idea where they were. She heard the gunfire long before she could see anything.

"Network online. Protocol Falair active. Loading." The voice in her head was male, but there had been no communication link established.

Sarah's voice reappeared. *"Restoring identity."*

All around her, the crodocs seemed to be hearing the same thing. They seemed less surprised than she was, though.

"Ma'am, I am required to inform you that I seem to have been subverted."

"How?"

"I'm not sure. It seems to be a subroutine that was hidden deep within my original design." There was a short pause. *"However, my main mission parameters do not appear to have been tampered with."*

"What's going on?" Lei asked as the soldiers around her started spreading out.

None of them were firing their weapons yet, but she could still hear gunfire and several resounding explosions coming from deeper in the cavern.

"The heart is online, so the aethernet is coming back up," Meela explained without really paying much attention to her. Instead, she was focused on trying to make her way around the unit so she could see. "Look up there." She pointed to a scaffold the two could climb to get a better view of what was going on inside the cavern.

Leilani followed her upward.

"There is some kind of network coming online in there," BB said. *"I'm having trouble linking to it. Give me a few."*

"Roger."

The cavern was smaller than most of the others. It looked like a newer dig site. Boring machines and sensor units were still parked around the area. The rock had been cleared in front of her, but it seemed to also have been cleared to the right. There was no telling how deep the cleared area went.

A bright light flashed into existence to her right, and a ball of fire easily thirty feet high came hurtling toward a group of corporate guards who were taking cover behind a nearby mining vehicle. They tried to run, but they didn't get very far before the fireball made contact with the vehicle and exploded.

Bodies and machine parts flew in every direction. Contact with the soldiers caused several secondary explosions, which told Lei that the ball of flames was far too hot to be merely fire; more likely, it was plasma. What had they done, found a sleeping dragon? Her eyes widened as she considered it. Nah—it would have to have been an infant to fit in this cavern.

"We need a better vantage point," she yelled over the gunfire to Meela.

Below them, a human security guard ran up to the major and pointed toward the source of the balls of plasma. The crodoc laughed in response. When the guard pointed a pistol at him, Major Thoris reached out, snatched the security guard by the neck, and snapped his spine easily. He tossed the man to the side and started giving practiced hand signals. The unit spread out and began to fire on the mining company's security forces.

Now it was a three-way firefight. The security forces seemed almost relieved to have something else to shoot at, and within seconds, they were all firing on the crodocs. No one really seemed to be firing in the direction of the rolling fireballs anymore.

Leilani sighed. *And the war begins anew.* Dorthy was going to toss her ass in the brig for this.

A familiar flash of light burst overhead as an IIS weapon fired past her and slammed into a security guard who had been turning toward her and Meela. They both looked up.

A railing-lined catwalk ran along the upper edge of most of the mining caverns. It allowed maintenance access to the air ducts and ventilation system. Now, there were more than a hundred soldiers up there in IIS coats. The closest one smiled down at her and waved.

"You didn't honestly think I was going to abandon you down there, did you?" General Horrison allowed a tiny bit of pleasure to slip through the silcomms.

"I wasn't sure what to expect."

"Helr and I weren't going to get along. He would have just shot you rather than listen. I needed to make sure I wasn't part of the equation. Besides, I brought backup."

"I see that. Don't shoot the major's men. They're marked as security."

He shook his head. *"No, they aren't."* Something seemed to dawn on him, and he held up a finger. *"That's right. You aren't cleared for the network."*

"Agent." Sarah's voice. *"I'm getting a request to join a local military network signal?"*

"Accept it, and have them extend it to BB as well."

"Understood."

Suddenly, the resolution on her HUD sharpened to amazing clarity, and the combatants below became clearly marked as green or red. She also saw several command channels off to the side. Each crodoc unit had its own; the security forces had one, the overall aether forces another. She joined the last one and heard Major Thoris acknowledging Horrison.

"Go ahead, General."

"I need you to push left to clear that flank. We'll cover you from above."

"Roger."

"Agent Falconi."

"Yes, General?"

"I want you and your team to slide in behind Thoris to the right and move inside the protective barrier. Your oracle will get you in. I need a recon."

23

THE HEART

The gunfight continued as Meela and Leilani slid between the crodocs and the wall of the cavern. Once Leilani had rounded the corner, she came to a stop, causing Meela to bump into her from behind.

Ahead of her was a massive, semitranslucent barrier unlike anything she had ever seen. It took up a whole quarter of the cavern and vanished into the rock. In shape, it looked like a sphere or a dome, but it wasn't hampered by the rock or the buildings around it. Inside, she could see people, both aether and kuldain, frozen in battle.

In the center was a crystal so massive that from where Leilani stood in the hollowed-out cavern, she couldn't even see the top of it. It was more than two hundred meters in height and at least a hundred meters wide, situated perfectly in the center of a vast room lined with magsteel and crystal.

The mining machines had bored a hole into the room. Around the edges of the translucent barrier were bodies wearing the gear of the local miners. The majority of them looked like they had been sliced apart from hip to shoulder. A couple security guards had also been cleaved in half.

Behind her, Meela pushed. When Leilani didn't budge, the crodoc strode around her.

The second she stepped through the barrier, it shimmered slightly, and the sole person moving within turned to glance in their direction. From his place at some kind of control console, he nodded to Meela, then went back to what he was doing. Reaching over to the far edge of the panel, he tapped the display several times, and a massive plasma ball leapt from a smaller crystal fastened to the wall of the chamber. It rolled through the barrier and out into the security forces, creating another loud explosion.

Meela waved for Lei to follow.

It took a moment for her legs to agree to respond. Small bits of rock sprayed down on her as something impacted the wall above her head. That was all the incentive she needed. Running through the barrier was like pushing her way through an enormous soap bubble. Inside, it was strangely quiet. The massive crystal resonated with power, emitting a soft hum.

The lone male was about a hundred feet away. Meela started making her way carefully in his direction, glancing over her shoulder at Leilani as she went.

"Make sure you don't touch anyone in stasis." She nodded toward the woman next to her. She wore a uniform and was frozen in midair, having been knocked back by some kind of explosion, if the burns on her armor were any indication. "Last thing any of these people remember is fighting, so they'll wake up fighting."

Leilani nodded.

As they made their way toward the man, several more plasma balls launched outward.

"Afternoon." The gentleman at the console spoke in accented Kassian, but at least he spoke it. "I believe you are called Agent?"

Meela looked confused. Lei wondered if she spoke the language.

"Yes. And you are?"

The male laughed. He was about six and a half feet tall with long hair, which meant he likely wasn't military. He was handsome and well built. Now that she was close, she could see the large, faintly glowing sword leaning against the control panel. It was covered in blood. That explained the severed bodies.

"I am known by many names, but you may call me Fendrick."

"Well met, Fendrick."

"That remains to be seen." He smiled kindly at her, though it didn't quite reach his eyes. He touched the fire button again, and with a roar, another plasma ball leapt from a nearby crystal.

"May I ask what you and your government are doing here?"

She frowned. That question was a trap. "That's a long and complicated story."

"Not really. I went into stasis while at war. I woke up eight hundred years later with a knife at my throat." He tapped something on the console and turned toward her. "There is a young man at my firewall losing his mind trying to reach you. Do you wish to speak to him? He seems very unbalanced but determined."

She smiled and nodded. "He can be annoyingly persistent."

"Leilei, are you okay?" The strange male was right. BB was pretty frantic.

"I'm fine."

"I lost you. I freaked out. You have to get out of there. They're bringing in the big guns and have requested military assistance. The navy is inbound."

"BB, calm down. Patch me through to Dorthy."

"Sec. Go ahead."

Hmm—Dorthy must've been close. That explained all the extra IIS units.

"Leilani?"

"Yes, sir. I need you to section-nine override the naval assistance inbound."

"We're already in contact with the navy. We're letting them come but planning to use them to police the system."

"Roger that."

"Is the situation under control?"

"Working on it."

"Understood. Proceed on mission. Dorthy out."

"I'm not entirely sure what happened there, but I assume you are?" BB asked.

"Yes. BB, I need something."

"Yeah?"

"There's a package I need you to find." She sent the name and picture she had of Mai Lenali, president of the Seef'aini government, who once controlled slightly less of aether space than Kass did of kuldain space.

"What am I, a mailman? Oh, wait, you mean a person. Hey, that's cool. So she's like an elected emperor. I'll find her."

Leilani sighed and shook her head. Fendrick, who was still patiently waiting in front of her, chuckled.

"Yes. I need you to find her and direct Major Thoris to her location and status. She's our proof. She needs to be recovered."

"Roger that. BB out."

She smirked. He was learning.

"I'm sorry about that."

The man smiled and nodded. "Young people are often difficult to potty train." He seemed amused at his own joke.

"You were saying?"

He smirked but nodded. "Yes. I think I have the situation correct. The planets exploded, which means my self-destruct worked. But since we are in stasis, it appears that some dumbass, white-winged, platinum-haired bitch decided to interfere." He shook his head. "We are no longer in aether space, which affects me and my gear more than it affects you." He waved a hand to indicate the firefight outside the protective barrier.

"Then, a couple hundred years later, someone decided to mine the—what I can only assume is an asteroid belt? And found this." He gestured to a nearby human who was still in stasis. The Seef'aini soldier had frozen in midair, his brains preceding his body by a good foot.

Leilani nodded. "So far correct."

"So my question remains the same: Why is your government here?"

The question was still a trap, but she couldn't ignore it either. "What the miners are doing is highly illegal. We're here to stop it, arrest those in charge, and straighten things out."

Fendrick narrowed his eyes at her response. "And who decides how things are *straightened out?*"

She took a deep breath. He had to be ex-military or a politician.

"That isn't my decision. My superiors will decide that."

"And if your superiors decide that this"—he waved his arm in a wide arc encompassing the bodies still in stasis around them—"should all just be destroyed to prevent this from happening again?"

She didn't answer.

He sighed and shook his head slowly. "As I suspected. Politics do not change, no matter what the year is."

"General?" Lei sent her message directly to General Horrison.

"Report."

"I have one conscious and at least seventy in stasis. Waking these up could be an issue, though. There was clearly an active battle going on in here."

The ground shook, and Leilani looked around. From the inside, the barrier was clear as glass—glass that was currently on fire. As the flames began to dissipate, she could see a large over-the-shoulder ordinance launcher being reloaded.

"Roger that. Identity of the conscious?"

"He says his name is Fendrick."

"Roger. Fendrick is now a package of interest. Maintain eyes on package while we find the other one."

The strange human chuckled.

"Please tell me your military has better equipment, because that was pitiful."

"Roger," Lei told Horrison, keeping her face blank. "My military wouldn't even come in here."

He nodded his understanding. "Orbital bombardment. Good."

Turning back to the console, he began to ignore Meela and Leilani.

"Do you know this guy?" Lei asked.

The crodoc shook her head. "I only know *of* him."

"Is he a politician?"

"I don't believe so, though he does deal with politicians regularly."

"Military?"

Meela shrugged.

"Then who the hell is he?"

"The heart."

Leilani frowned.

"I thought *that* was the heart." She gestured to the massive crystal.

Meela shook her head.

Leilani took a deep breath and let it out slowly. "I'm thinking he doesn't really need protection."

"I don't," he said loudly. "And you, Agent Leilani, may stay. You, Corporal, go tell your father that I found his wife. I will use this fascinating human named BB to help me confuse these corporate guards while he goes and gets her."

"Wh . . . what?" Meela stuttered. "His wife?"

Fendrick frowned at her. "Yes, why?" Then he looked annoyed. "Oh, good grief, child. It's been eight hundred years. I'm pretty sure secrets like your parents' love affair are pointless. Go rescue your mother. Her vitals are weakening at an alarming rate. I like her. I don't want her dying because you can't get your shit together."

"BB?"

"The major's already en route. I'm working with something that calls itself God to convince the security in the area to defend the far hatch. It will buy him time to get inside. But I'm not liking her vitals. The corps know they're losing the mine, and they are freaking. They've already started gassing sections while they evacuate personnel they consider important. I have the ventilation blocked for now, but it won't hold. People will start suffocating eventually." There was a short pause. *"Others, they're just shooting outright. I think that's what happened to her. They're aware that she's some sort of political figure. Her weakening vitals match those of someone who's been shot."*

"Do you have any speakers or mics that can play into the room?"

"Sure. Sec. Go ahead. You're live. I'll be back. I need to focus."

"Roger." Leilani switched from silcomms to regular kuldain comms. "Hello. Madam President, can you hear me?"

"Yes?" The voice was weak.

"Good. My name is Agent Leilani Falconi. We have units inbound to your location. We need you to hold on till we can get you out of there."

"My people?" Her voice was still weak, but it sounded stronger.

"Your people are as safe as we can make them for the moment. They need you to hold on. Major Thoris is en route to you. ETA four minutes." Leilani made a guess on the time; in reality, she had no idea, but the woman needed hope.

"Helr is alive?" The voice was much stronger now. Leilani wondered what had happened.

"Yes, ma'am."

"Who are you, again?" The voice now sounded normal, strong, and near the mic.

"I vouch for her, Mai." The man standing next to Lei nodded to her as he spoke over the link. "For now, at least, she and her government are helping."

"Ah, crap, *you're* alive?"

Fendrick laughed out loud, but that didn't come across the comm.

"Yep. Sorry, you old biddy. I'm not that easy to get rid of."

"Fine. Then open this damn door. I have some people I want to talk to." *Talk to* came out as more of a growl than real words.

Lei couldn't help but smirk. That was how she often dealt with people who shot her: a severe talking to—often one that left the other person bleeding from the ears, eyes, and nose.

"You will wait until Helr is in the area. You are unarmed, and . . ." His voice trailed off as the comm cut, and he shook his head. "Well, so much for waiting."

"What happened?" Lei looked around in confusion.

He waved his hand over the console, and a holo appeared above it.

A woman in tattered clothes was standing atop the broken-down door to her cell. Several security guards turned and raised weapons toward her, but her hands erupted in fire, which she threw at them with impressive force. It exploded on contact, taking out three of them at once.

Shaking his head again, Fendrick tossed the image aside. "An angry archmage is a dangerous thing. Hopefully, she'll stop at the security forces."

"Archmage?" That was a new bit of information for the history books. It also explained how she'd healed so fast after being gravely wounded.

He smirked. "It always amazes me how rarely secrets make it into the history books. Don't get me wrong; occasionally, a really big one gets figured out later on after everyone is dead, but it's rarely the whole truth."

He stated it so matter of factly that Lei suddenly realized the truth. "You're not human."

"Neither are you. What's your point?"

She furrowed her brow.

"I *am* human."

He laughed. Then, when he realized she was getting angry, he stopped and raised a hand. "I'm sorry, you didn't know?" Now it was his turn to be confused. "How can you not know? Don't you people have DNA scans?" He studied her intently.

"Agent, you have been scanned. Protocol One enabled," Sarah chimed softly.

He smiled as if he understood, then frowned and turned back to his console. His hands flew across the buttons.

"President Lenali has been recovered. She is alive and well. Your orders, General?" Thoris called across all comms.

"We will use the NCC as the base of operations for now. RTB with the package. And then come to me. We have a problem up here."

"Roger."

"General Horrison?" The man next to her spoke over the military silcomm in a channel she didn't recall joining. It seemed to include her, Horrison, someone named God, and the president.

She glanced over at the man next to her and grimaced. *God? Really?* She shook her head.

"I'm busy right now, Fen."

"I understand that, sir, but you have forty-nine agents of the IIS with you."

"Your point?"

"Their oracles have been subverted by an unknown entity. My base overlay has been altered."

"It's been eight hundred years, Fen." The female voice sounded tired. *"Things change."*

"Agreed, but these are my units. Each one clearly has my maker's mark. They should have been resistant to alteration. But these people found a way to overlay their own poorly designed spells. That means they are reusing oracles, by the way, which is a disgusting thought. Some of this overlay is specifically designed to lie to those agents."

"It wouldn't be the first time that a government lied to its personnel." The woman's humor came across the line.

"Are you saying that Sarah is lying to me about something?" Lei asked, knowing good and well that Sarah could hear everything she thought.

"Several things, Agent. But if I'm reading this horribly written overlay correctly, every single one of those agents has a kill switch."

"You couldn't start with that?" the general practically shouted across the comm. A faint feeling of pain came through with his voice.

Lei's hands closed into fists. She was rapidly beginning to dislike this person she was supposed to be guarding.

"I apologize, General." Fendrick didn't look at her as he spoke. *"Some of us are still trying to process the new information. I would like to reboot their oracles."*

"In the middle of a fight?" Lei and Horrison said in unison.

"It will be brief. Their command unit is in range. And I am not entirely sure that it isn't capable of making the agents do things against their will."

"The command unit isn't going to kill us in the middle of a fight. I happen to know for a fact that Dorthy has orders to take at least one person here to our emperor. He won't disobey a direct order," Lei growled.

The man next to her twitched slightly. He clearly didn't like her answer.

"Then I can't allow any of the agents near the president until I'm able to ensure that they are under their own power." Fendrick seemed a tad smug.

"Agreed," Horrison added.

As he did, a group of crodocs wearing corporate security garb walked through the barrier, their weapons drawn and pointed directly at her.

"Shit!" she mumbled to herself. "Are you kidding me?" Lei raised her hands. "Fine. I don't want to be down here with you nutjobs anyway."

A strange screeching noise sliced through the air. She spun to find Fendrick holding his blade pointed at her.

"No sudden moves, Agent. Just leave calmly."

"Gladly." She turned her back on him and his weapon and walked back through the barrier.

As she stepped out, she resisted the urge to tap several of the Kassian marines near the barrier's edge. It would just get the marines killed for no reason. She also contemplated sending Dorthy a direct message, but she wasn't sure it would be secure. Fendrick seemed to have a pretty tight grip on everything the oracles did.

24

NEW PLAN

As Leilani walked to the lift, a different comm unit chimed inside her bag. Pulling out the archaic device, she smirked, then stuffed the earpiece into her ear canal and tapped the answer button.

"Please tell me you have good news, BB?"

"Not really, no. He has complete control over anything and everything the oracles touch. When he decided we were a threat, he kicked me out of the network as well. Luckily, though, they hadn't had time to put an oracle in me. Near as I can tell, that massive crystal with him is an oracle. It's in low-power mode, though. It's designed to be fed by something called eldrich energy, and it's not getting enough, so it's sort of in trickle mode—able to do only basic wireless stuff, with a slightly wider range than our near-range network protocols."

"Is the ship in range?"

"No. When he tossed me off the network, I cut the relays. He has only what he got before I cut."

"Did you tell Dorthy?"

"Yeah, he's just coming in now." There was a muffled noise as the archaic phone changed hands.

"Leilani?"

"Yes, sir."

"Sitrep?"

"We currently have the heart secured and the president secured, and the mine is being contested. The corps are trying to kill everyone inside, so BB shut off the ventilation." She heard BB talking in the background.

"Looks like he was able to save only the people in the very center. I understand there's some kind of city down there?"

"Yes, sir."

"How long do you think the air will hold out?"

"Twenty-four hours, maybe less."

"Assessment?"

Leilani's HUD displayed an alarm from Sarah about the air quality. She pulled out her vac suit and flipped it on. The light went green again as the suit surrounded her and snugged up.

"They seem fairly well adjusted, sir. I can't, in good conscience, recommend cleansing. There are kids and full-blown families in there. They aren't even hostile. Besides, we have a few more complications that I can't explain on this circuit."

"Complications?"

"At least one class one and one class two."

"One of these days, I'm going to find that magnet of yours and have it surgically removed."

"Magnet, sir?"

"Yeah—that thing that attracts more shit to you than to any ten of my other agents."

Leilani chuckled. He was right. Stuff just seemed to happen around her. Most agents went their whole careers never seeing even one class-one complication. She had run into at least two in the last two weeks. She'd never really know what category the librarian fell into.

"All right, the navy is still a day out. I've lost comms with my agents, though BB here told me what happened. You are to stay low. Gorth is there, and he can handle the command. He was integrating well with the general. I need you back on mission. We saw four vessels leave as we were coming in. We need to know who is on them and where they're going. Leave the aether crap to Gorth. I'll give you back to BB. Just get me that damn info. We're having complications on our end, too, and I need to know."

"Understood, sir." Leilani took the lift to the level indicated by her HUD and came out into a rather spectacular firefight. She rolled out of the way and activated her stealth system as the lift filled with bullets.

One of them hit her shoulder, spinning her violently and slamming her into a wall. Thankfully, the suit held.

"Fuck!" She attempted to move her shoulder.

It still responded, so it wasn't shattered, at least, though it was sluggish. In her HUD, a display flashed 98 percent, alerting her to the damage. She stayed low and moved toward the green markers. Several times, the ground exploded around her. They might not have been able to see her clearly, but they sure knew she was there.

"Go left," BB said in her ear.

She did as she was told, and the wall where she was headed exploded.

"Up if you can," he added, clearly directing her someplace specific.

She glanced upward, kicked in her jets, and used the low gravity to leap through the air toward a sensor unit. Several explosions went off around her as the security forces tried to stop her from reaching it, but they couldn't lock on to her. Without computer guidance, they all seemed to be rather bad shots. She was fortunate they were civilian forces and not military. The military trained for equipment failure.

She grabbed hold of the sensor with her good arm as she flew past it. Ignoring the pain, she used her other arm to slap a flat circular device on it, then pushed off as hard as she could.

"Clear below!" she broadcast across the main silcomm.

Several IIS and crodoc military looked up, then started running as quickly as possible while maintaining cover. She had made it almost to a nearby platform when the explosion went off. The shockwave knocked her into the platform, and she felt a rib crack on impact.

"Damage level at 90 percent. Shall I enact repair protocols?" Sarah chimed in, exactly as she always had. Now, however, Lei didn't trust her.

"I'm okay, Sarah."

"Agent, I recommend that you remain at peak condition considering the threat level."

"Recommendation noted."

The oracle fell silent.

"Hey, Lei, look at . . . Ah, shit, I can't send it to your HUD. Wait! Your pad. Use your pad."

"Can he not see digital?"

BB chuckled. "Not since I took my converter off-line."

She pulled up her pad and tapped it open. On it, she could see several camera screens slowly rotating through the miners' quarters. Entire families lay dead wherever they had fallen. The corporation had killed everyone else; the security forces were all that was left. She looked down over the edge to the firefight below. They were doing their best to keep the IIS pinned down.

"Has the IIS announced themselves?" she asked.

"Yes, several times."

The realization punched her in the gut. "They're going to blow the place."

"Yeah, that was my thought too. I've been looking."

Leilani pulled out her binoculars. They wouldn't put the explosive where a camera could see it. They needed to crack the place open. She skimmed the edge of the asteroid. Finally, she spotted something—a long cable attached to some device buried in the outer rock.

She stood, still stealthed, and leapt off the walkway, using her jets at max power to boost her distance. Now that the aether sensor was down, she was ignored by those fighting below. It took several jumps to reach the line. She landed roughly against the rocks and slid, grasping at anything that might slow her down. Eventually, her hand caught on something, and she jerked to a halt with a painful yelp.

"Did you find it?" Concern permeated BB's voice.

"By the gods." She stared down at the massive bomb buried deep in the side of the asteroid. "What's the *Eldrich Sun*'s current distance?"

"We're in close orbit, I think. Why?"

"Tell Dorthy to move back! Now!" she yelled into the mic.

"On it." She was mildly surprised that he didn't question her, but she didn't have time to think much about it.

"*Gorth!*" She tried to maintain her calm on the silcomm, but some of her panic had to have come across.

"*Go ahead, Falconi.*"

"*They have nuclear bombs staged all the way around the outside of the asteroid. They've killed everyone inside already. They're planning to blow it.*"

"*Roger. Stand by.*"

Leilani looked over the strands of cabling that spidered out in a web away from the explosive she stood next to. This one bomb alone was probably enough to make a small crack in the massive asteroid. From where she stood, however, she could see at least twenty of them. If they were covering the whole outer surface, there wouldn't even be dust left over when they blew.

"Dorthy would like to know how far?" BB asked in her ear.

Lei lifted the pad and snapped a picture with the camera.

He gasped. "Holy shit! Yeah, I'll be back in a min. I'm going to walk this to him."

"Might want to make it a fast walk."

"*We're moving,*" Gorth finally replied over the silcomm. "*Thanks for the cover. We'll find the switch.*"

"Or we all die. No big deal," she mumbled out loud.

Farther down along the outside of the asteroid, she could see what looked to be some kind of hatch. It was far too large to be an air lock. Maybe a ship bay? She began slowly making her way toward it. She couldn't jump too hard; if she broke gravity, she'd find herself floating out into the asteroid belt. Another death sentence.

Leilani approached the hangar bay carefully, dropping to her belly to peer over the edge.

Inside the hangar were easily forty people rushing to load the last remaining gig. It was large enough to have a crew of probably ten plus maybe another fifteen passengers.

A hand reached up next to her and gripped the edge of the hangar hatch. She rolled away from it, pulling up her gun to aim at the smiling crodoc.

"It's been a few hundred years since I had to worry about being blown up," he chuckled into the digital proximity comms built into his IIS uniform.

It was a backup emergency comm. To use them, the agents had to be within ten feet of each other.

She glared at him. "Funny."

Horrison smirked.

"What are you doing here, General?"

He shook his head. "Just 'Agent,' thank you. I resigned a few minutes ago, turned it over to Thoris. He's earned it. Besides, I gave my word of honor to your emperor. Did I not?"

She couldn't help but smile at him, even as she rolled back into place and grunted in pain.

He said nothing about it. Instead, he looked over the edge and surveyed the area.

"The air scrubbers won't be able to keep up with that many." He pointed to someone walking into the hangar wearing a sidearm. "The loaders don't know they aren't going."

The person started talking to the man who'd been overseeing the loading. They both nodded, and the man with the sidearm raised it and began firing. The individuals loading the ship raced toward weapons or dove for cover, but it was too late.

"See?" Horrison shrugged.

BB came on the line again. "Back. We're moving further out."

"Hey, BB. Do you have a digital connection to the station anymore?"

"Nope, only what I can see from the sensors here, which is about to lose some resolution. If I bring my links back up, that God guy will have access to the *Eldrich Sun*."

Next to her, Horrison shook his head. "Don't let him anywhere near your ship. Right now, you're the enemy." Clearly, he could hear BB through the earbud in her ear.

"Did you hear that?"

"Yeah. You two must be pretty damn close to each other."

She glanced over at the crodoc, who was lying so close to her that they were touching, and chuckled.

"You might say that."

Rothar smirked in response.

"I really don't want the details of who's on top. You two need to focus on finding the missing foreman."

"Good to see that some things haven't changed. Crude humor is still crude." Horrison laughed and pointed at a new person moving into the hangar.

This one wore a different vac suit. It was clearly personalized, not a generic one.

Leilani couldn't easily see inside the suit, so she pulled up her binoculars. After zooming in, she nodded. "Okay, BB, we have the foreman."

"Um, wow. That was fast."

Lei tried clicking on the binoculars' microphone attachment, but the line was silent. They were obviously using comms.

"I really need to know what they're saying, B."

"You got your binocs?"

"Yes."

"Plug them into your pad."

She pulled out a cable and handed the binoculars to Horrison while she hooked them to her pad. He kept them focused on the people down below.

"Got it. Running translator now. Make sure you stay on their lips."

"What do you mean he's already gone?" The man in the tailored vac suit was clearly yelling at the other two.

The man who had shot the remaining security officers had his back to Rothar and Lei.

"I don't care what the bitch's orders were. I told him to wait for me!"

Lei could now see what the binoculars were aimed at on the pad, meaning she witnessed how the shooter's face paled.

"What do you mean?"

Then the shooter raised the gun and shot the foreman directly in the faceplate. Inside the helmet, his head exploded.

Lei raised an eyebrow and sighed. "How come I saw that coming?"

The crodoc next to her shrugged. "Experience?"

"All righty, then," BB said over the comms. "Nightmares for months for me. I just keep telling myself that none of this is real, but that isn't working anymore since they detoxed me."

"Side effect of being sober." She tried to be comforting.

The crodoc laughed. "Why do you think soldiers drink?"

"All right, that was the last loose end. Samuel is en route to his mission. We just need to clean up here, and we're out," the man with the pad said in response to the man with the gun.

"Yeah, last report I got, they were in range. The self-destruct should take them out neatly, along with the evidence." Again, he nodded to something the other was saying. "It's in place. By the time they realize it isn't the real one, it will be too late."

The other man holstered his weapon and gestured to the ship. They both strode aboard.

"Fuck! It's a ruse!" Lei said loudly. Across the local command silcomm, she called, *"Emergency evac. I repeat, emergency evac!"*

No one answered.

"Don't worry, Leilani. I already had Thoris evacuate everyone the moment I heard about the bombs."

She turned toward Horrison, frowning. "You had the ability to evacuate everyone all this time?"

He nodded. "Of course I did. I just didn't have positive control over everyone I was responsible for. Once they were all found and safe, I turned everything over to Thoris and came to find you. They cleared out about four minutes ago."

"What about the igranu?"

He smiled. "Who do you think I used to get everyone out?"

"What about those in stasis?"

The corner of his mouth turned down. "You've been at this a while. You know you can't save everyone in a situation like this." He gestured to the deck of the hangar. "There are always casualties. Besides, they've already been dead for eight hundred plus years, as far as the galaxy knows."

Her eyes narrowed. "You mean to tell me that we're the last ones on this hunk of rock?"

Chuckling, he nodded, then pointed to the slowly lifting ship. "And our ride is leaving."

"Jackass." She shot to her feet and leapt into the hangar.

As she fell toward the ship, she kicked in the magnetics in her boots. They crashed into the hull with a loud clang, jarring her injured bones. As a second clang sounded nearby, she gestured for Rothar to head toward a nearby hatch.

He nodded and unslung the rifle from across his back as he advanced. The ship was starting to pick up speed, and they both needed to get inside before it went into slip. If they were outside when it slid into one of the galactic slipstreams, they would both end up as paste.

25

CATCHING A RIDE

As they reached the bridge, Rothar remained off to the side, his weapon pointed toward the hatch to cover Leilani while she bent down and pulled a device from her bag. After setting it on the hatch panel, she tapped several buttons. The device sprang to life and began its override. Luckily, the old adage held true: professionals didn't make big mistakes—they made little ones.

The military override codes worked. The outer lock popped open, and she slipped inside, followed closely by her partner.

Rothar reached outside, yanked the hatch popper free, and snatched his hand inside as the outer hatch cycled closed.

Leilani reached into her bag and withdrew another device. Unlike the smaller one, this one had six interlocking points. She began setting them at equal distances around the outer lock, forming a net. When she'd placed the last, the net shimmered, then solidified, sealing itself against the hatch and locking it in place. No matter what the bridge did, the hatch wouldn't cycle back open until the devices were manually removed.

"They know we're here," he said flatly.

She agreed and pulled both pistols, positioning herself for the coming fight.

He moved to the side, using the bulkhead as cover, placed the hatch popper, then tapped the same three buttons she had.

"Forward shields to maximum," Lei told Sarah.

The oracle did as it was told. *"Shields at 196 percent."*

When the hatch cycled open, Leilani didn't hesitate. She stepped through the inner lock firing. The individuals on the other side returned fire, but they had not been expecting such blatant resistance. Likely, they'd thought they'd simply fire into the small air lock and clean up the mess later. Her first two rounds hit heads. Two weapons stopped firing as their owners fell to the deck.

"Rotate shields."

The shields toughened on her sides as she stepped all the way into the hall, one gun facing each direction, both still firing. Four more bodies dropped to the deck.

"Fuck. It's an agent!" One of the security people started backing away, though they continued to fire.

"Shields at 60 percent," Sarah's voice chimed calmly.

The bullets continued to bounce harmlessly off her. Three more down. One of them bolted around a corner; she changed the round in her gun's chamber and fired into the bulkhead. The round blew through the corner, ripping through the man's shoulder and then farther into the ship. It would stop after reaching a certain range from the weapon.

"Your turn. Left," she thought at Horrison through her silcomm as she dropped into a crouch. She aimed both guns in front of her, focused on the right-hand passageway.

Behind her, Horrison stepped out and opened his fully automatic weapon into the p-way to the left. Two seconds later, all gunfire ceased. Lei stood and turned to smile at the crodoc.

"A little sloppy, but not bad." She looked over the wreckage of what had been a fairly clean p-way.

It was now covered in bullet holes and bloody bits of humans. She gestured toward her end. There was plenty of blood, but only one hole in the bulkhead.

"Agents generally try to do minimal damage. Makes it easier to cover our tracks."

He glared at her and gestured to his side, shrugging. "Meh. Soldiers spray everything and sort it all out later."

"That is a crock of shit." She waved for him to follow her. "You are taught controlled three-round bursts."

He simply grunted behind her. "It's been eight hundred years since I got to shoot something."

"More like you're a general, and the last time you were in a gunfight where you had to shoot shit was a long time ago."

"You are annoyingly perceptive."

It didn't take long for them to reach the engine room. As she stepped inside, Lei was nailed on her already-broken shoulder by a huge steel wrench. It was enough to drop her like a rock. Her partner stepped in behind her, however, and was not happy. He caught the wrench as it swung again and lifted it up into the air. The kid on the other end, however, held on. The child tried kicking Horrison, but he didn't even flinch.

"Son of a bitch." Lei rolled and blinked the stars away as she tried to get the pain under control.

"Agent?" Sarah had been abnormally quiet throughout all of this.

"Go ahead, Sarah. Aw, man, this hurts like hell," she complained mentally to the oracle.

Subverted or not, she and Sarah had been through a lot in the last seventy years. If command was going to kill her, they would have done it years ago.

The pain began to subside as the drugs and nanites hit her system. She looked up at her partner and saw him holding a young human of about thirteen years old. He was about to snap her in half.

"Hold." She dragged her feet under her. "Not her fault she got a lucky hit." Leilani stood up and stretched as the last of the pain subsided.

"Luck, my ass!" the girl spat.

Leilani chuckled. "Quite a mouth on her."

Stepping up next to her partner, she met his gaze. He nodded in understanding.

"What are you doing here, kid?" Lei cocked her head at the girl, assessing her oversized clothing, dirty face, and hands.

"This is my ship, you damn pirate!" The girl swung at her, but Horrison just moved her small body out of range.

"Okay. I'll grant that this might be your ship, since I don't know who you are. But I am *not* a pirate." Leilani pulled her badge from her pocket and showed it to the girl. "I am IIS. Do you know what that is?"

"That's even worse." The girl sneered and kicked at her.

"I'll take that as a yes." Lei parried the well-aimed foot, then shrugged at her partner. "Toss her in one of the lockers, I guess."

The girl laughed. "This is my ship. There's no place you can put me that I can't get out of."

"What's your name?"

"None of your damn business, bitch!"

Lei laughed. "She reminds me of . . . well, me."

The ship shook violently, and the power to the deck plates and lights cut briefly as the electromagnetic wave washed over them. Lei's and Horrison's boots were designed for such an event; they automatically defaulted to holding them to the deck.

Lei looked to her partner and frowned. "The mine."

He nodded.

She pulled a metal band from her pockets, grabbed the kid's arm, and slapped the metal onto it. Then she grabbed the other arm and brought it close enough that the spreading metal caught it too.

"What the hell is this?" the girl shrieked.

"Shut up, or I'll put one over your mouth too." Lei gestured toward a janitorial closet.

Horrison moved to it and tossed the kid inside with a loud thud. Slamming the door, he turned back to Lei and motioned to the comm in her ear.

"BB? Are you there?"

No response.

"That hit us pretty hard." He pointed to a nearby panel that was showing extensive damage to the hull of the vessel, signified by numerous yellow and red lights.

If she had finally rescued her best friend from slowly killing himself with drugs only to get him blown up instead, she was never going to forgive herself. She moved to a different panel and began tapping buttons, bringing screens up to see the extent of the damage.

"Engineering, thirty seconds to slip," the bridge called back to them.

Leilani was surprised the large shuttle even had slip drives. She glanced down to check the status of the engine. The panel lights were emergency yellow. The bridge had to know that, but apparently they were willing to risk it anyway.

"Bridge, this is engineering. The drive is at 60 percent. We may not survive slip." As she spoke, she continued working to try to override the bridge consoles.

The man on the comm laughed. "Well, hello there, Agent. I had wondered where you'd gotten off to. Let's look at it this way: you die either way."

The ship jolted its way into the slipstream but managed to hold itself together. She lifted her hands off the panel carefully.

"Can't you take control from them?" Rothar asked.

She sighed. "Not once they're in the slipstream. It's like an eldrich line. One wrong move, and the ship rips apart." She shrugged. "And they have navs up there. I can't get us out of slip without navigation."

He gestured to the slowly flashing yellow light. "What about the drive?"

She shook her head. "I haven't taken an engineering course since the academy. Even then, slip drives weren't really my focus."

"What about the child?"

Leilani shrugged. "Might hurt to try, but it's either that or we risk that thing going off-line in slip. We're damned if we do, and we're damned if we don't."

Rothar reached into the closet and snatched the ankle that was disappearing into the vent on the rear bulkhead.

Leilani cocked her head and smirked. The kid had ingenuity.

Rothar was not as impressed, judging by the way he tossed her into the middle of the deck, where she landed with a loud, "Oof!"

"Aw, c'mon, you gotta give the kid props for that." Lei gestured to the vent as she knelt to look inside it. "Man, how were you planning on getting out of there?"

The girl, gasping for breath, didn't answer.

"Until you decide to give me a name, I'll call you Rat. Because that was impressive. You almost got away with it."

Sarah spoke up. *"Hostiles inbound."*

Evidently, her partner's oracle had told him the same thing, for he pushed his rifle around to his back and stepped toward the lovely little gun nest the engineering crew had set up for them.

"Look, kid. I'm guessing you're in here either because you're related to one of these idiots or because you're an engineer." Lei cocked her head slightly. "My odds are on both."

"Bite me."

Leilani knelt next to the girl and shook her head. "Nah. If anyone's going to bite you, it'll be him."

Rothar turned and grinned at the child, baring his lower canines. It was a frightening effect.

The girl looked away nervously.

"Look. I'm not sure what's going on here. But the people on this ship broke the law. They murdered thousands of innocent people. I'm here to arrest them."

The girl glared at her. "You're lying." The words had far less vehemence than they'd had earlier. "*You're* the murderer." She gestured with her chin toward the dead bodies.

"Touché." Lei shrugged. "Let me ask you this, though. You were in here while they set this up. If I had told them that I was IIS and I wanted them to surrender, what would they have done?"

The girl broke eye contact. "They would have shot you. Just like you deserve." She was still angry, but she was losing steam, which meant she was smart.

"Here's another thing to consider: If I were a cold-blooded murderer, would you still be alive?"

The girl blinked several times, obviously processing the question. Lei took the time to look her over. She was human, or at least she appeared to be. She was probably thirteen or so and was dressed in a well-worn jumpsuit that was several sizes too big for her.

"Agent. You still down there?" The man on the bridge sounded smug.

Lei took a deep breath and glanced to Rothar.

He shrugged.

Slapping the comm button, she answered, "Yeah, I'm here. What do you want?"

"Engine two is starting to drop. Since I doubt you kept my engineer alive . . . Do you know anything about engines?"

She looked over the panel. He was right. Engine two was orange, intermittently flashing red. Based on the readings, there was a coolant leak around the backside of the unit.

"I know you don't want to die any more than I do," the man on the comm stated flatly.

"I should just let us all blow up," she grumbled to herself. But she didn't answer the comm. Instead, she grabbed a tool kit and slapped her partner on the shoulder. "Watch the kid. I'll be right back."

As she walked away, she heard the chain gun spin up and send several thousand rounds down the p-way toward some unknown assailant. She couldn't help but bite back a comment about military boys and their toys.

When she'd maneuvered behind a large engine marked as number two, she allowed her shoulders to sag. It was definitely a leak. Coolant was spraying onto the nearby bulkhead, causing it to freeze and crystallize. If that bulkhead gave out, it was all over. Rummaging through her bag, she found a sealer. Now she needed to find a way to get close to the leak without freezing to death. She resealed her vac suit and frowned. It wouldn't hold out against the coolant for long.

"Agent?" the kid called to her from across the compartment.

"Yeah?"

"I can stop it for about thirty seconds. Any more than that, and it'll fail."

"All right, give me a second." Leilani positioned herself where she could quickly dart forward and patch the leak. "Go ahead."

The spray suddenly stopped, and she leapt in to start sealing the leak. As she worked, she kept an eye on the timer counting down in her HUD. At twenty-five seconds, she grew concerned. If she backed off, the sudden pressure would break the patch. Just as the counter ticked from twenty-nine to thirty, the last of the leak sealed. The coolant started flowing, and thankfully, the patch held. Either that, or it had exploded in her face, and she was dead and only dreaming of a happy ending.

She stepped away from the pipe and looked at her hands. Nope; she was still alive.

Her walk back to the front of the engine was accompanied by the sound of the chain gun spinning up again, followed by several bodies flying apart at high velocity. Patting Rothar on the shoulder, she stepped up next to the young engineer by the console.

"It got too hot and is out of sync." The kid frowned at her and held up her bound hands. "Unless you're a slipstream mechanic, I'm the only one left who can tune it."

Leilani didn't trust her, but she was also sure she wasn't suicidal. She tapped the restraints on her wrists once, and they articulated back into bracelets.

"And my name is Melissa." She snatched the tools from Lei's hand and jogged to engine two, where she crawled underneath it and vanished.

"Well done, Agent. Now hopefully we can hold out till we get to our destination." The man on the bridge was beginning to annoy her with his smug attitude.

Fifteen minutes later, Lei glanced over at the control console and saw engine two turn green.

"Got it!" Melissa exclaimed. "Damn, I'm good!" She slid out from under the engine and polished her fingernails on her chest before blowing on them. "No need to worship me, but I just saved all our asses!"

Lei hooked her thumb toward the kid. "Good to know she's humble."

Rothar shook his head and refocused his attention on the p-way.

"Hey. It's not like that's easy while the fucking thing is actually in use!" Melissa threatened Lei with a large electric wrench.

"Yeah, I can't imagine that it is." She held out her hand for the girl to give her a high five.

She glared at it briefly, then smiled and slapped their hands together.

"Good job, kiddo."

"Thanks, old lady."

Rothar laughed, and Lei smirked. "Touché. Good job, Melissa."

"Thanks, Agent."

"Do you happen to know who's in charge?"

Melissa frowned, then pointed to the console.

"Kevin James. The asswipe." The kid walked over to the console and made several adjustments. "Were you being serious? Did he really kill all the miners?"

Lei's eyebrows pinched together. "What makes you think it was him, specifically?"

"Because it sounds like something he'd enjoy doing. Mason is too much of a pussy to actually kill anyone himself." She shrugged, then shook her head and gestured to one of the dead bodies. "My uncle tried to tell me they'd evacuated all the miners. But they use me as the maintenance monkey because they're too lazy to do any actual work. I know how many ships we have and what shape they're in. There's nowhere near enough to evacuate everyone."

The voice from the bridge crackled over the speakers again. "I don't know what you did, but—"

Melissa reached over and muted the comm. "I really have no interest in listening to him anymore."

Lei smiled. "Well, Chang."

The kid lit up at being given the new title of chief engineer.

"Is there any way you can override him and give me ship's comms?"

"Of course. I have the entire ship from here." The girl tapped a couple of buttons on the massive console.

"Even navs?"

"You'll have to give me a few to swap them out, but yeah." She pointed to the all-comm button on the panel.

"Get to work on that."

Melissa nodded as Lei reached up and tapped the button. "Greetings, everyone. This is IIS agent Leilani Falconi. This vessel and all those aboard are hereby under arrest for multiple crimes against the empire, including several thousand counts of murder. If anyone wishes to surrender, please power down your weapons and remain where you are. When we arrive at our destination, the ship will be boarded by IIS agents, and you will all be taken into custody."

Leilani hated giving this speech, but as she was reminded so often, she was supposed to arrest first if possible. "If you wish to turn state's evidence, you will inform those agents at that time. The amount of sentence commuted will be determined by the value of your information. If anyone else would like to go out in a blaze of glory, I am in engineering and will be happy to oblige."

Under the console, Melissa chuckled. "That was impressive. It won't work, but it was still impressive."

"Why do you say that?"

"Because everyone on this ship is a James sycophant."

26

BOMBS, BOMBS, EVERYWHERE!

Horrison gave the hand signal for split entry, and Leilani slid past him to the other side of the hatch that led to the bridge.

It had taken the ship more than eighteen hours to arrive at the destination Leilani had plotted. For about twelve of those hours, all had been quiet. Melissa had locked the bridge down. Nothing digital or physical was getting in or out. She seemed eager to help do anything that made the captain unhappy, but she wasn't really interested in explaining why. Lei opted not to push too hard.

"Ready, Chang," Lei said quietly into the digital comm stuffed in her ear.

The hatch popped open, but there was no gunfire. Lei looked across the way to her partner, furrowed her brow, and took a quick peek inside. She shook her head when she saw that there was no movement. Stepping in, she cautiously surveyed the area, checking for hidden survivors.

"Look at this." Rothar nudged a person lying face down over their console.

The console was covered in blood and bits of brains. The back of the skull, however, had only a small entry wound. They had been shot in the back of the head.

They both slowly and meticulously checked the room. As they got to the captain's chair, they found a man with a small bullet hole directly between his eyes. In his left hand, resting in his lap, was a gun.

"Another person on the ship that we missed in the sweep?" Rothar asked.

Lei narrowed her eyes at the dead man in the captain's chair. She then looked to Rothar and held up a hand. "Don't move. Raise your shields."

She dug in her bag for the PG scanner. When she pulled it free and clicked it on, she wasn't surprised that it immediately began beeping loudly. Turning slowly to the bulkhead, her heart sank. She had stopped less than a foot from it. One more step, and she would have been in the direct line of fire. She took a step back and gestured for Rothar to stay where he was.

He nodded his understanding.

Putting the PG detector away, she pulled out the brightly painted jar instead. Once she twisted the top free, a tired-looking head popped up. She pointed to the device on the bulkhead.

He cocked his head and rubbed his eyes. "Squeak, click, pop?"

She bobbed her head in agreement.

Pulling himself onto the edge of the jar, the li'l guy stood with all four hands on his sides and began chittering and clicking at her.

Leilani sighed and held up four fingers.

All of his eyes opened wide in surprise. He stared at her hand expectantly.

She swung her open palm to the creature, and he walked onto it. Slowly, she turned her hand to the bulkhead next to the device. He scrambled from her hand to the bulkhead and carefully approached the device. From a small vest, he pulled several tools that could barely be seen by the naked eye.

She hadn't seen him work in a while, but she swore he put on a pair of goggles that made his eyes look disturbingly large. *Wow, has he gotten so old that he needs glasses? When did that happen?*

It took him almost a full minute of messing with the device before the small green light went dark, indicating it was off-line.

She and the crodoc sighed with relief. The small ulthari, though, looked up, tugged the goggles from his eyes, and began chittering again.

"Are you sure?"

He nodded.

"Pardon me, Agent?"

She looked to the crodoc. It was the first time he'd called her agent in a while.

"Why are you talking to dinner?" He shook his head. "No, the better question is: *how*. How are you talking to the . . . ?" His voice trailed off as he seemed to look for a less hostile word to describe what most aethers considered nothing more than an annoying pest.

"The li'l guy here is the best tool in my arsenal." She held her hand out to the small creature.

He hopped on and set the PG in her hand. He seemed to be ignoring the crodoc. Thankfully.

"We've been together for a long time." She shrugged and set him atop his jar. Reaching into her bag, she pulled out yet another specimen vial, dropped the PG inside, and sealed it with the stopper.

The small creature yawned and glanced over at her partner. He made several quiet noises, and Lei resisted the urge to laugh loudly. But she couldn't hide the chuckle.

"What did it say?"

"He told me to be careful with dumb partners. It's a good way to get stepped on." She couldn't help but grin at him as her li'l guy climbed back down into his home.

Rothar blinked several times as he stared at the jar.

"Relax. He's joking." She put the jar back in her bag and grinned. "I think."

"Hey, Leilani?" Melissa called across the comms.

"Yeah?"

"We're being hailed."

She moved over to the communications console and pushed aside the body of a heavily muscled female with dozens of tattoos. The side of her head was freshly shaved, and the words *Death to Authority* were inked on her scalp.

"Push it to the bridge."

"You got it."

The console came to life, and Lei tapped the flashing button.

"Grelashi Mine One, this is the IKS *Marksman*. Please stand to and prepare to be boarded."

"IKS Marksman, this is IIS agent Leilani Falconi, ID number 34A5F697 Indigo. We welcome your inspection. Please note when boarding that we may have a stray rat wandering around, and housekeeping has been lax in their duties lately."

"Roger that, Agent. Please state your status."

Leilani frowned and looked over at Rothar. She tapped the mute button.

"Something is wrong. Melissa?"

"Yeah?"

"Do we have visuals on that ship?"

"Not really. So much of the ship was damaged in the explosion, we don't have any operable sensors. Let me see what I can jury-rig together."

"*Sarah?*"

"*They are not broadcasting, Agent. I have remained in stealth mode, so I have not attempted to query them.*"

A familiar female voice came across the ship's comm panel. "Leilani?"

"Leka?"

"Yeah. We need to get you aboard quickly. How many do you have?"

"Three."

"Meet me at a lock. Wow, that ship is in bad shape. How did you survive getting here?"

"Long story."

"Roger that. Lock four looks like it's somewhat intact. We'll pick you up there." Aleka's voice was strained, and she was speaking far faster than usual. "*Marksman* out."

"Did you hear that, Melissa?"

"Yeah. I'll meet you there."

"Careful, there might be another person aboard."

"Yeah, I don't think so. I saw an anomaly when we fell out of slip." The kid wasn't kidding; *fell* was a good word for how the ship had exited the slipstream. "I had chalked it up to the damage, but after doing some checking, I think we launched a shuttle."

By the time Lei and Rothar made it to the lock, Melissa already had the hatch panel in pieces and was messing with the wires behind it.

"Do you have a vac suit, just in case?"

The kid shook her head.

"I'll be okay. There's enough pressure. I do have a question, though."

Finally, the inner hatch popped open.

"Hmm?"

There was a loud clang as the ship outside latched onto the smaller vessel and extended the hatch lock.

"Am I going to be arrested?"

Leilani put her hand on the girl's shoulder. "Not if I have any say in the matter."

The crodoc shook his head. "Don't make promises to the child that you can't keep."

She sighed. Her partner was right. "I don't know, Melissa, but even if you are, you helped agents. They'll be lenient."

The girl nodded as several loud clangs rang through the small lock.

Leilani stepped forward and tapped the button for the outer hatch. Miraculously, it worked. On the other side of the hatch were four heavily armed IIS agents and one tall, thin elar who seemed genuinely concerned.

"Leka, what's going on?"

"They told us you were KIA."

Lei turned and frowned at the crodoc behind her.

He shrugged.

"What do you mean?" KIA would make sense in reality, but BB knew they had cleared the station. At least, he should have known. Unless . . . "What happened to the *Eldrich Sun?*"

The elar nodded to the crodoc, then noticed the child standing behind him.

"A kuldain kid?" She shook her head. "You know I can't let her aboard."

"Trust me, this kid knows way more than you would think possible."

Melissa shook her head unhappily. "Isn't that the understatement of the century."

In their downtime, Lei and Melissa had talked. It turned out that her uncle was a real piece of work. He was the lead engineer for the entire mining asteroid, even though he had only a rudimentary knowledge of mechanics. His brother, Melissa's father, was the real brains behind the operation.

When her father died, her uncle had decided she would take her father's place. Though only ten years old at the time, she had already been a better mechanic and engineer than her uncle's entire team. She was also small and fit into places he and his people didn't want to squeeze into.

She had been forced to do all the work they couldn't or didn't want to do. For three years, she was the main engineer for the entire station. Crawling around in the ventilation system, she had seen things that adults shouldn't see, let alone a kid. The foreman had never even known she existed. She had even been smuggled aboard the ship they all escaped on, all because her uncle was too lazy or stupid to do the work.

"Trust me, Leka. The kid won't see anything in there that she hasn't already seen." Lei gestured past the four guards.

"All right, but she needs to stay in her quarters."

Lei glanced over her shoulder at the kid and frowned. "Fine. Put her in with me, though. She needs someone to keep an eye on her."

Melissa glared at her.

"Speaking of quarters. We really need to clean up."

Aleka nodded and wrinkled her nose. "No kidding. You guys stink."

$$\smallsmile$$

Two hours and four showers later, Lei sat in a conference room with Melissa, Rothar, Commodore Terrance Stevenson of the IIS, and Aleka.

"Leave it to you to find a loophole." Aleka shook her head and tapped something on the table.

"Trust me, she's qualified." Lei grinned at the newly minted thirteen-year-old IIS agent in her shiny, just-printed uniform.

"I make this look good." Melissa laughed and rubbed the black-and-red leather jacket.

"Well, honestly, having a kuldain kid on one of our teams is the least of our concerns right now." The commodore gestured to one of the panels on the far bulkhead of the briefing room. "This news story is eight hours old—not that it's hard to miss right now. It's being replayed constantly all across the empire."

One of the prosee panels lit up, and a recording of a female reporter appeared. She slid into the upper right corner of the frame as she spoke. "Today, IIS admiral Jason Dorthy was taken into custody by the Kassian Imperial Navy. He is accused of crimes against the empire, including overstepping his authority, six thousand counts of murder, and treason."

In the background, Dorthy was being led off the IKS *Eldrich Sun* in strip cuffs by several marines in combat armor. A long string of other agents was being led off behind him, all of them also in cuffs.

"Our chief naval correspondent, Tommy Gant, had a brief dialog with the senior arresting officer, Admiral Brigitta Gremm. We are presenting it to you for the first time, unedited. Roll the interview."

The screen changed to a headshot of a man with short, wavy hair. Behind him was the logo for the Kassian Navy.

"Thank you, Kelly. I'm here with two-star admiral Brigitta Gremm, currently in charge of Landari Sector. What can you tell me about this arrest, Admiral?"

The camera moved to Gremm. Her face was stern but smug.

"Admiral Dorthy has overstepped his authority for the last time. This time, thousands of innocent people died. He will, of course, be tried by a military tribunal, and if found guilty, he will be executed for treason."

"Admiral Gremm, my sources tell me that because Admiral Dorthy is Imperial Investigative Service, he falls under imperial jurisdiction, not naval. With such a clear jurisdictional line, what gives the navy confidence that its ruling will be upheld?"

"Generally, that would be true. But at this time, all attempts to reach the emperor have been unsuccessful. In lieu of the emperor's direct judgment, the navy will step in and do what is best for the empire."

"What the hell?" Leilani snapped at the screen.

The reporter blinked and furrowed his brow in confusion. "Are you saying you have been unable to contact the emperor?"

Gremm seemed pleased by the question. "Yes."

The reporter shook his head and went back to the issue at hand. "If that is the case, shouldn't he instead be held over until the emperor *can* be reached?" He placed heavy emphasis on *can*.

"You don't seem to understand the gravity of the situation." Gremm's voice rose somewhat. "He murdered several thousand innocent women and children."

"You have proof of that?" the reporter asked.

"That's for the military court-martial board to decide. But I'm sure they will see my evidence and agree with me." Gremm waved her hand to dismiss the reporter. "We're done. You have your sound bite." As she turned and walked away, two of her personal guards stepped between her and the reporter.

"Well, I guess we're done. According to our sources, as of right now, all of the Imperial Investigative Service has been put on temporary stand-down pending an in-depth naval investigation."

The man looked to watch Gremm walk away. "An investigation, I might add, that the media is being kept out of." Turning back to the camera, he frowned. "I don't know about you, but this seems peculiar to me. All we can do is hope that the emperor speaks out soon."

"That is crap!" Leilani yelled at the screen and turned toward the commodore.

The man sighed and scrubbed a hand down his face. "I've gotten my orders from headquarters. We're all to report to the closest naval station and dock. Most IIS ship captains are refusing to do so, though, since the navy isn't cleared for our vessels. All missions have been put on hold." He gestured to Aleka. "And that isn't the worst part."

"It gets worse?"

The elar nodded emphatically. "I'm here because about twenty hours ago, we had a sudden influx of aethers who had been held prisoner by a kuldain mining company. There were tens of thousands of them. I really don't know the whole story, but suffice to say that the antikuldain movement exploded. This was all the fuel they needed to start a full-blown offensive. Riots began; entire tram stations were taken off-line. We lost more than ten agents before we got the order to recall for our own safety."

Aleka shook her head and brought up some footage of riots. People being trampled; local city-state constable forces being overrun and beaten to death. "Then, about ten hours ago, we lost all contact."

The image changed. "Just before everything went off-line, we heard this."

"Network online. Protocol Falair active. Loading." The male voice was familiar, but Leilani didn't react.

"Then nothing." Aleka threw her hands into the air. "We still seem to have direct comms in kuldain space, but that's it. We've even lost contact with our agents who are still in aether space."

She sounded worried. Aleka had friends and family in aether space. They all did.

"And because of these new orders, we can't even look into it."

"Is that it?" Lei asked calmly.

"What, the galaxy falling apart isn't enough for you?" Leka snapped.

"Agent Aleka, that is enough. You're dismissed." The commodore's voice was calm and collected.

Aleka slammed her fists into the table and stormed out of the conference room. If a starship hatch could be slammed, it no doubt would have been.

The commodore drummed his fingers on the table. "The entire crew is in the same place as her. I, however, know a little bit about your mission. Jason and I are good friends. We talk." He smiled weakly at her. "You, Agent, are registered at headquarters as KIA. I have not logged your presence aboard my ship."

He pointed to the other two. "And I have no idea who these people are, nor do I wish to know. I am also not telling you to proceed on mission."

He tapped the table, and an image of the *Marksman*'s layout popped up on screen. "I *have*, however, been having the worst trouble in bay eight with intermittent power outages." He displayed the bay that held his personal gig, a small vessel capable of long-range travel. "I really need to do something about it before I lose my gig to space or something."

Leilani smirked. "Yeah, probably something you want to look into."

She, Melissa, and Horrison stood and started toward the exit.

"Well, Commodore, I guess we will head back to our quarters and wait to see what happens next." Leilani waved to him as she left the briefing room.

He nodded to her. "Leilani."

She stopped in her tracks but didn't turn around. "Yes, sir?"

"If you're caught . . ."

"I know. Don't worry, sir. It's hard as hell to catch a dead person. Didn't you know that?"

27

FOG OF WAR

"Hey, get out of here!" a male voice practically screeched at her.

Leilani slammed the door to the men's room and balled her fist. This was really starting to piss her off.

Rothar put his hand on her shoulder. "Easy, Lei."

"Easy?" she snapped at him. She wanted so badly to punch something. Even in her frustration, though, she knew that punching a crodoc was a bad idea. He may look like just a large human, but he wasn't.

"Another dead end, I assume?" Melissa chimed in from behind her.

She spun and glared at the young girl. She was dressed in jeans, a bulky sweatshirt, and a pair of glasses that acted as her HUD and oracle. Modifying children was strictly prohibited in Kassian space. On her back, she wore a large backpack. They were all dressed as regular civilians—just an average family out shopping at an annoyingly loud mall.

"Sheesh, just asking." Melissa shrugged. "Not like I know what we're looking for."

Leilani's shoulders slumped. "Yes. This one is dead too."

Melissa wandered back out toward the front of the clothing store.

"Take it easy, Lei. I'm sure Mai will get things under control soon enough. It's standard operating procedure to seal the doors when something this serious happens."

"That's my point! Eight hundred years is a long time. There isn't an SOP. They don't even have a centralized government anymore, let alone a network capable of taking the eldrich stations and doors off-line."

"Well, they do now."

"How?"

"What do you think Fendrick is?"

She frowned. "What do you mean?"

"He's called the heart because he's the network administrator. The entire oracle network—and all of the oracles on it—are his design."

"But that's what I'm saying. There isn't a network anymore."

He shook his head.

"Not when the heart was gone, no." He shrugged. "But as soon as he got back, he would have brought a new mother node online. First rule of war is what?"

"Communication network." She agreed, but it didn't make her any happier.

"Exactly. They'll get everything under control there, then reestablish with Kass. Mai won't break the treaty. Peace is too important to her." He grimaced. "Trust me. It's more important to her than the lives of two entire planets filled with people."

Leilani glared at him. "You honestly think that a president who's been missing for eight hundred years is going to be able to just show up and take back control from thousands of city-states?"

"Um, boss?" Melissa's voice sounded worried over the comm.

Glancing around, Lei found that Melissa had wandered off—again. "Yeah?"

"You might want to see this."

Two people who had been at a service desk nearby were running toward the large glass storefront. Several more ran after them.

Lei nudged Rothar and followed the crowd.

There, several people were standing near the third-floor railing just outside the shop, their hands over their mouths and their eyes wide with shock. One woman was on her knees, crying. Leilani followed their gaze to the jumbotrons floating far above the center of the massive mall.

There, under the headline "Breaking News," she watched as Emperor Steven Sargeras, who was standing at a podium and speaking to the press, rocked backward—once, then a second time—as two high-velocity rounds shattered the shield around him and slammed into his chest. IIS agents swarmed the emperor and rushed him off the stage. Two of the agents took several more rounds and also fell. The media panicked and began to flee.

Screams erupted in the mall as advertising screens all around them shifted to display the shooting. News stations were playing the clip on a loop.

"Hmm." Leilani took a deep breath, then released it slowly. "Well, this puts a new wrinkle in the fabric."

A woman nearby turned and glared at her.

"Oh, back off," she snapped at the woman.

Rothar put his arm around her shoulders and steered her away. All around them, people were in a state of shock.

Melissa pulled out a pad and plugged a pair of headphones in so she could watch the feed with audio. She followed slowly as the trio made their way toward a now mostly empty restaurant. No one even noticed when they entered; the employees were all watching vid feeds at the bar, all showing the same breaking news.

The audio from the vids was loud enough that the team could hear it even as they maneuvered to a table on the far side of the restaurant. "We have heard several conflicting reports, but the most recent one is that the emperor is dead. We will keep you updated as more information comes in."

Leilani let her head fall forward and hit the table with a loud thump. "You have to be kidding me. What the fuck did he think he was doing in a public forum like that?" Her growl came out muffled by the table.

"He was trying to talk to the press about the IIS," Melissa offered quietly.

Lei looked up, her forehead aching from hitting the table too hard.

Melissa's eyes widened and darted to the pad. "That's what she said, not me." She pointed to the female reporter on the screen.

Lei shook her head. "You're telling me that even after everything we told him, he still took the damn bait?"

She couldn't believe this was happening. A month ago, she had been happily going from mission to mission without any complications. Then she happened to get picked up by a random draft and landed smack in the middle of the largest political mess in more than eight hundred years. Not only that, but nothing she did seemed to make any difference.

"He couldn't ignore it forever." Rothar was trying to be comforting and failing miserably.

"Um . . ." Melissa looked from her pad to Rothar, then back at her pad, then back up at him with a pleading expression.

He took the pad and the headphones and listened to the reporter for several seconds. Then he actually chuckled.

"We have a break in the story!" a woman in the bar area exclaimed.

Rothar shrugged. "It gets worse."

"Awesome." Leilani put her head back on the table and covered her ears with her arms. It didn't matter. She could still hear.

"It appears that the man who was shot was actually a genie—a genetically engineered clone of the emperor. Where the actual emperor is or whether he is alive at this time is unknown." The reporter sounded almost angry, but Leilani tried her best to ignore that.

No matter what idea or plan Leilani came up with now, there was no recovering from this. The Kassian Empire had officially caught on fire. No amount of firefighting would be able to hide the damage the flames left in their wake.

"This is Admiral Damion McCarthy, first fleet admiral in charge of Kassward Sector. I am interrupting all broadcasts to inform the Kassian people that everything is under control. I am instituting martial law at this time until the emperor can be found and secured. Please refrain from calling emergency services about the shooting. Go about your daily business wherever you are, and allow the navy to do what it does best. We will find the perpetrators of this heinous act, and we will stop them."

Lei didn't even lift her head. She knew Admiral McCarthy. She didn't need to see him again. The last time they met, the circumstances hadn't been any more pleasant.

"Precisely what I would do." Horrison shrugged. "I'm going to see if I can get us some drinks."

"Something stiff, please," Lei added.

"Mmhmm."

"Soda, please," Melissa added as he walked off. Likely, she was not wanting a repeat of the last time he brought her a drink she thought was water.

Lei finally sat upright and pulled her pad from her bag. She checked her mail but found it was still empty. Then something dawned on her. Reaching in the bag, she found an old-model smart comm BB had given her. It took a minute to power the ancient device on. As it booted, a message popped up on the screen.

Took you long enough.

Lei smiled and brought up the texting application. *You okay?*

Of course I am.

The boss? She knew better than to use names on a secure line, even an archaic one.

He used one of those creepy copy things.

He's with you?

Yep. You watching the news?

Yes. What's going on?

We were hoping you knew.

What are his orders? This is kind of out of my league.

He needs you to get to ground. They're rounding us up by the handful. Starting to track doors, transportation, and any and all drop boxes.

Caris. Or some other insider. At the mine, they said he was killed, but it could have been a copy. No telling.

Yeah, the boss says it's an insider too. Likely someone pretty high up. They have the codes for the data. He says if you can get to Wonderland, he needs you to check it out. Right now, they think you're dead. That might be helpful.

Got it.

Hey, sis.

Yeah?

You remember when you were really little, and we used to play the hunt-and-seek game?

Frowning, Lei tried to think back to before she was taken away by the IIS. Then it dawned on her what he meant.

Got it. I have a plan. I'll be in touch.

Stay safe, kiddo.

She laughed and powered the unit off-line just as a drink was plunked down in front of her.

"You seem in better spirits." Rothar sat down next to her. "Couldn't get any food. The cooks refuse to return to the kitchen. So unless we want to cook it ourselves . . ."

"Yeah, drink up." She gestured to Melissa's drink. "Make sure he didn't spike that."

The girl sniffed it carefully and glared at the crodoc.

He laughed and shrugged. "What? She's funny drunk!"

"You're an ass," Melissa snapped at him.

Lei couldn't help but chuckle. He was right. The girl was hilarious drunk. It had all been great until she insisted she could fly and Lei had to catch her midleap from the fourth floor.

"So, it gets better." Lei waved her hand toward the vid screens in the bar area and took a drink of her scotch. "Gremm, I'm assuming, is using the chaos to round up every last one of us."

"The ship is a wash, then." Rothar downed his drink and grimaced. "And we were recorded coming off of it."

He narrowed his eyes and jutted his jaw toward two men walking in unison past the restaurant. Each held a pad, which they were checking regularly as they looked at people around them.

Leilani was glad she had changed her appearance before leaving the ship. If her picture got around to Gremm at any point, her KIA status would be revoked.

"Yeah, we need to get moving. Luckily, though, Gremm gave us a beautiful distraction." She downed the last of her scotch and stood up. "Let's go check out the kitchen."

The three of them headed toward the bathrooms, then triggered their stealth systems and slipped into the kitchen. Sure enough, there was a back way out of the kitchen that led to the employees-only area of the mall. They stayed stealthed as they wove their way through people and past security cameras. Kuldain space had its wonders, but facial recognition software, while a great invention, was not friendly to those trying to go unnoticed.

⌇

It took them almost five hours to get down into the fog—the lower levels of this heavily populated planet, Hemmer Moon—without being seen. Sociologists had argued for centuries about why the lower levels were called the fog. Some said it was because of the lawlessness or lack of education often found there. Others said it was because of the pollution. Either way, the fog was where you went when you didn't want to be seen.

Lei tossed her bag onto one of the beds in the dingy motel room. "All right, I'm going to shower." She pointed to the other bed. "Mel, get some sleep. We're all going to need it."

The kid didn't need to be told twice. She fell face-first onto the bed and was snoring within seconds.

Horrison followed Lei to the bathroom but leaned in the doorway, averting his eyes, as she undressed. "What are we doing here?"

"Well, I'm showering, and you're ignoring an order to get some sleep."

"You know what I mean."

She stepped into the shower and quickly washed off all the dirt and sweat. "My answer remains the same."

"Lei."

"Relax, big guy." As she stepped out, he tossed her a towel. "Have you ever heard of plausible deniability?"

He shook his head, frowning. "That's what I was afraid of."

"Look. I know I come off as a softhearted police officer most of the time." She handed him the towel, walked naked to her bag, and pulled out a set of clean clothes. "But that's only because, where I can, I like to make up for who I'm required to be every other day."

He stood quietly, staring at the wall next to her as she slipped on fishnet stockings and garters, thigh-high spiked heels, and a very short black rubber skirt that barely hid her backup firearm.

The gun was strapped between her thighs as high up as she could manage. She pulled on a bright pink top that covered slightly more than a bikini would, then slid on a very obvious shoulder holster holding her main firearm. Over that she placed a glossy white half jacket. It left her weapon visible but not overly showy.

Back in the bathroom, she began to put on makeup. "I am under no delusions, General. I am a criminal who happens to get paid by the government." As she finished her makeup and hair, she turned to smile seductively at him. "Make no mistake: I am a murderer, a trafficker, a smuggler, a prostitute, and whatever else I need to be to complete my mission. And nothing will ever change what I've done in the past or what I'll do in the future for my emperor."

She slunk toward Rothar, but he refused to back away from her. She smirked and stepped all the way inside his personal space, rubbing her breasts up the front of him. "And I am extremely good at my job."

She grinned and tapped him on the nose playfully. "Now stay here, watch the kid, and try to get some rest. I'll need you awake for the next leg of our trip."

She grabbed her bag and typed a sequence on its invisible runes. The bag changed to a small purse. She swung the thin strap over her shoulder.

"And don't try to follow me. You won't like what you see." As she got to the door, she turned back to him. "I'll be fine."

***

"Yo! Sammy! There is one fine-ass bitch here to see you!" A massive tattooed bouncer with gold and steel shoved through various parts of his body grinned at Leilani as she stood up and wiped off her mouth.

"I love me some fine ass. Send her in," the voice called from inside.

The bouncer zipped up his pants and gestured for her to go on in. Lei ran her finger along his chin as she passed him. Inside, she turned and blew him a kiss as she closed the door.

"Wouldn't want anyone disturbing us," she whispered.

Sammy smirked and turned back to the massive nightclub laid out below them.

She locked the door, then slid the bar across to secure it further.

As she strode into the large pleasure room and office of Hemmer Moon's most affluent slave trafficker and drug dealer, she took everything in to be sure there was no more security on the inside. This man was easily among the top one hundred of Kassian's most-wanted list, but what the Kass government didn't know was that he also trafficked aethers—a none-too-easy task.

That was how she and Sammy had met the first time. He had been trafficking in elari slaves, kidnapping them from aether space and selling them to affluent kuldain and aether buyers. They were a hot commodity and extremely expensive. The trick of smugglers like this was that they were among the only people who knew there was space in the aether. While it didn't use the same physics as kuldain space, it was traversable if you had the right ship and the right crew. And this man knew all the right smugglers.

The room was filled with overstuffed plastic couches, as well as flat surfaces for doing lines—and whatever else came to mind. Along the walls were solid steel rings with chains hanging from them, most likely for unruly guests and fleshy prizes that Sammy wanted to show off. Weapons were strewn everywhere, and toward the back wall was a large table with dozens of monitors and an impressive computer setup.

Spread across the couches were five women, none of them sober enough to even realize Lei was there. As she stepped through the last of the beaded curtains, she found the lone man. Like the one outside, he had tattoos and bits of metal pierced through his skin, though his piercings were not as prominent.

"Heya, babe . . . Oh, shit!" The bald man snatched a gun from the table in front of him and leapt over the back of the couch. From behind it, he pointed the gun at her shakily and shook his head.

He'd been sampling some of his product. She could tell by how hard it was for him to focus on her.

"Please, no! I've been good, I promise!" he pleaded with her.

Their last encounter had been, well . . . fun. For her, anyway. Lei walked through the room, slowly checking each of the women. She stopped in front of him and his shaking gun and smiled.

"Not bad, Samuel. You seem clean. I'm proud of you." Her voice was seductive as she pushed the barrel of the gun out of her face with a finger.

"See, I *have* been good!" He looked almost as if he were going to pee himself.

"Do you remember when I was here last time? I said I'd leave you alive but that you'd owe me one?"

The man suddenly stood up straight, the pistol hanging at his side. He knew it was useless against her. "No. Bitch, you are bad news."

Leilani smiled. She liked the sudden appearance of a spine. "Relax. It won't be hard. I need you to arrange a ride for me and two others."

He waved the gun toward a silenced vid panel that she hadn't paid any attention to. "You people are wanted all over the galaxy."

She nodded. "Yep, but by who?"

He frowned and tried to process what she was saying. Even when high, his intelligent mind still worked. It was one of the reasons she had left him alive. He was far too smart to waste, and besides, she'd known she'd need him at some point.

"If they arrest all of IIS, that just leaves the navy." The man laughed loudly. "And they're morons."

She nodded.

"It took me three years to recover from your last visit!" His eyes were clearing somewhat, which meant the drugs were losing their hold on his brain.

"And if you're a good boy, this trip will be simple and profitable." She stepped over the couch, and he backed away. "And if you're not, then it will take a lot longer than three years to recover this time."

"You're one evil bitch."

She gave him a sly grin. "Yes. Yes, I am."

"Fine. I'll arrange transportation, but your safety is on you. They've gone nuts in the aether. They're killing each other by the thousands. Movement in there is rough, even for my people. And you'll have to pay for the added complexity."

"Done." She tossed him a cred stick. "Three mil cover it?"

He stared at the stick in shock.

"Are you saying there's three mil on this?" He walked over to a computer console and plugged the stick in. He raised an eyebrow, then turned to her and smiled. "It's even clean. Well done, Agent."

"Leilani."

"What?" He was clearly shocked by the familiarity.

"Not Agent. I'm dead. Just Leilani now."

The color drained from his face as he considered the idea of her no longer being bound by the rules of engagement. He finally shook his head. "You as a criminal is not a pleasant thought."

"I know, right?" She winked at him and turned to head toward the door. "And Sammy?"

"What?"

"There's double that if you keep this to yourself. You and I both know that me as an enemy is not something you want."

The man shuddered and shook his head. "There's no way the military could stop you. And there's no IIS to turn you in to anymore, so you're safe with me. But I won't turn down cash." He followed her to the door and watched as she unlocked it. "You know the pickup. Be there in six hours. I have to convince a captain to do this, and that might be complicated."

"No prob, baby." She turned and gave him a kiss on the cheek.

He let her, but he stiffened, obviously unhappy about it.

She walked out and winked at the guard. "I think he wants to have words with you," she cooed at him.

The guard turned to look at his boss, and his face imploded as a bullet ripped it to shreds and spread the man's brains all over some nearby partygoers.

Leilani ignored the screams and strutted happily into the crowd.

28

ABYSS POINT

Leilani felt something touch her thigh and woke with her pistol in her hand. A tall crodoc stood over her. Rothar nodded and gestured to the far wall of the small cargo container. It had been three days, and the container was really beginning to smell. She stood and reached over to tap the child sleeping next to her.

"Yeah, yeah," the girl grumbled. "I know. I can hear it."

Leilani tugged the girl upright and pushed her behind herself and Rothar.

She and the crodoc each withdrew a yellow marble from the hidden compartments in their jacket sleeves and waited. As the door swung open, at least nine heavily armed crodocs pointed weapons inside. Their uniforms looked familiar, and each wore a suit of full combat armor that Lei envied.

At the door itself, the captain they had paid to smuggle them into aether space had a gun pressed against his head. His hands were in the air, and his face held a look of fear and, oddly, apology.

The crodoc with the gun to the man's head looked into the box and smiled.

"Well, hello there, General." She seemed genuinely happy to see him.

The captain frowned and started to say something, but the female hit him in the back of the head with her pistol.

"I will admit, this was not what I expected to find." She laughed and beckoned for Rothar to come out. "Who are your friends?"

The small unit behind her hadn't lowered their weapons. The hairs on the back of Leilani's neck stood up in warning.

"Jaena." Rothar stepped in front of Leilani but didn't climb down.

The female's smile faded.

"Don't make this complicated, sir."

"Oh, it won't be." His voice came out calm and cool.

He and Lei had agreed to take their oracles off-line before coming into aether space. That meant they had no silcomms, but Lei could read his body language. This was about to go very bad very quickly.

"Fine. If you want it that way, sir, you are under arrest for crimes against the Seef'aini Republic, including treason and working with the enemy." She pointed to Leilani and Melissa behind him.

"Jaena, don't do this."

"Yeah, your words don't mean shit anymore, sir."

"I'll apologize to your son, then." He flicked the ball, and it exploded in a cloud of powder.

Leilani reached back and grabbed Melissa, tossing her unmoving body over her shoulder as she fired repeatedly at the soldiers in the rear.

Rothar hopped down from the crate and fired his pistol into the female crodoc's forehead. The round buried itself within her skull. Lei jumped down after him and threw her ball before the other cloud could fully dissipate.

Several more shots were fired as the three of them evacuated the area. Luckily, they were on the station, so it wouldn't be too hard to get where they needed to be.

"This way!" Lei turned down a dark hallway. The kid on her shoulder was rousing, so Lei set her down. "Move it!"

They wove their way through hidden maintenance tunnels, alarms screaming around them. She knew good and well that her security codes wouldn't work now. She just hoped they hadn't found the tram.

They were on Theris Graxin, a planet run by one of the stronger criminally backed city-states. It was on the very edge of known aether space and was truly lawless, with little government structure and no security forces. At least, it hadn't had any the last time she was here. The presence of a crodoc army was a bit of a surprise. She turned down another p-way and slid to a stop.

"Well, isn't this just peachy!" Melissa snapped. "You ran us to a dead end. I thought you were supposed to be the all-powerful, all-knowing agent?"

Three days in a box had really soured the kid on the whole secret agent thing. She had complained constantly about the sheer boredom of it all.

Lei reached up and slapped the wall hard. A light flashed beneath her hand, and there was a soft chime. The wall slid aside, and she gestured for them to go first. It was pitch-black inside, save for a softly lit circle on the floor no more than ten feet in diameter.

Melissa rubbed her arm uncomfortably. "Um, yeah. I, um, I deserved that."

Lei pushed her inside. The crodoc followed, but his head was cocked to the side, as if he were listening to something.

Suddenly, he nodded like he understood and locked eyes with Lei. "I know what's going on."

"Good. You can tell me in there. Hurry. They're almost here."

He rushed past her. As she stepped inside, the wall slid closed behind her, and a soft voice spoke.

"Welcome back, Leilani. I assume there's an emergency I need to be aware of?" A tall, elegant woman stepped out of the darkness and into the small lit area where the three of them stood. Both her hair and the robe she wore were long and white. As she moved, her image flickered slightly, making her seem translucent.

"Careful," Leilani whispered to the other two. "Don't move until she gives us permission." She stepped forward and bowed.

"Greetings, my lady. Yes. There is an emergency. We need to get to Wonderland."

"Ah, Wonderland. A magical place indeed. A place of unicorns and fire. Why do you seek such a place?"

"I've always wanted to play with fire." Leilani smiled brightly. "But the unicorn I can die happily without ever meeting."

"Then the fire it is." The woman nodded and faded from view.

The area suddenly lit up completely, revealing a small tram station. A single car capable of holding no more than twenty people sat alone on the softly glowing eldrich line.

"Um. Lei, what was that?" Melissa asked.

Lei chuckled and beckoned for them to follow her. "You mean you finally saw something new?"

"Well, yes, but I meant that weird-ass conversation."

"It was coded communication." Rothar nudged the kid and pointed to a series of crystals lining the walls of the tram station. "Those are weapon systems."

He raised an eyebrow at Lei as he followed her onto the tram. "Systems that are several thousands of years old, I might add. Even older than me."

"Your point?" Lei hated running this tram. It was an antique, and she was always afraid it was going to fall apart under her. Death by eldrich line was not a fun way to go.

"I'm merely curious." He shrugged and shoved Melissa into a seat.

"Hey, watch it!"

Ignoring her, he reached down and began fastening her multipoint harness. She slapped his hand when he reached between her legs for that strap. "Hey!"

"Shut up, child. You let me do this, or you die. Your choice."

She snatched the strap from him. "I choose strapping *myself* in!"

"Will you both shut up?" Leilani finally got the tram to power up with a violent shudder. "This thing is hard enough to operate."

Rothar stepped up behind her and shook his head. "That's because you're doing it wrong." He gestured to a switch she had never gotten to work.

"It doesn't work."

He reached around her and pulled a lever she'd always ignored. He then flipped the switch. There was a soft roar that faded to a softer purr as an engine she hadn't even known existed came online.

"It's called a clutch." He pointed to the lever.

His arms were still around her; she glared at him over her shoulder. "Fine, you drive it, then."

She ducked under his arm and shuffled toward a seat.

"What's a clutch?" Melissa asked, but Lei ignored her.

Rothar sat in the pilot's seat and strapped himself in. "Where am I going?"

"This line only goes one place."

He frowned. "Are you saying this leads to an abyss point?"

"Yep."

"That will kill us."

Leilani smiled. "Well, at least we won't have to worry about the mission anymore." She gestured to the way out of the station. "Get moving."

He did as he was instructed, but he was clearly uncomfortable with it.

As the car lurched forward, Melissa looked up at her curiously.

"What's up?" Lei asked.

"I'm not much of a bedtime-story girl, but I thought unicorns were unique—that there's only one of them."

"That's true. Why?"

"The creepy woman said we were going to a land of unicorns—you know, as in more than one."

"There's only one at a time. But when one dies, it's replaced by another."

"Oh." She still seemed confused.

The tram was running much more smoothly than any other time she had used it. She would have to suck up her pride at some point and ask Rothar to show her how to use the thing he called a clutch.

As they approached the main line, though, Leilani grimaced. No matter how good a pilot he was, this part was never gentle. She reached up and held on to the straps of her harness in preparation. Their car crashed into the line and was jerked sideways as the main eldrilin threatened to shear them in half. The car held, though, as it always did. Across the aisle, Melissa threw up all over the deck. As the car settled, a miniature brass ball rolled out and began to clean and sterilize the mess.

Lei undid her harness and walked unsteadily to the crodoc. "You said you know what's going on?"

He nodded. "Mai sent me a message. That stupid winged bitch decided that if they were evacuating, they should evacuate everyone, even those still in stasis. They flooded into Gorlish City. There was no way to manage an influx of that many refugees. No matter how hard she tried, the city just didn't have the infrastructure to handle it. So the aethers were spread out to other cities. It took two days to get the mother node online, so they had no military comms."

He shrugged while shaking his head sadly. "A lot of the military joined up with the resistance because they still believe kuldains are the enemy. The antikuldain zealots were able to spread their message too fast." He looked up at her apologetically. "Mai is trying to reestablish control, but she is being fought by various city-state leaders and the resistance. They're claiming she's a kuldain plant, because evidently aethers don't have mae'lacans anymore. Or those that *are* mae'lacan"—he gestured to Lei—"don't know it."

"Okay, that is not the first time someone has called me something other than human. What is a mae'lacan?" She held on to the back of the chair as they went through a rough patch in the line.

"Elari come in several different subspecies." Rothar leaned back in the chair and crossed his arms behind his head. "Tre'dalmor, fae'ana, yel'adari, and mae'lacan. They're all unique. Fae'ana are tiny, brightly colored, and annoyingly cheerful. Tre'dalmor are like your friend Aleka: tall, thin, and elegant. Yel'adari are much smaller but otherwise a lot like their taller cousins. Then you have mae'lacans, like yourself. You look human, though you're generally larger, stronger, faster, and smarter."

She shook her head. "I *am* human. I've seen the DNA scans."

"Before your oracle?"

Frowning, she considered the answer. Her oracle had been placed in her when she was very young, almost immediately after she was kidnapped. Long before she joined the IIS. "No, I suppose not."

"Fendrick said the oracles had their base overlay changed to hide all mae'lacans. Even from themselves. They always show them as human on every scan, eldrich or digital."

"Why?"

He shrugged. "No clue." He tapped the panel. "We have two hours to the destination. I'm going to catch a nap."

Unfastening himself, he stood and took her arm. "And Lei, if I die in two hours because you're wrong, I'm going to hunt you down in the afterlife and beat you senseless."

She laughed and nodded. "Roger that. I'll be waiting." She took the seat, then looked back at the crodoc. "Wait, did you say they evacuated *everyone*?"

He sat down in one of the larger reclining seats and began strapping in. "Mmhmm."

"Even the Kassians?"

He looked up at her and shrugged. "I assume so."

Lei frowned. She didn't want to think about that right now. If the Kassians survived the chaos to be rescued, it would be a miracle.

An hour and a half later, Lei woke her companions and smiled brightly at Melissa. "Hey, kiddo, I think you'll want to see this."

Back at the control panel, she tapped a sequence into a keypad. A whole new panel twisted out from the side and made itself available to her. This one had far more modern piloting controls.

"Interesting aether-physics lesson for the retired general," she yelled over the noise of the eldrich beneath them. "Abyss points, as he calls them, are really just breaks in the eldrich line, or eldrilin, as it's also called." She gestured to Melissa. "Anyone who knows anything about energy knows that energy, in any form, is cyclical."

Melissa smiled. "Yep."

"But when you break a power line, the energy pours out into nothing, looking for a way to continue its cycle."

The roar of the line suddenly stopped, leaving an almost deafening silence. Lit only by the eldrich line, the tram launched from the dark tunnel into open space.

True space was a vast darkness filled with suns, planets, moons, and, in general, orderly chaos. This space, however, was a completely different creature. There was no order to this chaos. The area itself was large—not quite the size of a typical solar system, but similar. True space would be black, but here it was more like entering a massive cloud.

All around them were wisps of clouds in all shades and colors of the light spectrum. The effect was the most bizarre rainbow of cotton candy. Thousands of sparks of light peppered the clouds, each blinking and flashing in its own colors.

Occasionally, an arc of brightly colored energy would flash from one spark to another, much like a massive lightning bolt. It was beautiful and utterly dangerous. Such things were why all flight in the abyss point was done manually. No computer could keep up with the split-second decisions necessary to stay alive.

Lei tapped a button on the new panel, and magsteel wings unfolded from the side of the car. She pulled back on the pilot's yoke and tapped another button. A rocket fired from the rear of the tram as they pushed forward and entered a nearby purple cloud.

Melissa reached her arm out of the tram to run it through the purple cloud. "How are we breathing?"

"Aether space is not like kuldain space. Physics is not the same." They broke free from the cloud. "Some people believe that these breaks in the line are the homes of the gods."

Ahead of them was the most amazing view in the universe. It was as if a planet had exploded, but the devastation had proceeded only so far before the explosion was somehow halted. As such, the planet was in millions of pieces, but they still formed a somewhat roundish shape. Each of those pieces thrived with life—mountains, jungles, waterfalls, and beautiful plains filled with flora and fauna.

The whole planet was lit up like midday even though there was no sun. Occasionally, a piece would shift colors as a bright wisp of cloud lazily passed over it.

She drove their tram car between the pieces of floating planet. "As you're about to see, there are no gods here. I doubt there ever were, but if gods really do exist, I would like to think they lived in places like this."

The tram car flew through a waterfall that was flowing from one large piece of planet to a smaller piece far below.

"Grelashi almost became one of these abyss points. The line is slowly leaking there, so it was removed from the normal tram lines."

They wove their way through the debris, carefully avoiding the more active wisps of clouds. As they rounded a smaller chunk, another massive piece came into view. It had rolling plains, a slowly winding river, and a massive forest filled with visible life. It also had a heavily fortified compound. Several massive gun turrets spun and began tracking the vehicle.

"Welcome to Wonderland." She reached for a comm panel. "Wonderland, this is the *Phoenix*, inbound. Please respond."

"Roger, *Phoenix*. How's the weather out there?"

"Kind of on fire right now. But I'm sure the magenta will fill the moon soon enough."

"Roger that. The unicorn has been informed of your presence and is waiting for you. Land on pad three."

"Thank ya kindly." She chuckled.

"Another code, I hope?" Melissa glanced at Rothar, who simply nodded. "This place is amazing! Are unicorns real?" Melissa unfastened herself and moved forward to stand next to Leilani.

"Not in the storybook way, no. At least, not that I've ever seen."

"Then what *is* the unicorn?"

The weapons continued to track them until they landed gently on a flat, grassy area that had been planted with pansies manicured into the shape of a sizable number three.

Rothar stood and hiked his thumb toward the kid. "What about her?"

"What *about* me?" Melissa snapped.

"Well, I don't know about you two, but I think food is in order. I'm starving for something other than ration bars."

"Please!" Melissa squealed.

Lei laughed and nodded to her partner.

He stepped out onto the grass. "Well, I see why our scouts never returned from abyss points."

A human woman in a Kassian marine uniform was heading their direction, an IIS soldier in combat armor behind her.

"Well, hello there, Captain." The woman pulled to a stop and saluted her.

Leilani returned the salute.

"He's waiting to see you."

She nodded and gestured to Melissa. "She's starving. You think you can oblige her?"

"Of course, ma'am." The woman grinned and waved to Melissa. "Hello, young lady. My name is Lieutenant Cailet Harrison. What's yours?"

Melissa put one hand on her hip and pointed the other toward the woman. "Now, see? *She* has manners!" She smiled politely at the woman. "My name is Melissa Drakesmith. Nice to meet you, ma'am."

The marine lieutenant laughed and shook her hand. "Don't worry about them. IIS field agents rarely have time for manners." She waved for the girl to follow her. "Let's go see what we can find in the kitchen."

"Sounds good to me. But let's get one thing straight. I'm well aware that you adults are just trying to shove the annoying kid out of the way."

The marine looked back at Leilani. "I like her."

Lei smirked. "So do I. That's why I'm keeping her away from *him*."

The woman nodded her understanding. "So, what do you like to eat?"

"I want a damn soda!" The girl glared over her shoulder at Rothar as she walked off with the lieutenant.

"A soda it is."

29

WONDERLAND

As they wound their way through the massive compound, Lei noticed a serious lack of physical security—which wasn't a good sign. Rounding a corner, they approached an open door with a single IIS security guard outside.

"Get in here, Leilani!" a male voice shouted.

She grimaced and lengthened her stride. He didn't sound like he was in a good mood, which always seemed to be her luck.

"Your Imperial Majesty?"

Inside the smallish room, a shirtless human male was sitting on a medical table while a woman in a white smock rummaged around in his shoulder with surgical tools. He gritted his teeth against the pain. "Why is it whenever we talk to each other face to face, something awful has happened?"

"Because those are the only times you need me, sir." She shrugged, then bowed deeply. The crodoc behind her simply nodded to the human.

"Sarcasm not appreciated."

"Yeah, well, we each deal with crap in a different way."

"Watch your language in my presence."

She rolled her eyes. "At least I didn't say 'shit.'"

"And now you have." Emperor Steven Sargeras glared over his shoulder at the woman as she dug deeper into the wound. "That hurts, Clarice."

"I'm sorry, Your Imperial Majesty. The bullet seems to be moving." The woman looked flustered.

Leilani walked around the table and pushed the woman out of the way. "Who shot you?"

"One of my own marines. It was unbelievable," he grumbled.

"Your entire empire is coming apart around you, and you're surprised that one of your own people shot you?" Over the emperor's shoulder, she caught Rothar's eye and then cast her gaze to the table.

He smirked and nodded. Reaching into her bag, she pulled out li'l guy's jar and removed the lid.

On the other side of the table, the crodoc stepped forward, grabbed hold of the emperor, and spun him facedown onto the table—probably a little more roughly than necessary.

"Hold still, sir. Or this will hurt a lot more than it has to."

"What are you doing?" There was a tinge of panic in his otherwise stern voice.

A head popped up from the jar in her hand. The ulthari looked from her to the person on the table and then back to her. "Squeak?"

"Yep. It's starting to run. We need you to stop it before it gets to his heart."

"Click, squeak snap." The creature disappeared into his jar, then came up wearing a long white coat and a belt full of tiny tools.

"Amazing." Rothar watched in awe as the creature leapt onto the man's back and skittered toward the wound, pulling his goggles down over his eyes as he went. "Please tell me this creature is unique."

"What the hell is *that?*" Sargeras roared, pushing up against the massive crodoc.

Rothar held him to the table, and both he and Lei ignored the emperor's ranting. A guard stepped into the room, but Lei pulled her pistol and pointed it at him, shaking her head.

Using a tiny laser scalpel, the ulthari began cutting into the man's back, slightly below and to the right of the original wound.

"Not really, no," Lei said, finally responding to Rothar. "But if it helps you rationalize it, he *is* highly trained, and I paid . . . well, technically, *he* paid"—she cocked her head in the direction of the man writhing on the table—"a lot of money for his equipment."

"Leilani, I order you to stop whatever you're doing!" Sargeras screamed, trying to force them to pay attention to him.

"Your Imperial Majesty, I took an oath a long time ago to protect your grandfather. Then I took it again to protect your father. Then again for you. I am not going to follow your order, because it goes directly against that oath. I swore to protect you against all enemies and to uphold the honor of the empire, yada yada, and some other garbage I don't care about. But you, sir, I do give a rat's ass about. Therefore, you will shut up and just lie there like I told you to."

The doctor walked into Leilani's view. "Can we at least give him a sedative?"

Leilani shook her head. "No. The bullet is programmed to move in for the kill if his heart rate slows down even a little. It's waiting for surgery to trigger its programming. Luckily for him—well, for all of us, really—he's a stubborn ass who refused to be sedated after being shot in the first place."

The woman watched the tiny, spiderlike creature in awe. "What is that?"

"It's called an ulthari. Most aethers consider them a pest. But despite their reputation—and annoying propensity to reproduce in huge numbers, steal, and be potentially lethal—they're highly intelligent. With the right training and tools, they can do just about anything." She shrugged. "This one is actually a trained intrusion and assassination specialist."

That revelation made the guard twitch and power up his weapon. Lei clicked a button on the side of her own weapon, changing from armor-piercing to nonlethal rounds, and pulled the trigger. Energy leapt from her weapon and slammed directly into the man's chest plate. He shook violently and fell to the floor, still twitching. She waited till his eyes rolled back in his head, then shut the weapon off.

"Sorry, sir. I'm not letting some edgy idiot risk your life." She looked to the doctor. "Mind shutting the door?"

The woman looked scared, but she scrambled around the unconscious guard and did as she was bid.

"Falconi, you are out of control," the emperor growled through clenched teeth. He had stopped fighting and was clearly focusing on the pain as the creature buried itself to its thorax in the newly cut wound in his back.

She shrugged. "I feel in perfect control." Then she glanced down at the small creature. He was in deeper than she was comfortable with. She waved with her gun for the doctor to come to her.

The woman did so hesitantly.

Lei leaned forward and whispered in the woman's ear. "He might need a transfusion. Do you have any blood stocked up here?"

The woman shook her head. "We barely had time to get out. I couldn't grab anything more than a basic emergency bag."

"Didn't that have some in it?"

The woman nodded and pointed to two empty plasma bags in a nearby recycler.

Lei shook her head and sighed. "Fine. I'm a match. Use me."

The woman frowned at her.

"Trust me. I've had to do it before, but he was very little at the time." She hopped up on a nearby table and yanked her coat off. Reaching into her bag, she withdrew a small vial. "When the ulthari comes out with the round, the bullet will need to go in here immediately. Then put the cork in. If you're not fast enough, it will look for another target." She handed it to the woman.

Rolling her shirtsleeve up, Lei glanced over at the crodoc. "Roth?"

He raised an eyebrow curiously.

"When he's done, see if you can find the li'l guy some fish. I promised him fish for the work. He prefers anchovy, but in reality, he doesn't know the difference. Any fish you show him will work. Just tell him it's anchovies." She laid back as the woman slid the needle into her arm.

"Got it. What's an anchovy?"

"A small, stinky fish," the emperor, facedown on the table, growled. "They swim—ugh—in large schools—arghhh!" He screamed through the pain.

Suddenly, the ulthari popped up, screeching loudly. He held a bucking bullet in all four hands.

The doctor leapt toward him with the vial and held it out. He wrestled it into the vial, and she slammed the cork down just as it tried to leap out toward her. The second the vial sealed, the bullet fell to the bottom and stopped moving.

The doctor stared at the now inanimate bullet. "Well, that was horrifying."

"Be happy I didn't tell you the rest," Leilani slurred. The world around her was beginning to flicker.

"Has she eaten anything lately?" the doctor asked.

"Not for about forty-eight hours."

"Shit! This could kill her."

"She knew the risk." Rothar stepped into Lei's darkening vision and smiled down at her.

Lei simply nodded as the world around her finally went dark.

Leilani awoke sometime later in a large, comfortable bed. It was the most comfortable bed she could remember ever being in. She must've still been dreaming. Looking around, she saw Melissa sitting in a large chair in the corner of the room, typing rapidly on some small device.

"Hey." Her voice felt weak. She cleared her throat and tried again.

The girl's head snapped up, and she smiled. She hopped off the chair, ran the couple of strides to the bed, and leapt up to sit next to Lei.

"I've been talking to this guy. He's awesome!" She spun the small comm unit and showed her the archaic text program that Lei and BB used in emergencies.

"Where did you get that?"

"It was in your jacket pocket, making a funny chirping noise. I found it about an hour ago."

"How long have I been out?"

"About eight hours." Melissa gave a dismissive wave of the hand. "The doc said to let you sleep. You needed it. My mom was a doc. I know better than to argue with them."

That was the first time the girl had said anything at all about her mom.

Leilani reached for Sarah, then remembered she was off-line. With a mental flip, she triggered the oracle. It would take her several minutes to boot all the way.

"Rothar?"

Melissa grinned mischievously. It was a weird look on her. "He's with the emperor. They're both fine. They're going over the next few steps."

Lei threw back the covers and found herself clean and naked. She glanced down at herself, then over at the young engineer.

The girl shrugged. "Wasn't me."

Shaking her head, Lei found her freshly laundered clothes draped over a chair nearby, then began getting dressed.

"Have you met him yet?"

"Yep."

"Please tell me you were polite."

"Like you were?"

Leilani grimaced. Rothar had a big mouth.

"Hey, BB wants to talk to you."

Lei took the device and typed as she finished dressing. *Yeah?*

I like the kid.

Okay.

Boss says well done, but we're running out of time. They're getting seriously out of control. Come pick us up. We have a plan. I'm at home.

Roger that.

She tossed the device back to Melissa as she finished putting her boots on. Turning, she swiftly left the room with the young engineer on her heels.

As Lei and Melissa approached the war room, the guard she had shot earlier glared at her from his post outside the door. She grinned and patted him on his chest plate as she passed. "No hard feelings, big guy."

Stepping inside the tactical command room, Melissa chuckled behind her. "Wow, that made him maaad."

Lei just laughed.

Retired general Horrison, Emperor Sargeras, and Colonel Jhonnas Maxwell looked up from the table they were studying.

Melissa stepped past her to high-five the emperor and stand next to him at the table.

Lei nodded to each of them men individually. "Gentlemen."

"Agent," the emperor acknowledged her. "Agent Horrison here was informing us about what he knows regarding President Lenali, General Thoris, and the sad state of affairs in aether space." He cocked his head. "Suffice it to say we aren't getting any help from them any time soon. They have their own problems to deal with.

"And what we know of kuldain space is limited. We do know that as we were evacuating, Kass Prime and the three surrounding systems were completely locked down by the Kassian Navy. No one is coming in or out. Anyone who tries isn't even being warned. They're just being destroyed."

Leilani frowned. That was a severe overreaction, but sadly, it was within the navy's rights while the system was under martial law.

Rothar leaned forward and moved the holo map showing the imperially held worlds. "Gremm was last known to be here," he said, indicating the location, then shook his head. "Nowhere near Kass Prime at the time of the shootings."

"Perhaps, but we know there are, at minimum, two PGs and shooters unaccounted for," Leilani chimed in.

He nodded. "And as of a week ago, there was a shooter in this area." He tapped the solar system that they had come from.

"Which leaves the question: Who's next?" Sargeras added.

Lei leaned across the table toward him. "I have to ask a question, Your Imperial Majesty."

He shook his head before she could ask. "No, the genie didn't belong to me or any of my people."

Leilani frowned. "That means they had this planned all along. It takes time to grow a perfect clone. It also means they had access to your DNA file, which narrows the field a little as well."

"I mean no offense by this," Rothar said, though his tone contained a hint of arrogance, "but that's a pretty complicated scheme for a human."

All three of the people at the tactical table glared at him.

He raised his hands in surrender. "I'm sorry, but it's true. This takes years of careful planning and implementation. Humans are usually short-term thinkers."

"Offense taken," the emperor grumbled.

"That's your problem, Your Imperial Majesty." Rothar chuckled. "It wasn't intended. I was merely stating facts from my experience. I have a hard time believing that a human is behind this."

"The average human lives to be about two hundred years old." Based on her new revelation about what others considered her species to be, Leilani wasn't willing to argue too hard. She had never known her parents, so she couldn't be sure either way.

Rothar folded his arms as he considered her words. "That sounds about right. But that's still not enough to do this." He jerked his thumb toward the map. "This plan included taking control of not only the Kassian Empire but the Seef'aini Republic's network as well." He shook his head. "That takes knowledge that apparently no human has any longer, which in and of itself is suspicious."

He zoomed the map out until it included the entire Kassian Empire, all 1,231 worlds. "A true coup in an empire this size would take generations. It cannot happen over one human lifetime."

He reached off to the side and pulled out several images of Gremm with her father and mother. "This is the closest line, yes?"

All three Kassians nodded.

"There are no children here." He spread his hands. "The parents are old or dead, and she is in her own career with no spouse or children."

"What are you getting at?" the commodore asked.

Thankfully, Leilani wasn't the only one confused.

"He's right." Sargeras absently tapped the edge of the table. "When changing the royal line, which has happened in the past, it takes generations for the empire to finally settle down. If these people were planning such a coup, they would be doing it for their children and grandchildren. But they don't seem to be planning that far ahead, or they would already be training kids for the next step."

She and the commodore looked at each other. They were both IIS. They would live much longer than typical humans. She was already more than a hundred fifty years old; odds were that he was at least two hundred or more. But neither of them seemed to fully grasp the idea of planning that far out.

"Did it ever occur to you two that they're just idiots?" The room fell silent as she spoke. "Maybe Rothar is right, and they thought this through like a human would. They might have missed an important piece of the puzzle, such as progeny. You do realize that us mere mortals don't think like that generally, right?"

This time, it was the crodoc's turn to glare at her.

Sargeras laughed. "She has a point. Doesn't really change the annoying mess we're in, but I'll admit it makes me feel a little better."

Rothar shook his head but said nothing.

"All right, then, so the next step is to start tying the pieces together so we can make some arrests."

Leilani locked eyes with the commodore, then shifted her gaze to gesture to the office behind him.

He nodded.

"Agreed, sir," she said. "I'll take my team to Kass Prime and see if we can't find your PG and hopefully your shooter. Then, if we can, we'll see if we can tie them in with the Shovalli family, like the rest of this."

"Sounds good. We'll stay here until we get confirmation." He rubbed his shoulder. "I think I'd like to avoid getting shot again."

She nodded and smiled.

"I'm going to go get something to eat and maybe take a nap," the emperor added.

The three IIS agents stood to attention and saluted him.

"At ease." He waved his good hand dismissively toward the group and strode from the room.

Leilani waited until she was positive he was out of earshot. "Have you checked the rest of them?"

"Yes. We had to shoot four of our own after the incident. Two more royal guards, an aide, and one of the medical staff." Colonel Maxwell shook his head. "How they got that many that close to him, I have no idea."

"Yeah, well, do you know Agent Caris?"

The man nodded. "He's an insider, and we aren't entirely sure he's alone. We do know that one of ours has been feeding Gremm and her people the data for everything. Caris is responsible for the PGs, and if he's still alive, then he's likely where the leak is coming from." Maxwell frowned. "Caris has access to the Wonderland files."

Leilani massaged the back of her neck. "I know. Don't let anyone else in. Change the pass phrases, and don't trust anyone."

He reached out and tapped something into the tactical table. The edges of the table turned yellow.

"Done."

"We need transport."

The man rested his hands on the table. "I have the perfect ride for you."

30

CATCHING A RIDE

One of the benefits and detriments of an empire that spanned more than a thousand solar systems was that things happened slowly. Even with slipstream travel, news took time to disseminate. What might take seconds to spread within a solar system might take hours, days, or even weeks to reach farther out.

It had taken them two days to get to Kass Prime, and much to her team's frustration, Lei couldn't help but be cheerful the entire trip. She enjoyed the feeling of walking into the belly of the beast unnoticed. The Kassian Imperial Palace was abuzz with military and staff, even without the emperor's presence.

A large corporal escorted her through the busy hallway. Rothar didn't excel at subterfuge, so she'd found him a part that was easy enough for him to play . . . such as an officer in the Palace Guard.

"Corporal?" a stern female voice called from behind them.

The guard snatched her arm, yanking her to a stop. The strip cuffs on Lei's wrists chafed painfully, and she gritted her teeth. When Rothar turned toward the voice, he noticed the woman's rank and snapped to attention, saluting without letting go of Lei's arm.

The lieutenant returned the salute and nodded toward the prisoner he was holding. "Where'd you find that one?"

"Hiding in a closet," he sneered.

Leilani glared up at him.

"Typical." The woman laughed. "Take her to holding."

"I apologize, ma'am, but I can't comply. The admiral wants to question her."

The lieutenant looked surprised but merely shrugged.

"I doubt she knows anything, but I just saw him go into the private quarters." She gestured in the direction they had been going.

The guard saluted the woman again. "Thank you, ma'am."

"Proceed, Corporal."

The guard shoved Leilani, causing her to stumble forward. They continued down the hallway and entered a beautifully lavish wing of the palace. She had the entire palace memorized, but she had never been in this section; she had just never really had a reason to enter the personal quarters until today. She couldn't understand how anyone lived like this.

"I'd be afraid to touch anything if I lived here." She eyed a vase, ten feet tall and intricately carved and inlaid, as they walked past.

The guard knocked her in the back with the butt of his rifle, causing her to take an extra-large step forward.

"Easy there, big guy. I don't think the royal family would appreciate blood on their gorgeous rugs."

He simply grunted at her.

"Gotta love the stimulating conversations we have." She rolled her eyes. Further down the way, a lone marine stood outside the private imperial quarters. She veered slightly toward him.

He watched them approach but wasn't concerned.

"The admiral wants this one," the guard behind her said, and the marine inclined his head toward the door, allowing them inside.

The two of them stepped into an open common area featuring several overstuffed couches, two large wooden desks, a massive fireplace, and—of all things—a kitchen and wet bar lining the walls. They could hear someone talking in one of the connecting rooms.

Leilani popped her restraints free and gestured to that room's door. The disguised Rothar nodded and stepped up next to it. Silently, she slid over to a painting and placed her hands on the panel hidden behind it. At its soft chime, she quickly tapped in an override code.

The odds that Caris had made it to Kass to manually change the palace security codes were minimal. The code was accepted, and she sighed with relief. Quickly moving to the private bedroom, she paused to listen.

"There has to be a clue around here about where you went. I swear, man, when I find you, I'm going to wring your scrawny little neck," Admiral Damion McCarthy grumbled loudly.

Leilani glanced into the room to make sure he was alone. He was, but an admiral never stayed that way for long. She slid behind him, gently placing her hand over his mouth.

He startled, like any normal human being would, and reached to yank her hand away. Stepping around into view, she held her finger to her lips. Taking the hint, he frowned but said nothing. She pulled a device from her pocket and scanned him thoroughly. His coat was bugged.

When, pointing to her scanner, she motioned for him to take the jacket off, his frown deepened, but he did so and handed it to her. She mimed talking to her hand, hoping that he'd understand that she needed him to keep talking to himself, then gestured for him to follow her back out into the main room.

He followed her, continuing his ramble. "Seriously, man. This is ridiculous. What were you thinking?"

After laying the jacket over one of the chairs, she began noisily opening and closing desk drawers, rummaging through papers within to make sound. She then waved for him to follow her back into the bedroom. Once the door was closed, he glared at her.

"You have thirty seconds before I call the guards."

She cocked her head. That was reasonable, considering.

"All right. Let's start with that Maxwell says you're loyal and that I should at least give you a chance."

"Is the emperor alive?"

"For now."

"All right, I'm listening." He folded his arms across his chest.

"As I'm sure you know, there's a coup going on."

McCarthy glared at her, clearly annoyed.

"The clones were not made by Sargeras's people. It's a setup. They managed to get insiders into his staff, and he was shot, but he survived. He's now in a secure location." She held up her palms. "Well, semisecure. We need you to continue on task. Martial law edict 9315 allows you to take over as regent until either the emperor or a suitable replacement can be found."

"I know the law, Ms. Falconi."

Nodding, she continued, "That's the plan." She pointed to where she'd put his jacket outside. "You have insiders on your staff as well. Doing this may put your life in danger, and if they find out you're working with the emperor, it will be forfeit."

He took a deep breath, still annoyed, but she wasn't sure his annoyance was with her this time. "My life is always in danger. Such is the way of politics, but I understand the risks. It was my next step anyway, but I will admit, I'm much less worried about doing it now." He rubbed the stubble on his chin. "I will play my part. I assume you need more, or you wouldn't be here."

"I need access to travel records around the time of the shooting. And I need transport to a recon-class vessel in system." She pulled her backup portal scanner out of her bag and handed it to him. "They're using microwormhole technology to assassinate their targets. This finds the device."

"Please tell me you're joking." He took the scanner and looked it over.

"Nope. That should find both ends so long as they're powered. They can hear, see, and shoot through those holes." She raised her chin.

"You said you needed travel records?" He was still staring at the device, obviously trying to process the idea.

"Yes. The shooter had to at least be in low orbit."

"Then they're still in system." He finally looked up at her. "I had a bad feeling about the entire thing. My people were already picketing, ready to seal the system. The second the first shot was fired, I locked the whole system down." His grip tightened on the device, and he held it up. "This finally gives me a focus. I'll take care of the shooter or shooters." He glared at her. "You take care of whoever is doing all of this. And Leilani . . ." He turned toward the door as he spoke.

"Yes, sir?"

"If my emperor dies, I will hunt you to the ends of the universe."

"Sounds reasonable." She gave half a shrug. "Nice to know you don't hold a grudge."

A marine, a rather annoyed prisoner, and an invisible child all sat aboard the naval shuttle silently. The bruise on Leilani's cheek was beginning to swell, and once again, she resisted the urge to kick the large man sitting across from her in the face. Up front, the naval pilot was talking to the IKS *Hoganmeyer*.

As the shuttle docked and the back hatch lowered, the marine stood up and reached for her. She yanked her arm away and turned to walk down the ramp unassisted. At the bottom were a lieutenant and two marines.

"Welcome aboard, Agent Falconi. I assume your guard has orders to transport you the whole way?" The lieutenant held out his hand to the large marine corporal next to her.

Rothar handed him his orders.

The lieutenant glanced at the orders, then nodded before looking up at the pilot of the shuttle. "Roger that. We accept the responsibility of the transport of one marine and one prisoner. You're clear to return to your post, Ensign."

The pilot walked back aboard the small shuttle.

The lieutenant waved his pad at them. "The captain would like to speak to you two."

As the shuttle turned and left through the atmo shield, the group walked across the bay and entered the main part of the ship. Inside, the executive officer pointed to Leilani's strip cuffs.

"You can take those off now."

She popped the cuffs off. Then, before anyone could realize what she was doing, she spun and backfisted the large marine. He didn't even try to block it, though he also didn't allow it to connect with the nerve cluster she was aiming for. Instead, she connected with his incredibly dense cheekbone.

The lieutenant raised an eyebrow, then jumped as a thirteen-year-old girl in an IIS uniform appeared next to him.

"He had that coming." The girl folded her arms.

Leilani cradled her now-broken hand in her good one, and her foot came up between his legs.

The young engineer flinched. "I'm not so sure he deserved *that*." She looked up at the lieutenant. "They clearly have shit they need to work out. You were saying?"

The doubled-over retired marine started laughing. It was a deep, angry sound, but it wasn't the type of sound that usually made a person's skin crawl. Lei chuckled and shook her head at him.

The naval officer grimaced, first at the young engineer and then at the other two, who were nursing their injured parts and now laughing.

"Well, I was going to ask where the third member of your group was, but I see now." He raised a hand to greet the young engineer, then jerked his thumb in the direction of the other two. "Should I take them to medical before the captain?"

"Nah, they'll be fine. They'll likely take a few more swings at each other." She tucked her hands in her pockets. "You got any chow?"

He took a deep breath and looked past the two injured IIS agents to the ship's marines standing behind them. "When they figure it out, meet us in the galley. The captain needs coordinates."

"We should leave them be. This has been a long time coming." The girl bounced on her toes. "Besides, I'm starving. And actually, I know where we're going."

The lieutenant chuckled and pointed down the p-way with his pad. "All right, we'll grab food on the way to the bridge."

31

WARRANTS AND ARRESTS, OH MY!

Leilani and Rothar were led into a small office. Behind the desk sat Captain Greggory Bains of the Imperial Kassian reconnaissance vessel *Hoganmeyer*. He was in a crisp, neat uniform and had clean-cut hair and steel-gray eyes. Sitting cross-legged on the desk, facing the captain, was the young IIS engineer. Their attention was currently fixed on a holographic display Melissa was showing him.

"If you change the power output here, you can get almost 6 percent yield over time." She shrugged. "It wouldn't seem like much in the short run, but in the long run, it could mean outrunning someone or something when you really need it."

"I'll talk to my engineer about it. Thank you, Melissa."

"Yep." Turning toward them, she grinned. "Heya, agents!"

"Come in and have a seat, agents." The captain smiled at them. "Feel better after a shower and some sleep?"

"Yes, sir." Rothar nodded to the captain, then sat down. "Thank you."

"No problem. I was enjoying this young lady's company. This is an impressive little genius you have here."

As he gestured to her, Melissa beamed with pride.

"Make sure you take care of her." He turned from the girl to a pad on his desk. "My crew and I have been assigned to you for as long as you need. That being said, I should tell you that we might have some issues in the system you asked for."

Leilani frowned. "What's wrong?"

"The IKS *Empress's Dream* is currently in Theryia System." When they didn't seem to understand, he clarified, "Admiral Gremm's current flag vessel."

Lei and Rothar both looked at each other.

"Dorthy," she said quietly.

He nodded.

"Do we know why she's there?"

The captain furrowed his brow and began sifting through his reports. After several moments, he shook his head. "All right. Ideas?"

Melissa smiled. "We could wait till she leaves."

"That's a possibility, but let's consider it a last resort." Lei didn't really feel like explaining fleet etiquette and management to the kid at the moment.

"How long do you think it will take to pick up the package?" The captain leaned back in his chair.

"Not more than twenty-four hours, I hope," Leilani said.

"Well, I need to refuel and resupply before I continue on mission. In reality, the fleet should ignore me."

"Aren't you assigned to Kass Home Fleet?" Rothar asked.

"No. I was recently assigned to the Eleventh Fleet." The captain crossed his arms. "It was far enough out that no matter where I went en route, I wouldn't be questioned. I have a year to get there."

"I assume you were given a response when challenged?"

The captain nodded. "Yes, I was asked to deliver some fleet mail on the way." He grinned. "You know, various crew members sending things home from their travels." He tapped the navigation map on his display that showed the system they were headed to. "Coincidentally, I have three packages to deliver here."

Melissa smiled. "You mean us?"

"No, besides you three."

"Oh." The girl hopped off the desk and walked over to the nav board.

"All right, so that should restrict the questions. Now we just have to get our packages up here and figure out where to go next." Lei tugged at her earlobe.

Even with military-grade engines capable of using the gravitational pull of black holes without tearing the ship apart, the trip from Kass Prime to the outer edge of the empire, far to the galactic east near the Geloran border, still took a week and a half. On a civilian vessel, the trip would have taken a minimum of four weeks.

Very few ships had the structure and engines capable of handling larger gravitational pulls, let alone using them to increase speed. This ability was one of the main reasons the Kassian Navy was so powerful. Entire fleets could use gravitational anomalies to slingshot themselves into the slipstream at a higher velocity than a normal vessel could handle, allowing them to travel across the massive empire far faster than most other vessels.

"Any bets on what we've missed?" Leilani leaned back on the exercise machine and crossed her arms as Rothar lifted weights that would crush a human.

"I don't bet. I take in information and make educated assessments," he grunted out.

"Well, that's something to look forward to, I guess." She laid her head back on the machine and made a snoring noise.

"What?" He set the massively overloaded barbell back in its cradle, allowing the magnetic locks to kick in place. Nothing on a ship was ever left to sit free. Everything had to be bolted to the deck when not in use.

She snorted herself awake. "Oh, I'm sorry. Were you talking? You're just so boring, I guess I fell asleep."

He glared at her and walked off toward where his gear and towel were stowed. "You know, I had a lot of soldiers under my command." He pulled the towel out and wiped his face and hands off.

One of the local marine lieutenants walked by and nodded to him. "General."

Rothar smiled broadly at the lieutenant, but Lei rolled her eyes. The crew had managed to find out that he was a retired general, and now, no matter where they went, he was a general and she was an agent, even though they were technically both agents.

"I even had special operators, much like yourself." He swung the towel around his neck. "And I can't help but wonder if they were as much of a pain in the ass behind my back as you are to my face."

The young marine laughed quietly.

"We can hear you, marine."

He stopped suddenly.

"Leave him alone. It's not his fault that you're a pain in my ass."

"Who's the superior here?" she grumbled halfheartedly.

"The captain." He pulled her gear from her locker and tossed it to her. "And I mean the ship's captain. Not you."

"I knew what you meant." Glancing at the clock, she gestured to the hatch. "I may be a pain in the ass, but at least I'm good at my job. We need to go get cleaned up."

Rothar laughed, scratching his chin. "Agreed, Agent Leilani. You are amazing at your job. And I'm honored to fight alongside you. But I'm sad to say that I might always end up your straight man. I'm too old to change my ways too much."

Lei smiled at him. "Yeah, but maybe I need that. Besides, at least I'm a bitch to your face. I've never been a behind-the-back kind of person."

Once they were back in their quarters, Rothar started up the conversation again. "Are you this much trouble in front of your command staff? You're a direct report to an admiral, right? Dorthy?"

"Yep and yep." She stripped off her clothes and headed to the freshers. While in slipstream, the water-based units were shut off, so the crew used sonic showers instead.

"Hmm." He followed her to wait for his turn.

"Don't stress over it. I came into the IIS later in life. Like you, I was kind of set in my ways. And the IIS isn't as rigidly military as a group of marines would be."

"So all of the agents are this relaxed with their superiors?" He tossed her a towel as she got out of the shower.

She pondered how to respond as she rubbed the cloth across her skin even though she wasn't wet. It was somehow still a part of the routine. He stepped past her into the unit.

"I'll take the silence as a no."

She let it go and left the bathroom to get dressed. They had only about fifteen minutes till they were out of slip. Navy ships didn't generally have space for passengers. The marine officers who were usually stationed in this room had been moved and now bunked temporarily with their enlisted. She and Rothar had the room to themselves.

Fifteen minutes later, they were walking onto the bridge just as the ship slid perfectly out of slip and began to bleed off the extra speed. The bridge became a buzz of noise as the crew went about the business of moving into a heavily populated system. Communications and navigation got their course from the system traffic control, and the ship maneuvered into the traffic lanes and began the slow process of going deeper into the system.

There was a small fleet in system, but that wasn't unusual. On the rim, pirating activity was fairly common, and fleets were kept in the more heavily populated areas to help patrol and police the borders.

Captain Bains smiled at them. "Hello, agents. It looks like we made it intact."

"Getting updated newsfeeds, sir," one of the crew called to him.

"Toss it to my console."

"Aye, sir."

A new holographic display appeared in front of the captain's chair. There on the cover, under the headline "Emperor a Phony!" was a picture of the emperor in handcuffs, being led by two marines.

"Not a flattering picture of him." The captain shrugged.

Rothar grimaced and shook his head. "I wonder if he's seen this?"

"We can hope not." Lei rubbed her arms.

The same communications officer stood and walked up to hand a pad to the captain.

He chuckled, shook his head, and handed the pad to her. "Welcome to the top-ten most-wanted list, Agent Falconi."

She stared at the pad and her slowly rotating image.

Rothar looked from it to her in surprise.

Sighing, Lei ran her fingers through her hair. "Wish I could say it was a first."

"Look at the signature." The captain folded his arms and leaned back in his chair.

At the bottom of the list of charges was the tightly scrawled signature of Admiral Damion McCarthy.

Leilani tapped the pad on her forehead, resisting the urge to toss it back at the captain. "Figures."

The young lieutenant frowned, obviously confused. "Sir?"

"Relax, Watson." He jutted his chin toward Leilani. "The agent was sent to us by the admiral. He knows exactly what ship she's on. If he wanted us to arrest her, he would have just sent the message directly to us, don't you think?"

The lieutenant took a moment to consider, then nodded his understanding.

The captain crossed his legs and inclined his head toward the lieutenant's station. The younger man returned to his station while the captain held his hand out to Leilani. She handed him back the pad, and he bounced it in his hand as he spoke. "This does complicate things a little. Either I read my entire crew into the mission or I shouldn't be your ride. They will follow orders, but I have some pretty loyal crew members on this ship. At some point, someone is going to start asking questions."

Leilani nodded and held up a finger to indicate that he wait a moment. *"Sarah?"*

"Yes, Agent? I'm in range to establish communications."

"Go ahead."

"Dorthy here. Took you long enough."

"Sorry, sir. We're in system. The captain here is loyal, but the new warrant may cause complications."

"What captain?"

"Captain Greggory Bains."

"A loyalist. Okay, I assume he knows the emperor is alive and well? He is alive and well, right?"

"When I last saw him, yes, sir."

"Okay, your comm should be ringing."

The device that she had been carrying in her pocket began to vibrate. She reached in and pulled it up. It said *BB* on the front.

She lifted to her ear. "Yes?"

"Give the comm to the captain." It was Dorthy.

She handed Bains the device. "Admiral Dorthy for you, sir."

Rothar looked at her curiously, but she just shrugged.

"Yes, Admiral. Give me one moment." Captain Bains stood and waved to his executive officer, who was standing nearby, then pointed to the seat. "You have the bridge, Samson."

The XO nodded, stepped up to the chair, and sat down, logging himself into the system. The captain pointed at the two agents, then at the door to his ready room. As they all three stepped inside and closed the hatch, the captain continued talking into the comm.

"Go ahead, Admiral." He was quiet for a long while, but he nodded several times. "Yes, sir." Several more nods. "No, sir. Of course, sir."

Leilani turned to Rothar, ignoring the other conversation. "If we have to find new transport, you have any suggestions?"

"All the people I knew are dead." He folded his arms. "At least, I assume they are. A couple of them might still be alive. But I know nothing about them anymore, including their loyalties."

"You knew people in kuldain space?"

He furrowed his brow. "Of course I did. Just as you know people in aether space."

She scratched her chin. "I know people in aether space because it's my job to police the two. But how would an aether marine know kuldains?"

He unfolded his arms and splayed his hands. "The policing of the two used to be done by the military. We worked with the Kassian military in a joint-patrol action. We had a cross-training process in which officers would spend a year or two in the other military to gain an understanding of what the differences were."

Leilani leaned against the bulkhead, jamming her hands in her pockets. That wasn't information in the history books on either side. She couldn't help but wonder if he was pulling her leg.

"Then how did you end up at war?"

His shoulders sagged. "The military never chooses war. Politicians do. Protests were getting out of control on both sides. The media was blowing it so far out of proportion that the regular people lost track of reality. They voted in politicians who made poor choices."

Lei shook her head. Politicians and nobles—both were fallible, and sadly, the types of people attracted to those jobs tended to be extremely more so.

"The first shot was by a civilian at a Kassian ambassador. But the Kassian military had to respond. They were just following orders and trying to save lives. But in the scuffle, they accidentally killed the wrong person. Later, we found out it wasn't the Kassian marines who killed that senator; it was one of our own. By that time, though, the war was already in full swing. The truth had become irrelevant." He shrugged sadly. "Two years into the war, Mai was elected president on the platform that she would bring peace to both sides. She brought in outside mediators."

Leilani nodded her head in understanding. "The igranu."

He bobbed his head. "We got the fighting to stop long enough for both sides to meet on Grelashi to have peace talks."

He furrowed his brow, looking away from her into the empty air. "What happened after that, I'm not entirely sure. I was in the talks on Grelashi, but I got pulled out because something strange was happening. My people said that individuals dressed in the armor of Kassian marines were on Shevalis, Grelashi's aether sister planet, and shooting their way into the heart."

He locked eyes with Lei. "The Kassian general and I were good friends. He promised me that it wasn't his people. His were all still on Grelashi. Damn Fendrick, however, sent an alarm through the net that the Kassians were attacking his command center. He sent it to every oracle he had access to, which, I'd like to point out, was all of them.

"I was halfway there when the shooting started again. Honestly, that's the last thing I remember . . . Well, not the last thing. The last thing is how angry I was when I saw that Fendrick had overloaded one of his damn crystals."

He balled his fists tightly at his sides.

Lei reached up and patted him on the shoulder as the captain behind them cleared his throat.

"The admiral has a plan." He sounded pleased by it, smiling. "Since the IIS has lost every ship they had, he's commandeering us. Which means I get to tell the crew the truth. Or at least as much of it as they need to know for now." He handed her the comm device. "That is one seriously archaic piece of junk."

She tossed it lightly, then caught it again. "It works."

"True. We're going to continue as if nothing has changed. We're dropping off mail and picking up a crate or three." He walked the few steps to the small conference table. Tapping it several times, he activated a holo of the current solar system.

"The *Empress's Dream* left four days ago. Apparently, she is heading to Shovalli System. There, she's having some sort of party. The admiral said he would brief you when he got aboard. Until then, stay out of sight." The captain shrugged. "His words, not mine."

She rolled her eyes. "I figured."

"It'll take me three days to get restocked, refueled, and ready to leave. I'm sorry to say it, agents, but you're stuck in marine country for a few more days. We're going to put the other two in with you. I hope you don't mind."

They both shook their heads.

"Good. Oh, and Agent Falconi?"

"Hmm?"

"Thanks for letting Agent Melissa work with my engineers. They love her. She's already made some adjustments to the performance of my ship that my crew had no idea were even possible."

"No skin off my nose." Lei shrugged. "The kid is annoying as fuck. I'm just happy she's bunking with someone else right now."

Rothar agreed emphatically.

The captain looked at them both strangely but just chuckled.

"Well, that's it for now, unless you have questions."

"No, Captain," they answered together.

"Then you're dismissed." The captain strode out of his ready room back onto the bridge. They heard the call of, "Captain on the . . ." as the hatch closed, leaving them both in the ready room alone.

"I'm never going to get used to that," Rothar grumbled.

She patted him on the back. "I never did."

32

PLANS, PLOTS, AND PROBLEMS

"Okay, so McCarthy has proclaimed himself regent. But we all know he won't and can't hold it for long." Dorthy leaned back in his chair at the small conference table.

Melissa, BB, Dorthy, Rothar, Leilani, the ship's captain, and the ship's executive officer all sat around the small table in the ready room. Along the bulkheads stood several other ship's officers, including ones from medical, the marines, and engineering as well as the officer in charge of supplies.

"So we have no more than six months to find Gremm and prove that she or her father or both are behind all of this." Dorthy crossed his arms. "And that's assuming McCarthy drags his feet that long."

"What about the emperor?" the marine major standing behind Rothar asked.

Dorthy waved his hand toward Leilani.

"We spoke to him two weeks ago. He's in a secure location that isn't really capable of receiving comms. But last we checked, he was safe." She looked up to see if that was what the major wanted.

"Yes, we know that he's safe, but what I meant is: What were his orders?"

Lei gestured to Dorthy. "Those were his exact orders. He needs the leaders of the plot taken out so he can resurface and try to straighten all this crap out."

Sitting on the table in front of the admiral was a stack of portfolios, papers, and digital media. He glanced down at it, then up across the room. "All right. To that end, Admiral Gremm is throwing a birthday party for her father at their resort home on Shovalli Minor. So, Captain, if you wouldn't mind setting a course there?"

Captain Bains locked eyes with his executive officer. After a brief, wordless communication, the XO got up and headed through the side hatch to the bridge.

"Falconi, you and Horrison will be attending the party." He looked to BB. "They'll need identities and invitations."

BB was still skinny, but fairly healthy looking. He tapped his pad and stuffed it in the bag next to him as he packed to leave. "On it."

"Major, they'll need a driver and a couple of guards, just in case they need evac."

The marine stood and saluted before leaving.

"Jaina, they'll need attire befitting the setting."

The ship's supply officer stood up straight and saluted. "Aye, Admiral." She too left.

When he turned to Melissa, Dorthy's face softened slightly. "And if you and the chang could come up with some kind of scanner and backup comms that won't be noticed by the household security, that would be great."

"In other words, get out." Melissa chuckled and tucked a lock of hair behind her ear. "Sure thing, boss." She smirked at the chief engineer as the two of them left.

After the majority of the people in the room had left, Dorthy patted the table next to him, looked over his shoulder at the chief medical officer, and handed her a pad. "I need you to go over this and tell me your opinion."

She sat next to him and began reading the data.

"You two. You'll need new faces, of course." Dorthy shrugged; he was more covering his bases than anything else. She and Rothar were both well versed in disguises at this point. "I've been looking through these papers. You're right. We can't arrest either of them on this. They were careful not to mention names, and BB's information, while incriminating, isn't admissible in court because of how it was obtained. It *is* enough, however, for an arrest warrant. The problem is that there is no authority right now that can give us the warrant. Because of martial law, there isn't any authority at all right now save for the navy, which is firmly in Gremm's pocket."

He leaned back in his chair. "Which leaves us needing undeniable proof that we can take to McCarthy. Then we hope he has enough loyal people to back his plays."

Lei furrowed her brow and rapped her fingers on the table. "That may be difficult."

"More than you know." Dorthy gestured to the doctor. "Doctor?"

The woman looked up, her face twisted with concern. She tapped the pad with her index finger loudly. "If I'm reading this correctly, there's no way the duke can be behind anything. Unless they've done a damn good job of faking these scans." She shook her head. "But I'm not seeing any signs of tampering."

"What do you mean?" Rothar asked.

"According to this, the duke has been in a coma for just over ten years."

The whole room fell silent as everyone got lost in their own thoughts.

"Maybe a copy?" Lei looked to Dorthy, who leaned back in his chair and folded his arms across his chest.

"That was my thought. But if so, then where is the actual duke?"

Leilani groaned. Magical copies—like the one she had used at the mine to cover her naval counterpart—were often mistakenly thought to be in a coma because once their orders were fulfilled, their brains stopped. They maintained life in the body, but until they were given new orders by the operator, they simply didn't have any brain activity—something often mistaken for a comatose state by medical personnel.

"So we have to get in to her estate, find the body, and see if it's a copy."

"If it *were* a clone, there would be telltales in the scan," the doctor interjected.

"Thank you for the expert opinion, Doctor. If we find a body, we'll call on you again for an assessment. You're dismissed."

The doctor stood and nodded to the admiral before walking out.

"I assume that a clone and a copy aren't the same thing?" Captain Kelly asked.

"No, they aren't." The admiral folded his arms across his chest. "I mean no offense, Captain, but may I use your ready room alone for a few minutes?"

"Not a problem, Admiral. I understand completely. The more I know, the greater the risk to myself and my crew." He stood and walked out to the adjoining bridge.

Dorthy turned to the two of them. "Find me that body. If it *is* the duke, then there's someone else in play here. If not, then we still have to find the duke. " He lifted his pad. "In one of his reports from the Grelashi mine, Caris says that they knew what they were mining for, which leads me to believe that there *is* something we're missing."

Rothar leaned back in his chair, crossed his arms, and grinned at Leilani. She grimaced and tried to ignore him.

"Yeah, Rothar said the same thing." She reached across the table and pulled the leather portfolio from the pile of papers. "However, I maintain that our mysterious party isn't the major concern here. Right now, we're in the middle of something that could rapidly turn into a civil war. If we don't reestablish some sort of order in this chaos, people are going to start turning on each other. All of us have serious loyalties to both sides, but we are first and foremost guardians of our emperor and his people."

She tossed the folio onto the center of the table with the royal seal facing upward. "Let's assume for a second that we have a hidden party and that they're after only the heart. Then why all of this?" She knew good and well that the evidence pointed to something far deeper than a simple coup, yet sometimes her bosses needed a gentle nudge from underneath to see it.

"A distraction." Rothar didn't move as he responded, still convinced that he was right.

Lei turned toward him and raised an eyebrow. "Really? You think someone would spend more than ten years just working on a simple distraction?"

"It's not simple by any stretch of the imagination, but I agree with the general," Dorthy added.

Leilani sighed. They were a little more stubborn than she had hoped. This would take more effort on her part.

"Okay, then. Let's assume this is just a distraction. Who is it distracting?"

"Us." Dorthy leaned forward in his chair, resting his elbows on the table. There was the spark of an idea in his eyes. "Someone is trying to remove the IIS from the picture."

Rothar cocked his head slightly, then turned to Leilani and furrowed his brow. "Didn't you say that the Seef'aini Republic doesn't have a military anymore?"

"The Seef'aini Republic doesn't even exist anymore. There is no unified government. So no, there is no military. Only local city-state security forces, and those are pretty weak in most areas. If something serious happens, the IIS steps in at the request of the city-state and deals with the issue."

Dorthy grimaced. "Shit."

They both looked to him curiously.

"We recalled everyone when things started getting bad. I tried to convince Senator Fathrin and Admiral McCarthy that it wasn't necessary, but they insisted. They weren't willing to risk losing agents' lives to a bunch of protesters." He shook his head. "The senator managed to convince the emperor, who ended up putting a signature on the order that I couldn't ignore."

"Which means that the heart has no protection." Rothar's voice was flat, and his jaw clenched slightly.

"It has Thoris," Lei said, trying to be comforting, though she doubted it helped. They both knew that the aether was a wreck right now, and the military that was still loyal to Thoris was stretched thin.

"Well, whoever is behind this, they've caused chaos on both sides, which is likely the distraction for whatever their real goal is." Dorthy tapped the portfolio with a finger. "Because we all know that this coup is a short-term issue. As long as the emperor is alive, we will recover the throne."

"Agreed, but until then, distraction or not, we're useless to anyone but the emperor."

Dorthy scratched his chin, shaking his head slowly. "They've successfully tied up any resources we could have provided." He tapped something on the table's surface. A holographic image of an e-invite popped up. "So, for right now, we have to focus on recovering control of the IIS. To that end, we have the party that you two will be attending." He gestured to the floating invitation. "It's on Shovalli Minor, which evidently is 100 percent controlled and owned by the family. It is a small class-M moon that's generally cooler than the larger main planet."

The holo changed to a picture of a man and woman in formal attire. "This is Countess Renee Gerthias and her husband, Gordon. Gordon is a retired marine—something that should be easy for you." He pointed to Rothar. "They do not know Gremm personally, so researching the portfolios that BB has put together should be enough to get you by. They own a small planet on the Geloran border."

The image flickered to show a tall woman with light-bluish skin, long white hair, and bright blue eyes that seemed to sparkle even in the holographic image. She was amazingly elegant and adorned with gems and jewelry that would make most noblewomen jealous, but this geloran female had toned down her decoration to just above what she would have considered disgustingly plain.

To gelorans, their bodies were an empty canvas. A geloran without artwork was considered offensive. And humans . . . Well, they were plain, even in formal dress.

"This is Ambassador Shelai of the Maythendi Confederacy." Leilani kept her face carefully neutral, not indicating that she knew the woman personally. "The ambassador and her entourage will be at the party. I'd steer clear of her. She will likely know the countess personally since the gelorans trade with her planets regularly."

Dorthy locked eyes with Leilani, but neither of them said what they were both thinking: it was a little odd that the ambassador would be at a party of Gremm's. But the geloran did have a knack for being where the most information could be gleaned.

"This is Ambassador Nofutu Meshana of the Sudalif League. He—at least, I think he's male—will also be at the party."

The image flipped to a creature with light-gray skin, a massive domed head, and huge black eyes. It wore a human-style suit in dark gray with a white shirt and a black tie, along with a mask over its face. Many outsiders mistook such masks for breathing apparatuses, but in reality, they were merely a device to make humans more comfortable with the messari's lack of a mouth.

Like humans, messari required oxygen, but they absorbed it through a very advanced membrane covering their whole body. They communicated with their minds using a psionic wavelength. And where a humanoid generally had ocular organs, the messari had full-spectrum sensory organs. Humans, however, automatically assumed they were eyes.

Leilani smirked and shook her head. "Female."

Dorthy shook himself. "I really don't understand how you tell the difference."

Next to her, Rothar cocked his head. He was being unusually quiet.

"Well, he . . . she . . . it should keep whatever they know to themselves. I hope. They've never really involved themselves in our politics, and this party is clearly political. Honestly, I'm surprised they're even going to be there. So until we know more, I'd avoid them as well."

He scrolled through the list of guests. It was a virtual who's who of the Kassian elite. Wealthy corporate CEOs, holovid stars, and the upper echelon of noble families were all invited.

"BB is getting together your packets of all the people the countess will know or know of. It should be pretty detailed, but you have about ten days to go over it all. We'll be in system in nine. You have RSVPed for that Saturday morning. That will give you about four hours to explore and look around before the party."

"So we're supposed to be staying at the estate?"

Dorthy nodded.

"And what about the originals?" Rothar cocked his head, his arms still firmly folded across his chest.

"They've been delayed. By some of BB's friends. He assures me they will be unharmed."

Leilani raised both eyebrows. That Dorthy had believed the hacker's assurances was impressively naive, especially for an IIS agent. BB didn't have nice friends. Hell, he didn't have friends. He simply had people who could be blackmailed.

"I am going to leave you two to discuss your plans." Dorthy stood and moved to the hatch. "Good luck, agents."

33

A HORSE IS A HORSE, OF COURSE, UNLESS . . .

"Greetings, Countess. Lady Gremm was not able to be here herself to greet you, so she sent me. I have a car waiting for you." A tall, thin, elderly man in a perfectly tailored gray suit bowed respectfully to her as he swung his arm toward the large aircar stretched out behind him. On his lapel he proudly wore the insignia of House Shovalli.

The countess was a tall woman with long black hair and a thinner frame than Leilani was used to—a side effect of being in the public eye, most likely. Leilani wondered if she had ever eaten anything more than a bite or two per day. Luckily, the item that she was using to mimic the woman's physical appearance didn't actually affect her own physiology. She doubted the woman had enough strength to lift even one of her dozen bags. Why any human being needed twelve suitcases for two days, Lei had no idea.

She spun her hand in a circular motion between the luggage and the aircar as she glanced back at the skycap who had followed them from the shuttle. His gravcart was so overloaded with luggage that she could barely see him. She didn't wait to see his response before moving toward the door that the Shovalli chauffeur was holding open for her.

Leilani had been surprised, as she read the portfolio BB gave them, to learn that the countess was genuinely compassionate. She did several charity events each year and even volunteered as often as her staff would allow at local orphanages on all four of her planets. Her political programs and agendas were almost always in the best interest of the people.

Her husband was a retired marine general and had originally been the head of her security before they fell in love and got married. The couple almost restored her faith in nobles. Almost.

"To your left are the hunting grounds that the duke and his daughter used to hunt on every summer." The aircar was flying low enough for her to easily appreciate the snowy landscape below. The driver's voice slowed and dropped slightly in volume as he continued his practiced explanation. "Before the accident, anyway."

Leilani looked down at the snow-covered forest. It was truly beautiful—from up here in her nice, warm car, anyway.

"We will be approaching the compound on your right shortly."

Compound was a good word for it. Hell, the emperor's compound in Wonderland didn't have this much security.

Rothar raised an eyebrow at her, and she shrugged.

"Does Admiral Gremm really need this much security?" he asked the driver.

"Lady Gremm does not wish anything to happen to her father. She implemented this security after his original injury." The man's voice was oddly flat.

The car floated to a stop on one of the landing pads, and the doors on either side were opened by house staff. The two of them were given a tour of the estate as their bags were delivered to their room. Leilani couldn't help but smile as they were walked through the barn to see the prize-winning horses.

The stable master explained that the Shovalli family was using a rigorous breeding campaign to preserve a species of equine that had almost been lost. In the last fifty years, the horses had gone from critically endangered to threatened. They hoped to eventually pull them off the list altogether.

"Does Lady Gremm ride?" Lei couldn't help but wonder more about the woman's private life.

"No." The stable master folded his arms. "This project was her mother and father's. While the lady allows the program to continue in her father's name, she herself is not particularly interested in horses."

Leilani shook her head slowly. Losing the breed because the woman stopped caring about keeping up appearances would be disheartening.

Lost in her own thoughts, Leilani pet a particularly curious stallion on the nose. She hadn't even noticed that Rothar and the stable master had wandered ahead.

"Lovely animal, is it not?" A soft, feminine voice startled her out of her thoughts.

Leilani spun and saw Shelai, the tall, elegant geloran ambassador, towering over her. The average geloran was between nine and eleven feet tall. This woman was on the lower end of that spectrum but was still easily more than three feet taller than Leilani.

"Madam Ambassador." Leilani bowed politely. She was in trouble.

The woman smiled sweetly and waved her left hand in the air. Magic surged through the area.

"Renee is afraid of horses." The geloran chuckled and pet the animal on the nose like Leilani had. "Though I never really understood why." The woman shrugged. "Something about a childhood accident."

Leilani stood slightly taller, trying to resist the urge to stand at attention in front of the woman.

The geloran placed her hands together and grinned. "Relax, Leilani. I am here because I want you to know that I approve of why you are present." She pointed to the animal, even though they were no longer talking about it. "I have secured the immediate area. You may talk freely, but make it quick. The staff here is very nervous, and my wards against surveillance have set off their alarms."

"How do you know about my mission?"

The ambassador smiled. "It is my job to know what is happening in the empire." She shrugged. "Of course, I do not know everything, but I do keep up on things that might directly affect my people."

"Reasonable. I'm here to assess Duke Shovalli."

The blue-skinned woman smiled, but there was something else in her sparkling eyes. "That is what you think you seek. But it is not the whole truth."

Leilani cocked her head and pulled her coat snugly around herself. Dealing with this particular geloran often reminded her of her conversations with Krelor: annoying riddles and puzzles that required endless patience.

"You will find what you expect with the duke, but he is not the true secret here. *That* is what you seek. You will find it far below, hidden from the demon." She reached out and patted Leilani on the shoulder—a very personal gesture for a geloran. Because humans were mortal and, as such, a lesser species, gelorans touched them rarely, if ever. "My scout will tell you more."

The woman turned and walked back toward the main house, leaving Leilani alone in the barn to try to piece together the new information.

<hr/>

"Are you telling me that the ambassador actually used the word *demon?*" Rothar seemed skeptical. The tour had lasted several hours—likely just to keep them occupied till the party—but they were now changing for the celebration.

"Yes," she called from the bathroom.

"I know very little of gelorans. They left the aether when I was just a child . . ." Rothar stepped into the bathroom, his tie in his hands, and froze when he saw Lei in the mirror.

Leilani had secured the room the moment they entered, which the security staff would have expected. They were letting their disguises recharge while they got ready for the party. Their disguises were subtle ones, changing just enough to make their sizes and facial structures correct; the rest was up to them. This meant they still needed to dress appropriately and, in Leilani's case, wear makeup. In the past, the IIS had tried full illusions, but they'd found that the failure rate was higher.

She had brought a rather spectacular strapless gown in a geloran-influenced style that hugged her body in all the right places. The dark gold accentuated her olive-skinned complexion, black hair, and hazel eyes. The effect was evident in the crodoc's sudden lack of focus. She straightened and walked over to finish tying his tie.

"You were saying?"

"I . . ." He shook his head. "I do know, however, that if the gelorans are using the word *demon*, it's something we should take seriously." He took a step back and adjusted his tie, then smiled his thanks.

"Perhaps, but in Kassian, *demon* is used to replace a more vulgar term, such as *bitch*."

He cocked his head. "A female dog in heat?"

"Or a horribly nasty woman. Yes."

"Regardless, we should test her for dimensional interference."

Leilani chuckled. "With what?"

"You don't have a tool for detecting demons?"

She furrowed her brow slightly. "Wait. I think there might be a translational issue at play here." She folded her arms. "Are you saying you want to check her for an M-theory deviation?"

"That is exactly what I'm saying, I think. M-theory is multidimensional theory, yes?"

"Yes."

Just then, there came a knock on the door. They both grabbed their camouflage systems and turned them on. Their shapes adjusted into the handsome human couple. Rothar walked to the door and opened it. Outside was the chauffeur who had picked them up at the space dock.

"Good evening, my lord and lady." The man bowed deeply. As he stood, Lei noticed that he had an odd look on his face and was absently tapping his leg with his hand. "I am here to escort you downstairs."

She spoke up before Rothar could answer. "We aren't quite ready. Why don't you come in and wait?"

The man bowed his head respectfully and stepped inside. As the door closed, the room resealed, and the small crystal on the coffee table changed colors to green.

Rothar looked at Lei with a confused expression, but she merely smirked at him and walked to the chauffeur.

"Jornis?"

He grinned and extended his arm toward her. They clasped forearms, then hugged each other.

"Took you long enough." The chauffeur's voice now held a tinge of humor and was far less respectful than it had previously been.

"I expected something . . . bigger." She held her hands with the palms down and raised them above her head, suggesting the height of what Jornis actually was: a geloran.

He pointed toward Rothar. "They finally gave you a new partner?"

"Kind of. May I introduce retired general Rothar Horrison."

The chauffeur and Rothar sized each other up briefly before the man at the door nodded approvingly. "The councilwoman will want to know that tiny bit of information. She's been wondering whether the rumors were true." Turning back to Leilani, he shook his head slowly, his face growing more somber. "It's bad here." He rubbed his hands on his thighs. "Well, in the human sense, anyway."

"Yeah, I know."

"I doubt that."

"What do you mean?" Leilani was confused. "What are you doing here in disguise anyway?"

"I've been here for six years." He gestured to the floor with an open palm. "The ambassador grew concerned when a project of hers stopped communicating with her." He rolled his eyes. "You know our kind.

Sometimes it takes us a bit to realize things. She didn't notice until too late that Lord Kelly Shovalli had stopped sending his correspondence."

Lei shook her head. "The duke's name is Ferdis Steven Shovalli."

He nodded. "That's true, but his firstborn son and only legitimate heir's name is Kelly Gordon Shovalli."

Lei and Rothar looked at each other in shock.

"Are you telling me that Gremm has managed to utterly wipe her older brother's existence from every database and oracle in Kassian space?"

Jornis shrugged. "I don't know about that, but I do know that Brigitta Gremm thinks he's dead."

"And he's not?"

The man folded his arms. "No, I know he's alive, but I don't know where." Clearly annoyed, he waved an arm in a sweeping gesture around them. "The staff is very tight lipped here. And extremely compartmentalized."

"I've noticed. They're all terrified of Gremm."

He splayed his hands. "Rightly so. She literally shoots anyone she doesn't like or who argues with her."

"Are you kidding me?"

"No."

Rothar finally spoke up. "We're taking too long. We need to get moving or risk rousing suspicion."

The three of them agreed and made their way to the party.

Several hours later, Leilani was standing with Ambassador Meshana and her human interpreter. On the surface, they were talking about the economic possibilities of a treaty with the Kklikra Heiarate, but through silcomm-like communication, the three were having a separate conversation.

"It is not the place of the messari government to get involved in Kassian politics," the human translator reiterated.

"Has anyone told you that you're annoying?" Leilani snapped at the human, and she felt humor from the small messari female in the dark-gray-and-white tuxedo.

"Perhaps, but he is correct. I cannot get involved."

Leilani sighed, and her shoulders slumped as she ended the surface discussion curtly as well. Her years of silcomms had given her plenty of practice with having two conversations at once, but the messari version utterly removed her oracle, which made it more complicated. Instead, she was required to use pure telepathic communication, which she had only limited experience with.

The messari's translator was a traditionally raised human psionic and, as such, was far more experienced and educated than Lei was. Luckily, she had enough training to secure her thoughts from bleeding into the conversation, though she knew her frustration was coming through clear enough.

"Nothing?" Rothar asked as she approached him by the bar.

She shook her head. She suddenly had an overwhelming desire to visit the stables, specifically at night, and in the next few minutes. She furrowed her brow and looked around. Her gaze passed over the small gray ambassador, whom she caught nodding her large head ever so slightly toward her before fading into the crowd and out of sight.

"Well, I'll be a unicorn's tail feather."

Rothar smirked and raised an eyebrow. "Where to, my lady?"

"I think I'd like to go for a walk."

They had easily avoided the admiral all night. It was clear that the woman had no interest in a boring sector on the far edge of the empire.

Rothar held out his arm for her, as they had practiced for days, and the two of them left the party quietly.

34

SECRETS BURIED BENEATH

The handsome couple meandered through the garden, though Leilani had this nagging suspicion that she was about to miss something important in the barn. She veered Rothar in that direction suddenly.

"I'd really like to see the horses again."

The two of them strolled quickly to the large, closed barn and stepped inside the warm building. The lights were on, even though it had looked dark from the outside. A man with a backpack and a white coat stepped out from an empty stall and began to pull the coat off, neatly folding it.

Leilani cleared her throat, alerting him of their presence.

He leapt into the air and spun, his face white, then calmed as he realized he didn't recognize the two.

"I, I am . . . I'm sorry, are you lost?" he stuttered.

"No." She shook her head and walked toward him. She glanced in the empty stall, then back to the man.

He was beginning to sweat. As he stashed the white coat in his bag, Lei glimpsed some basic medical equipment among his supplies as well.

"Relax, Doctor. We aren't here to cause trouble."

He stumbled backward into Rothar, who had stepped around him without being noticed.

"Invisible mare giving birth?" She chuckled and hiked her thumb in the direction of the empty stall.

The man laughed nervously. "A stallion belongs in there, actually. He's down there." He pointed down the barn to a horse currently fastened into the cross-ties.

The stable master stepped past the stallion and into the aisle, carrying a hunting rifle that looked like it could drop a grizzly with a single shot.

Hearing a soft whoosh behind her, Leilani stepped to the side, out of easy reach of the door to the stall. When she glanced in, she now saw a heavily armored guard with a far more advanced aether weapon. In the center of his chest was a royal symbol. She pinged the guard with Sarah.

A stern male voice spoke across the silcomm. *"Identify."*

"Agent Falconi, ID number 34A5F697 Magenta."

There was a long pause. Then the guard stepped forward and opened the stall door. Looking down the hall toward the stable master, he nodded, and the other man relaxed slightly.

"Doctor, you're dismissed."

The panicked man with the backpack did everything in his power not to run from the barn.

"Agent, follow me." He waved his rifle in Rothar's direction. "With you?"

She nodded.

The two of them followed the guard into the stall and passed through the back wall, which was clearly an aether illusion. It was far too good to be a hologram. As they stepped into a small, metallic room, a door slid closed behind them. Apparently, the room was a lift of some sort, but it had no buttons or any other method of interaction.

Royal guards were notoriously quiet. This particular guard was no different. They rode the lift for a good four minutes in utter silence.

Finally, the lights brightened, and another wall opened up. In the hallway stood a man who looked like an exact duplicate of the chauffeur who had brought them there. This one, however, wasn't the geloran agent.

"Greetings, Ms. Falconi. I can honestly say that I am relieved to see you." The man's voice was tired, but his smile was genuine. "I was beginning to lose hope." He waved for them to follow him.

The facility that they were being led through was filled with royal guards. She was amazed at the sheer number of them. If she hadn't known any better, she'd have said this was a backup imperial bunker. It looked so much like the facility at Wonderland. The doors and walls had the royal seal emblazoned everywhere. The entire place was heavily decorated with artwork almost as old as the empire itself.

The man held his arm in front of him and stepped out of the way so they could precede him into the room. Outside, two royal guards snapped to attention as she passed.

"As I'm sure you've figured out by now, this is an emergency bunker used for royals. It is equipped to handle the emperor himself, but alas, we were unable to find him. We do hope that he has made it to Wonderland, at least." The man stepped into the large office after them and smiled weakly.

"Please have a seat." He walked around to the back of the large wooden desk but did not sit down. Instead, he pulled the chair safely out of the way into a nearby corner. Picking up a remote on the desk, he pointed it at the wall to their left.

Leilani turned to look just as the wall went clear. Through it, they could see into a room where a man was lying on a stiff-looking bed. His hands were folded neatly on his chest, and he was covered in a sheer cloth from head to foot.

"This, of course, is the real Duke Shovalli." The man picked up a leather portfolio and held it out toward Leilani. "And this is the autopsy report from eleven years ago."

Rothar had moved to the wall after it went clear and was studying the body carefully. "It appears he was shot."

Leilani opened the papers and scanned them. Only true royals actually wrote things down to prevent digital copies from being hacked. In fact, the art of handwriting had been lost throughout most of the empire, used only by royals and the occasional eccentric individual.

"Well, yes." The man hung his head. "But you might be interested to know that it was done at point-blank range while he was on his knees with his hands tied behind his back. Whoever did it also beat him pretty good before shooting him."

"While I appreciate this information, may I ask who you are?" Leilani folded the papers up and handed them back to him.

"I was the duke's personal aide. My name is Joshua Jefferson." He rubbed his fingertips along the edge of the pad as he talked. "Though I understand that I am now the chauffeur assigned to people Her Ladyship doesn't like."

Leilani chuckled. "I think the countess should be offended by that."

The man laughed, but Rothar just glared at her.

"Probably." He shrugged. "Six years ago, I agreed to allow the geloran agent above to take my place. It gave me time to focus here. Of course, I gave him only enough information to keep him looking. He no doubt told you that the duke's body above was a fake?"

Leilani shook her head. "Not in so many words. No."

"What made you check the barn?" His voice hardened as he focused on the obvious security breach.

"Luck."

"I don't believe in luck."

She smirked. "Neither do I."

Joshua furrowed his brow and pursed his lips. Leilani realized she wasn't going to get away with keeping her source secure. At least, not without more information. The royal guards and staff did not take security breaches lightly.

"You're not the only one in the galaxy who has concerns about the current political climate in Kass."

He looked to the side as he considered her words. "Ah." He pointed the remote to the other empty wall to their right.

It, too, went clear, but unlike the room on other side, this room was bustling with people. In the center was a large cylindrical vat. In it was a naked man floating in some sort of liquid or gel. Cables and wires protruded from all over his body. It was a full life-support and regeneration system, also called a regrowth tank.

"What's wrong with him?" Lei asked.

"Do you know who he is?"

She nodded. This was who Jornis was looking for, though she wasn't about to tell the duke's aide that. Standing, she strode to the wall and began scanning the scene for clues as to what had happened here. Finally, one of the staffers walked into view with a data pad. The naked man's vitals were 100 percent stable. The life support appeared to consist of physical and mental stimulators to prevent atrophy.

"He's in a coma." That was the only answer that fit all of the clues.

"Yes. No matter what we do, we can't wake him. I was hoping *you* could, actually."

Leilani turned and leaned her shoulder on the glass, crossing her legs. "I'm not a doctor."

The aide walked over to stand near her. "I didn't assume you were. I don't think he needs a doctor. I think he needs an aether specialist."

She furrowed her brow. "Why do you think that?"

He strode to the door and waved for them to follow him back out into the hall. "We've had every doctor we could smuggle in come look at him. There's nothing at all medically wrong with him. But our aether sensors occasionally sense minute spikes in aether energy emanating from him."

The door to the medical room opened, and the four medical staff inside turned to see who was entering. Three of them reached for weapons until the aide lifted his hands to dissuade them.

"They're agents."

One of them kept his hand on his weapon and narrowed his eyes dangerously. "What makes you think they're safe?"

"Because they went through way too much effort to avoid her." His gaze traveled upward, then back to Lei and Rothar. "We've known Gremm had an insider for some time. The first agent we contacted . . . Well, he made quite an impression on all of us. I lost nine people that day."

He shrugged and walked over to a technical display on the wall. "I was hoping that with everything going on, eventually someone would look into Gremm and end up here. Seems I was right." He pointed to the display.

Leilani stepped up to one of the security panels that monitored the firewall of the medical lab. After she'd tapped several buttons, the display asked for her credentials. She logged into it and began accessing the aether section of the technology. It would have scans that they likely couldn't read without an actual full aether on staff. A display appeared with detailed scan data, and her eyes widened before she furrowed her brow and bit the inside of her cheek.

"Is that what I think it is?" Rothar asked behind her.

"Yes."

"Fuck." It was the first time she had ever heard him use the Kassian cussword. Or any cussword, for that matter.

"I don't think this is aether tech." She looked over her shoulder for his assessment and saw him shaking his head.

"I've seen this before. If we cut it, they'll know."

Leilani ran her fingers through her hair as she considered her options.

"If we stay too long, they'll know we're here." Rothar looked to the human man next to him. "How often are the spikes?"

"They used to be about once every few months, but since the whole assassination mess, they've been about twice a week."

"When was the last one?"

"Three days ago." Leilani pointed to the detailed graph. "I have an idea."

She closed her eyes and loudly thought the name of the messari ambassador. Another mind heard her first.

"*Hello, Agent. May I ask why you are trying to link out from a secure location?*" The mind was carefully controlled and highly trained, but she could clearly feel the royal guard imprint.

"*I need a relay to a friend who can help.*" She knew the intelligence officer was checking her for the truth.

"*Please don't involve the ambassador. I will relay for you.*"

"*Thank you.*"

There was no reply, but suddenly she felt Jornis.

"*You must have found him. Is he okay?*"

"*No.*"

"*She will not be happy.*" His mind projected the image of the geloran ambassador.

"*I know. I hate to say this, but I think we need her.*"

"*She is not allowed to get directly involved.*"

Leilani opened her eyes and looked the panel over, allowing Jornis to see what she was seeing.

"*Sa falian!*" he exclaimed in his own tongue.

She knew what it meant: basically the same thing Rothar had said but far more elegant sounding.

Everyone in the room stopped moving except for Leilani. A tall, thin, blue-skinned woman shimmered slowly into view next to her.

Leilani instinctively reached for her weapon but stopped before actually touching it. Glancing back at Rothar, she grimaced. He was frozen along with the others, which shouldn't have been possible.

"How?"

The geloran was wearing a mostly see-through silk gown from one of their own planets. Her long hair hung free, which no geloran would ever let happen in their own space, but she was trying her best to be as plain as possible for the humans—if several pounds of diamonds, sapphires, and platinum could be considered plain. She clearly had come directly from the gala still happening overhead.

Ambassador Shelai smiled and lifted her finger to her lips. "Shh. I am not here, Agent. You and I both know we are not allowed to interfere in mortal matters." She walked up and placed her hand on the glass of the large tank. "However, I love this young man like my own child."

Humans were passionate and easily offended, but Ambassador Shelai was very difficult to upset, which was why she was a Kassian ambassador even though she was one of the few Maythendi Confederate council members. So when the ambassador turned a steely gaze on Leilani, Lei's skin literally crawled, immediately growing goose bumps to warn her of the impending danger. She'd seen that look only once before, and it had been as horrifying then as it was now. Thankfully, though, the emotion wasn't directed at her this time.

"When I find the creature who did this, I will punish them for centuries. When they beg my forgiveness, I will continue for another hundred before I finally end their existence." The words were dark and carried with them sheer power that actually crackled slightly in the air.

The ambassador began to drag her fingertips along the tank in intricate patterns. Her touch left a trail of pure eldrich energy across the surface of the tank. It looked like a beautiful trail of blue-and-white fire, licking at the air with soft hisses and crackling noises.

This went on for several minutes. The air grew so loud that it began to hurt. Leilani could feel the pain in her lungs as the eldrich power grew in intensity. Her skin already itched as though millions of tiny bugs were biting her all over. She contemplated pulling out a rebreather but decided against any distracting movements.

Even the tiniest distraction could cause the ritual to fail, and considering the sheer amount of power being imbued into the tank, the result would likely wipe out anything in a fifty-mile radius.

Eldrich, like electricity, was only stable in very controlled circumstances. However, eldrich was unique in one very special way. Those in very select circles could physically manipulate it with mind and body. The number of wizards, as they were called, who could manipulate it manually was very small, though according to the history books, it hadn't always been that way. The geloran ambassador, however, was from the old school, where all engineers were taught to manipulate eldrich manually first.

"Interesting." Ambassador Shelai finally spoke as she tapped the last bit of the ritual and the eldrich faded into the tank with an anticlimactic fizzle. "It is another master."

The geloran smiled happily and looked at Leilani. "I do love a challenge."

She walked around to the front of the tank and tapped the glass with her finger. The body inside twitched, and the eyes popped open. The ambassador waved for Leilani to come where the man in the tank could see her.

She did as she was bid.

"This one is with me. When you are done with her, come talk to me, my dear. In person," the woman said loudly, likely not knowing that he could hear her through the built-in microphone.

He nodded his understanding.

"When you are ready to leave, Jornis has orders to take you anywhere you need to go." The woman patted Leilani on the head like she would a pet. Lei twitched slightly but didn't move away. "Take good care of him. If he is harmed, it is you I will punish."

Leilani tried to smile but didn't quite manage it.

The woman walked around the room, then suddenly took a step backward to look intently at Rothar. When she tapped him on the shoulder, his disguise fell, and she grinned broadly.

"Little Roth. How wonderful! The rumors were true. You *are* alive," she said in Crodoc.

Leilani moved till she could see him clearly. He was frozen, but unlike the others, his eyes were still moving. He had heard all of it—likely because of his antitime protections. That meant this wasn't a time-stop spell but something different.

"You, too, must come speak with me when you are free of this mess. We have much to discuss."

He closed his eyes, but his facial expressions were frozen.

The woman lifted her hand off his shoulder, and his disguise returned. She then shimmered out of view, much as she'd shimmered in. The doctor near Leilani suddenly stepped directly into her as everyone started moving.

"What the . . . ?" the woman said.

But then a male voice filled the room with its excitement. "He's awake!"

35

EVACUATIONS

Leilani and Rothar stepped out of the way as the staff leapt into action. Oddly, they weren't missed as they slipped back into the office.

"Gremm is going to notice when we don't return to our rooms." Rothar was sitting in one of the two chairs facing the desk.

Lei, however, was leaning against the desk, facing him and the door. With the sudden activation of a royal, she had lost her access even to the psi officer who had been relaying for her. They were stuck until things calmed down.

The door opened, and a person appeared in the frame. Leilani chuckled—not because someone was walking in, but because they had used the IIS trick of literally appearing in the doorway when the door was fully open. The cameras would see them walking into the room but never up to the doorway itself. It was a traditional tactic used to fool less attentive security officers. Considering the state of the facility, it might work, but then again, it might set off the heightened security. They would find out either way soon enough.

The gentleman walking into the room looked like Joshua Jefferson but was, in fact, Jornis.

She smirked at him. "You come to tell us how we're getting out of this mess?"

Rothar glanced over his shoulder and nodded to the human.

"I would never presume to tell you what to do, Lei." Jornis smiled brightly and flopped into the chair next to Rothar.

"Well, that would be a first." She shook her head.

He merely chuckled.

Rothar seemed slightly confused, but then, he hadn't seen the way the man entered.

"Jornis." Her voice was flat, letting him know that now wasn't the time.

The use of the name gave Rothar all the clarity he needed, and he relaxed in his chair.

"Sorry, Lei. I made arrangements for duplicates of you two to go back to your rooms, where you will no doubt do what couples do, pack, then leave the same way you came." He shrugged. "Your Kassian sensors are primitive, to say the least. They won't notice the golems."

"I can do without the insults."

"What insults?"

Leilani rolled her eyes, then shifted her attention to Rothar. "So that just leaves this mess. I know from experience that they have multiple evac plans. They will be able to get everyone out without Gremm noticing." She furrowed her brow and turned back to the geloran. "Why are *you* here?"

He rubbed his hands together happily, as if she had finally figured out his little puzzle. "Ah, there you go."

Leilani took a deep breath. Jornis and his mistress had been assets to the empire, even friends, but they required a lot of patience. They never truly intended offense; they just never really saw Kass as an equal.

"The councilwoman has offered you the use of myself and a vessel." He reached into a bag at his side and handed her a Kassian pad. "I intercepted this. The method of communication set off our alarms, so naturally, we monitored it. Honestly, we're very impressed with this.

It's almost enough to improve your standing, but then, the technology has a long way to go before the council will even consider upgrading your status above primitive."

Leilani ignored most of what he said, but she took the pad and skimmed it.

"They found the unicorn. They need assistance with evac."

Rothar nodded. "It was only a matter of time before they found him."

She turned to Jornis just as the door opened and several royal aether guards poured into the room, weapons at the ready.

"We're going to need that ride." She looked up at the guards and chuckled. It had taken them longer than she'd expected. "Hello, boys."

She raised both hands but spread her feet as she prepped to move.

Before she could do anything, however, another person walked into the room from between the guards. "Stand down, everyone." The man was incredibly handsome—almost more so with clothing on. Of course, it could have had something to do with the lack of tubes sticking out of him.

"Your Grace." She stood all the way and bowed slightly, but the two in chairs remained seated. "How can we help you?"

"Let's start with information. I've been somewhat briefed about my little sister and father." He walked around the room to the desk, much to his security's distress.

After pulling the chair back over to its place, he sat down and began shuffling through the data stacked neatly on the desk. Finally, he slid all of it aside and steepled his fingers. "Relax, Agent. Why don't you introduce me to these two."

Lei had turned to face him as he walked around the desk, which put her back to the guards—a literally painful move. She could feel the muscles in her back complaining at putting a threat behind her. She gestured, palm up, to Rothar first. "This is Agent Rothar Horrison. My partner."

The duke nodded to the seeming human sitting in the chair and still disguised as the count.

"And this is . . ." She contemplated how to explain Jornis. "A personal friend who was bringing me some intelligence."

"A friend?" Jornis replied sarcastically.

She didn't need to look at him to know he was grinning like an idiot.

"I'm a friendly agent who has been given to the IIS on loan until this matter is sorted out, Your Grace, due to the councilwoman's personal interest in keeping you alive and well." He chuckled. "And preferably off your imperial throne, if at all possible."

The new duke took a deep breath and tapped his steepled fingers against his lips. "Ah. I see." Turning his attention back to Leilani, he tried to pretend the last statement hadn't been said. "And what information about my cousin, Agent?"

"The IIS has no comment at this time as to the status of the emperor."

"Is he at least alive? Or do I need to begin preparations for assuming the throne?" His response was stern.

"Last I checked, yes, he was alive."

"Very well. It's my understanding that you are investigating my sister?"

"Yes."

"If it helps, she was the one who shot my father and me eleven years ago. Though she wasn't alone at the time. There was a man with her. He never got close, merely talked quietly to her the whole time. We were out at the lakeside. He stayed about thirty feet away under a nearby tree. He wore some kind of cloak with a hood masking his face. Very antiquated, but effective.

"I was never able to see him clearly. His voice, though, made my skin crawl, and since this was only yesterday for me, it might affect my dreams for a few years to come." The man rubbed his arms briskly. "Brigitta seemed to be following his orders. It was strange. She kept calling him 'Father,' which I'm not sure I understand."

"Thank you, sir. That helps." She needed to get moving, meaning she needed to hand this part of the investigation off to someone else. That left her with only one person.

The empire was not a fragile entity, but it did have strict rules to ensure stability. Only the immediate royal family was allowed to know about aether, which left the more extended lines, such as the Shovalli line, out of the informational loop. In the current situation, however, someone higher than her pay grade needed to be around to make decisions.

"There's a naval ship in orbit called the IKS *Hoganmeyer*. You and your people need to rendezvous with that ship as soon as possible. It is a royal-cleared vessel, though it might be tight quarters. You need to stay with them until we get this investigation straightened out. Admiral Gremm has most of the navy working for her. If they find out you're alive and now above her in the line of succession, this will get ugly very fast." She watched him to make sure he understood what she wanted.

"Very well. I will take only a few of my people and will go to this vessel. I understand that you need to get going, Agent. But I would like to say one more thing before you leave."

She folded her hands behind her back, waiting.

"Thank you. And please keep my cousin alive. I have no desire to be emperor."

Her face softened, and she smiled at him. Before she could speak, however, the office faded around her.

—⌇—

They became corporeal again aboard the geloran ship. She spun and glared at Jornis, who was now ten feet tall with black hair and dark-blue skin. "You do realize you just had us vanish in front of a noble who knows nothing about the aether?"

He smiled brightly, showing white teeth that stood out in bright contrast to his darker skin.

"That was simply technology, Agent. You need to relax. Besides, it's been used on him dozens of times. The man is well versed in geloran tech."

"Why?" Her voice was pitched lower than usual. Foreign interest in a royal would have to get reported. Eventually.

"That is not for me to explain. I would not dare to speak for a council member." He pointed to the hatch in the distance.

A female geloran in a military uniform was at the control console. She ignored the humans, almost pretending as if they didn't exist—something that would be the case all throughout the ship. To acknowledge the presence of a lesser species aboard one of the geloran council's military vessels would, by law, require sterilization . . . which was a polite way of saying elimination of the vermin. In the past, various geloran captains had simply refused to log the presence of the lesser species—a rather ingenious method of circumventing the archaic law.

"Agent?" Sarah had been quiet ever since the incident in the mine, but Leilani had been too busy to talk to her oracle about it.

"Go ahead."

"You are receiving a communication from BB."

"Put him through."

"Hey, Lei. Dorthy said he has his package en route. Your package, however, is getting tossed around pretty hard right now."

"Are you in contact with my package?"

"Yes."

"How?" She couldn't help but wonder how her best friend had managed to communicate with Wonderland. It was designed specifically for that to be impossible.

"Actually, Melissa did it. While you were there, she took one of your PGs and made a comm unit for him."

Leilani actually grinned as they walked through the ship. *"Give her a hug for me. And patch him through, if you can?"*

"It doesn't really work quite like that, but we can give you voice."

"Maxwell here."

"This is Falconi. What is your status?"

"We had to evacuate Wonderland. We are pinned down in a small medical facility on Gomashri. It's bad, Agent. I'm not sure how long we can

last. *Most of my people are injured. Some of them seriously. There's some sort of creature here destroying everything in its path using tech we've never seen before.*"

Leilani frowned. "*Does it look like a humanoid lion with wings?*"

"*How'd you know that?*"

"Unicorn is pinned down by a crashilor," she said out loud.

It was enough to stop the geloran in his tracks. He spun and looked down at her in shock.

"What?" His usually cheerful expression fell to become serious. "Please tell me you're kidding."

"No."

Jornis turned and began to sprint through the passageway. As he did, the lights on the vessel changed to red, and a siren began to sound. Leilani bolted after him, having to work hard to keep up with his much longer stride.

"*Shoo fa!*" he yelled, and several people up ahead leapt to the bulkheads to move out of his way. They then also turned and ran to their own duty stations.

"*Agent?*" the commodore's voice called through her silcomms.

"*Stay alive, Maxwell. We're on the way! Unicorn?*"

"*Alive.*" She heard weapons fire over the comm. "*For now.*"

"*Roger that.*"

"*ETA?*"

"*Unknown. I'll keep you posted if I can.*"

"*Roger.*" Over the comm, she could hear the firing of weapons grow louder and the creature roar.

"*Leilani?*" It was the young engineer.

"*Yeah, Melissa?*"

"*Please save him. I like him.*"

Leilani chuckled. "*Most of us do, kiddo.*"

The trio ran through the hatch onto the bridge just in time to see the stars sprinkled across the black abyss of space fade from existence.

"Hello again, Agent Falconi. Welcome aboard." The tall female geloran in a military captain's uniform nodded at her. It was the first time the creature had even acknowledged that Leilani existed, let alone talked to her. "I need a destination."

"Makiel," Rothar answered from behind her.

Leilani spun to glare at him.

He held up a hand, palm toward her. "Trust me. I may be new to all of this, but as the tactician of the team, I know we need more than just the two of us."

The captain of the ship pointed to another geloran, who began plotting the course, then turned back to them. "We can help with the crashilor, but we're not allowed to interfere outside of that." She crossed her arms and looked to the tall agent next to the two humans. "Go get suited up. This one is just a scout. You should be able to handle it. Try not to damage too much."

He saluted her by placing his fist on his chest, then turned to jog off the bridge.

"You two will be my guests." She nodded to the general. "It's about time you got a real partner, Agent. General, it's a pleasure to meet you. Welcome aboard the Council Ship *Starlight*. My name is Captain Fae'ael Jemmarial."

"As in Torvis Jemmarial?" he asked, clearly surprised.

"My grandfather, yes. He will be pleased to know you're alive, sir."

"Grandfather?" Rothar's voice rose slightly.

"Yes. Much has happened while you slept, sir. But I'm sure that will be a discussion for a later date. We're here."

A floating planet snapped into view on the table in front of her. Leilani stared at it with her brows furrowed in confusion. She knew that smugglers used ships in aether space, but she had never really understood how. Now it appeared that the gelorans could also move between aether and kuldain space in ships.

"Bring up frequency 291-0546," Rothar called to the comms station.

The geloran looked to the captain for permission, but she simply nodded.

"Hailing 291-0546. We have an acknowledgment."

He gestured to the display of the planet. "Put it on the table."

An image appeared of a female crodoc in uniform. The woman snapped to attention when she saw Rothar.

"General?"

"Get me Thoris."

The crodoc saluted, then ran off-screen.

A large, familiar male crodoc stepped into the camera, his eyes sunken and with dark bags under them. "What do you want, Roth? We're kind of busy."

"I know, Helr. I need as many marines as you can spare."

The other male shook his head. "I've got nothing *to* spare."

President Mai Lenali stepped into view next to the crodoc. She also appeared exhausted, but makeup covered the bags under her eyes. She smiled warmly to the two agents, but as her gaze traveled to the geloran captain standing next to them, she arched an eyebrow high on her forehead.

"Is that a geloran in a military uniform?" Her voice was pitched slightly higher than usual.

"Yes, Madam President." Rothar nodded curtly.

A slow, sly smile spread across Mai's face.

"I'll give you Seef'aini troops if we can get geloran assistance." She turned her attention to the captain. "I invoke the Treaty of Stazz'na."

The captain's eyebrow raised as she glanced to the side. A male geloran nearby seemed to be looking for something on his display. Then he tapped the alternate-reality interface and tossed it toward her. Captain Jemmarial rubbed her hands together as a similar smirk spread across her face.

"That is perfectly acceptable to us, Madam President. I will check with my council, but I highly doubt they will decline the treaty. I do need to officially ask, however. Are you claiming that the Seef'aini government is intact and intends to reclaim aether space, as per the Agreement of Gefshoo?"

"We are, but right now, we are dealing with a heavy terrorist resistance. Not to mention an increase in attacks by a species cataloged as crashilor. We believe the two are linked."

"Understood. I have relayed this to the council, and they are rerouting military assistance. Until then, how may the CS *Starlight* assist you, Madam President?"

Thoris locked eyes with Rothar and mouthed a thank-you.

36

LOST UNICORNS

Leilani looked from one massive crodoc to the other. Up to this point, the meeting had gone smoothly. There had been no arguments, not even a disagreement as they discussed plans on both sides. Thankfully, the president hadn't come. The geloran ship had dropped Lei, Rothar, and Jornis off on-world while the rest of them escorted Mai to a meeting with a neutral city-state leader.

"I've given you a single Seef'aini platoon," said Thoris. "That should be enough to deal with the fighting in Gomashri. Our intelligence indicates that the resistance forces there are scattered and disorganized. They shouldn't be too much of a threat."

"Thank you, General." Rothar nodded to his successor. "That should be plenty."

"Honestly, I should be thanking you. None of this would be possible without you, and while it may not be pleasant at the moment, it's better than the alternative."

Both men nodded and clasped forearms, then patted each other on the back in a combat hug.

Leilani moved off to stand next to a geloran clad entirely in powered armor. On his back was a rather nasty-looking serrated sword. In his hands was the traditional energy weapon used by the ground troops. The armor gave him easily three more feet in height and almost doubled his overall mass. In truth, it was a horrifying visual, but his presence was more comfortable than standing between the two crodocs.

"I even managed to get you all a ride." Thoris swung his hand, palm up, toward a tall, winged person in a familiar uniform as they strode into the room and bowed to everyone.

It was unclear whether the officer was male or female, since the simple, single-color uniform carefully concealed the subtle differences between the sexes. Likely, that was by design.

"I am Captain Sai Gelleri. I have hereby been ordered by the Hodair to give transportation to agents Leilani Falconi and Rothar Horrison for so long as they should need during this conflict. It is important to note, for the purpose of our records, that we may not engage in combat. We are authorized for transportation only." He bowed his head politely to Leilani. "We have enough room for one thousand mortals." He shook his head vigorously. "I do not believe that translation is accurate. Humans?"

The geloran next to Lei laughed, a disturbing sound coming from the speakers in the suit. "That's better than what we call them."

The igranu bowed its head and shoulders in agreement. "That is because we are far more polite and respectful to the younger species." Its pleasant expression drooped slightly into what appeared to be a frown. "We all start someplace. And your people often forget this fact." The accented Kassian was not hard to understand, but translating was clearly difficult for him.

"Touché." Jornis chuckled again. "Though I am not sure that's the real reason," he mumbled to himself.

"We're on a timetable," Rothar stated firmly. "We have people currently trying to stay alive, waiting for us to give them backup."

"Understood." The winged captain bowed. "We stand ready. The Seef'aini troops are already aboard."

The conference room faded. At the other end of the transport, a lavender-winged igranu, also in uniform, stepped up and handed the captain a pad. He skimmed it and tapped near the bottom.

"Make way," he said in Kassian.

"ETA three minutes." The igranu bowed her head and shoulders, then stepped out.

Around her, a platoon of crodoc marines began checking their weapons. Rothar walked over and began talking to the commander of the unit. Leilani didn't really know the Seef'aini ranks, but the other crodoc was likely a lieutenant or some such. She and Jornis, on the other hand, didn't move. The plan was that the two of them would go down first. They were the only two with the actual training, equipment, and experience to deal with the crashilor quickly.

She would be the bait. When they were done, the marines would flood the area. Then they would evac the unicorn and head to the next point.

"Transport in sixty seconds." The winged person at the console tapped several AR buttons, not even looking up.

Across the room, Rothar held up a reassuring fist. *"Good luck,"* he said across the silcomms.

She nodded and pulled her sidearm.

"Thirty seconds. The area is hot. I see forty combatants, not including the target."

Leilani took a deep breath, rolling the small yellow time-stop grenade between the fingers of her left hand.

The ship and people around her faded from view, and the quiet chatter was replaced with the roar of gunfire and the scream of a very large and very angry crashilor. Luckily, the teleporter tech had put her about ten feet from the creature, facing its back.

"Roarish ne falitha!" she roared through the sound amplifier in her jacket.

Jornis had taught her how to taunt the maned scout in its own language.

When the crashilor spun on her, she was slightly shocked at the sheer rage in its eyes. She couldn't help but wonder what Jornis had told her to say. Whatever it meant, it'd worked. She threw the ball high up into the air. As it popped and the dust scattered wide over the combat area, she leapt to the side, rolled, and came up alongside a large troll in makeshift armor. It appeared to have been made out of metal street signs over a cardboard backing.

She fired her weapon at the troll's head, then leapt again as the crashilor roared so loudly she could feel it in her bones. As it charged after her, she couldn't help but chuckle. The time-stop powder hadn't been for him. Crashilors had technology that protected them from time altering. She'd simply needed him to focus on her exclusively so she could get him into position for Jornis.

In the distance, Jornis's weapon let out a high-pitched whine as it spun up. Thankfully, the black-maned creature was too focused on ripping her to shreds to notice. Their plan had worked. The geloran weapon was extremely powerful, but to make the shot, Jornis needed to get through the scout's armor, which meant he needed time to charge it. They'd only get one shot.

A ball of plasma from the enormous cat creature's weapon roared overhead as she dove into the crowd of rebels again. The rebels simply ceased to exist where the ball passed through them, leaving cauterized body parts to fall bloodlessly to the floor. She could feel the heat on her back as she quickly pulled her feet back under her and began running. A display in her HUD flashed a warning that she couldn't take a direct hit from that weapon.

"Agent . . ."

"I know!" Diving again, she barely dodged another ball of plasma. It slammed into a nearby shop, utterly destroying the entire front and burning a rather nasty hole deep into it. She hoped the bystanders had evacuated already.

"Jornis!" she hollered.

A beam of plasma leapt out from between the two buildings where Jornis had been transported. It slammed into the seam of the winged lion's chest plate under its right arm, burning a hole directly through. It screamed loudly and fell to its knees.

As it did, Leilani leapt to her feet and fired several explosive rounds with both pistols. The rounds tore through the hole that Jornis had already made in the armor, exploding on impact and knocking the crashilor to the ground with another scream of pain.

People nearby were starting to come out of the effects of her time stop. She glanced around and realized she was standing in the middle of the enemy. *This might hurt.*

As if on cue—which it likely was—Seef'aini soldiers materialized throughout the battlefield. Shots rang out as they began to open fire, clearing the area of any remaining rebels within seconds.

Leilani diverted her focus to the two rebels in front of her and fired without waiting to see what they would do. She didn't have time to see if they would surrender. Less than thirty seconds later, it grew quiet.

"Ma'am, I am detecting Colonel Maxwell nearby, but he is not responding to communications."

Leilani turned toward where Sarah was indicating and took off at a run. She could hear at least one set of footsteps behind her—likely more.

"Maxwell?" she shouted as she vaulted over an improvised barrier. Luckily, she caught sight of the body on the other side while she was still in the air and was able to adjust her trajectory to miss him.

"Here," a female voice answered.

Lei looked and saw the woman who had taken Melissa for food back at Wonderland.

"Lieutenant?"

The woman nodded but didn't look up from where she was giving chest compressions.

Leilani stepped up to the commodore and saw that he had several large holes through his armor. They didn't look like crashilor damage. She put her fingers on the man's neck and checked his pulse. There was none. Putting her hand on the lieutenant's shoulder, she shook her head.

"Stop, Harrison," she said softly. "Where is the unicorn?"

The lieutenant's eyes teared up, and she gestured inside with her head.

Leilani stood and strode into the warehouse. The area just inside the door was littered with injured. One of them lifted his gun and tried to point it toward her.

She put her hands up in surrender to help him relax. "Easy, Gunny."

He was missing a leg, the wound already cauterized. Now, that was likely from the crashilor. Most of the injuries in here, though, were not from an energy weapon but rather from the local slug throwers.

As she scanned the area, her gaze landed on three people currently working on someone on the floor. The doctor, at least, was alive; the others looked like some young female aide and a marine corporal who was bleeding everywhere himself.

"Area secure," Rothar said on the silcomm.

"Roger. We need medical assistance as soon as possible. This is really bad."

"Roger."

Leilani wove quickly through the bodies toward the field surgery in progress. As she glanced down at the person being operated on, she was relieved to see it wasn't the emperor. That meant, though, that he was still missing.

As she approached, the bleeding corporal snatched a pistol off the ground next to him and held it toward her in a bloody hand. She smiled as she recognized his face.

"I have the package," she called across the silcomms.

"Roger that," Horrison replied.

"Easy. Corporal?" Her second word carried a hint of humor, but she resisted the urge to laugh. The man in the marine armor relaxed, the pistol falling to the ground next to him again.

"What took you so long?" he spat.

"Sorry. We were in Messarin Sector." She shrugged. "I got here as soon as I could manage."

He clenched his jaw.

"Want me to take that?" She pointed to his hand, which was buried inside the injured man's chest. He appeared to be acting as a rib spreader for the doctor. "You look injured. I have a medic inbound."

She pointed over her shoulder to the door just as several crodoc soldiers poured through. The reaction from the wounded Kassian soldiers was not friendly; the gunny actually fired at them. He missed, however, and managed to shoot a hole in the ceiling.

"Stand down!" the man next to her bellowed loudly.

Not that it was really needed. The kick from the shot had been enough to injure the gunnery sergeant even further, and he fell unconscious. The few other conscious marines who had been trying to reach for weapons, however, paused at the order.

"Easy, sir." Lei put her hand on his shoulder firmly enough that he could feel it through his armor.

Several crodocs bearing bags clearly marked with blue crosses moved through the room, doing triage as they went.

Leilani beckoned to two of them. As they came over, one of them assessed the surgery and carefully stepped in to take the emperor's place. As the second medic helped her pull the emperor away, he struggled to stand, and Leilani realized that the only reason he was even conscious was sheer force of will.

"You'll be okay, sir. I need you to rest," she said as he weakly fought being laid down. The corporal's uniform was covered in both dried and fresh blood, and she couldn't help but wonder how much of it was his own.

He looked at her, tears in his eyes. She had expected some smart-ass response, but even in his position, he had likely never seen this much death. Especially the deaths of people he knew and trusted. It would change him. It always did, no matter how well trained a soldier was.

He reached out and took her hand, squeezing it as the medic put him to sleep. When his grip finally loosened and fell away, she looked across to the medic.

"Sergeant?"

The crodoc looked up at her.

"Don't make me a liar."

He chuckled and shook his head. "He'll be fine, ma'am. The damage is minor. He's just lost a lot of blood."

All around her, medics and even full-blown doctors of various races were beginning to go through the injured. The warehouse turned into a temporary hospital and surgery center. The lone human doctor was now on a table of her own, being operated on.

Someone stepped up next to Lei, but she recognized the movement and didn't look toward him.

"They lost twenty-three of a forty-one-man team." Rothar handed her a local aether tablet. "But you'll want to see this."

It was a recording of the initial attack on the Kassian royal guard, taken from an odd angle. In the video, a team dressed mostly like Seef'aini marines moved in carefully and took up positions. When it started, the fire was concentrated and simultaneous. The shooters knew exactly who their targets were. The four royal guards dropped first, then the man in imperial armor who had been between them—obviously a double.

"This was an assassination attempt." Her gaze lifted to Rothar, anger and confusion beginning to set in.

He nodded and pointed to the pad.

"Keep watching."

She returned her gaze to the video as the person holding the camera moved in short, quick bursts to get closer to the attackers.

"We got him. Why are we still here?" a young crodoc asked a person entirely enclosed in Seef'aini military armor.

"Standard protocol. We kill them all just in case that was a double."

The person's accent turned Lei's face a deeper shade of red as her anger welled up. That wasn't a crodoc. That was a Kassian in Seef'aini armor.

"I'm not sure I want to kill everyone just because you're paranoid," the kid grumbled.

The man in the armor turned his weapon on the kid and shot him, then turned back to his target.

The camera got a small spray of blood on the lens, and the operator quickly darted away from the marine. Whoever was managing the camera was insane. Leilani actually grimaced as the cameraperson slid deeper into enemy territory. Toward the back, they found two people talking quietly. These two, also wearing Seef'aini marine uniforms, were not speaking crodoc, however.

"Are you sure it was a miss?" a female voice asked in Kassian.

"Positive." The male tapped a pad. "I'm still seeing his beacon."

Leilani looked up at Rothar, her fingers so tight on the pad that her knuckles were white. The only people who had the frequency of the emperor's location beacon were IIS.

"Are you sure that isn't some sort of spoof?"

"Why would they spoof that?"

"I don't know, but we can't stay here much longer. We're going to get caught."

"By who? Gremm took care of anyone who might come to his rescue."

The female reached up and smacked him on the helmet. "You know you aren't supposed to say her name out loud."

He laughed. "Who's going to . . . ?"

There was a loud pop and a roar. The two soldiers turned toward the sound, as did the camera. The crashilor had literally appeared in the middle of the firefight.

The rest of the video consisted of the cameraperson darting and diving for cover repeatedly as the creature began to fire into the pretend crodoc soldiers.

"Whoever this was"—Leilani paused the footage and looked up at her partner—"please tell me they're alive so I can thank them?"

Rothar smiled. "He is. In fact, he asked for you by name."

She shook her head, confused. "How?"

The crodoc shrugged. "No idea. He's outside waiting for you. He brought me the footage and asked me to give it to you. Said you paid well for info."

Leilani followed him outside. A defensible perimeter had been set up by the real crodoc marines. Outside of that was a second perimeter set up by what looked to be locals with weapons, all of them looking outward. There was also a large group of individuals circled around a smaller person.

As Rothar led her in that direction, the group moved off, obviously having gotten their orders. When they'd cleared, she could see a familiar-looking dwarf. Gordon Markes grinned up at her through his bushy beard. Next to him stood a small black imp.

Max flapped his wings, hopped up on the shoulder of a nearby elar, and waved at her.

Lei chuckled. "Well, I'll be damned."

"You *know* it?" Rothar asked.

"Don't be rude." She hit him on the arm and grinned as she approached the other two. "Heya, Max. Gordon. What are you two doing here?"

The dwarf shifted his feet, then suddenly stood firm and folded his arms. "I couldna hide in mah hole fereva." He shrugged. "You kinna made tha clear." He gestured to the imp next to him. "When tha shit hit tha fan, I came up an foun this thief and his li'l gang."

Max sat up proudly and crossed his arms.

"So I took advantage of 'em. And their tiny size." The dwarf gestured to several electronic devices on the table in front of him. "I asked mahself wha Elaris woulda done. I came ta realize tha even if I didna agree with his job, he loved his unicorn. So I decided ta help." He gestured to the warehouse.

"I started trackin' 'im. When I saw the others usin' another tracker tha Elaris made, I spoofed it. I kept makin' the thing jump around. It didna stop 'em for long." He shrugged. "But it was long enough."

She looked to Max. "And I'm guessing you caught that amazing footage?"

The imp grinned happily. "Yep."

"Good job. You'll end up wealthy in no time at this rate. Where's Masha?"

The imp frowned but didn't answer.

"The war's been rough." The dwarf shrugged. "The rebels are killin' everythin' in their path, kids or anythin' else. It's bad. It ain' right."

Leilani rubbed her hands on her face, then allowed them to drop to her sides.

"You in charge of these people?" She gestured around.

The dwarf nodded. "They's locals wantin' to prove tha' not everyone's goin' crazy. Some of us are just good people tryin' ta survive."

One of the crodoc medics walked up and tapped her on the arm.

"Ma'am, he wants to talk to you."

She nodded and pulled a small pouch from her bag. She tossed it to the imp. "Don't use it all in one place." She chuckled as he almost fell off the elar's shoulder under the weight of the bag. "And Gordon, wait here. I'll see if we can evac you as well."

The dwarf shook his head. "No. Mah place is here, tryin' ta help these people. Elaris was in love with 'is unicorn. I did muh part an gave 'im a chance ta survive till 'elp coulda come. Now I'm gonna 'elp 'ere."

"Understood." She found a slightly larger pouch in her bag and tossed it on the table. "For you and your people. Make sure everyone gets supplies and food."

The dwarf nodded his understanding, and she turned to follow the medic.

37

PAINFUL
LESSONS IN LIFE

"I understand, sir, but you're mistaking me for someone who gives a damn." Leilani balled her fists at her side, then relaxed them as she tried to calm down.

"Damn it, Leilani. This isn't a request. It's an order." The emperor, still refusing to rest, yanked against the restraints that held him to his bed.

Rothar smirked at her from just outside of the emperor's view.

"Let me up!" the man bellowed, then grunted in pain as he injured himself yet again.

She glanced over to the medical officer standing next to Rothar. The woman was the only original staff member the emperor had left who was willing to come in the room with him.

"You two are dismissed. Rothar, keep the gunny out of here, no matter what you hear. I won't kill him." She waved her hand to indicate the emperor. "I promise. Though, stay nearby, doc, just in case."

The woman looked horrified, but even she was at her wit's end.

"Come on." Rothar pulled the exhausted woman out of the room.

Leilani locked the hatch from the inside, using her own security code so that no one could override it. Then she walked into the middle of the room and pulled a knife from her boot.

The emperor narrowed his eyes as he watched her approach. "You wouldn't dare."

Instead of just releasing him, she cut his bindings and took a step backward. "You want up? Fine," she stated flatly. "You want out of this room, though, you go through me." She turned her back on him and, making her way to the small kitchenette area, began to pour herself a cup of coffee.

She had been awake for more than forty-eight hours at this point, and she was beyond exhausted. They would reach their destination in another five hours. While the ship had the ability to move more rapidly in emergencies, it was a massive strain on the engines; she and the captain had agreed that their next destination wasn't that dire.

Steven Sargeras shuffled to the hatch and tried to open it. It buzzed softly, alerting him to the lock.

"Agent Falconi, you will let me out of this room this instant."

"Nope." She leaned back against the counter and sipped her coffee.

"How dare you refuse a direct order!" he growled at her.

She didn't even look up from her coffee. That was something she loved about this particular ship: the food was amazing and tasted exactly how she wanted it to, no matter what she ordered. The printers were well beyond anything aethers *or* Kassians had.

The man stormed over to her with a slight limp. Yep, he had definitely hurt himself again. If he didn't rest, the nanites were never going to be able to finish the repairs, and he was going to keep hurting himself over and over. But in his anger at losing everyone and everything, he didn't care.

The coffee went flying from her hands, and she glanced up at him with one eyebrow raised.

"You will look at me when I talk to you!" Even as he shouted, he grimaced in pain.

Without saying a word, she turned her back on him and poured herself another cup of coffee. As she turned back around, he took a swing at the new cup. This time, she blocked the blow and took a drink.

He stood still briefly, stunned by her action. Odds were that no one had ever raised a hand to him. He shook himself and focused all of his rage on her. One of the fascinating things about royal nobles was that while they had martial training just in case, they never truly fought anyone. Emperor Steven Sargeras was no different. He swung at her several times with practiced moves, but she blocked each one. On the third swing, she lost her coffee cup again. This time, she was annoyed.

The man continued to swing and kick at her, adrenaline covering up his pain. She simply kept blocking, allowing him to vent his frustration.

"I will have you executed for this!" He picked up a chair to throw at her.

She parried the metal chair and wondered how much he had damaged himself by trying to throw it. It crashed loudly into the coffee pot, shattering the glass and spilling the precious liquid all over the counter and deck. She felt her annoyance growing and resisted the urge to punch the man. As her attention returned to him, she saw him snatch up a knife.

Her shoulders slumped slightly. He had to be kidding. This temper tantrum was getting out of control. She still said nothing, however, as he advanced on her.

He swung with the knife, and she dodged, stepping into his bubble. She punched him lightly in the face, bloodying his nose.

He took a step back and wiped his face. The sight of his own blood drew him to a dark place. She could see it in his eyes; he was now planning to kill her. He lunged into her parry, and she punched him again, this time slightly harder.

"You lost almost everyone today," she finally said. "How far are you willing to take this?"

He swung at her again with the knife, then managed to connect a kick into her side. His hatred was now fully directed at her. "I'll kill you myself for striking your emperor."

"That's not how this works." She dodged as he swung at her again. Stepping around him, she punched him in the kidneys.

He stumbled forward.

"The moment you picked up a weapon, you stopped being my emperor and became one animal attacking another." Her voice was calm, and she kept her hands in front of her with the palms open.

He turned, but he was moving more slowly now.

"You're angry." She began shifting her weight to her back leg as he readied himself again. "And you have every right to be. You've been shot several times now. You've had to sit by and watch your friends and family die around you. You may even have lost your crown. It feels like your entire existence is unraveling." She took a step back and dropped her hands to her sides. She was out of easy range, but if this was going to stop, she would need to be the one who submitted. "I know how that feels," she added quietly.

His gaze flickered as he realized that she was referring to what he had done to her after the Kamorian incident.

"How you recover from this is up to you. You can give in to the hate and kill everyone around you, or you can learn from it and grow into a stronger person." She tapped herself on the chest. "Trust me, you don't want to go down that first path. You lose part of who you are in the process."

The man looked down at the knife in his hand, then back up at her. "I'm sorry."

Leilani stepped forward and held out her hand for the knife. "I wasn't aware you knew how to put those words in that order."

He dropped it in her hand and scowled. "Smart-ass."

"It's a coping mechanism. I don't recommend it." She shook her head and moved to put the knife in the sink. "It's not worth the trouble."

He chuckled, then flinched in pain. "I think I need to lie down."

"Astute observation, sir." She put his arm around her shoulders and helped him to the bed.

"Leilani?"

"Yes, sir?" She fluffed the pillows behind his back so he could sit up.

"I really am sorry. For all of it."

She gave him a weak smile. "You did what you thought was best, sir. We all have our places in life." She'd had years to contemplate what had happened to her after the Kamorian incident. She hadn't deserved it, but someone had had to take the fall to preserve the peace. She still didn't like his decision, but after several years of contemplation, she understood it. "And I don't envy yours, sir."

"Nor I yours." He grimaced. "I think I could use my doctor now."

"I'll let her in, but might I recommend that you apologize to her as well. You've been a real jackass."

He nodded, but his jaw was clenched against the pain as the last of the adrenaline began to wear off.

Leilani walked over and unlocked the hatch. When it slid open, she found a gun barrel in her face. Lifting both hands, she backed away, and the doctor rushed past her into the room.

"Easy, Gunny." She backed up to where he indicated and stood quietly as the gunnery sergeant looked toward the emperor.

"Give me one good reason why I shouldn't put a hole right through your skull?" the man growled at her.

"Because I would be very annoyed," a weak voice called from the bed.

The gunny's attention wavered, and Leilani glanced past him to the hatchway. Rothar was lying unconscious on the deck, and she was fairly sure she could see blood pooling beneath him.

The gunnery sergeant frowned at the man in the bed. "Your Imperial Majesty?"

"Leave the agent be. We were simply talking."

The man's gun lowered somewhat, but she didn't wait to see what he would do if she left. She ran past him to the crodoc's side. When she checked for a pulse, she found one, thankfully, but it was weak.

"I need a medic and three guards to the emperor's quarters," she called across the Seef'aini silcomms. *"I have a man down."*

"Roger that," the officer in charge of the Seef'aini marines answered.

"Roth. C'mon, big guy. I need you to wake up." She patted him on the face roughly, trying to shock him awake. "Damn it, General! You really want the history books to read 'war hero taken out by a lone human'?"

The crodoc stirred slightly, and his eyes opened. He tried to smile at her, but it rapidly turned into a grimace.

A female igranu medic showed up behind her and pushed her out of the way. The medic set a crystalline object on her partner's chest, and several tiny, metallic threads leapt from it and buried themselves into his chest cavity.

"I need you to back off, Agent," the medic said to her.

Leilani moved away and watched as her partner was lifted onto a floating gurney and rushed down the hall toward the ship's medical.

One of the several Seef'aini marines drew her attention. "You asked for us?"

She nodded and pointed to the hatch.

"No one comes or goes." Her eyes narrowed dangerously. "No one!"

The marine smiled, baring slightly sharper lower canines.

"Our pleasure, ma'am."

"And put guards on the rest of the Kassian marines as well. I don't want them leaving their locations."

His grin grew, and he gave her the chest-pounding Seef'aini salute.

Leilani turned and stormed off. She knew better than to go back in and check on the emperor. Unlike him, she was a trained killer. She was likely to do something stupid.

Leilani walked onto the bridge of the large igranu vessel. The presence of so many of the beautiful winged creatures made her shake her head. She had to wonder what they considered attractive or ugly.

"Ah, Agent. Welcome to the bridge. We are forty-eight minutes from destination. We *are* in comms range." The executive officer smiled warmly at her and waved an open hand at the backless chair empty next to him. "Please join me. The captain is in a meeting. He will join us when he's done."

Lei hopped up onto the backless seat and yawned. Exhaustion was taking its toll. She needed to sleep soon, or she was going to hurt herself.

The XO reached over and tapped something on her chair, and a holographic display appeared in front of her. It was an exact duplicate of a Kassian military comm panel. That the igranu had this much intelligence on Kassian military hardware bothered her only slightly. She was just too tired to care.

Reaching up, she typed in a frequency and a destination.

"Ground Team Alpha, this is . . ." She hesitated as she tried to figure out how to refer to herself. "Please patch me through to General Marshall."

"Unknown vessel, this is Ground Team Alpha. You have entered into restricted space. Identify yourself, or be fired upon."

Almost immediately after the standard warning, a deep male voice responded. It belonged, Lei recognized, to Gunnery Sergeant Lairn from the ground headquarters on Mathious Moon. "Hold for the general, Agent."

"This is Marshall. Go ahead." The voice sounded pleasant, and Leilani found herself smiling.

"I have a situation and was wondering if we could talk face to face?"

"We'd be happy to have you again, ma'am. Come on down. We even had a door installed if you want to use it. It's in the main house."

"Roger that."

Several minutes later, she was stepping through a door into the secure building in the center of the Mathious Moon base camp. Marshall and the gunny were waiting for her. The general stepped forward and wrapped his arms around her in a surprising hug.

"You have no idea how relieved we are to see you." He hugged her a little longer than she'd expected. "We may get ignored for the most part, but we do get media boats. It's looking pretty bad out there."

He stepped back and seemed to regain his composure.

She smiled at both of them. "I need your help."

"Whatever you need, we're happy to help."

She cocked her head. "Be careful about agreeing to anything until you hear what I need."

The gunny chuckled and shook his head. "No, ma'am. We owe you too much. We're all willing to die for you." He pointed out the window at the gathered marines. "Every last one of us."

There were easily more than two hundred soldiers out there, milling about as if they were waiting for orders.

"Well, here's the situation . . ."

38

THAT WHICH IS NECESSARY . . .

"What about Sitharus?"

Leilani and Anthony were walking through the hall of the massive ship as they chatted about more personal matters.

"That is one interesting creature. I've learned a lot from him." Anthony smiled warmly. "My entire team loves him. He's entertaining, to say the least." He laughed and shrugged. "He calls us his ant farm."

Leilani chuckled. "I'm surprised he knows that concept."

"He didn't. One of my privates explained it to him." He shook his head. "And it's been his pet name for us ever since."

"Okay, that's funny." She paused outside of a hatch guarded by two Seef'aini marines in full armor. "We'll have to catch up more after this gets situated."

General Marshall straightened the lapel on his jacket. "Perhaps over dinner?"

"I'm sure we can arrange that." She returned the smile. "Let them know that I'm here with a guest." She bowed her head to the marines, and one of them placed his hand on the panel next to the hatch.

Anthony tilted his head toward one of the Seef'aini guards. "These aren't ours."

"No. We're having some issues with the royal guards. Like I said, tensions are high. I'm not sure what to expect inside."

"Understood."

The marine with his hand on the panel waited for her to acknowledge that she was ready before he opened the doorway. Lei took a deep breath and pointed to the hatch.

As it slid open, the gunnery sergeant inside lifted his weapon and pointed it directly at her head.

"Stand down, gunnery sergeant!" General Marshall barked, stepping between the marine and Leilani.

The gunny blinked in surprised at the Kassian general, but he lowered his weapon, albeit hesitantly.

"Your Imperial Majesty! It's a pleasure to see you alive and well," Marshall called to the man lying on the bed at the far end of the room. He strode up to the marine gunnery sergeant, stepping all the way into the man's personal space, their eyes locked. "You, gunnery sergeant, will conduct yourself in a reasonable manner or be dismissed. Do you understand me?"

"Yes, General." The man put his weapon away and went to attention.

"General Marshall. You are honestly the last person I expected to see." The emperor sat up carefully, with his doctor's assistance, and held his hand out toward the general.

Anthony was clearly surprised by the gesture but quickly stepped forward and shook his hand.

"We thank you for your loyalty to the crown."

Anthony grinned broadly as Leilani stepped up next to him, keeping him between her and the gunny.

The emperor smiled warmly at her. "Falconi, you keep good friends."

She chuckled. "Thank you, Your Imperial Majesty."

"I have four hundred and thirty-five soldiers ready to take over as your royal guards in your time of need, sir." Anthony didn't look at the man to his left as he added the next part. "It's my understanding that your people suffered some serious losses and could use some downtime. My people are ready and able."

"While I thank you for your offer, I am not sure . . ."

Leilani interrupted the emperor by handing him a secure pad.

He looked the report over and raised both eyebrows in surprise. "I take that back. I accept, General. And I can't possibly thank you enough. We, Emperor Steven Sargeras, hereby assign General Anthony Marshall as head of our royal guard until such time as we are able to reestablish control over the throne and arrest all those involved in this attempt to overthrow us."

Sitting on the edge of the bed, the emperor slumped as if a serious weight had just lifted off his shoulders. He took a deep breath and let it out slowly.

"I, General Anthony Marshall, do hereby accept the appointment to royal guard commander. It is my honor and duty as a loyal marine to serve." He hiked his thumb at Leilani. "I will have guards assigned and give your people some much-needed rest. When you're ready, the agent here has told me of her plan. I think it's a very good one. We would like to go over it and get your input."

Emperor Sargeras folded his hands in his lap, shaking his head. "I don't know why you're so damn loyal, but each passing day, you amaze me even further, Ms. Falconi."

She smirked. "All part of the job, sir."

"I do not wish to overextend myself at this time. How about we set up a temporary operation center here?" He gestured broadly with his palm around the room.

The general stood tall and saluted. "Understood, Your Imperial Majesty. I will see it done within the hour." He turned toward the gunny. "You are dismissed, gunnery sergeant. Go get some sleep. And that's an order."

The gunny saluted but glared at her as he slunk from the room.

"Team One into position," Marshall said across a Kassian comm unit.

Several soldiers filed into the room, each wearing combat armor and carrying aether-modified combat rifles. They took up positions around the walls and near the hatch, and the doctor and emperor seemed to relax a little.

"I will be back shortly, sir." General Marshall gestured to one of the soldiers. "This is Lieutenant Chase. She will be your liaison for this shift."

The woman stepped up and snapped a salute.

The emperor nodded to her, and she returned to attention.

"Thank you, General Marshall. May I ask about the Nine Pillars?"

"They are secure, sir. I left the rest of my unit there."

"And the entity?"

"Napping at the moment, sir."

"It naps?"

Anthony chuckled. "Yes, sir. We have about nine months before it wakes up and wants another game. I left my second-in-command. The entity prefers to play against her, anyway. Something about her mind being more open to the multiple dimensions needed for a good game."

The emperor furrowed his brow. "Somehow, I think I'm missing something. What's this about a game?"

Anthony glanced at her and grinned. "You can thank the agent here. The entity is happy and content with life and the empire. But I will brief you about it later, if that's acceptable? Right now, we're on a timetable."

The emperor bobbed his head in agreement and signaled that they were dismissed.

"We'll be back, sir."

Once outside, Leilani spoke to the Seef'aini guards posted there. "It's secure now. Work with General Marshall's people, and assist where they need it."

The two guards snapped to attention and saluted before turning their attention to Anthony.

"For now, just keep the original royal guards in the barracks, including the gunnery sergeant who just left here." He pointed over his shoulder to the hatch. "My people will take care of security. Until we know more about what's going on, the rest will remain secured."

Both soldiers turned and marched off, but they weren't headed toward the barracks.

"Corporal?" Lei called after them.

One of them stopped and looked back to her while the other kept moving.

"The gunny went that way?" Lei ran her fingertips over one of the weapons strapped to her leg.

"Yes, Agent."

Lei took a deep breath, resisting the urge to draw the weapon and follow the Seef'aini marines. "Stop him before he does anything stupid."

"Aye, ma'am." The guard jogged off.

"Isn't medical that way?" Marshall asked her.

"Yes. And the agent he shot." She allowed her shoulders to droop slightly as she yawned.

Marshall rubbed his chin absently. "Do you think he could be on the wrong side?"

"I don't know what to think anymore."

As Lei ran her fingers through her hair, Marshall paused and focused his gaze on empty air. Leilani chuckled. Apparently, he still wasn't comfortable using the silcomms.

Several Kassian marines ran past in the p-way, likely headed for medical. Two of them slid to a stop and saluted the general.

"Reporting for duty, sir!" a female marine barked loudly.

Marshall hiked his thumb over his shoulder toward the hatch behind them. Both marines snapped a salute. He returned it and held his palm up, gesturing in the direction the marines had come from.

"All right, let's get a command center set up," he said as the two of them walked away from the royal quarters.

Several hours and a nap later, Leilani was leaning back against the kitchen counter, sipping her coffee while Admiral Dorthy, Duke Shovalli, Agent Horrison, and General Marshall talked around and over each other. Dorthy and Duke Shovalli were represented holographically via the new command center that had been set up in the room. The admiral was catching everyone up to speed on the activities of Gremm and her devoted followers. Agent Horrison was catching everyone up on activities in the aether, and General Marshall was adding in what little he knew.

They had already gone over Max's footage and caught the emperor up on the missing Shovalli heir. That had revealed its own problems, since it became apparent to everyone present that the emperor had lost his memories of when he and Kelly Shovalli had met in their teens. Tampering with the emperor's memory was a treasonous action on its own, but not one that surprised Leilani.

"What about McCarthy?" the emperor asked.

"My people say he's loyal, but he's bound by his duty. And he's surrounded by the enemy," Dorthy added. "We need to be careful if we deal with him." His holo shrugged. "My people have been attempting to contact him, but it's sketchy."

"I can't believe he would turn on me, but I also don't want him dead. So be careful there. And Gremm?"

The conversation continued, but Leilani wasn't paying attention. There was a light flashing in her HUD. She took her cup of coffee and stepped out into the p-way of the ship.

"Yeah?"

"Hey, Leilei. I have someone on the comms who's asking to speak directly to you." BB's voice sounded tired.

That didn't surprise her. They were all exhausted. When she glanced at the name tagged to the comm, however, she raised an eyebrow in surprise.

"How did you get to him without alerting his staff?"

"You don't want to know. It was so far from legal it almost comes all the way back around. Plausible deniability and all that crap."

Lei chuckled and shook her head. Very little of what they were doing these days was legal. However, *quod est necessarium est licitum*—that which is necessary is legal. She had already spent time pondering how this would all turn out and who would have to take the fall for breaking the laws they all had.

"Falconi?" The man on the other end seemed agitated. Reasonably so; right now, the fate of the empire was resting squarely on his shoulders.

"Yes, Admiral?"

"Unicorn?"

"Secure. Angry as all get out, but secure."

"Sounds like him." McCarthy calmed slightly. *"All right. Here's the deal. It'll be taking place in the palace. Friday at 1:00 p.m. Three days from now. The media will be here in force. They have been given a week's notice to ensure that everyone is here. I've arranged to put Gremm up in the Green Wing. She's insisting on her own guards, and I'm allowing it. However, I'm also removing the security locks on the back door. I'm sure you know the one?"*

Leilani chuckled. She knew exactly what he meant. Inside the palace were hallways and doors that no one, save very specific security personnel, knew about. They were often called the evac tunnels. You either knew them from experience, or you didn't.

"Please note: if you are caught, there is nothing I can do."

"So, SOP. Got it." She shrugged even though he couldn't see her. "You get caught, you're on your own" was standard operating procedure for all special agents like herself. IIS would always try to bail her out if possible, but it was always better not to rely on that safety net.

"I've given you all I'm going to. Don't fuck this up. There's only one way to recover this. And I'm giving you a stacked deck. How you play the hand is up to you."

"Thank you, Admiral."

"Yeah. McCarthy out."

Leilani looked down at her almost-empty cup of coffee and contemplated going to the galley to get a refill instead of stepping back into the command center behind her.

"We good, BB?"

"Yep. I have an idea; sending it to Dorthy now."

"Got it." Leilani stepped back into the room and walked up to the table to stand next to the hologram of Dorthy, where she waited to be acknowledged.

"So now we just have to find out where she'll be next and how to intervene," the emperor was saying as Lei raised a hand to interject.

Dorthy turned toward someone off camera, and a hand reached into view to give a pad to the admiral. As he looked it over, a sly smile played across his lips.

"Agent Falconi?" The emperor bounced his hand in her direction.

"Yes, sir. BB and I have an idea." She cocked her head to the side slightly. "And I'm betting they're pretty close to the same idea."

The emperor bowed his head for her to continue.

"Gremm is on her way to the palace to be sworn in as empress."

All of them glared at her, but none of them said anything. Everyone knew it was the next part of the equation.

"We need to let her."

The emperor raised an eyebrow and folded his arms across his chest.

"She's feeling pretty confident right now—positive that even if you do show up, she'll still have the upper hand. She isn't afraid of us. And we might be able to use that."

"You plan to trick her into confessing?" Anthony chuckled, tapping his fingers on the table.

"Yes, but it gets better than that."

A data packet showed up in Lei's HUD, and she dragged it to the table so everyone could see. The media blip was muted, but the headline was easily readable: the inauguration of a new empress, live on all channels.

"I plan to have her confess everything on intragalactic news."

Each of the men looked from one to another, except for General Marshall, who just kept grinning at her. He leaned on the table, slightly crossing his legs. A text from him appeared on her HUD.

You did it again. Nicely done.

She smiled at him but didn't reply. She hadn't pulled it off yet.

Dorthy lifted the pad in his hand to draw attention to it. "My computer specialist has the same plan. He says he can set it up so the media gets a live feed of the confession."

"That solves the problem of killing her." Duke Shovalli pointed to several items on the tactical table. "If we can indeed convince her to admit everything in front of witnesses, it will clear the emperor, and I won't even have to get involved." He appeared relieved. "And I can honestly say that I prefer to stay out of this if at all possible."

"Agreed. Very well, Leilani. It's on you. Get with Marshall, and take what people you need." Sargeras pointed to Anthony. "We'll wait just outside of system for the aftermath. Then, once the IKS *Hoganmeyer* has rendezvoused with us, we'll switch to her and come in to clean up."

"Understood, sir. ETA on the *Hoganmeyer*?" Lei glanced to Dorthy.

"Four days."

She took a deep breath and turned to her partner.

Rothar folded his arms. "Just try to go without me."

Chuckling, she bobbed her head in agreement. "Good. Meet me in my quarters when you're done here." Leilani strode from the room.

As she walked down the p-way, she heard the men stifling laughter.

"I'll never get used to that woman ignoring my station," the emperor grumbled.

"The best agents rarely have the best manners." General Marshall chuckled. "Your Imperial Majesty."

39

SACRIFICES

The ship faded from view, replaced by the dark hallways of the evac tunnels under the Imperial Palace. Leilani switched her vision to ultraviolet. Around her, fifty of Kass's aether-resistant marines did the same. It wasn't long before every name in her HUD was green, indicating they were ready to proceed.

"All right. There are no cameras or sound sensors in here, but there are movement sensors. Hopefully, the admiral either has those shut off or has only his reliable people on the consoles." She gestured for the teams to begin moving. "Unit Two, secure the exit. Three, the barracks. Four, the royal suite. And Five, hold here."

Leilani started toward a dark tunnel. *Melissa?*

"Roger," the young girl responded. Lei could sense her fear.

"You in place?"

"Yes, Agent. I'm ready."

"BB?"

"Yep, we're a go," he replied almost cheerfully.

Leilani bobbed her head to Rothar, and they both jogged down the hallway directly in front of them with two special operations marines on their tail. The marines' job was to stay out of sight and only act if something went very wrong.

"You going to be able to do this?" she whispered to the disguised Rothar next to her.

"I'll be fine."

Leilani had her doubts. Lying was not one of his strengths.

They turned several corners until she finally stopped at a door. She held up her fist for everyone to stop. Placing her ear against the door, she could hear muffled talking on the other side. She pointed to the two marines and gave them the hand signal to deploy here. They nodded their understanding and began to set up the equipment they'd brought with them.

She and Rothar continued down the hall and turned a corner. After a quick check, they slipped through another door into a brightly lit corridor and began sneaking quietly along it.

It wasn't long before they came to an intersection with guards. She pressed her back up against the wall, held up her fist, then signaled for Rothar to move. He slid silently past her and across the hall, pulling up his pistol.

They leaned around the corner together and fired their silenced weapons. Both guards dropped with minimal noise. She gave another hand signal, and she and Rothar began to slink forward, carefully staggering their movements to check ahead of each other.

It took ten minutes to get to the door they were looking for. There hadn't been enough guards along the way, which gave her a bad feeling. They both stood on the threshold for several seconds, looking over the unguarded door.

"There's no way it's this easy."

She approached the door alone with her partner covering her. She could hear muffled talking on the other side. The evac tunnels were all manual, with nothing digital to be tracked. She reached forward and pushed the door open slowly.

She wasn't all that surprised when she felt the barrel of a weapon press into her forehead. She was glad, however, that they didn't feel the need to pull the trigger right away like they probably should have. She took a step back, pulling her hands into view. Behind her, Rothar stepped into the hallway with his hands raised as well.

"Weapon," the female voice on the other end of the gun demanded.

She loosened her grip on her weapon, allowing it to spin around on her finger, hanging harmlessly by the trigger guard.

The woman reached forward and took the gun by the barrel. She was obviously well versed in IIS weaponry and their safeguards.

"Please have the agents come in," Admiral Gremm cooed from within the private room.

The petty officer holding the weapon stepped backward and, with the barrel of her gun, waved for them to enter the room. Like the other royal quarters, this room was extravagantly lavish. It was large enough for a family of eight to live in comfortably.

"Ah, Leilani." The admiral sighed and shook her head. "Have I told you how annoying I find you?"

Lei stood with her hands in view as the naval officer slid around behind her. "No, ma'am, but I assure you, the feeling is mutual."

She was punched hard in the kidney, which caused her to grimace. But she managed to resist making any noise.

Next to her, Rothar stepped into view.

"Ah, and this must be the famous General Horrison. You know, before a few weeks ago, I had never even heard of you, but after some research, I have to admit: if even half the reports are true, you are an impressive man." She waved her hand at him. "Let's see the real you. Drop the disguise."

Leilani glanced at him.

"It's on a timer. I have no control over it." That lie was perfect. Even Leilani believed him, and she *knew* it wasn't true.

Gremm frowned, then shrugged. "No matter. Whether the blood be red or green makes no difference to me."

She returned her attention to Leilani. "You know, when you first showed up on my radar, I was annoyed. But it turned out to be beneficial. So I let you live. But as the weeks rolled on and you kept showing up over and over, it grew more and more tedious. I grew curious, so I pulled your secure IIS file." The woman's grin was filled with malice.

She strode to her desk and picked up a pad lying there. "You made your debut on the IIS radar at four years of age . . . by murdering more than five hundred civilians."

Leilani frowned, but the woman continued.

"You derailed a train going more than three hundred miles an hour." She made a clucking noise as she flicked her finger across the screen. "And that trend continued. One hundred dead here, forty there." She flicked again. "Until finally you were captured by IIS. But instead of euthanizing you like he had been ordered to do, the now admiral Jason Dorthy hid you in aether space."

She turned the pad so both of them could see a picture of her holding a sign and angrily yelling at the person taking the picture. "Where you joined several anti-Kassian terrorist groups and even carried out raids on IIS-held facilities."

Turning the pad back, she flicked her finger across the screen and laughed at the image on it. "Did you know, General, that for three years, Agent Leilani here was the president of your fan club at Eldrich Line University?"

She held up a picture of Leilani at the age of eighteen, dressed up as the great General Rothar Horrison for All Hallows' Eve. Lei was afraid to glance over and see whether Rothar was looking at her.

"Yet again, IIS command—or, rather, Dorthy specifically—refused the kill order on you, something I'm currently using against them in court." The woman grinned broadly.

"The case is progressing nicely, I might add. IIS will be disbanded within the year." She made a circling gesture with her finger in the air. "Regardless of what happens here today."

Crossing her legs, Gremm leaned back against the desk with a large, happy grin and continued to flip through the files on the pad.

"Even after you joined the IIS, your career of destruction and mayhem continued. Your death toll is phenomenal. I mean, if you had been anyone else, you would have been labeled a serial killer long ago and tossed into space without a vac suit." The woman shook her head, pursing her lips. "Yet you managed to not only live but thrive."

She held up the pad again and showed the bloody face of a thirteen-year-old boy. The forensic photograph clearly showed the bullet hole between his eyes. "Recognize this young noble?"

Leilani didn't answer her.

The woman nodded to the petty officer behind her, and Leilani felt another punch to her kidney. She grunted and stumbled forward.

"Answer me."

"Yes." Leilani coughed and tasted blood.

Gremm showed the image to the crodoc. "This young man was the heir to the planet I happened to pick Agent Falconi up from. That was just before we first met. She shot the young man in his sleep. He was a perfect student and a loyal imperial noble. But his father wasn't playing nice, so the agent here was ordered to kill him to bring the father in line. Isn't that right, Agent?"

Leilani refused to answer and received another punch, this time much harder. She doubled over and began coughing up blood.

"You see, General, you have unwittingly associated yourself with a known murderer and assassin."

There was a pause, but Leilani was too focused on not throwing up to see what the admiral was doing. She wasn't sure what the guard behind her was hitting her with, but it wasn't a fist, that was for sure. While bent over, she took the time to try to get a glimpse of what was behind herself. The guard had a stun baton set to just below lethal. Well, that, at least, made more sense.

"And now the good agent is here to kill *me*. Not that it will make a difference. My plans are already in full motion." Brigitta Gremm leaned back against the desk with a large grin and folded her arms.

Leilani forced herself upright, ignoring the pain.

The admiral waved to the side, and three naval personnel walked into the room. Two of them trained weapons on the agents while the third began scanning them. The woman with the scanner reached into Leilani's pocket and pulled out a recording device. Leilani grimaced. Gremm, however, laughed and stepped up to take the device from the ensign.

"I see. Not to kill me, but to trick me into telling you everything?" Gremm cackled gleefully and snapped the device in half. "How unlike you."

"You don't know anything about me," Leilani growled.

The slam into her side came so hard that she crumpled to the floor and began vomiting blood. She wouldn't be able to survive another hit.

"Don't I?" Gremm walked up to Leilani's crumpled body. "I know more about you than you would like. Face it, Leilani, you're just like me. You're tired of being trod upon. Especially by people who think themselves better than you. Sargeras fucked you over and over again, using you for his own needs and then throwing you to the dogs to be shredded apart until there was nothing left but a cold-blooded killer."

Leilani hated how true that statement was.

"There is *one* difference," Leilani managed to cough out.

The other woman crouched down next to her. "What's that?" she asked softly.

"I still believe in doing what's right."

Gremm patted Leilani's shoulder gently. "So do I, my dear." She stood and strode back across the room to her desk. "Which is why I'm doing this in the first place. The royal family was out of line. Our so-called emperor had overstepped his bounds. And I, being the good, loyal imperial noble that I am, stepped forward to remove his totalitarian regime. Honestly, it shouldn't have been this easy. Another perfect example of how much the people wanted him gone. They happily believed that he was dumb enough to use a genie as a body double."

She steepled her fingers in front of herself and tapped them together several times. "Even if he *does* manage to survive my purge, when he comes forward, the people will eat him alive."

Gremm stepped forward and spun once, arms wide, as she reveled in her success. "The new regime will be glorious! I will rule with an iron fist. The people will either love me or die!"

The grin plastered to her face was dark and dangerous. "The navy is already so deep in my pocket that they will do whatever I say. Power is an intoxicating feeling. I'm sure it's much like how *you* feel just before you murder an innocent child."

Leilani coughed. She was having trouble focusing.

"Ma'am, you are starting to lose consciousness," Sarah chimed softly in her head. The oracle had been ordered into stealth mode to avoid any sensors Gremm might have had.

"Go ahead."

"Nanites being released now."

"Is everyone ready?" she asked weakly.

"All units reporting green."

Leilani felt the pain subside as meds ran through her system and the nanites began to repair the damage. She brought her shields online. The oracle dampeners that Gremm had put in place had already been overridden by BB before they even transported into the palace tunnels.

"He was *not* innocent." She more coughed the words than said them as she pushed herself upright.

"Excuse me?" Gremm raised an eyebrow in surprise as Leilani slowly stood.

"The boy—he wasn't innocent. Much like another young girl who shot her brother and father at point-blank range. He strangled his mother and sister to death at his father's request."

Gremm shot to her feet at the accusation. "How dare you!"

"How dare I what? Suggest that you're not only a murderer but one capable of killing her only remaining family members?"

Gremm glared at the woman behind Leilani, and Lei felt the weapon slam into her force field. The shield, however, was designed for high-power energy weapons, so the stun baton did nothing.

"Kill them!" Gremm shrieked, and the guards in the room pulled their triggers.

At the same moment, Leilani and Rothar tossed the time-stop grenades they'd hidden in their cuffs into the air. They exploded into a yellow cloud, freezing the rounds in midair. The four aether genies, however, didn't freeze. But they lacked the agents' experience with this method of combat.

It was all over before the smoke cleared. All four aether guards were dead. The two naval personnel who had been directly behind the agents took the four rounds meant for them.

The only people left alive in the room were the usurper and the two agents, who now stood on either side of her.

Gremm glanced around at the dead bodies, then turned to face Leilani defiantly. "Even if you kill me, it will stop nothing. The greater plans are already in motion. Nothing can stop us. If not me, it will be someone else sitting on the throne."

"Your brother, perhaps?" Leilani stepped forward and slapped a metal band around the woman's wrist. It immediately grew to encase her hand.

"What?" Admiral Gremm was so shocked that she didn't resist as Leilani slapped the second band on her other hand. The two metal bands linked together.

"Your brother, Kelly Shovalli? I'm sure he'll want a few words with you at some point during all of this." Leilani slapped the woman roughly on the back. "Or maybe he'll just ignore you and pretend like you don't exist, like you did to him."

"But that's not possible," Gremm mumbled to herself. "I know I killed him." She shook her head slowly, repeating it over and over.

The door opened, and several Kassian marines stepped inside, scanned the room, then moved aside to allow the man behind them to enter.

As Admiral McCarthy stepped into the room, Leilani bowed respectfully.

"Regent."

"Agent Falconi." He waved a pad at her. "I have stopped your transmission. Nice trick, that. It took us a while to find it."

Leilani giggled. "I hope the reporters got enough, at least?"

The man furrowed his bushy brow. "Far more than I would have preferred. But I was able to get it stopped before she claimed to have all of the navy in her pocket, at least." He glared at the mumbling woman sitting on the desk. "I'm disappointed in you, Brigitta."

The woman's head snapped up. Her eyes seemed slightly glazed over. Leilani recognized it as a symptom of eldrich influence. She needed to get her to Dorthy as quickly as possible.

"You have nothing! I am invincible! He will kill you all." Gremm's voice came out as a low growl. The sound made Leilani's skin crawl.

The admiral raised both eyebrows in alarm and took a large step backward.

On the other side of the raving lunatic, Rothar met her gaze and pulled something from his pocket. He slid what appeared to be a silver choker around the woman's neck, and she slumped unconscious in his arms.

McCarthy looked to the two agents and shook his head to clear it. "Okay. Well, that wasn't disturbing at all," he lied, then pointed to the open door that the two agents had come in through. "Your people started that broadcast sooner than they probably should have. There's blood in the water, and the media is looking to place blame. I would recommend you leave the same way you came. I'm not sure what they would do if they got a hold of you right now."

Leilani tossed a hand in the air, then let it fall to her side. Well, it looked like she would end up being the scapegoat once again, despite everything. She glanced to Rothar and saw him nod as he lifted the unconscious woman and tossed her over his shoulder.

McCarthy folded his arms across his chest and frowned. "You're not leaving her with us?"

"You'll get her back after IIS clears her of external influence," Lei called over her shoulder as she stepped into the evac tunnel.

"Agent." McCarthy's tone left no room for argument, and at the moment, he was still the imperial regent. She turned to lock eyes with him. One day, maybe, they'd have a conversation that didn't end with her sneaking out afterward.

"Thank you for your service to the empire." He bowed deeply.

As he did, the remaining marines all snapped to attention and saluted her.

Rothar put his hand on her shoulder and urged her out into the tunnel. Pulling the door closed behind them, she glanced up at him briefly, then turned to jog back the way they had come.

40

GAME, SET, MATCH

"Duke Fathrin!" the woman yelled, trying to get the attention of the chair of the House of Lords.

A short, kind-looking older man who was graying at the temples and dressed in an expensive suit turned and stepped toward the reporter. He waved aside his unhappy security personnel, who were trying to herd him into the waiting vehicle.

"Mrs. Withers?" He smiled warmly and bowed his head respectfully to the camera.

"Does the House of Lords have anything to say about sanctioned assassinations and the people who carry them out?"

He took a deep breath and looked directly at the camera. "The House of Lords cannot, of course, respond to comments about sanctioned assassinations. What we can and will say is that governing is not an easy task. No one person is infallible. Recent events are clearly proof of that. Our government has special councils for secret actions for a reason. No one person knows everything that goes on. The one who comes closest is the emperor, but even he isn't privy to everything, mostly because it would be impossible for one person to keep up with it all. That's why there are so many dedicated women and men in service to this great empire. We strive to keep it running smoothly and to catch and fix problems like those experienced in the last few weeks."

"But it's clear that this problem *wasn't* caught. Why is that?"

"Are you sure about that?"

The woman looked confused. "What do you mean?"

"Lady Gremm never made it to the throne. The checks and balances worked, thanks to several loyal imperial investigators and military personnel."

"Are you talking about Agent Falconi?"

"Among others, yes."

"Are you saying that we owe this government win to a known murderer?"

The duke smiled at the woman. "I'm saying that Agent Falconi went above and beyond the call of duty, putting her life on the line not only to protect her emperor but to ensure that the woman trying to murder him was arrested and tried in a court of law. Those don't really strike me as the actions of a murderer, do they?"

"So you're claiming that the duchess's accusations are false?"

"I'm saying that at this point in time, Lady Gremm's words are suspect." He refused to acknowledge her as a duchess. "And until a court of law determines the truth, we should all accept Agent Falconi for the hero she is." He smiled at the reporter. "There is no such thing as the whole story. We each only have our version of it. It's our duty, as seekers of the truth, to examine as many sides as we can. Not just the side with the best ratings."

The woman raised an eyebrow and smirked. "Well said, Your Grace." She gestured for the cameraman to stop recording. As the camera lowered, she held out her hand to the duke. "Well played, Your Grace."

"Same to you, Glenda."

"Can you tell me anything off the record?"

He grinned and leaned in closer to her. "Keep your ears peeled. You'll love our next announcement."

Her eyebrow rose again, and she shook her head in amazement. "I'll be around when you come out, then."

He chuckled. "You do that."

His guard stepped up and whispered in his ear. "They're getting anxious, sir."

Duke Brentley Winston Fathrin patted his guard on the shoulder as he stepped into the waiting vehicle. Inside, his aide handed him a cup of coffee and a pad.

"Here's the bill."

Brentley sat down and began skimming it as the vehicle headed toward the House of Lords building within the imperial compound. When he was done, he leaned back in his seat, crossed his legs, and smiled contentedly. At least something positive would come out of all this mess.

As Duke Fathrin walked toward his seat in the middle of the massive dais, a countess stepped out in front of him.

"Are we really going to pass this?" She waved the pad in her hand, displaying the bill awaiting a vote.

"You have concerns, Countess Terris?" His face remained neutral.

"What if what the duchess said was true?"

He raised an eyebrow in curiosity. "Like everything else she's told us was true?"

The countess fidgeted nervously.

"Even if she *was* telling the truth, which murderer would you prefer to back, countess? The one working for us or the one working against us?"

The woman narrowed her eyes. "To be blunt, neither."

"If you think politics is bloodless, then you are in the wrong profession, my dear." He pointed to the pad in her hand. "That woman has sacrificed everything, including her life and her career, for the emperor she loves. You think she didn't know what she was getting into when she arranged that broadcast? You'd punish her for following orders and loving her emperor?"

Realization passed across the countess's face as she stared down at the pad. She placed her thumb on the scanner, adding her signature to the thousands of others.

He patted her on the arm and continued to his chair. Once there, he turned to the crowd and glanced at the corner of his heads-up display. The bill would pass, but the numbers still weren't good enough.

"May I have everyone's attention?" he called loudly.

The automated systems kicked in and fed his voice through speakers throughout the massive, theater-like room. Slowly, it grew quiet as the various senators turned toward him. The House of Lords was enormous, and due to the coronation that was due to take place this week, all but one or two of the seats were full. This was an event that happened once in a hundred years, if that. It was a chance to make history, and they all knew it.

"I know we are not officially called to order, and I respect the last few minutes you have before we begin, but I would like to speak from the heart before the house recorders bring us all under the political strings we're so used to.

"In the last few weeks, everything we have come to know as order and reason has been brought into question. The rumors and sheer amount of data that has crossed our desks, accurate or not, have been astonishing."

The room grew loud for a brief moment as just over fourteen hundred people murmured their agreement.

He raised his hand to bring them back down to quiet. "Whether or not we agree with Gremm is not relevant at this time. We can argue that at a later date. Right now, each and every one of you has a bill in front of you. A bill that will decide the fate of one single person. This servant of the empire has given more than any one of us. Conceivably more than most of us combined."

He waved a hand toward a group of individuals who sat in a box separate from the main body. They were the group dedicated to imperial secret matters.

"For some of us, this person's name has come across our desks multiple times. And it has never been dealt with in a benevolent manner. Each time, this person has been sacrificed to cover up something we cannot or will not speak of." He paused briefly for that thought to settle in.

"In this time of crisis, we, the lords and ladies of this empire, have the chance—and the choice—to step up and say, 'Enough!'" His voice rose on the last word.

"We have the chance to unanimously speak as one voice and say that we understand that the cost of service is high. And for once, we have the ability to say thank you to all of those soldiers and individuals who put their lives on the line for us every day." He spread his arms wide, gesturing to the massive hall of senators.

"All I ask of *you* is that you set aside your political views and recognize those whose lives are put on the line for our great empire. Acknowledge, just this once, that their lives matter. That this one woman's willing sacrifice matters. Let her stand for us in this time of need as a beacon for all of history to remind us that no matter what comes, we shall stand, and we shall fight for our way of life!"

In his HUD, the numbers began to climb steadily.

"Thank you for listening to the words of an old man. Please enjoy your remaining five minutes."

There was a soft chime throughout the room as the five-minute warning reminded everyone to head to their seats.

Brentley moved to his chair and sat down to watch the counter. The last number clicked over about ten seconds before the final chime sounded. In front of him, down on the main floor, a woman stood, called the house to order, and began reading off her pad. He ignored her. His speech had worked. For the first time in more than a thousand years, a bill had been passed through the House of Lords unanimously. He drummed his fingers on his pad and smiled down at the image on it—the image of IIS agent Leilani Falconi.

"House Bill 23497615 has been passed with a unanimous vote of 1,405, with zero abstaining and zero dissenting. We do count three members absent. This is an imperial record," the woman announced.

The house erupted in a thundering ovation as everyone stood.

$$\_\int\_$$

"Today, there was a standing ovation in the House of Lords for an Agent Leilani Falconi, the woman responsible for arresting Duchess Gremm. Despite disputes over Agent Falconi's service in IIS, a bill pardoning her for all of her past actions has been passed with a unanimous vote of 1,405 to 0. An astounding achievement. Not only does this make the first unanimous vote in the House of Lords in more than 1,003 years, it is the first bill ever in the history of the empire to pass with this many votes." The video on the holovid screen switched from the standing ovation to reporter Glenda Withers.

"It is clear that the House of Lords intends to make a statement with this bill, but it remains to be seen what that statement really is. Even as the fate of the IIS hangs in the imperial court system, one thing is certain. Agent Leilani Falconi has definitely reminded us that there are people out there willing to sacrifice everything for the empire. Perhaps that is something the courts need to keep in mind as they make their decision. This is Glenda Withers for Imperial World News, Kass Prime. Best wishes to all of you watching from home."

Duke Brentley Fathrin reached up and switched off the holovid with a flick of his wrist. In his other hand, he held a pad showing the rotating image of Agent Leilani Falconi. A hand appeared in his vision, holding a crystal glass filled with scotch on the rocks. He took it and set the pad on the table next to him.

"Well, that didn't go as planned." His aide stepped into view, and Brentley smirked up at him.

"On the contrary. It went *exactly* as I planned."

The man looked confused. "You meant to have her arrested?"

"Of course. Can you imagine someone that easily manipulated and unstable on the throne?"

The aide shrugged. "I thought chaos was the point?"

"Ah . . ." Senator Fathrin swirled the scotch in his glass slowly. "No. I needed only enough chaos to make my prey run. I'm not interested in mass instability. That's insane. The dumb child did exactly what I needed her to do: find my prey, then create enough chaos to flush him out into the open."

"Now what?" The aide folded his arms uncomfortably.

"Now we use our new tool"—he tapped the pad on the table—"to corner him and return what is rightfully mine."

ACKNOWLEDGMENTS

I'd like to acknowledge and thank my friends and family for reading copy after copy of the manuscript and helping me flesh out this universe. A thanks to my publisher, Brown Books, for helping me put this all together and get it into your hands. And thanks especially to Erynn Newman for helping me refine my book in that tedious and terrifying editing tradition.

WENDI COFFMAN-PORTER

Wendi Coffman-Porter grew up an only child in a military family. She spent a lot of time as a child inventing new friends and sharing them with others. She began writing her stories down at the age of ten, and by the time her first child was born she'd written her first novel. Her passion has always been the colorful canvas and creative freedom of fantasy and sci-fi.

Wendi is always developing something new and colorful to share with others, whether she is role-playing or writing in her office at home in Texas in the middle of her pack of furry friends. Her fervor for incredibly rich realities that are as authentic as the one outside your own window is what drives her to constantly find out what's happening around the next corner. She strives for a deep new understanding of the nature of life, no matter what form that life might take.